TOMATO BOY

TOMATO BOY

BY GARY McKEE

A BOB McGREGOR MYSTERY

ABQ PRESS
Albuquerque, New Mexico

For Mary and William

Copyright © 2009 by Gary McKee

ABQ Press Trade Paperback Edition 2009

Cover illustration by Marigail Mathis and Tommy Mathis
Cover design by David Sims

ABQ Press
Albuquerque, New Mexico
abqpress.com

garymckee.com

Library of Congress Cataloging-in-Publication Data

McKee, Gary
    Tomato Boy by Gary McKee
    ISBN 978-0-9774161-5-8

Library of Congress Control Number: 2009905706

CHAPTER 1

The heavy old car practically steered itself at forty-five and under. So with left palm on the steering wheel knob, Bob McGregor shifted around to stretch his right arm along the seat back. The arm with the plaster cast. Today, prickly itching had replaced the usual pain in his broken wrist, but he was thinking he'd rather have the pain. The cast allowed full movement of his fingers, and he used them to twiddle the long hair of his dozing passenger, his friend Janet Hood, causing her to stir.

They were away from the holiday traffic of the interstate now, traveling an undulating two-lane highway that was taking them north into the greenwood foothills of the Poplar Mountains of Tennessee. On each successive hilltop, tremulous heat waves rose from the pavement and conveyed to McGregor the impression he was heading into a series of mirages without end.

Just inside Calvin County, their destination, a temporary road sign with red flags attached warned, "Caution Bump Ahead." It was Hood's annoying habit to read road signs aloud, and she woke up in time to perform the ritual.

McGregor brought his right hand back to the wheel and tapped the brake. He wanted no harm to come to his new ride, an expertly restored 1953 burgundy Buick Skylark convertible and a gift from his new client. But Hood the worrier had never trusted another driver in her life.

"Slow down a little more, McGregor! Want to ruin the alignment? You see those workers up there, don't you?"

"Yes. Now take it easy!" He wiped rolling sweat from his face. The third-of-July heat had his nerves on edge, and Hood's fretting didn't help.

Hood's concern for the car he understood, though. She owned All Hood's Cars, the best automobile restoration business in the South, and with her own hand had restored a neglected heap into the like-new machine his car was today. She loved it like a baby, even naming it Edgar after her deceased father; it reminded her of his brawn and his forceful character, she explained. Never mind that McGregor held title, he knew his Buick would always belong to Hood. But having known Hood well for fifteen years, McGregor sensed that something else was on her mind, the fussiness and her lack of exuberance all day being strong indicators.

McGregor looked her over. They'd put the top down at the last fill-up, and the bright sunshine glimmered off the sunscreen oil sheen on her tanned bare legs. She had black hair pulled behind her ears now in a pony tail, which showed her slightly elongated earlobes, good for nibbling, which she liked for him to do—well, when they were on good terms. She had a high forehead, sharp nose, a more rounded chin, dark eyebrows and dark eyes that managed somehow to blaze with life no matter her mood. In her beauty she didn't look like a steadfast steely guru, but that was what she was to him.

Hood more than once had taken over his life, this time by secretly engineering his move to Tennessee's outback Calvin County and its tiny burg of Calvin Station—his new job representing an old college professor of theirs with the accompanying fat salary, the bonus of Edgar the Buick and time off to write his historical novel. She'd done it all a few weeks back, before he'd resigned as chief prosecutor for Alabama's Task Force on Automobile Theft. If McGregor had gone from that job to a position with a Montgomery criminal defense firm, he'd be making only half the money he'd get by working up here the next two years. Hood might be prone to anxiety, grumpy and obstinate at times, but she turned events.

Ahead in the roadway stood a man wearing overalls cut off at the knees. He waved a red flag and then spat hard on the road. McGregor knew the gesture indicated he meant business. So McGregor braked to a stop, having to steer around a part of the pavement apparently washed out from recent rain. There they waited while six other men finished packing gravel in a trench across the road.

The flagman finally waved them on, calling out, "Good-looking car!"

McGregor pulled alongside him, saluted, and then asked, "How close are we to a place called the Tomato Emporium?"

The man leaned on the car. His face sun-darkened, the creases on either side of his chin ran with tobacco juice. "In about two miles," he said, showing incongruous white teeth, "you'll come around a curve, come to a clearing in the woods. It'll be there on the right, across from a county park that's up that way. Can't miss it. Big sign. Now hold on a sec." He trotted to an ice chest on the roadside and came back with two cold bottles of water labeled "Trust Rust."

McGregor thanked him, and the man grinned and spat another puddle, this time with an easy grin.

As they drove away slowly, Hood reclined again, tasting the water and reading the fine print on the bottle, which she said was about voting. But their attention was drawn to a white-shirted man with a bulldog scowl who had jumped up on the sideboard of an orange county work truck. Bulldog called to the workers, "Come on boys, time for my loyalty speech. Now I want some good, loyal volunteers to get more campaign signs up. Election's right on us!"

Loyalty was on McGregor's mind, too. He was taking on Roland Poteet as a client out of loyalty as much as for the money. The now retired Poteet had mentored him through some difficult periods in the years since college, and McGregor never forgot that it'd been Poteet who'd introduced him to Hood when they were both students in Poteet's geology class.

Back then, Poteet had donated his way into a teaching position with a hefty contribution to the college following some tight string-pulling by wealthy friends. His wife of many years had died suddenly, and he'd needed a complete change. So he'd dusted off an old G.I. Bill-fueled PhD in Earth sciences and opened his checkbook. He turned over his several businesses to managers and retired to academe. Still, he couldn't keep his hands out of the businesses, couldn't turn loose, and as a teacher he'd lasted only a year. His current retirement was supposed to be for keeps.

Hood tossed the empty bottle into a trash bag and scooted over beside McGregor to talk directly in his ear over the wind noise. Her breath was wet and cool from the water. "I guess I only have two miles left to tell you what I need to tell you." She yanked a wad of his hair, a favorite method of gaining his full attention.

"McGregor, I'm feeling less and less enthusiastic about this move of yours. I guess it started with that damned crazy thing we did of jumping into the hammock together. It'd have been funny if you hadn't cracked your wrist. I don't know. Seeing you in so much pain. It was like a bad omen. Maybe I feel like I'm gonna lose my sweet Lumpkins. I've always had you in Montgomery, and now—"

Releasing his hair, she sat up straight. "I'll stay with you the two weeks, help you catalog Poteet's antique cars, all the ones he has warehoused out west. But then I'll have to leave. Can't stay away too long from All Hood's or things'll go sour. You know how it is."

He put his cast around her shoulder and tried to hug her, but she moved back to her side of the car where she

propped her bare feet on the dash, not having a seat belt to
worry about, and pitched her knees back and forth in a pout.

McGregor tried to think of a response to re-excite
her. This move was making him feel as if he'd just escaped
prison, sailing three feet off the ground. He was now over six
years out of Alabama law, class of 2002. He joined the Task
Force right out of school. So he'd had six years of Force
politics, stacks of case files, staff shortages, budget cuts; dim-
wits on the juries, idiot defense lawyers, and yes, some cor-
rupt judges. The burn-out came last year and the blow-out
came this year. Yeah, gathering all Poteet's property, managing his estate planning, and at the same time being allowed
to work on the book that only existed now somewhere over
the rainbow—well, Hood didn't realize that she'd orches-
trated *this* lawyer's heaven. One time, a car thief had told him
that freedom was driving off in somebody else's brand new
Toyota. Today, he understood that and smiled in satisfaction,
but he said nothing to Hood, his thoughts sounding too un-
McGregorish. He had a reputation.

In short order, they came to the promised clearing on
the right where indeed a large sign in curled red neon
boasted: TOMATO EMPORIUM. The earthy smell of the
summertime forest gave way to that of wafting smoke from a
barbeque pit. McGregor coasted to a halt on the roadside
without entering the parking lot. He put the car in park and
turned to Hood. Pleasant odors always instilled pleasant
thoughts.

"Princess, I've been thinking about my loyalty to
Poteet, how important it seems to him that I come up here.
But your loyalty to me ... just when I need you. Well, you're
always in my head. You make me happy and I'll *always* be
around for you." It hadn't come out exactly right, but it
made the point.

Hood further darkened her eyes with her brows and
smiled, giving him that bubbly giggle of hers, the one he always wished she'd reserve for him and him alone. She said,

"I love it when you try to be earnest. Makes you sound so silly, Lumpkins. And damned irresistible to *me*."

Poteet had instructed them to stop at the Tomato Emporium to meet a woman named Mama Limbo, a friend of his, he'd said. He'd given no reason, just told them to do it; then afterward come to his home, which he called his camp. It would be McGregor's first face-to-face meeting with Poteet in over a year.

The large parking lot was gravel-on-mud, evidently still under construction, and was full of cars and trucks parked in untidy rows. Beyond the lot was a rambling structure, the far-back part of it a two-story job and the front a single story in two zigzag sections, the combination making it hard to estimate the exact dimensions of the building. But bright red paint and white trim mitigated the crude design. You take away the new landscaping and fresh coat of paint, the place would look like a low-down 1950s roadhouse. McGregor approved, liking most things from the fifties.

Hood said, "A solid restoration job!" Then she grabbed his cast as he eased the Buick between two rows. "Easy does it. Look how mushy! They've had one hell of a rain up here lately. There's a good parking spot way over there next to that fence just to the right of the building. See it? It'll be close up and we can keep an eye on Edgar."

The fence was eight feet high and woven with ribbons of green fabric, the color of a line of pine trees on the other side. And the empty parking space turned out to be a marked off area for an electronic fence gate. As they approached the gate, it was sliding open fast. The fence and trees had concealed an automobile junkyard, and a rusted-out orange pickup truck came jerking its way out, forcing McGregor to hit the brake. The whine of the truck's revved up engine said the driver was trying to take off in high gear.

Behind the wheel they saw a bearded, heavy-set man, steering with one hand and pounding on the dash with the other. Seeing them, the driver slung the wheel to the right in a lightning-quick move. The truck skidded to a stop in the gravel, barely missing the Buick's front bumper. One rear truck fender was held on by nothing more than wire and duct tape, as far as McGregor could tell. Grinding into the correct gear, the driver gunned the truck, kicking up grit and spattering mud over the front of the Buick. He took off around the back of the building,

Hood sprang up from the seat, stood over the windshield and shouted, "Hey, you asshole!"

As the truck hit the highway pavement with a lurch, a thick arm came out of the driver's window with a middle finger pointed skyward.

"That son-of-a-bitch!" Hood jumped out the door and started searching the front of the car for gravel cuts. McGregor killed the engine and joined her.

They found nothing but a few globs of mud. Nevertheless, Hood kept up a steady stream of profanity directed at the highway until her gaze shifted to the junkyard through the gate. For a moment the junkers absorbed her full attention. As the gate closed on its own, she started stomping feet and cussing again.

Then they heard a voice, mild and sugary, calling, "Hello over there! Hey, y'all."

McGregor turned toward the building's front veranda to see there a good-sized woman who was wiping her hands on a clean white apron held high over a waitress-style dress. She was probably mid-sixties, but the red high-top sneakers she wore gave her a youthful flair. The forehead bangs and fluffy hairdo helped, too. Coming their way, tip-toeing across the mud-gravel, she radiated a large, friendly smile.

"Are you Miss Hood and Mr. McGregor?" She pronounced McGregor delicately as McGregah. Hood once had said that charisma was a projected personal aura. Mama had it, and he felt it. As they accepted her offered hands, McGregor's anxiety over the car melted away before her maternal warmth. Hood looked disarmed, a rare condition for her. But mood shifts came easily to Hood.

"Well hello," McGregor said. "That's us."

"Well I'm Zora Limbo. But y'all don't ever call me Zora. Call me Mama. I even sign my name that way."

Hood giggled and said, "Hi, Mama. Let us be Janet and Bob, okay?"

"I'm the owner here, and I saw what happened. Was your car hurt in any way? It's such a beautiful thing! And a convertible! What make is it, a Buick?" Mama touched a fender tenderly.

Hood blurted, "Yes, a 1953 Skylark. I restored it myself, and then I named it Edgar." She said it like a child happy from adult praise.

Mama said, "Edgar. I had a beau once named Edgar. Real nice name for a stout, good-looking one. The car I mean." She and Hood blinked at one another, and Mama's face turned slightly pink. They had to be making some kind of female connection, McGregor thought.

Hood said, "Uh, Mama, I'm ashamed at cussing. I had no idea you were standing there. And to answer your question, I don't believe the car was hurt at all."

"Think nothing about cussin' Poker—this time. He's my son, my flesh and blood. But I've been known to use my own rough words on him." Her eyes suddenly watered as she averted them toward the highway. "Poker is a real good boy, but I'm here to tell you, behind the wheel of that old truck of his, he can turn into a mean, ugly rat."

"So that was your son?" asked McGregor, not meaning to sound so pitying.

Mama shot him a split-second look of suspicion. "Yes, sir," she said. "But what I need to tell you is that Potty—that's my sweetname for Roland—he called me not ten minutes ago. Said he couldn't recall your cell number and knew you'd show up here right about this time."

Poteet was known for perfect timing. *And* for never forgetting a phone number. He was the only person of McGregor's acquaintance who survived without a contact list in his cell.

Mama took a deep breath and said that Poteet had been sitting in his kitchen drinking a glass of sweet tea this afternoon when somebody shot out his big kitchen window.

"Shot out his window?" they both asked.

"That's not all. He found a death threat note in his mailbox this morning when he went to get yesterday's mail. He's with the sheriff in Calvin Station, and he says for y'all to hold up right here until he calls me back. Our young Sheriff Buell, he's starting a big investigation. And that brings me back to my son, Poker."

She sucked in air, but held up her hand conveying she was all right. "You see, Poker was sent up for ten days for fighting at last year's Fourth of July picnic. Now back then, they claimed Poker sent a death threat note to old Red Wiley. Red is our county attorney."

She paused for a snort. "That note, it seems, said Red was gonna be skint and his hide posted on the courthouse door as a warning. Sometimes, the pompous little dandy does need his whiskers pulled at least; it'd get him back down to Earth from whatever planet he's on. Now, mind you, nobody ever proved my boy did it. But they said that the note to Red was cut from letters in a magazine like in the movies, you know, and that this new one, Potty's note, looks a lot like it."

Alarmed but spellbound by her non-stop delivery, McGregor opened and shut his mouth. Mama held up her hand again. Hood locked fingers with McGregor.

"Then Sheriff Buell, he comes on the line after Potty and told me to have Poker get himself down to the substation right away for some quick questions, or he'd send the deputies out for him. I had to use some words like yours, Janet, to make him go. Found him out there in the junkyard a while ago, hidin' in his truck and sweatin' like a hog. I hope I'm making sense here, but what I'm trying to do is to ask you to forgive how he acted just now, seeing as how he's a suspect and being wrongly accused and all."

Stopping for breath, her face paled. McGregor thought she might faint and clutched her arm, but she pulled away gently.

"I'm here to tell you both that Poker would never do anything to hurt Potty. Potty's the best friend we have. Without him, we'd never have built up this place like it is." She waved her arms to encompass the parking lot and building.

McGregor wondered what to do. He couldn't help second-guessing his decision to come up here and sensed an opportunity, perhaps a final one, to turn around and go home. Poteet was brilliant at business, maybe a genius. But his behavior often didn't square with his brains.

He said, "Mama, let's get out of this heat before we melt. Hood, if you'll escort Mama inside, I'll park the car and call Poteet. I don't care what he said about us waiting."

McGregor received a stern look from Hood. The message registered and he said gently, "I'm sorry to be so brusque, Mama. I know you're worried about your son. Tell you what, since I'm coming up here to be Poteet's lawyer, after I talk to Poteet I'll see what I can do about Poker's situation."

Mama relaxed but said, "Whenever something happens, they pick on my Poker. Like he's a usual suspect! Know what I mean? It's not right! It's just not right!"

McGregor gave her his best professional smile and nod of reassurance, and Hood led her away by the hand.

McGregor found a spot for the car, put the top up and locked the doors. A strong breeze began blowing the hot air around, and McGregor gazed across the road where a grove of tall tulip poplars swayed his way. The poplars suddenly shed a cloud of withered spring blossoms, and in a giant whirlwind the blossoms crossed the highway to engulf McGregor briefly before scattering high into the air. The modest scent they left behind caused him to wonder if he'd just received some kind of message from Calvin County.

McGregor started absently wiping Edgar's headlamps and grille with a handkerchief. What might Poteet have done to cause someone to fire a shot at him? To hear Poteet tell it, he did nothing but fish all day and luxuriate in his retirement. And what about Mama Limbo? She seemed as deceptively domineering as Poteet, but McGregor suspected she was going to be instrumental in handling his new client. Poteet had insisted they stop here first, so something was going on between him and Mama. McGregor called both Poteet's home and cell but heard nothing but voice mail. He wondered exactly how he was being hoodwinked.

Inside the Tomato Emporium, McGregor found a large, handsomely decorated room, best described as an upscale country café turned afternoon beer hall. The crowd was a jovial mix, equally male and female, with business dress shoulder-to-shoulder with overalls and T-shirts. Most customers were drinking red drinks from giant mugs.

Beyond the big room, behind a half-wall partition, McGregor could see a bar and lounge where a throng whooped it up over a TV baseball game. The tables and booths were full, and the many stand-up drinkers forced the wait staff to push their way through. Today was Friday, and the Tomato Emporium was definitely *the* place for an end-of-the-week stopover. But the lawyer in McGregor wondered if Calvin County had a fire marshal.

A row of large, nearly floor-to-ceiling windows to the left of the front door lined the wall that ran parallel to the main highway. A group of stander-uppers near the windows parted to reveal Hood and Mama apparently admiring the window view, their arms around one another's waist. Mama was pointing and talking. McGregor hustled over to see what was going on.

Mama took his hand without skipping a beat, saying, " … and so the whole reason for having y'all stop by here was to show you the county park over there where the Fourth of July picnic will be tomorrow. We want you to come, and so we wanted you to meet some nice folks today and not feel so out of place tomorrow. Our Big Turkey River runs on the other side of the park down the hill, and we'll have riverboat rides. From the bottom of that hill you can see way across the river to Potty's place. Potty has arranged for a bunch of county bigwigs to serve an early breakfast of pancakes and sausage. You know, get five, ten dollar tips for charity for being servants and taking friendly abuse. But before that, just after dawn to start things off, the bigwigs are all meeting right here in my little old café. Y'all come early and join us. Even the Tomato Boy himself is supposed to show up and be a server. I'm taking a picture of that!"

Hood asked, "Who's the Tomato Boy?"

Beaming, Mama said, "He's our big celebrity here. Fact is he's a cousin of mine on my daddy's side. The family sent him to California right after he graduated high school. Some teenager things happened; heaven knows what. He stayed out there until he inherited the Calvin House Hotel in Calvin Station. Folks love him. It's his face, you see, that's on all the can labels and the posters, the advertising and what not, for our Calvin County brand of tomatoes, the photo made back in the 1970s when he was eight years old. Face of an angel if you ask me. His real name is Clyde Thacker, and y'all just might get to meet him today.

"He called me this morning and wanted to drop by around five, about now. Wouldn't say what he wanted. He's only been here once since I opened. You have to understand I'm now his biggest competitor against that bar and eatery of his at the Calvin House. Place called The Thumb—"

She interrupted herself with wide eyes and dropped chin. "That's him coming now!"

McGregor saw a car approaching from the north, from the direction of Calvin Station. Recognizable at once, it was a 1956 Buick, a red-and-white hardtop.

Hood shouted, "Crazy! A Roadmaster Riviera. Look at it! I wonder if it has the 255 horsepower engine. Your Tomato Boy knows how to pick his antique cars, Mama. That one's exceptionally hard to find."

The stand-up drinkers began to gather around Hood, and everybody watched as the car halted in the fire lane near the windows. The driver waved, and before shutting down the engine he raced it a couple of times to the delight of the elbowing, guffawing crowd.

Then the Tomato Boy stepped out of his car and stood for a long moment as if in a pose, one hand behind his back, the other in his trouser pocket, his gaze directed at no one in particular. He turned slowly away, shielding his face from the western sun, eyeing the park and, McGregor guessed, providing his audience an extended viewing opportunity. Looking no more than forty and in height maybe six feet, he sported a plume of shoulder-length blond hair combed straight back from a high forehead. Apparently undaunted by the heat of the day, he wore a striking, double-breasted red suit, to McGregor's eye perfectly tailored. Add to it the green bow tie and the white shirt with red cufflinks, along with the cream-colored shoes, and McGregor thought that on any other man such attire would amount to nothing but a zany costume. But on this tanned, handsome-faced and straight-backed man, it seemed tasteful, even elegant. Highlighting the overall effect was a daring smile of self-assurance. With head up, the Tomato Boy came forward in firm steps.

Mama spoke, a note of bitterness in her voice. "Look at him strut! He's probably here to gloat about stealing Leslie. She's my best waitress. Probably here to pick her up. Today's her last shift with me."

McGregor said, "I thought you liked him."

"Oh, I do. I love him to death!"

Behind Mama's back, McGregor and Hood engaged in some silent eye rolling.

The Tomato Boy was greeted with a dozen outstretched arms, hands holding napkins and pens for autographs or cell phones for photographs. Several nervy women edged close to him and received a pat on the arm. A couple of them, starry-eyed, shoved napkins at him. He gave them tiny pinched hugs as he pocketed the napkins in a slight-of-hand movement. The Tomato Boy quickly maneuvered himself to stand directly within a narrow sunbeam coming through a window. In the yellowish sunlight his glowing face said he was having a blast.

Mama stood arms akimbo for a few minutes, but then stuck two fingers in her mouth and stopped the ruckus with a screeching whistle. "Stand back! Let the man breathe!" She grabbed the Tomato Boy's coat sleeve and elbowed him through the gabby mob, beckoning to McGregor and Hood to follow. When Mama had them tucked away in a booth against the wall in the back bar, she caught the attention of the bartender and held up four fingers.

Following introductions, the Tomato Boy said, "All this nonsense about folks calling me the Tomato Boy is just that—silly nonsense. So y'all call me Clyde like my close friends do. Mama's my cousin and I've become quite fond of your Mr. Roland Poteet in the last year since he moved here."

Mama said, "Janet told me that Bobby will be here two whole years lawyering for Potty, and that she herself will be with us a couple of weeks to help catalog Potty's antique cars to get him and Bobby ready for a big estate planning."

Clyde said, "Roland just mentioned the other day that he wants to use those cars along with my collection to start an antique car museum here, a tourist attraction."

McGregor hoped the car museum idea was merely the whim of the day for Poteet. He could hear Poteet saying, "Oh yeah, that museum thing. You can take care of setting that up, can't you, McGregor?"

Clyde was continuing, "At any rate, it's great to have y'all here. Now I've heard what's happened to Roland today. Sounds terrible. Is he coming here, or do y'all need to go find him? What's the latest?"

McGregor said, "We were to stop here to have Mama introduce us around, but that was before we heard the news. As soon as Poteet calls we'll have to go. I know he will be pretty upset."

"Well let's plan, all of us here, to make Roland join us for dinner on me at The Thumb after a while. That's my bar and restaurant over at the Calvin House and it has a great chef. Mama's not the only person with a good place to eat in Calvin County." He planted a kiss on Mama's forehead. "Mama, you must come," he begged. She nodded a reluctant yes, as if she'd lost a round in a game they were playing. He added, looking at Hood, "Shorts are fine. It's summertime."

A waitress with a tray of red drinks materialized inches from Clyde's shoulder. McGregor looked up at her to find blue, questioning eyes. Velvety lips spread into a cool smile that she directed solely at him for an instant before she turned to face Mama and gracefully set the mugs on the table. She was brunette, five-six or so, and her skimpy server's uniform revealed much of a perfectly proportioned body. No power in the universe could have kept McGregor from eyeing her up and down.

Mama recited their names and said, "And this is Leslie Rion. She's been helping me run the bar. As I told them earlier, Leslie, I'm sorry to have to lose you to Clyde, but I know you'll like working for him."

Leslie said, with no trace of a southern accent, "Good afternoon, Janet. Bob. I hope you enjoy these drinks. They're called Mama's Tomato Potions and they're made from a secret recipe of hers. I wish I could join you, but there are so many customers today."

And with that she moved on. McGregor watched her at length as she wiggled around the swinging arm of a cigar-waving joke teller at one table to take orders from another table where four boisterous, middle-aged women hollered for more Tomato Potions.

Beneath their table Hood squeezed his thigh hard enough to leave fingerprints through his slacks, and that jolted him back to face the group. Ah, God, they were all looking at him—caught with his secret thoughts hanging out. Hood had an I'll-get-you-back-you-bastard scowl. Mama's face crinkled in mirth.

Clyde had leaned back, though, and unseen by Hood or Mama, he flamed his eyes at McGregor, then turned his face cold. McGregor had crossed a line, it seemed. And there was more to this Tomato Boy than a red suit and a bow tie smile.

It was all over in an instant. Clyde's face thawed and returned to its Tomato Boy look. McGregor recovered and took a long swallow of his drink. He exclaimed, "Okay, now! That is one fantastic piece of work, Mama. Tomato juice never tasted so good!"

Mama's phone rang from her apron pocket. It was Poteet calling and Mama handed the phone to McGregor. He listened and then relayed Clyde's dinner invitation before disconnecting. He informed the group that Poteet was at Clyde's hotel for a club meeting and that dinner would be fine in about an hour. "This club meeting of his seemed to be more important than talking about getting shot at."

Mama said, "That'll be his Firstplacers Club. He started it months ago after he got bored fishing. It's a booster-type thing. The whole county's involved, practically. Potty worked through the club to get me financing for my Emporium."

"Oh, and Mama," said McGregor, "I'm to tell you that the sheriff released Poker."

A conversation ensued between the Tomato Boy and Hood about her car restoration business and Clyde's renovation of his hotel back in the nineties. They went on and on. Relief came when Mama butted in.

"Clyde, what was it you wanted to talk to me about? Your reason for coming?"

The Tomato Boy hesitated, lightly tapping his lips with a fist. He shrugged. "Nothing private, I guess. I wanted to make a stab at *not* finding Poker here so I could ask you something, Mama. Is Poker acting peculiar lately? He said a few strange things to me this morning. Weren't the words so much as his attitude. He was real antagonistic and I can't figure it."

Mama became interested in her fingernails. "I don't know, Clyde. All I can say is he's been acting funny ever since the spring, right after we opened up here. Should I talk to him?"

"No. And come on, y'all, let's be on our way. It takes a good twenty minutes to get downtown and over to the Calvin House, what with the holiday tourists roaming the streets. Mama, please go get Leslie for me. It's time I take her to her new job."

Out front, McGregor and Hood joined a couple dozen Potion drinkers to watch Clyde grandly seat Leslie, then himself, in his Buick. Honking his horn and waving, he drove away. Mama followed in an eighties Oldsmobile, a derelict badly in need of its own restoration.

McGregor and Hood, having obtained specific directions to the Calvin House, took time for the restrooms and then went out to hop into Edgar, leaving the top up this time. Back on the highway, McGregor was about to ask Hood to size up the situation when she sucked in her breath. Up ahead, a rusty orange pickup truck was idling at the side of the road in a cloud of blue exhaust.

CHAPTER 2

The truck was parked front-to-highway at a slight angle to-ward Calvin Station, as if Poker was lying in wait for them. As they swept by him, Poker revved his engine to a loud, hacking cough. McGregor couldn't read the man's expression. Was he was laughing at them or simply baring his teeth?

"You see that, McGregor? The man's a wolf."

McGregor kept an eye on the rearview mirror for some distance. "He's not following us," he said, "and I've an idea for dealing with Mr. Poker. Tomorrow while I'm meeting Poteet's friends at the picnic, suppose you obtain Mama's permission to look at that junkyard you found so interesting. Arrange for Poker to guide you through it. Size him up for me so I can talk to him later and maybe get a backdoor handle on Poteet. If I'm right about Poker, he'll have connections to the wolf paths of good old Calvin County. You're not afraid of him, are you?"

"You don't have to goad me into it, McGregor. For once, you have a good idea. I know how to sweet talk big bastards like him. I might even talk him out of some of those junkers at a good price."

"All right. And now let's think of how we're going to deal with Poteet. On the phone he was all matter of fact, but he has to be rattled."

"Poteet's always hard to figure. Let's wait and hear what he has to say."

McGregor said, "He has a thing going with Mama, it's pretty clear. What's your take on her?"

"Mama has a tender side to her. You're probably thinking she's a tough old bird like Poteet, but she's not. I get the feeling she's a bit frail emotionally—and Poteet better not hurt her. We had a real good talk before you walked up." Hood cut her eyes at him. "Women's stuff, so don't ask me. Mama has a mother's perspective on things."

Hood as a young child had lost her mother, and McGregor knew he would be entering dangerous territory if he were to hint that Mama might be manipulating her. So instead he asked, "What about the Tomato Boy?"

Hood's mood took a one-eighty. "My God, yes! What about that man! The red outfit and that car of his. Now that's a combination! And I loved his hair. And I'll tell you, that voice of his sounded like a soft trombone. It tickled my ears."

McGregor blinked at her in pretended astonishment. "What'd you do, fall in love with the guy, Hood?"

"Love! It was you who fell for that hot little Leslie, wasn't it?"

"No, Princess. I was just looking."

"Looking is one thing. Dropping your eyeballs on the table; that's a bit different, isn't it?"

She reached over and pulled his short neck hair. "You should grow your hair long again, Lumpkins. Like in college. Like the Tomato Boy. Long hair these days gives a man an outlaw look. Intriguing. Maybe sort of dangerous. You know?"

They crossed a long bridge. The river was the Big Turkey River that Mama had mentioned, and Hood read the posted sign aloud. And then the Firstplacers Club sign that welcomed them to "Historical Calvin Station."

"Historic would be the better choice of words," Hood commented.

According to Poteet's rendition of history, Calvin County was created in the 1820s, cut out of Manskar County to the east. It was named for its first sheriff, one Clayton Calvin, who either had been a crook or a saint depending on which historian told the story. In an off-handed way Poteet had told McGregor to take note of Sheriff Clayton Calvin for future reference.

Calvin Station long ago lost its county seat status to the centrally located and much larger railroad town of Finneyville, located in the flat farmlands. But the tourists flocked to the smaller town with its restaurants, playhouses and festivals. Plus, it had the scenic beauty of the Poplar Mountains and the Big Turkey. And the grand landmark, the Calvin House Hotel.

In the late nineteenth century when the tomato became an American favorite, farmers found that it grew well in Calvin County's fertile soil. The weather often was perfect for tomatoes. Even now, during each growing season, weather fronts out of the west tended to push up against the eastern mountains around mid-day to cause a cloud cover to form over the farmlands just when ripening tomatoes needed hot-sun mornings but shadier afternoons.

Decades ago the tomato growers formed an association and adopted the trade name "Calvin County Tomato." The name had since taken on a meaning in the grocery stores and roadside stands reminiscent of the famous Vidalia Onion from Georgia.

This evening, as McGregor and Hood rolled along the narrow cobblestoned streets of Calvin Station, the lanes were clogged with strolling tourists. From several walkers they received thumbs-ups and admiring looks for Edgar. The shop fronts were of red brick and painted trim, neat and tidy. But the town had been hit by a blizzard of advertising.

Posted signs and flapping banners announced an upcoming August Tomato Festival. Interspersed among these were political posters. A local election was scheduled for August.

Reading aloud, of course, Hood made fun of the election campaign placards. She favored "Eskew to the Rescue" over the less imaginative "Trust Rust" until they came to "Sweep Calvin County Clean with Grooms—Vote Dimpsey Grooms for Road Superintendent."

"There's you a winner!" she exclaimed.

McGregor laughed but wasn't amused. In his experience politicians were sniveling bloodsuckers. Exhibit Number One: the legislators who cited this year's revenue shortfall to cut his task force budget in half only to divide up the spoils later as pork for their home districts. How many times through the years had those hacks forced him to beg for money?

Once, he'd almost lost Hood, had not married her when he should have. In the middle of yet another fight over his budget. These days, he and Hood had a connection but not a tight bond. They were tied together with something like a wire from a worn-out spring. Rationally speaking, it was not the fault of the legislators that he hadn't married Hood, but he enjoyed blaming them just the same.

They found the Calvin House Hotel on a hill east of the town common. Standing above a manicured lawn bordered by hedgerows and tulip poplars, the hotel looked like a three-story ante-bellum mansion, complete with Greek Revival columns. Signs directed them to parking in the rear.

At the entrance to the back lot McGregor braked in front of a sidewalk statue, ten feet high, of a man attired in nineteenth century garb and animated so that one big arm moved at the elbow in a come-on-in gesture. The thumb was missing from the much over-sized moving hand, the hand carefully painted to show a bloody amputation. Lights flickered at the base of the statue, the whole of it distasteful in the extreme.

Hood asked, "Where the hell are we, Podunkville or Las Vegas?"

Two modern five-story wings had been added to the back of the hotel. The rooms on the top floors had balconies. Signs named one wing the Tomato Tower; the other, the Big Turkey Tower. Small trellised gardens, an open-air bar and grill, and a pool with separate hot tub enclosures filled in the space between the wings.

McGregor parked near the security guard hut where he hoped his car would be safest. Hood spied the guard over by the pool. She said, "We still have a few minutes, so let me go slip him a twenty to take special care of Edgar. Bet you never thought of that, McGregor."

He had not. Hood glided away along the sidewalk, and McGregor got out for a better view. He could see why the locals might think of the Calvin House as a community centerpiece by the way it was serenely perched on high ground overlooking the town and the commons in front and the river to the rear.

At the pool fence, Hood already had the security guard slapping his knee and grinning. Hood's charm, when she chose to use it, could give a man a mighty heartthrob.

McGregor ignored a flinch of jealousy and turned back toward the parking lot and beyond. Tall trees shaded much of the asphalt. To the left, a walkway edged with animal topiaries led to several tennis courts, sure to be a favorite hangout for Poteet. He loved tennis as much as old cars and often bragged about having knees as good as any twenty-year-old's.

It was getting cloudy and cooler, and the sun had dropped below the buildings behind McGregor. In the air above the long field down toward the river there were sky-to-ground shafts of sunlit haze burning reddish purple and bright pink like iridescent melting rainbows. The water of the Big Turkey was becoming obscured by low fog.

McGregor heard Hood call. She walked up with the guard marching behind her, his eyes following each bounce of Hood's perky hips. Uniformed in a tight khaki shirt and a dangling nightstick on a belt, he was somewhere in his mid-twenties. Under tousled, longish hair he sported a fixed smile, which lent him the air of a recent lottery winner. He had weight-lifter arms and pectorals, a real man of steel.

McGregor worked out each morning but never wanted the over-developed, steroidal look. He concealed his disdain with an offered hand.

Hood introduced the guard as Tomás Hernandez. "I'll take good care of Edgar, Mr. McGregor," he said through his smile.

McGregor thanked him, understanding but not liking where the man's true interest might lie, given the watch he'd put on Hood. McGregor was more concerned, though, about the chesty-breasty body language Hood was giving back to Tomás. McGregor knew all her moves. This was one of her classics.

Suddenly, a green and white 1955 Ford Victoria came swerving into the parking lot. It raced in their direction before screeching to a halt. The driver was a thin-faced man with bugged-out eyes and gray-black hair that stood out straight. McGregor thought he looked like a horror flick actor running from a chain-saw lunatic.

Tomás lunged into the lot, shouting, "It's that idiot Trussell! Hey, you!"

The car reversed, peeling to the back end of the lot to dive neatly into a parking space. Tomás was running at top speed when an orange pickup careened into the lot, the now familiar orange pickup. Poker jumped from its cab, yelling incomprehensibly. Waving a tire iron, he ran toward the weirdo.

The weirdo tumbled out of the Ford and took off across the field toward the river with Poker running hot on his trail. Tomás screamed into his radio and chased Poker, the three of them soon disappearing into a blur of tall grass and haze. McGregor and Hood were left to shake their heads in amazement.

"Woo, McGregor! What do you make of that?"

"Ah, God. I don't know. Poker's getting interesting, though. That Trussell—was that his name? Is he out of a horror movie, or what? Did you see his hair?"

"Yeah, I'm beginning to think we've stepped into a village of maniacs. Damn, look at the time! Poteet's probably in agony. To him a minute late is an hour late. Let's go."

When McGregor and Hood turned they had to walk through a gathering of onlookers from the pool. A stocky man in a too-tight swimsuit who must have overheard their comments purposely stepped into their space, blocking their way. With the look of a forced smile, he said, "Don't be alarmed, you two, we're not all maniacs here. Those thick-heads are just the town crackpots fighting again. Nothing to worry about." Then, in what sounded like an understated command, he said, "So don't worry."

The man stepped away to peer hard into what was now an approaching fog. His smile withered into a scowl of teeth and pinched lips. They left him pounding his fist into his palm.

"Whatever's happening out there," McGregor muttered to Hood, "that man has a huge stake in the action. And do you recognize him?"

"Yeah, sure, he's the preachy boss dude from back at that road construction site where our nice Mr. Spit Juice gave us directions to Mama's. I hope this guy's not one of Poteet's friends. I don't like him, and he better not get in my way again." It was always a mistake to trespass Hood's path.

To get to the rear entrance of the hotel lobby they had to go around the pool. A horse playing boy cannon-balled into the water to splatter Hood's legs. Hood pointed playfully and yelled back at him, "If I were in there with you, kid, I'd get you back good!" The kid laughed.

Recently Hood had adopted an ostentatious adoration of children. She said, "The adults around here may be goofy, but the kids are normal."

Under the portico they were met by two men in uniform pushing out through the hotel's glass doors. The first
one said in a drawling baritone, "Hi, folks, I'm Sheriff Buell.
Y'all seen a security guard running around here anywhere?"

They pointed to the parking lot and McGregor
briefed him on what had happened.

"Thank you very much, sir. You're Mr. Poteet's new
lawyer, aren't you?"

Word got around fast. McGregor confessed, and he
and Hood introduced themselves with Hood doing her
chesty-breasty act again. She seemed suddenly into uniforms.

Pulling eyes away from Hood, Sheriff Buell turned to
his partner and said, "Jimmy Henry, why don't you take off
down there and see if you can find out what's going on?"

Buell seemed too young for a sheriff. But he was
beefy, short-necked and well on his way to developing the big
round belly a proper southern sheriff needed for the part.
McGregor guessed he was an ex-football player slowly getting
fat. Buell escorted them into the lobby and then excused
himself with a nod to McGregor and a swift but full-length
glimpse at Hood.

CHAPTER 3

The Calvin House lobby was spacious with a high ceiling. The walls were decorated in mural paper and wood paneling probably adapted from nineteenth century designs. A great stacked-stone chimney topped a tall fireplace with a heavily carved mantel. Above, a grand crystal chandelier filled the entire space below the opening to a mezzanine.

Beneath the chandelier was a furnished area where perhaps fifty men and women wearing name tags were hugging cocktails and socializing. Roland Poteet suddenly sprang from the center of the group. He was the only one wearing a coat and tie. "Here they are," he crowed, "and damned near on time! We were just talking about you two."

He gave McGregor and Hood hearty hugs. For their ears only, he said, "God, it's been an awful day. I'm sure glad to see you!"

In his early seventies, Poteet was tall and McGregor thought him dashing with his thick white hair and athletic frame, which was a good match for his peppery disposition. Poteet tended toward gesticulation as he spoke, and having a strong personality accompanied by a stage voice, he normally commanded the room. Today was no exception. Bankers, lawyers, doctors, farmers and, of course, politicians rushed to assemble around McGregor and Hood for introductions.

To McGregor and Hood, Poteet said for everyone else to hear, "All these friends are in the Firstplacers Club. I had to miss our meeting this afternoon because I was over at the sheriff's, but they kindly stayed on and waited for me."

Three women tore Hood away from McGregor, and he heard them talking about the fog coming in from the river, referring to it as "an itty-bitty tomato fog." He made a mental note to ask about that.

A man gulping a tomato juice drink cornered McGregor. The drink looked heavy on the vodka and light on the juice. The man's guest badge, hanging sideways, identified him as Red Wiley—County Attorney.

"Red hair, red beard," the man said, "and believe it or not, it's my actual name. So call me Red. I like my drinks red, too. So you're Bob McGregor. May I call you Bob?"

McGregor nodded.

"Okay, great, Bob. Listen, I want to recruit you to run in our marathon in the Tomato Festival coming up. What do you say?"

Red, probably fifty, had a body that looked chiseled by a goodly number of multi-mile runs.

"I don't know, Red. I'd have to train for a marathon."

"You look in great shape to me. Are you a swimmer? You have the shoulders for one and I don't see an ounce of fat on you."

"As a matter of fact," McGregor answered, "I was a swim coach back in college."

"Well, we're going to have the annual Shoot the Big Turkey swim race during the festival. With that arm in a cast, I guess you won't want to swim, but you can be an official. You interested in that? How about getting your butt out in the walking half-marathon. You're up to that, surely. Come on, you gotta do something."

Maybe Red was drunk, McGregor thought. But more likely, Red was badgering him on purpose to get a lawyer's quick fix on his fortitude, his ability to withstand an onslaught of bullshit. McGregor decided to turn the table and test Red's ability to bust a lawyerly stonewall. Asshole lawyers enjoyed playing this kind of game, and McGregor had to admit to himself that he enjoyed it too.

McGregor politely refused a drink from a server, but Red snapped up one from the tray without a glance or nod at the human being carrying the tray.

McGregor said, "You know, that marathon idea is growing on me. What's your best time, Red, your best run? You planning on winning this year?"

"You know what, Bob? Let's switch subjects. New drink, new topic. What do you think about people who sue the county to have their roadway potholes filled in when they know the county has no money? Now Eli Rust—you met Eli Rust yet?—he spends the county treasure on crap like used Bobcat earth movers—nothing but salvage in my opinion—and then complains about the high cost of maintaining road repair equipment. We end up with no money to repair potholes, but we have great equipment—except for those stupid Bobcats."

McGregor realized he'd given Red too much credit. Red was blithering drunk. Looking for a way to bolt, McGregor saw the Tomato Boy slip into the crowd. Red stopped yakking as Clyde raised a hand. A hush fell on the whole lobby and Red melted away into the crowd.

Clyde spoke in admiring terms about the Firstplacers Club and how each member was always welcome at his establishment. Then he announced drinks on the house.

Poteet sought out the elbows of McGregor and Hood. "Clyde says he's met the both of you. Let's go find Mama. She's probably in The Thumb waiting for us. Clyde will join us in there."

McGregor said, "Are you going to tell us what's going on with this shooting and that death threat, or not?"

"In a minute. I know you're both full of questions." He paused to wave to his club members.

McGregor and Hood watched a cocktail server approach another group. McGregor recognized the movement of her hips. Wearing eyeglasses and dressed in black slacks and a starched white shirt with her hair in a bun, Leslie seemed much older.

She looked their way and they waved to her, but she was watching someone or something behind them. Fear swept across her face, and she turned on her heels to speed away through a swinging door with a sign that read "The Thumb, Employees Only." They looked behind them, but saw nothing more than the club members handshaking with Clyde.

Hood said, "I wonder what that was all about."

With Poteet in the lead, they went down a corridor and around an interior corner to the entrance of The Thumb. Elaborately carved dark wood and stained glass decorated the bar's doorway. Mama was nowhere to be found, and as they were being seated at an isolated table in the rear, Clyde walked up.

He said, "I couldn't find Mama, so I took the liberty of starting without her. I've ordered drinks. I want to be the first to serve you newcomers our specialty of the house." He winked at Poteet. "It's a tomato-based drink, of course. We named it The Calvin County Quiddity—fancy word for the essence of the place. I know you'll love it. Like a meal in itself." He snickered. "Mama tried to copy it."

Once drinks were in hand, Clyde kept up the chitchat, again paying most of his attention to Hood. And Hood was receptive. Too receptive, scooting her chair ever closer to Clyde as she answered his questions. She'd be in his lap soon.

McGregor subdued his annoyance, and although not forgetting the intimidating stare the Tomato Boy had thrown his way back at Mama's, McGregor tried to see Clyde now through Poteet's eyes. He guessed what Poteet saw was an affable guy, a regular guy who enjoyed the small-town life, with the added touch of celebrity status. Poteet likely would see the wit, the charm, the casual southern grace, a fellow comfortable in his own skin, not unlike Poteet himself.

Then McGregor, as he munched on a celery stick, amused himself with the supposition that the Tomato Boy had some vegetable rot, a dark side of the Moon, one never revealed to his fellow worldlings. He'd have a chat with Poteet about that, and soon.

But now was now and feeling more and more left out, McGregor interjected, "Clyde, tell us how you came up with a name like The Thumb for this place."

"Didn't name it, Bob. Happened a little bit over a hundred years ago." Clyde ran his fingers all the way through his hair two times and then leaned forward. "Seems a well-dressed fellow, a dandy type from over in Manskar County, started gambling in the old bar here. Got drunk and lost heavily. Thought he had some good cards, but he was out of money. He called a local boy's raise by wagering his right thumb. You can imagine what happened. The Manskar man lost!

"Janet, hope this doesn't make you think ill of the place. But a bunch of old boys held him down and whacked off his thumb. Right over there on that bar. For years they kept it in alcohol in a jar on top of the bar. Like a shrine. The bar's been called The Thumb ever since. You see my statue out front? I had that awful thing made in Reno when I inherited the place some years back. How's that Quiddity, Bob?"

McGregor swallowed and wiped a spill off his chin. "Ah, God! It's great! This one's different from Mama's but just as good. The importance of tomatoes around here can never be understated, I guess."

"Clyde," Hood said, "you tell a great story. While McGregor's working with Poteet, he's going to attempt writing an historical novel. Maybe you could help him come up with more local lore he could use."

Clyde drawled, "Shoo-ah! How about just tell the whole story of this hotel, how it got built and what all's happened here. You tell that story and you tell the story of the whole county. Nothing important has ever happened in Calvin County unless it had something to do with this place. Still that way today.

"Fact of the matter, just tell what all's happened underneath the Clayton Calvin chandelier in the lobby. You'll have to learn about ol' Clayton, Bob. He's my ancestor, the one who originally built my hotel. He had that chandelier out there brought over from London and was sitting under it one time with a friend when the friend got his head blown off. That'd be a story!

"When I was a kid, I saw some old family journals, which were supposed to tell how Calvin County was run in those days. The shenanigans they pulled around here and such. Don't know where the books are now, but if we could find them for you, bet you'd learn a lot. Nothing's probably changed. Same shenanigans, just better covered up."

The maitre d' walked by pointing to his watch, and Clyde said, "I must run to a five-minute meeting. Y'all excuse me, please. I'll come right back, but if Mama shows up, go ahead and order the chef's surprise. It'll be a feast!"

He seemed preoccupied for a moment. Then he walked away, head low and looking at the floor. McGregor noticed Leslie on the other side of the bar trying but failing to gain Clyde's attention.

After fresh Quiddities and an appetizer were brought to the table, Poteet re-adjusted himself in his chair. He said, "Clyde's away for five minutes, and that's just enough time for a business meeting."

McGregor said, "First, I want to know about that death threat note. Then give me the details of the shooting."

"Well, the note was done up in capital letters cut out of magazines. It said, LAY OFF OLD MAN OR GET SHOT."

"What does the 'lay off' mean?"

"Okay, here's the short version," Poteet began. "I retired July first, last year, see? Fishing was all I wanted to do at the time. I'd heard about this place because the state had just announced that a huge portion of the Poplar Mountains would become a state recreational area. Parks, boats, fishing and what not. I was just poking around, you know, and bingo! Found my camp. It wasn't for sale, but it was perfect! You'll see. Anyway, I made an offer to the lady who had just finished building it. She couldn't refuse. No sane person could. Well, I moved right in. It was completely furnished, kitchen stuff, you name it. I bought it all. Turned out, this lady was the county clerk. Her husband's in the real estate business and he's probably the one who talked her into the deal, you come right down to it. Now, she hates my guts with seller's remorse. She bad-mouths me a lot, but she's a real go-getter and I wish she'd join the Firstplacers Club—"

"Stop!" McGregor interrupted. "This is not a short version. We want to know why somebody's trying to kill you!"

"Okay, okay. Fast forward to this last spring. I've told you my camp is up in the Poplars on a hill above the Big Turkey. Well, my neighbor's a fellow named Dimpsey Grooms. Can't see his house from mine, but anyway he's my closest neighbor. Any rate, last winter was cruel to my road and I couldn't get Eli Rust—he's the road superintendent—to pave the potholes in it. To this day, there's a giant hole right at the entrance to my driveway. Watch out for it when you get up there. It'll swallow that Buick whole. By the way, how did the Buick do on the way up here? Like it, McGregor? You did a fantastic job on it, Hood, from the pictures."

Hood squeaked, "Poteeet!"

Poteet sipped his drink and waited with a smile for Hood to quit squirming.

"Dimpsey, he's an engineer, just retired. Not born here, but been in the county for years. He says to me, long story short: 'If you back me in the August election for road superintendent, I guarantee you'll get your road repaired. It's my road, too.' So I do. I back him. Hell, I threw money at him like there was no tomorrow."

McGregor and Hood both sat back in their chairs and shook their heads at one another.

"Well, it turns out Calvin County has a good old boy network in place like any other Tennessee county, I guess. The tomato growers over on the west end usually get all the road money. And none of them want anything to do with any new growth on the east side of the county—development of the mountains, the recreational area and such. They figure the county gets on the map, there'll be a bunch of newcomers and they'll lose their hold on local politics, and they're probably right. What they didn't factor into the fight they chose with me was that I'd spent months putting together my Firstplacers Club. County boosters. A get-things-done club. Those people you met out in the lobby and a bunch more. The growers finally wise up to my power, because my Firstplacers balk when the growers ask them to stop me from backing Dimpsey Grooms."

"Wait, wait, wait!" McGregor interjected. "The growers don't want growth, if I can put it that way, and you landed in the middle of their politics because your road has potholes? And you want us to believe then that *farmers* are trying to kill you?"

"That's exactly what I'm thinking, the gist of it."

"But, Poteet," McGregor said, "that's no reason to murder somebody. Have you any proof? Do you know any particular individual behind it?"

"Well, the Manskar County people—I believe I told you Manskar County is over to the east of us—they don't want this area developed either, because they want the state development money over there. And ... wait a minute. What time is it? It's been a lot more than five minutes. Where the hell is Clyde? And where's Mama?"

Suddenly, Leslie ran up to the table. "I need to see Mr. Thacker as soon as he comes back. Please tell him to find me!"

Poteet asked, "What is it, dear? Can I help?"

Leslie was flustered. "No. I mean, thanks, but I have to talk to him. I have to run!" With that, she was gone.

Poteet said, "That girl is a dynamo! Until today, she worked for Mama and was practically running the bar. Now that she's here, she'll be the manager of The Thumb in short order. Something worries me about her, though. She has some kind of fixation on the Tomato Boy. Can't figure it."

Hood said, "We met her at Mama's a while ago and I got weird vibes from her. But McGregor's in love with her."

"I can understand that!" Poteet said, seeing McGregor's grin. But then he scrutinized his wristwatch. "I'm going to find Mama and Clyde and get their butts in here."

Before either McGregor or Hood could object, Poteet was striding toward the hallway. They sat staring at one another. McGregor finished his second drink. "Did you get anything out of what he told us?" he asked.

"No. You said it. Said he had to be rattled."

"Let me rephrase," McGregor said. "I think he's crazy!"

The server appeared with more Quiddities, which nobody had ordered. After several minutes of silence, McGregor couldn't help fuming. He pointed a finger at Hood and said, "You're to blame for this, you know. At the defense firm, I'd have a bunch of clients lined up already. Poteet's world is always full of ridiculous chaos—you should have known it would be no different now. Tomato farmers trying to kill him. Bullshit!"

"Now hold on a damn minute!" she retorted. "Were you in a coma? You didn't have to agree to his offer. Now you blame me for helping you stay on your feet?"

"Stay on my feet with a broken wrist!"

Hood jumped up from the table. "All right, I'm not going to put up—" She stopped short and sat back down. "McGregor, I think we're getting tanked."

McGregor looked hard at his third empty glass; then let out a temper-deflating breath. "Yeah, you're right," he said. "I'm sorry, Princess. I'm tired. Let's excuse ourselves from dinner and try to get a two-bedroom suite. With Mama and the Tomato Boy here, I bet Poteet won't talk any more, anyway. We can get room service tonight and get some sleep. We're supposed to be at Mama's at dawn."

Hood cringed. "I forgot all about that. But we get separate rooms."

McGregor made a face. "Be that way. First, though, I'm going to the restroom."

Across the hallway he opened the door to a spotless but exceptionally stinky restroom. He thought about searching for another one, but he couldn't wait. Holding his breath, he dashed to a urinal. Then, he heard somebody making shushing noises in a stall. With a quick peek under the stall door, he saw two pairs of feet.

He heard scuffing noises as he went for a fast hand-washing, and the stall door opened a crack. Trussell, the guy from the parking lot, squeezed out. His hair was still sticking out every which way. McGregor tensed.

Trussell walked toward him and said in a guttural rattle, "Hi, man, how am I?"

McGregor repressed a chuckle and replied, "I don't know, fella, you look a little strange to me. How about leaving me out of whatever's going on here. I'll just slip out the door."

As the restroom door was closing behind him, he heard someone in there yell, "What did you have to talk to him for, you goddamn idiot?"

He'd only heard Poker shouting earlier during the parking lot chase, but the gravelly voice from the stall sure sounded like him.

McGregor stopped mid-way in the wide corridor and stared at the wallpaper, a mural-like painting of an eighteenth century lawn party and a pastoral scene of running horses, fences and forest. Down at the floor, he saw marble. Tennessee marble, like in the National Gallery of Art or one of those D.C. places.

The two men in the restroom never came out. They had to be up to something.

He stepped over and peeked through the glass enclosing the vestibule of The Thumb. Hood sat alone, her head resting on her fists. No Mama; no Clyde; no Poteet. He ran his fingers over the smooth mahogany framing the entrance and wondered how many men and women had come here, for how many years.

He was imagining the sound of loud voices, of a corridor full of farmers and merchants and politicians marching through the years. Had he ever heard of a farmer committing murder?

Then actual loud voices exploded from the direction of the lobby and reverberated throughout McGregor's corridor. Somebody screamed. His hand automatically reached for the .38 on his right hip. Not there; not there for months. Couldn't have handled it anyway with the bad arm.

Then there was more screaming. Diners emerged from The Thumb, Hood behind them. They and McGregor ran as one to the lobby. Fearing that something had happened to Poteet, McGregor elbowed his way through the crowd with Hood holding onto his cast.

In the lobby under the chandelier, Leslie was dancing around in circles, stumbling over tables and chairs. Stumbling and screaming.

And Poteet was chasing her.

In protective bodyguard fashion McGregor grabbed Poteet and flung him into Hood's arms. He had blood on his coat sleeve.

Leslie slumped into a chair, her new glasses gone. Her hair had frizzed out of its neat ball. She looked up at

McGregor in a pleading silent scream as if trying to transmit to him her thoughts, the sexy flash of her blues stolen, he could tell, by something she'd seen.

Sheriff Buell appeared out of nowhere to hover over Leslie and order McGregor and the crowd to stand back. McGregor, shaken by Leslie's eyes, retreated to where Hood held Poteet.

"What the hell happened, Poteet?" he asked. Poteet just shook his head, looking faint.

Deputy Jimmy Henry came over to take possession of Poteet, but Poteet pulled away from him and said loudly, "Clyde's dead up in his room. His head's sliced open!"

The crowd heard him and moved en masse toward the elevators for the Tomato Tower, but the sheriff froze everybody with a yell to halt. "... and stand still and don't move until I tell you to!"

He shouted to his deputy, "Jimmy Henry! Turn Mr. Poteet loose and get over here and hold onto this girl!"

Buell told the two scared desk clerks that they were now his deputies, that they were to guard the front and rear doors—nobody in or out. He radioed for an ambulance and backup, all available officers. Then he ordered the crowd to assemble at the front desk, the better for Jimmy Henry to watch over them.

Buell hustled the pale Poteet to the side of the room. McGregor and Hood went with them, Buell not seeming to mind. Red Wiley came over.

"Mr. Poteet, what's going on?" Buell asked.

"I left McGregor and Hood in The Thumb and walked all around the hotel looking for either Clyde or Mama, see. They were supposed to be with us. Finally, I just went to Clyde's suite. The door was ajar and I found him on the floor. Pool of blood. His head's caved in, Sheriff. I checked for a pulse. Nothing. You know how the kitchen's out in the room there, and I heard something from behind the counter. I went over to look and noticed the refrigerator had been pulled out from the wall. Beside it and squatting on the floor was Leslie. She jumped up screaming and ran away, yelling about me killing Clyde. Except she didn't say *Clyde*. She said Daddy!"

Red Wiley said in a hard whisper, "Damnation. Daddy?"

Poteet paled again. Hood pulled a chair over for him, and McGregor put him in it and told him to take a few deep breaths.

He continued, more slowly. "I jumped in the elevator with her at the last second. You see, I'm thinking she's the one that killed Clyde. She fought me like a tiger in there and then came running out here. So I chased her. Didn't want her to get away, if that was what she was trying to do."

Buell said, "I've heard enough. Wait. Did you close the door to the suite?"

"Yes. I mean, I don't know."

Other officers arrived, followed by paramedics and EMTs. The desk clerk handed Buell a passkey, and Buell quickly organized his deputies. Jimmy Henry was to stay with Leslie, take her into the hotel office. He ordered a paramedic to check her to see if she needed medical attention. Again he shouted to the crowd to stay put.

To Poteet, he said, "You feel like coming up with me?"

Poteet assured him he was fine but wanted McGregor and Hood with him. Buell reluctantly agreed. With Red Wiley, the deputies and the paramedics, they took the elevator to Clyde's fifth floor Tomato Tower quarters.

Seeing the door ajar, Buell cursed. He cursed again at the bloody tracks on the corridor carpet. He eased inside the doorway and called for the paramedics, then caught Poteet gingerly by the arm and led him just across the threshold. Red went in with a deputy. Another deputy stayed in the hall, but he let McGregor and Hood peek in.

Clyde lay sprawled; blood in his blond hair; his bow tie now green *and* red; the slender fingers of both hands clenched into fists. On the side of his face not bloody, the eye was open in the same cold, hard stare McGregor had received at Mama's restaurant.

McGregor shivered. Hood put her arm around him and wiped tears on his shoulder.

The paramedic who was checking Clyde shook his head gravely. The police photographer came up behind them, her hand covering her mouth. She went in. Poteet repeated to Buell his version of events, pointing to where he had walked and where he'd found Leslie.

McGregor's attention was drawn to an old-style cassette tape recorder, the portable kind about a foot long and a relic from twenty years ago. It was on the floor beside Clyde—the body— with its casing cracked. Several cassette tapes were scattered about. No CD's? A large television hung on the wall; surround sound speakers were in the ceiling. Modern stuff—and yet ...

The sheriff told McGregor and Hood to take Poteet back downstairs and have him examined by one of the emergency crew, away from the crowd. And to keep him quiet.

In the lobby, cameras and several reporters holding out microphones greeted them with shouted questions. The security guard from the parking lot, Tomás Hernandez, was there to help. He stiff-armed away the press, being especially attentive to shield Hood, McGregor noticed. Tomás situated the three of them in a corner and an EMT came over to take Poteet's blood pressure.

A tall man in a deputy's uniform stalked to the center of the lobby. The crowd shrank from his glare. Tomás whispered in pride that this man was his brother, Carlos Hernandez, Sheriff Buell's chief deputy. Carlos was approaching McGregor's group when he received a call on his radio and cocked his head to listen. McGregor was sure he heard the radio voice crackle the word Limbo.

Tomás conferred with his brother and reported back that Carlos wanted to interview Poteet, but was being called to a disturbance down at the Big Turkey Bridge. They were to stay put until Sheriff Buell spoke with them. The medic said Poteet needed the rest anyway.

Mama materialized. She asked, "What's happened here? I heard Carlos's radio say Limbo and something about a wreck at the bridge. Is Poker hurt? Somebody have a heart attack? Potty, you sick? Somebody say something!"

They all spoke at once. Mama took the news in silence, her eyes darting side to side, hands shaking. Then, without an explanation of where she'd been, she kissed Poteet on the head and told Tomás she wanted out.

Tomás hesitated. "But Sheriff Buell said—"

"You unlock that door, young man, or I'll slap the flour out o' you!"

He quickly complied.

The lobby crowd had divided into cliques; lawyers and bankers were in one huddle, farmers and merchants in another. The politicians dashed from group to group, the better to be caught on camera, McGregor surmised. Ears were glued to phones, and several sets of fingers tapped away on BlackBerries. A chant arose from one cluster: We want liquor! We want liquor! Finally, a harried server from The Thumb came out bearing trays of Quiddities.

Those present eventually signed a roster with their names and addresses and where they were when Leslie had come in screaming. Told they were free to go, nobody left. Indeed, more persons were arriving at the hotel to stand in gangs on the front and rear porticos, some peeking in with hands cupped against the glass.

A short, thin woman banged on the door so fiercely that Tomás gave up and let her in. Immediately, the politicians ran to cluster around her. Tomás received radioed orders to escort the medical examiner upstairs and had to leave the Poteet group unprotected.

Poteet's color came back to his face. He said, "That woman who just came in, she's Tipsy Alcorn, the county clerk, and the person who sold me my camp."

Hood cautioned him, "Just stay quiet for now, Poteet. We can talk later."

But he said, "Ah, let me talk—about something, anyway. Y'all watch Tipsy over there. She won't even look my way. She goes around saying I stole her house from her in a moment of financial weakness. McGregor, you can talk some sense into her. By the way, she's also the county historian. She'd be good for your book." He leaned back in his chair to close his eyes.

Hood patted his drooping shoulders and whispered to McGregor, "All of a sudden, he's talking as if nothing happened. He may be in shock."

A man in an ill-fitting blazer walked up. It took a moment, but McGregor recognized him as the roadblock boss and the man from the parking lot who had assured them everybody here wasn't a maniac. Poteet sat upright and introduced them to Eli Rust, the county road superintendent.

Poteet and Rust shook hands, Poteet weakly, Rust with enthusiasm. Rust, with the smarmy grin of a campaigning politician, allowed as how everybody was real concerned for Poteet. He volunteered to report on Poteet around the room so no one would come over to pester him.

"Do that, Eli," Poteet said. "Tell them I'm fine. And thank you. I appreciate the kindness. It means a lot to me."

Rust turned to McGregor and Hood. "Roland's probably told you that him and me are in a bit of a battle. I've told him I'll pave his potholes soon as there's money for it." He gave Poteet's knee a patronizing pat. "But no, he has to go and run Dimpsey against me. Well, I just want y'all to know that politics is one thing, but when it comes to something like what's happened tonight, we're all one big family. If I can do anything for you, Roland, you call me. Most of the people here are staying the night, planned to do it in order to be at Mama Limbo's early tomorrow. Hope you all feel like coming. Word is that the picnic's still on."

McGregor cut Rust off. "If the sheriff approves, we'll leave. I'm sure you've heard somebody shot out Poteet's window today. He's had a rough one and we're all tired."

"I get it. Be seeing you. Bye, Roland."

Before leaving, Rust met McGregor's eyes briefly. McGregor had the feeling he was being assessed for strengths and weaknesses. It was the same sensation he used to get from defense counsel before an important trial.

Sheriff Buell came out of the elevator and told Poteet he could go as long as he promised to come in for a complete statement early tomorrow. Poteet agreed, with assent from McGregor, and Buell headed toward his deputies.

Hood said, "Poteet, let's get you to your place. I'll drive you. Are you in that red '59 Caddy convertible I sold you last year? I'd love to wheel my sweet baby Chesterfield around one more time." Poteet nodded.

But before they could leave, Buell shouted to the television reporters. In front of the cameras he adjusted his belt up on over his paunch and thrust out his chin.

Clyde Thacker was dead, he pronounced. They were treating the death as a homicide. No arrests had been made, but he was taking into custody a person of interest and material witness, one Leslie Rion. She was a newly hired cocktail server at the hotel with a California driver's license and a local address. Because the roster was complete, they should all go about their normal activities. The hotel would be open for business as usual immediately after they escorted Miss Rion from the premises. The Tomato Tower's fifth floor was off limits. Anybody trying to take a look-see would be arrested for interfering with a police investigation.

Deputy Jimmy Henry led Leslie to the front door, but when there Leslie pulled away and spun back to face the milling, whispering gawkers.

"I'd never kill my own father!" she shouted and started crying again.

Jimmy Henry whisked her through the doors as the lobby erupted into pandemonium.

McGregor, Hood and Poteet listened to the speculations of the crowd for a while, and then slipped along the wall to the rear exit. As they pushed through the doors, Poteet's phone rang. He answered, stuck a finger in his open ear and listened, saying, "Fine. Good grief! Fine, see you there in less than twenty minutes."

He shrugged and rasped, "Mama will be meeting us at the camp. It's something about Poker. Said it was an emergency!"

CHAPTER 4

In the fog of the hotel parking lot, the security lamps glowed in sagging fuzzy balls of light. They spotted the Cadillac convertible, and Hood gave her Chesterfield baby a peck on the windshield. She was annoyed to find his doors unlocked.

Poteet said, "No need to lock. Not supposed to be any crime around here."

They'd be taking the main drag, Ferry Road, Poteet directed, and just east of town they would turn left to go south into the mountains. He said that the road to the camp, the pothole-filled road, was called the Old Military Offshoot. It dated back almost two hundred years.

With Hood driving Poteet in Chesterfield and McGregor driving Edgar, they were soon in the high foothills where the fog diminished with the elevation. In the lead, Hood swerved frequently to miss as many holes as she could. The road had been well buttressed, even straightened and widened in many places. Shoulders had been tacked on where feasible along the hillsides. But much of the pavement in long stretches was a mess and in spots nonexistent.

Because the rear lights of a 1959 Cadillac are affixed to great flying tailfins, McGregor found them easy to follow. He put himself on automatic pilot and stretched tight neck muscles. Nighttime odors, earthy and pungent, filled the warm air blowing through the car and assaulted McGregor's always intolerant nose, causing his eyes to water. He was used to the reaction, and wiping with a tissue he thought of Leslie crying. He could hear the screaming. As screams went, hers weren't screechy but were rather agreeable to the ear. "Fetching, in their own way," is how Poteet would put it. Screams of fear shouldn't be agreeable, though, so McGregor took back the shameful thought. With a smile.

So, the Tomato Boy was Leslie's father. The prevailing theory overheard back at the hotel was that she must be a love child because she was from California, where the Tomato Boy had lived for so long, and nobody had ever heard of Clyde having married.

McGregor knew criminals, and there was nothing about Leslie he could point to that said she could kill anybody. One thing was sure. Mama liked her and trusted her—as far as that went. Before tonight, Poteet seemed to like her. Maybe tomorrow McGregor would try to see her and offer his assistance for whatever good it might do.

They crossed a bridge, the third one by McGregor's count, and the road straightened for a distance, apparently bringing them to a plateau. An unbelievably pleasant fragrance hit McGregor with a wallop. The essence of a million flowers was the only way he could describe it. He wished for daylight because this place had to be beautiful if it looked like it smelled.

At the end of the plateau they slowed to ascend another hill, and McGregor was certain he heard the sound of rushing water. At the top of the hill the road flattened once more and within a mile the brake lights on the Cadillac lit up. Hood stopped completely. Poteet exited the car and walked back to McGregor.

"We have to drive up on the lip of the hillside on the right at an angle for just a few yards," he said. "That will get us around the giant pothole I told you about. It's hard to see it in the dark, so take care. Then we'll come back on the other side of the road to my driveway."

The paved driveway snaked slightly downhill through landscaped woods. It ended in a parking area large enough for five or six cars. A short sidewalk led to a wide front porch.

Poteet's camp was a mansion. It was a wood-shingled two-story house with a one-story smaller attachment connected by a windowed walkway. The whole place possibly contained living space of eight, nine thousand square feet.

Hood parked next to Mama's vintage Oldsmobile. McGregor pulled in and switched off his headlights. On the front porch Mama sat taut in a rocking chair, the single overhead light washing out her wrinkles and making her face look spookily white.

They hopped out quickly. Poteet pulled a tiny remote from his pocket and with a click lit up the whole front of the house.

Jumping up, Mama waited for Poteet. She grabbed him and whimpered into his chest, "Oh, Potty, they called me to go over to the jail in Finneyville. They got my Poker in there!" Then she began to sob, pushing away from Poteet and into Hood's ready arms.

She explained that "crazy Trussell" had rammed his car into Poker's truck at the Big Turkey Bridge. An argument had turned into a full-blown fistfight. Chief Deputy Hernandez—Carlos—had arrested them for disturbing the peace. When searching Poker's truck he'd found a piece of plastic, something that connected Poker to the murder of the Tomato Boy. "They're holding my boy on suspicion of murder!" she cried.

Poteet keyed open the door. Hood pulled Mama past McGregor into the living room. In the ten minutes that followed, Poteet brewed Mama a cup of hot tea. McGregor poured her a glass of brandy, and Hood patted her back and hugged her.

Eventually Mama was able to add that after meeting with the picnic committee she had shut herself away in a hotel conference room to review the last-minute details of her upcoming dawn party. There had been so much to do that the time had slipped away from her. Poteet accepted her excuse, obviously taking her word without any doubt whatsoever. McGregor wanted badly to question her, but in the awkward moment he gritted his teeth and said nothing.

The smaller section of Poteet's house was a guest quarter with three complete bedroom suites, and a large, comfortable den, complete with a television and wet bar. McGregor brought in the luggage from the Buick. Hood found a pair of pajamas for Mama to wear and put the distraught woman to bed, staying to comfort her. Poteet left to change out of his bloody clothes; McGregor went to work in the kitchen preparing scrambled eggs and bacon. It was past eleven o'clock.

When Poteet came into the kitchen he was wearing a silk robe. For a long moment he stared at the plywood board covering what had been his large picture window facing the backyard.

He said softly, "Mama will start grieving for Clyde now that she knows nothing can be done for Poker until morning. Have I told you Clyde was her cousin? I assured Mama we'd get her to the café in the morning in time to greet her guests. She has a steady hand there as a head waitress, woman name of Helen, who'll open up the place about four. But I'm sure Mama will want to be there about then. Might need your help to drive her, depending on how she's feeling when she wakes."

McGregor said, "I'll take care of it. You should stay in bed and get some sleep. Right now, go sit at the table and let your nerves settle. Food'll be ready soon."

Poteet sat down and folded his hands in front of him. McGregor knew the stalwart could face just about any adversity. He needn't worry about Poteet, but he did.

Fumbling about the range and scorching his cast, McGregor one-handedly flipped bacon in a skillet and stirred eggs in another. He let his thoughts drift back to college days. Back then, he had admired Poteet's strength and kindness. Hood's father had died suddenly, leaving her with no family at all. It was Poteet who had helped her through her grief. McGregor had acted childishly, inept, and was useless in comforting Hood.

He was still no good in such cases. He felt supremely self-assured handling legal challenges, but rendering aid and comfort in the face of grievous tragedy was beyond his abilities. Hood had once described him as passionate but without much compassion. He flushed thinking how twice he'd already considered reneging on his commitment to Poteet.

Poteet, not one to stay motionless long, put a kettle of water on for coffee. Without planning to, McGregor gave him a hug. An attitudinal change seemed in order if he was to be of any assistance to the old fellow.

McGregor said, "Look, I really think everything will turn out for the best." It was the only platitude he could think of, and it sounded phony.

Poteet stopped in the middle of picking up a jar of decaf, hands in mid-air. He looked at McGregor with reddening eyes.

"Thanks, McGregor. Somehow, when you say it, I believe it. I appreciate that."

McGregor placed the bacon on a paper towel and scraped up the eggs. Encouraged by Poteet's response, he took the coffee jar from Poteet's hand and set it on the counter. Facing his friend and erstwhile mentor, he said with feeling, "Look, Poteet, I know you're in trouble and I know you've suffered a great loss. I'll stand beside you and be here for whatever you might need. And I'll do my best to disentangle you from this mess and get you back to normalcy. The idea that there's a silver lining behind every cloud is really not a bad way to look at the future. In the next few days, perhaps we can find some positive meaning to this death of the Tomato Boy."

Poteet had been slumping, but McGregor's attempt at eloquence straightened him up. "You're absolutely right. I've been thinking the worst. Couldn't help it with Clyde dead and that poor Leslie in jail and Poker there, too. If Poker goes down for this, it'll kill Mama!"

McGregor wanted to ask him exactly what was between him and Mama, but Poteet kept talking.

"Therefore! ... Therefore, we must turn what's happened into an opportunity for the future. That's why I need you, McGregor, to keep me focused on the big picture. You stir up these coffee mugs for me. I've just had a tremendous inspiration!"

Poteet turned about-face and went to the hallway where he pulled from a drawer a silver plated .45 pistol. Heading out the door to the back deck, he said, "I want to check around the house. Won't take long."

McGregor heated several muffins and took the opportunity of being alone to eat more than his share. When Poteet came back, Hood was with him. Taking a plate and a seat at the table, Hood said simply, "Mama's fine."

McGregor decided to push Poteet. "Now talk. Tell us the full story or I'll whop you upside the head with one of those skillets over there."

"I really and truly don't know much more," Poteet replied with renewed vigor. "The tomato growers are a tight-lipped bunch. After I backed Dimpsey Grooms, some of the Firstplacers in the know warned me that the growers take their politics seriously and so I'd better get out of their way. Well, it raised my hackles. I told them right back that I take my road seriously. I paid over a million dollars for this property and at first a few potholes didn't seem to matter. I guess I can still live with them if I have to. But I'm paying a hell of lot of property tax for this paradise, and I went to the courthouse and told them just that.

"The Firstplacers were considering my whole package of ideas; the planning for the August Tomato Festival had just begun. You probably saw the signs we put up in town. The county officials were all helpful and cooperative with the festival. I expected a positive response to my road complaint. But I hit a brick wall. All I got was one administrative excuse after another. Finally, Red Wiley told me flat out that the growers always received the available road money and always would. He said he was passing the word to me. The growers said I'd better lay off.

"Maybe I'm just a spoiled old rich boy, but I made my money all on my own and did a lot of good in the process. Y'all are familiar with my old businesses. I built low-cost housing, post offices, that sort of thing. Remember that car dealership in Nashville? I sold a lot of Dodges. I was one of the first to start HMOs for the laboring man and woman. After I partnered in that asphalt and paving company, we paved dozens of farm-to-market roads.

"I told Red Wiley I knew my way around the road business and that I didn't like being bullied by the powers that be. I threatened him with a big lawsuit."

McGregor interjected, "Now I understand why ole Red was so wild about potholes this evening at the hotel. I thought he was a babbling idiot, but I see he was pumping me for information. How sly an old fox is he?"

"Well, he's been county attorney for years. He's real close to the sheriff. Don't ever say anything to Sheriff Buell unless you want Red to know it, too, and vice versa."

Then Poteet laughed. "The older I get, the more I start revealing about myself. I never told y'all the true story of why I had to quit teaching college after that first year, did I? Well, faculty members hated the gravel parking lot they had to use. Grumble, grumble. I was still in the paving business on the side, a silent partnership, you see. On impulse, I up and paved the lot one weekend out of my own pocket, like a donation. I really thought they'd be ecstatic, but all hell broke loose. I didn't go through channels; the college didn't get bids, and the other paving companies were up in arms. I simply brought back my equipment and dug up the asphalt and hauled it off. Made so many higher-ups mad, they 'bullied' me out of my retirement job." Poteet doubled over in laughter, slapping both knees. Hood joined in.

McGregor relaxed, feeling cozy in the big room filled with laughter. With all his wealth, Poteet was still just another guy getting the shaft from petty politicians and self-serving bureaucrats. Suddenly, his appreciation of Poteet swelled. He said, "Tell us about Dimpsey Grooms, and then we'll quit for the night."

"He seems a fine fellow, but sometimes fine fellows make sorry politicians. He has a weight problem and can't give a speech for jerking up his pants all the time. Says he can't win without more road signs and more newspaper ads and more free barbecues. The truth is, though, he does have an excellent chance to win because nobody really likes Eli Rust, you know, as a person. Too much like one of his bulldozers. I heard just recently there was a groundswell for Dimpsey, so I guess it was time for the political skunk work to start. Today I get the death threat letter and then my window gets shot out. Part of the reason tonight's dinner with Clyde was so important was that he was close to hopping on our bandwagon. I expected to get his endorsement tonight for Dimpsey. Then that all went down the drain and he's dead in a pool of blood."

Hood patted Poteet's hand and McGregor asked him, "Did Leslie kill Clyde?"

"I don't think so," replied Poteet. "I like her. We've played tennis together at the hotel. I don't know what that means, but that's my feeling. Poteet placed his hands on McGregor's wide shoulders. "What if the murder is tied to the stuff happening to me?" he asked. "If you're going to help me like you said, start nosing around for connections first thing."

CHAPTER 5

By four in the morning McGregor was up and showered. He tiptoed to Mama's suite and found her ready to go. She wanted him to follow her to the Tomato Emporium because driving in the dark made her nervous and she needed his backup.

It was clear and moon-bright as McGregor pursued Mama's Oldsmobile around Poteet's driveway pothole and back down the Old Military Offshoot toward Calvin Station. His sleepy mood freshened considerably when they hit the aromatic air of the plateau where last night he'd imagined so many flowers. He was convinced they were out there, out in the silvery moon-glow, and that they were calling to him in a strange way, as if from an old dream.

He shook his head and focused on Mama. "Look at her go!" he laughed to himself. If Mama was nervous driving in the dark it didn't seem to affect her speed one iota. She dodged the potholes with skill and pulled ahead of him on the straight-aways. Watching her lights swerve side-to-side made his thoughts bounce around.

He had prosecuted cases in several small towns and knew they were fishbowls. You were watched, talked about behind your back, reported on about what you bought at a store, be it clothes or groceries. In short order you learned to be cautious. A prudent newcomer would never take the exterior shell of a town at face value. He'd take care to ferret out the bonds of family, of marriages and former marriages, of professional, business and religious connections. Connections mattered.

He began thinking of Calvin County as a whole, as a network of people and soil, of people and rivers and mountains and rain and tomatoes—a system, every single thing tied to everything else. And there was more, he knew, something deeper, something he needed to discover. Something that would fill the small black hole in his mind, settle his soul. He wanted attachment. With the re-commitment of loyalty to Poteet, he was finding a new sense of strength, a pride of self not felt in some years. At thirty-three years old, he was changing. And, ah God ... he was feeling it happen.

Mama swung right, toward town, ignoring the posted 30 MPH signs. McGregor figured she was going to stand and fight anyone trying to pin Clyde's murder on Poker. Last night, they'd helped her through her initial motherly anguish. And now, his bet was she'd start punching. What about Poker? Hood's visit with him in his junkyard wouldn't happen today, but he thought he should arrange it shortly. Suddenly, he thought of the restroom stall incident with Poker and Trussell. Hmm.

His mind jumped to the piece of plastic supposedly found in the Poker Limbo's truck. Perhaps plastic from the recorder that he'd seen on the floor by the body? No. He shouldn't go nosing around in the murder investigation. Pretending to be a simple estate planner while investigating anything would be problematic at best. He'd look for connections. Yet, what if he found the murder was indeed tied to the shot fired through the window and to the threatening note?

Crossing the Big Turkey Bridge out of Calvin Station, he thought about Eli Rust. Poteet would probably assign him the task of negotiating with Rust on the pothole issue if Rust won the election. He didn't like Rust. Then the shutters closed in his brain as his stomach rumbled. He was hungry and desperate for coffee. He'd get a bite at Mama's before heading back to Poteet's.

At the Tomato Emporium a woman came out the back door to greet them as Mama and McGregor parked their cars in the rear of the building, near the junkyard fence. Mama introduced the woman as Helen, her café manager.

"Bobby, you stay for coffee," Mama said. "Give me a minute and I'll join you."

She nodded to Helen and went up a staircase in the back that McGregor had not noticed the day before.

Helen had a pleasant face topped with a helmet of sprayed hair. She seated McGregor in the empty café, then brought coffee and a plate of fluffy-looking biscuits to him. As he accepted the plate, the ash of the cigarette dangling from Helen's mouth fell atop a biscuit. She blew it off for him with a wink and took an ashtray from her apron.

Kicking a chair out for herself, she sat down straight-backed. "Mama called me last night," she said, "and filled me in on the goings-on. I tell you, I thought she was gonna flip out. First thing she thought of was that Mr. Poteet would find a way out of this mess for her. She goes running to him anytime something odd happens around here, which is all the time."

McGregor poured molasses over three biscuits and ate heartily. Helen sipped her coffee and puffed quickly through the cigarette, her eyes inviting a question.

McGregor lit another cigarette for her and took one from her offered pack as a gesture of neighborliness. "Helen, I bet you have your finger on the pulse of this place. What do you think is going on between Mama and Poteet? I mean are they a couple, or what?"

Helen smiled coyly and leaned over, her big nose almost touching him. "I came here to live with my sister, who's the county's police photographer, but I'm from up north and I've been around. I'll just say that if I make it to sixty, I hope

I can muster the drive that Mama does. You know the kind of drive I'm talking about, don't you, Sugar?"

Helen wolf whistled softly, and then glanced over her shoulder as the back door slammed. She snorted and said, "Back to work for me. The other girls are coming in. Do we have a day in store for us! What about this Tomato Boy thing? Ain't that a mess? And Poker getting arrested. The gossipmongers are gonna have a field day and I'm gonna listen!"

She rose to leave but reached to touch McGregor's hand. "You're kinda cute, Bobby Biscuit. As you southerners say, y'all come back now, hear?" She pushed over the ashtray to him. "Now put that thing out. You know smoking's not allowed in the restaurant!"

McGregor didn't smoke often, but cigarettes were great for sudden anxiety attacks. He watched the bouncing retreat of Helen's attractive buns all the way to the kitchen's swinging door and saw her peek back at him as it closed.

Several minutes later, Mama scurried into the cafe, wrapping herself in a fresh apron. "Don't think I told you, Bobby. Me and Poker, we live up on the second floor back there. Had a quick shower and now I'm ready for the Fourth of July! Business-wise, should be the best day of my life. Hate to say it, but Clyde's murder can only help. Come on back here to my office now, Sweetie. I have a proposition for you."

She led McGregor to the rear of the café and held aside a tapestry of finely woven tomatoes, hung in a doorway like a curtain. The room they entered was small, and she put him in a chair in front of a desk with just enough room for his knees.

"Bobby, you're a lawyer and supposed to know all about crime and such, right?"

McGregor nodded as the hairs on the back of his neck stiffened.

"Did you meet Red Wiley yesterday? Like him?"

"I met him and he seems okay."

"Good, 'cause you'll be working with him. You see, I want you to get my Poker off this charge the sheriff's got him on."

She held up her hand to object. "Just hear me out. Potty tells me you want to write a book. Says it's gonna be about history. Well, I have a set of journals which go back to the founding of this county. Nobody's ever looked at them, I mean no professor type, anybody like that. Just a few family members. And not many of them. I keep 'em hid real good."

"What kind of journals, exactly?" McGregor asked with caution.

"I see Potty kept my secret, didn't he? Just like I asked him to. That sweet old boy. I can tell from your reaction. I've been wondering if you being so kind to me and all had to do with your knowing that I had those darned old things. An ancestor of mine named Clayton Calvin wrote 'em. Twenty leather-bound volumes. He founded Calvin County in 1828, built the Calvin House Hotel and was the first sheriff. Died around 1860, if I'm not wrong."

McGregor was nonplused, his mind racing in excitement.

"Here's the deal," she continued. "You get my stinker of a boy off, and I'll let you look at 'em to your heart's content. Long as you need to. Long as it's you and nobody else. I figure they're worth a lot of money, but I'll let you look for free, and if you come up with something you don't have to pay me any royalties, if that's what they're called."

Mama rocked back in her swivel desk chair to lock in McGregor's eyes with the bargaining stare of a tough rug merchant.

McGregor pondered, knowing blood was boiling to his face. Nothing had inflamed ambition in him this way in years and he was fascinated by the stimulus. It was hard not to get up and dance. Nothing could be better than writing a book based upon original research.

"I'll have to think about it," he said. "I need to talk to Poker, of course. I can't do anything on his behalf without his consent. And I'd have to peek at the journals first."

"Bobby, listen to me. You talk to folks around here about me and you'll never hear anybody say I'm mean or vindictive or anything like that. The word you'll hear most is crafty, probably. I admit it. I'm crafty and I already got you figured out. You're a sweet boy, smart as they come. And you're loyal. Potty says so."

McGregor couldn't help fidgeting. Crafty was a good word for Mama. Tricky might fit her better.

"I made you an offer," she said. "Now you take it or leave it. Right now!"

McGregor said, "There are a couple of things you might not be clear on. First, I'm not licensed in this state yet, won't be for several weeks. Now, I can represent a client like Poteet on the quiet for a while, but if I go to court I'll have to get the judge's permission. Second, I cannot enter an appearance for a client without an agreement with him, personally. And another thing, I've never tried a murder case. Besides, what if this connection to the murder isn't real? I mean what if they drop the charges quickly? May I still have access to the journals?"

"Okay, Bobby, take a breath. I see I didn't make myself clear. I don't need you as an attorney. We have scads of them over in Finneyville. They come in here all the time, and I know two or three who'd love to handle a case like this. What I want you to do is clear Poker's name—my name— completely. I don't even care if they drop charges. I don't want the name of Limbo or Calvin dragged through the mud. What you're going to have to do to get my journals is to find the real murderer."

"But, Mama, I don't have the authority to investigate an open murder case. That's up to Buell and the state investigators. They'd have *me* in jail!"

"You have my authority and you have Potty's authority. That's all you'll need in Calvin County, believe me.

Buell's too young and inexperienced, and I don't trust the state, not one whit. As far as Buell's cooperation is concerned, he'll cooperate with you as soon as I have a chat with the boy."

"Well, let's assume you're correct on that. All I could offer is my best efforts, keeping in mind that I'm supposed to be here working for Poteet."

"Bobby, half the damn county's gonna be here any minute for the kickoff party. Make up your mind. Find the murderer—get the journals. Is it a deal?"

The Emporium's front door opened with a bang and loud voices reverberated throughout the café.

McGregor wanted to acquiesce, but his mind was fumbling with the ramifications of such a contract. He said, "Mama, you've put me on the spot. Give me some time!"

"Hellfire, young man!" Mama growled. "I don't have time to give. My Poker's in jail for murder, and I want to know if I can count on you and I want to know right now! Deal or no deal?"

The dawn revelers in the café were yelling, "Mama? Mama? Where are you?"

McGregor heard himself shout, "Deal!"

"C'mere, then." She stood and held out her arms.

McGregor rose and leaned down to her, expecting a motherly hug. She kissed him hard. Squarely on the lips.

McGregor sank back to his chair and licked lipstick. Mama patted his shoulder, victory all over her face. He *could* have just said no and later figured out how to get the journals. Should have. Becoming entangled in the lives of the locals was not his intention. He wanted to be an observer, not a player.

Mama said, "Next day or two, Bobby, I'll let you take that peek you want at one of the journals. You've been awfully kind to me and I appreciate it so much."

The clamor outside the office escalated. A man burst through the tomato tapestry.

"Mama, there you are! Oh, sorry, didn't know you had company. Anyway, what's this about Poker being arrested?"

Mama responded in friendly anger. "Camper, did I invite you in here? Get back out there and tell those yahoos I'll be there directly, answer all their questions in my own good time."

Camper nodded.

"Wait, Camper, I want you to meet Mr. Poteet's new lawyer, who just moved up here from Montgomery, Alabama. Meet Bob McGregor. Bobby, meet Camper Eskew."

The simple introduction required more composure than McGregor had, but he rose to shake hands and focus. Camper had a forelock of gray hanging down over the top of a pair of thick glasses. Wrapped around his toothpick body was a chest-to-knee apron covered with campaign buttons screaming, "VOTE CAMPER!" McGregor assumed the man was doing a dress-up political parody for the audience outside.

Mama said, "Camper is our county property assessor, and he's running again. I guess Potty's filled you in on this flapdoodle they call an election."

"Actually, Poteet's hardly had time to say his hellos." To Camper, he said, still having trouble taking the man at face value, "So good to meet you. If you have a voter registration form on you, I'll register. Be glad to vote for you, but tell me who your opponents are."

"Don't have any forms, Bob, and don't have any opponents. I sure do need your support, though. I appreciate it. It's a great pleasure to meet you. Anything I can do for you, you just say the word."

"Go now Camper," Mama said, "and do as I asked."

When he'd left them, Mama whispered, "The man's been a bit cockeyed ever since he lost his wife last year. Just look over it; everybody else does. Like he said, he's unopposed, but he keeps campaigning. We all feel sorry for him.

And do you mean to tell me Potty's not said anything about his backing old Dippy Dimpsey against Eli Rust?"

"He's mentioned it, but with few details."

"Well, the detail is he's in hot water with the tomato growers and that's a big detail. You ask him about that first thing today and get it all straight. Me, of course, I'm voting with Potty, but don't tell anybody. Don't want Eli to get wind of it. A lot of my customers are thinking like me, but just keeping it hush, hush. Good for business. Eli has a side to him that I don't like."

Mama went out to face the restless crowd and answer their questions. From the murmur of voices, the words "Tomato Boy" resounded loudest. As McGregor listened to Mama speak of sadness in the heart for Clyde and how Poker was being "misused," questions came to mind.

Had he seen in Mama any real display of grief for Clyde—the grief that Poteet had predicted? Was she simply accepting the death? You generally accept a death more readily when you expect it. Had Mama been truthful about being tucked away in a closed-off conference room when Clyde was killed?

On his way to the back door, McGregor recognized several faces from last night at the Calvin House lobby. Over to the side, though, an unfamiliar, rotund man sat alone at a table. His apron bore a single button that appeared to say "Dimpsey Grooms." He had sagging jowls that pulled down his lower eyelids to reveal the red of each eye. The man was staring at the back of the head of Eli Rust, who in turn was watching Mama from the crowd's edge. Rust suddenly turned to stare back, which seemed to force the big man to blink wildly and avert his eyes to the ceiling.

Camper Eskew sidled up to McGregor and started whispering, but McGregor couldn't make out what he was saying. He squeezed Camper's arm goodbye and quietly slid out the back door. As he did, he noticed Eli Rust backing out the front door.

CHAPTER 6

Edgar was waiting patiently for McGregor in the post-dawn light. With his Buick grille of chrome-capped teeth gleaming, Edgar smiled mischievously as if he had surmised that McGregor had just been plucked like a big turkey.

The sun was rising fast and a breeze stirred the air with an electric potential. McGregor felt a mix of relief and anticipation.

"Edgar, old boy," he said under his breath, "you're wrong. Mama may have hustled me, but I think I needed a good kick in the butt so I took the gamble. For the time being, destiny is on my side."

Over in the county park, birds chirped at several workers, a merry bunch preparing for the picnic. A woman whooped as a squirrel darted from underneath a table to skitter up one of the stone entrance posts. In the breeze the treetops merged into one lush dancing canopy, and the dew-covered grass twinkled in lively winks. Mama was going to have a beautiful day. McGregor found himself actually looking forward to meeting more of the local folk, to mingling at his leisure, to hearing more about Clyde Thacker.

The death of the Tomato Boy was stirring emotions in McGregor, making him feel good and bad at the same time. Good because he had feelings *at all*. Bad, of course, for Clyde. He posed the question to himself, What am I really feeling? He settled on disappointment and annoyance. He had wanted to know Clyde. The apparent dual personality of the man had intrigued McGregor and still did. What was it like to wear the Tomato Boy crown of regality? He tried to imagine Clyde in jeans and sweatshirt with a cold tomato beer in hand and talking incessantly about the history of his hotel. Yeah, he could feel the emptiness all right

McGregor shrugged. He popped the latches on Edgar's ragtop and buttoned it down. On the road back to Calvin Station he put the pedal to the floor, enjoying the loud moan of the Dynaflow transmission. He met a couple of sedans, running bumper to bumper and zooming toward Mama's. The drivers threw him friendly waves. He whistled a made-up tune as loud as he could—into the wind.

Poteet had to be in on the fast one Mama just pulled, McGregor reasoned. Poteet put a bug in Mama's ear at some point last night—most likely when he'd had his "inspiration" and had gone out to check on the house. The pistol was a great prop, the old geezer.

McGregor knew that Hood would be irritated to learn he'd accepted Mama's deal without consulting her. So what? But why did he assume Hood's first response to him would be one of irritation? The question was worth considering, for today Hood felt more precious to him than ever. Today would be a good day to start a new relationship with her, to begin seriously including her in this serendipitous adventure Poteet had set him on. Maybe he could keep her here longer than her two-week commitment.

The air turned cooler after he wound through Calvin Station and ascended the hills of the Offshoot. The darkness last night had hidden the beauty of the mountains and their growth of oak, poplar and cedar. Higher up, a couple of near breathtaking vistas opened up through the roadside trees, rolling mounds of misty forest cut with ponds and pastures. Here and there birds swarmed in flight, countless birds, forming ever-morphing patterns that looked like fractals of nature thrust up and spread against the blue of the skies. "Nature at its best," McGregor murmured aloud and realized he'd never before uttered any such phrase.

When he approached the bridge over the third creek, he saw the water there was at banks' brim and flowing fast. The road sign said Pullwater Creek. Sitting opposite the sign were two boys with fishing lines hanging over the bridge abutment. McGregor slowed and waved to them, receiving big grins in return. Across the bridge, he went a ways and braked.

Pullwater Creek flowed northerly, he could see. From the higher elevations where the camp was located, it ran on the eastern edge of a flat meadow that was about a mile long and perhaps a quarter-mile at its widest. The meadow contained several small groves of trees, mere islands in an ocean of wildflowers showing off mostly bright colors of milky white and snow white; hot pink and orange; lemon yellow. The reds were rose and cherry, the purples magenta, and the blues were sunshiny blue.

McGregor took so many quick breaths through his nose he almost hyperventilated. The scents turned to strong flavors in the back of his mouth. He fantasized about buying an easel and paints and coming back here to spend the day painting. He'd never painted before, but that didn't seem to matter, the idea was so enticing.

As he moved on, slowly because of the potholes, he wondered: yeah, if I painted this meadow, would I not—in a sense—possess it? At the south end of the plateau he climbed the long hill to the next level plain. The camp would be a mile or so up the road. At the hill's top he turned back for a high-level look at the field. Magnificent. Light buffets of wind sent long waves of clashing colors rippling across the field in the direction away from McGregor, then back toward him, then away again. A *beckoning* field of flowers?

He became aware of the roar from Pullwater Creek, and with that in his ears he returned to the mundane world and drove on. Arriving at Poteet's driveway, he surveyed the giant pothole. A heavy rain could wash the entire roadbed down onto Poteet's property. You'd think with all his money Poteet would simply repair it himself, but McGregor knew that Tennessee law prohibited private citizens from working on county roads.

On the front porch of the camp Poteet and Hood were together in a wooden swing, laughing merrily and drinking coffee.

"I have a piece of news that'll make you flip," he said.

Hood asked with nonchalance, "What, Mama's going to let you use a set of journals for your book if you solve the Tomato Boy murder?"

"Damn it! You two really piss me off, you know that?"

Poteet said, "There now, Laddie. We agreed we'd try to make the best of a sad situation. I had to offer Mama something for the journals. She's so attached to them I don't think she'd take any amount of money for them. I couldn't think of another way to cajole her. It's a tough assignment, but I think it'll be worth it to get her journals. You did agree to the deal, didn't you?"

"Have you ever had your arm twisted by Mama? What else was I going to do?"

Poteet smiled a knowing smile.

Hood said, "Come on, grab a mug. This murder case is the most exciting thing I can imagine. And you thought you were moving to Dullsville, huh? Truth is, I've been interrogating this old bastard here and we've developed several leads for you. Clues!"

Faced with Hood's lightheartedness, McGregor said, "Hold it a minute. This thing is serious. I've put away some miserable pieces of human debris in my time, and I'm not getting involved in solving a murder with my eyes shut. We're not playing a board game."

Hood said, "Oh, McGregor, don't pout. We're adults, too. It's just that I had my first good night's sleep in a long time. I'm feeling great, and Poteet's all relaxed now. He's lost a good friend, but we've been getting over it by hooting about the old days. Back when Professor Poteet paved the parking lot at the old alma mater and was canned in the process. There's probably more to that story, huh Poteet?"

"Later on, I'll tell the rest of it," he replied, punching Hood in the ribs. "I paved over a few of the details this morning."

McGregor sniffed the coffee carafe before pouring. "Did you two put whiskey sweetener in your morning coffee? You sure act like it."

Hood said, "So what if we did? It's a holiday and God bless America. Come on, I've had the tour of the camp. You have to see this place!"

Sipping coffee, they walked around the corner of the house where Hood held out her arms to the river and sang, "Ta-da!"

It was a pretty scene. The back lawn sloped far down to a tall boathouse that stood sentinel over a fishing dock extending several feet over the water. Woods bordered the lawn on either side. The grass, the trees, the river with its blanket of low morning fog, and the forested steep hill on the other side with its ten shades of terraced greenery all combined to form a halcyon nest for an old bird like Roland Poteet. They walked on down the yard, admiring the picture.

McGregor said, "If I lived here at your camp, I'd come out and just breathe. The fragrances in this whole area are like nothing else."

"As far as I'm concerned you do live here," Poteet said mildly.

McGregor flared his nostrils in deep satisfaction.

Hood made them look at a line of ducks swimming out of a bank of river fog. The ducks took off in flight as one, and Hood asked the men to ponder where the birds might be going and if they would come back. Hood was high *of* spirits as well as on spirits.

"I've an urge to go skinny-dipping," she said and hooked elbows with Poteet to jostle him.

McGregor was sure his own face lit up hot and red as salsa, in relish of the idea.

"Not that I'm going to, my good *Pater,*" Hood said. "It's just an urge."

But the good *Pater* was staring at the river and paid no attention to Hood's coyness. He seemed lost in distraction, but then blurted, "I've a map of this whole watershed I need to show y'all. The Appalachians are folded and faulted and deformed. The Poplar Mountains are part of that chain and resulted from a geologic rift, which is like two Earth-doors opening up, making the space in between a valley."

Poteet had taken on a lecture-style monotone, or "monodrone." "Now in the case of the Big Turkey here, the 'valley' is narrow and deep, making a perfect place for a river. As rivers go, it's a relative short one. There are long rivers arising from rifts. For instance, the Congo River, or the Zaire now, I guess, arises in a rift but then flows thousands of kilometers. Our river may not be as long, but it does run north, which I know you find as interesting as I do. If you think about it, you could spin the valley around forty-five degrees, and the Big Turkey would flow west. It would thus be referred to as a gap."

McGregor and Hood remained silent. McGregor put his hands in his pockets and looked at Hood's bare feet and the grass protruding at the top of the vice of her toes. He imagined her naked, just as he used to do when he was whiling away the clock ticks back in Poteet's geology class.

"There's a creek called Pullwater Creek between here and Calvin Station," Poteet said in normal voice, his impromptu lecture apparently over. "It runs somewhat parallel to the river for miles before eventually emptying into it. I almost put a place on it like this one, but I thought it might flood. Up here, I have the hill to protect me." Then he stuttered, "I ... I sure felt secure here until that gunshot."

They looked in unison back up to the deck at the kitchen's picture window and its thin, ugly plywood cover.

"I figure," Poteet continued, "the gunman must have stood over there on the other bank. See that sandy spot across the water? That's the bottom of a dirt road that leads from the river up the hill to the county park where the picnic is today. Mama's Emporium is over that hilltop a ways. Bet the guy just drove down that road, sighted in on the house, and fired his round. Finished in seconds. With a scope, he could've seen my silhouette in the big window. But Sheriff Buell says that Jimmy Henry questioned a couple of young smoochers he found in the park right after I called in. They saw nothing, and there was no reason to suspect them. Still, I'm betting I have it right."

McGregor said, "He might not have been trying to hit you or he would have come a lot closer. Think he was just trying to scare you?"

Poteet muttered, "Maybe."

Hood pulled on McGregor's cast and said to him, "Let's be happy again. Come with us back to the house and see Poteet's art room. Poteet, tell him the story."

They climbed the deck steps to the kitchen door.

"Well, okay." Poteet said, perking up. "I was in Montgomery that time picking up Chesterfield from Hood, and I drove back sightseeing through the small towns. When I saw the sign for Florence, Alabama, it reminded me that the Tomato Boy had commissioned a portrait of himself with a lady artist in Florence, named Marigail Mathis. The name has a ring to it and it stuck in my mind—along with the idea that I might get myself painted. Clyde had gone on and on about how beautiful she was and how she was a fashion designer who only painted portraits on a limited basis. She does it all from one sitting and large photographs. I found the art gallery he'd mentioned, but instead of her I found her husband, Tommy Mathis.

"He was friendly as friendly could be, and it turned out he's a full-time artist. He paints in this impressionistic style with lots of yellows and oranges and purples and teal. Beautiful stuff! His gallery walls were floor-to-ceiling with paintings of southern France and Tuscany. With those colors, you get purple fields, yellow houses, teal people, what not.

"I told him I'd thought of retiring to Tuscany, but that I couldn't really leave America. Fought for it in Korea, and gonna die *in* it. No use spending my money with foreigners. He suggested I buy his paintings and create an art room. Have the best of both worlds, sort of."

They had come to an upstairs room, and Poteet opened the door to a mini-art gallery. There were maybe a dozen paintings, all professionally hung and lighted.

Hood exclaimed, "Don't you just love the lemon yellows? The last Buick I had before Edgar I painted a lemon yellow."

Poteet laughed, his face beaming. "I asked Tommy Mathis if he'd accept a commission to come up here and paint my back yard. Ha! He looked at me like I was crazy. Anyway, I bought half his paintings. The other day, I registered him for a prime booth in the Calvin House for the Tomato Festival next month. Probably won't come, though. He's a hell of a high-powered artist and only goes to the big shows, you know."

Poteet scrubbed his chin with a hand and said, "I guess I'd better call the gallery and tell them that the Tomato Boy's dead. I may be the only one who knows about his portrait."

They continued the tour with McGregor receiving coaxing elbows from Hood to make him ooh and aah properly for Poteet's benefit as they peeked into decorative bedrooms and spa-like bathrooms with Poteet voicing his pride in the place as though he'd planned and built it himself. In the master bedroom Poteet pointed out the favorite of all his paintings. It was a colossal Tommy Mathis, the scene a Tuscan-like village drenched in yellow and orange sunlight.

McGregor wondered, why so many paintings from one artist? An understanding hit him. To Poteet, simply acquiring material stuff was not enough. He had to adopt it. Cars, houses, paintings. What about human beings? A little money bought their services. A lot of money bought them, made them eligible for adoption. Was that the reason Poteet was paying him a jacked-up salary? The reason for the Buick? And the journals deal? Did Poteet view the soul of Bob McGregor as an item on the market, ready for purchase and adoption? Should he have laughed off Poteet the way Mathis had.

Annoyed at his disloyal thoughts, McGregor said, "Poteet, it's after seven. We'd better get ready to go to the sheriff's."

Poteet looked at a wall clock and rushed off without a word. McGregor and Hood went to their guest suites to spruce up.

McGregor followed Hood into her room. "Did you squeeze more information out of Poteet while I was gone, or did you spend the whole time giggling at me for getting skewered by Mama?" Still smarting over Hood knowing about the journals, he was wondering exactly where *her* loyalty might lie today.

"Yes, Master Cocky, I did get more info from Poteet. And I'll have you know that I had no idea Mama had those journals until Poteet told me this morning, way after you'd left."

He said, "Oh."

Hood started undressing as she headed toward the bathroom. McGregor turned his face away as a courtesy and sat on the bed.

She said from the bathroom, the door ajar, "Here's my take. Your helping Mama is good for two big reasons. First, it gets you the journals. Second, if the murder is solved, Poteet will get taken off the death threat list—probably.

Why? Because I bet all events in this bizarre place are tied together in some fashion. You have the chops to get it done; it might as well be you who gets the glory."

McGregor wasn't convinced. "I'll need your help. You with me all the way?" He waited for an answer during a tooth-brushing session.

Finally Hood said, "For God's sake, McGregor. Yeah, sure, for the two weeks I'm here. But after that, it'll be up to you and your remaining testosterone.

"Now listen, Poteet told me he played a lot of tennis with Leslie. She threw a good deal of attention his way but was transparent as hell. Said she pumped him for details about the Tomato Boy all the time. He thought she had a crush on Clyde. The way men think, you know? Everything's about sex! Anyway, Poteet believes he's the one who talked the Tomato Boy into hiring Leslie away from Mama. Don't tell Mama. He thinks it's a good chance Leslie is indeed Clyde's daughter, having heard Clyde confide how he philandered around out in California. It's Poteet's guess that he was told things that Clyde never revealed to anybody else."

Hood came out dressed in tight silk slacks and a sleeveless shirt with her hair brushed. Her face was freshly made up in that certain minimalist style that Hood had perfected. McGregor couldn't help drooling inside. And no emotion of his ever went unrecorded by Hood.

"Ooh, McGregorrr," she purred with a hip wiggle. "Maybe everything is about sex. How do you feel about that, you being a maaan?"

"All depends on who the womaaan is," he shouted, as he came off the bed on his knees and made a playful grab for her legs. "You doubt my testosterone?"

She jumped back, giggling. "Stay, Lumpkins, stay! I'm saving myself for marriage."

McGregor hauled himself to his feet. "Since when? Oh well, I'm going to my room before I lose what's left of my dignity."

Hood followed. He asked her, "Anything else from Poteet?"

"Poteet said Trussell is a ne'er-do-well but in a different category from Poker. Mama controls Poker most of the time. He says Poker is rowdy but smart in many ways. Trussell has something seriously wrong with him, though. He has brain damage from an accident, Poteet thinks. Has a sister named Terri who watches out for him at times. He lives in a shack, a literal shack, up on a hill above her place. You're supposed to be able to see the thing from the Offshoot when you cross some field Poteet described to me that's down the road a piece toward town, near that Pullwater Creek he mentioned a while ago."

"I know the field. It's a flower meadow. You'll love it."

McGregor decided to wear a coat and tie to look like a lawyer. Hood, of course, would not deign to turn her head for him to dress. She kept talking as if he were nothing more than a mannequin in a store window.

"Poker and Trussell hang out," she continued, "fishing and goofing off together, and such. The sister encourages it, saying Poker's the only other person in the whole county who pays any attention to her brother, even if they do fight a lot. Besides, Poteet says they never really hurt one another. It was Trussell who Poker was fighting at last year's picnic. You know, the time Mama said Poker was arrested. Never would have been arrested if he hadn't smashed into a picnic table full of food, right in the middle of the Methodist preacher saying grace."

She started laughing. "Poteet said the preacher jumped out of the way and a half-pint of booze popped out of his coat pocket!"

Poteet peeked in the doorway. "You two decent? What's taking so long? Let's go. Hurry up!"

CHAPTER 7

In the driveway, hurrying to lower the top on his car, Poteet said, "We should take separate cars again. Soon as I finish with the sheriff, we'll head over to the park for the picnic. McGregor, you might want to stay longer over there than I do, meet some more of my friends, what not. Hood, you'll drive me again?"

Poteet gave McGregor directions to the sheriff's main office. They'd take the Old Military Offshoot back to Calvin Station. Then left, to the west, on Ferry Road. Then fifteen miles to Finneyville. "There's a shorter way and I know we're in a hurry. But I want y'all to see my scenic road, understand why it's crazy for them to refuse to fix it up. It could be a mighty big tourist attraction."

McGregor said, "Yeah, yeah, you two go ahead. I'm putting the top back up on my car, to, uhh, to keep my hair from blowing."

"You need a cap like mine," Poteet said, positioning an English driving cap on his head. "Top ought to be down, day like today."

With Hood at the wheel of Chesterfield, they raced up the drive.

McGregor quickly raised his ragtop and clamped it shut. His mood swings were becoming somehow related to the raising and lowering of the car top. Proportionally or inversely? Ah, God. What was he thinking? Things were happening too quickly and the last person he wanted to see was the sheriff. He found a bottle of ibuprofen pills and tossed down four of them dry. He'd been working his arm far too much lately, and why had he not brought along a bottle of water?

By the time he reached the head of the drive, Hood and Poteet were out of sight. His temper flared, and to save a few seconds he tried to pass Poteet's giant pothole going to the right instead of circling around it the other way as Poteet had taught him. He had to crunch down into it a bit in order to miss a gatepost and heard a clunk from underneath the car, but the car drove and steered just fine. He'd let Hood inspect it later.

Coming out of the trees at the top of the grade overlooking the Pullwater meadow, which he was beginning to think of as his own meadow, he saw the Cadillac as a red streak speeding across the bridge where the boys were still fishing, at the meadow's other end.

Hood was flying across the potholes far too recklessly even for her, he was thinking, when he saw the flash of an orange pickup come out of nowhere from the right side of the roadway, just ahead of Hood and Poteet. To miss it, Hood swerved all the way to the left shoulder, but she never came back onto the road. The Cadillac sailed off into the field of flowers and disappeared around one of the groves of small trees.

Having been intent on watching the Cadillac, he realized he was going down the hill too fast. When he stepped on the brake pedal to miss an upcoming hole, the pedal went to the floor. He had no brakes.

Going past fifty, the Buick hit the hole and yet another—then another. On the third one, the steering wheel wrenched itself from McGregor's hold and the car slung to the right to head full-tilt across the meadow and mow through the flowers. The meadow at this point was narrow, probably dropping off downhill at a good thirty-degree angle. The creek started coming toward him fast and roaring louder.

McGregor got his good hand firmly on the wheel and flipped it fully around to the left. But the car refused to turn in the slippery vegetation. He started stomping his foot for the emergency brake but couldn't find it. In seconds he was thirty feet from the creek's bank, which looked ten feet high off the water.

This could not be happening; no way was he going into the creek—not with Edgar! As the Buick hit air he was wondering exactly how Hood might kill him. He himself was in the air when the car dove for the creek and the world went dark.

McGregor came to in a swirl of water, water rushing so fast his legs were splayed out in the direction of the current, away from the car. He wiggled his toes. No shoes. Somehow, he was attached to the car, which was half in the water with its driver's door ajar. It was stuck in a mass of creek debris, seeming to have run over a large sapling as it cleared the bank.

Twisted onto his right side, McGregor's head rested on his shoulder, out of the water. But water foamed just at his nostrils. He tried to let go of the car, but found he wasn't holding onto it; it was holding him. The wrist cast had been wedged in the hinge end of the half-opened door.

It took a strenuous effort to pull himself toward the car, but he did it and tried to open the door wider. It was stuck. He let himself float back out. The good thing was he heard sirens. At least he could hear and could see. Rescue was probably only minutes away, so maybe it was best to stay with the car. Out in the swift water there was no telling where he might end up. Maybe nobody would find him. Maybe he would hit his head and drown. One clear thought welled up. As a swimmer, he was comfortable in the water. He'd survive.

If sirens were coming, though, McGregor wondered how long he'd been unconscious. No answer formulated itself. And just then, his head started throbbing. He touched his free left hand to his forehead and came away with a handful of blood. So there was injury and there was pain. It was becoming terribly hard to think. Almost instantly, a deep coldness permeated his body.

The sirens ceased. He yelled for help and his head seemed to split wide open, as if he'd been axed. His thoughts jumbled together so much, leap-frogging one another, that he had to concentrate just to be sure where he was. Yeah, Pullwater Creek. An excellent name. He wondered who had named it and at the same time wondered why he was wondering such a thing. Was he delirious? Because he was aware he might be delirious, he couldn't be delirious. That was some kind of rule, wasn't it?

After a long time he decided he was dying. On the other hand, perhaps he was merely dreaming he was dying. That had to be it. Another rule. The sirens started up again way, way in the distance. Saved again.

But nobody ever came. And he was cold.

Suddenly, his mind cleared completely. He was in a courtroom. A funeral was in progress; the mourners were dressed in black. He saw himself as the judge; his bench a casket. At least, it wasn't Judge McGregor's funeral.

From the bench, Judge McGregor saw himself over at the prosecutor's table holding an orange pickup truck high in the air, showing it to the crowd. Each person in the courtroom now held a bouquet of bright flowers. He heard himself demand that the pickup be admitted into evidence as state's exhibit number one. But before he, as the judge, could render a decision the pickup turned into a red Cadillac.

A red Cadillac. Hood and Poteet had been flying through flowers in a red Cadillac. In an instant he was himself again, his real self, swimming on the college swim team. What a relief. His coach, running along the poolside above him, was not his coach but was that Janet Hood he'd recently met. Nice girl. Good rack. She urged him to swim for his life, to forget the red car he was dragging behind him. To win, she yelled, he had to get rid of the car!

He became lucid in a rapid mind-shift and he blinked himself to full reality. The solution to his predicament was clear. The creek might be deep, but it was narrow. If he could untangle his arm, in a few good strokes he'd be on the bank. He pulled himself up to the car again. His cast was weakening, becoming mushy. If his arm wasn't actually caught in the door hinge, only his cast, then he should be able to pull his arm out.

The car shuddered.

Slowly, his old Buick rotated in his direction. If it refused to release him it would take him down as it flipped over.

"Edgar, you bastard. *Turn me loose!*" He put his knees against the car and pulled. "*Please!*"

The cast crumbled. He was free.

Immediately as the car rolled, McGregor pushed off and plummeted through the water. The current was a live monster, an alligator clutching the body in a death roll and giving no chance for swimming. Rolling over and around, time and again, he finally righted himself on his back, feet first. Trees flew by on either side, but there was a clear blue sky above.

It was in this moment's rush that McGregor felt it. An energy flow of mercy. Not fearing it, not fighting it, he had the giddy feeling of freedom, of exultation, of invulnerability. In whimsy, he was a steel butterfly in a hurricane. Though colliding with slick, waterlogged tree trunks and crashing against smooth giant boulders, nothing hurt him. Once, the weight of the water stood him upright for a thrilling instant in a shallow, and he dug his stocking feet into the gravel on the bottom. Then he was swept away again.

The creek spread out wider and the crush of water weakened considerably. McGregor saw dark shadows ahead. Human forms? As he closed on the forms a stick of wood appeared, and in the split second necessary he grabbed it. It was slippery, but before it left his cold fingers, another hand, a small hand, grabbed him. He was out of the water and more hands pulled on his clothes. Life was moving in a series of short nows, there being no past and no future. And he was aware of each of them. Then he was on his back and sunshine blinded his eyes shut. Persons were talking with mouthfuls of cotton, sounding like bees buzzing. That was fine with him. Life was good.

He jerked his eyes open to an angelic female face. Its beauty, surrounded by a corona of fierce light, was beyond imagination. Its soft lips constricted in worry as hands smoothed his hair back and placed something on his forehead. A brain spark ignited. With the flash of insight he understood the connection between life, love and beauty. The understanding itself faded, but the memory of having had it lingered.

When McGregor came fully awake and more aware of his surroundings, he realized how cold he was. He was wrapped in a dirty tarp and was sitting on a seat in a truck. The faces in front of him cleared up. The words coming out of the face-mouths began to make sense.

"Looks like you're gonna be just fine, fella, soon's we get you warmed up a bit more. I got the heater running full blast. You'll be okay."

They were such comforting words and were coming from a man he recognized, a face with a sideways grin on it. He looked around.

He was in the passenger seat of a pickup. The understanding that the pickup was an orange one rang bells and he remembered Edgar, his dreams, the water, and the searing pain in his head. That pain now was hardly noticeable. He felt his forehead to make sure his head was still there. He found a bandage.

In addition to the talking man, there were two boys watching him. A woman was standing next to the boys. McGregor squinted at her. It was she. It was his angel. She had blond hair and gave him a sweet smile set against perfect buttery skin.

"You remember me?" the man asked, tugging McGregor's attention away from the angel. "I'm Eli Rust. We met last night at the Calvin House when you were tending to Roland Poteet. You remember? You okay now? You coming around?"

"Yes, I remember you," McGregor heard himself croak.

The man gave him a drink from a water bottle.

"Thanks. Are you the one who pulled me out? I thought I was going to die."

"Nope. Wasn't me. These two boys got a holt of you. I drove up just as they were draggin' you out."

The boys grinned.

"This here's Charlie and over there, that's Dewey. And that's Charlie's mother, Terri Williams. They live just over yonder. The boys were here fishing when all the excitement happened, they tell me."

The angel-woman said, "Eli says you're Mr. McGregor. So glad to meet you."

She stuck out her hand, but Rust waved it away.

"I'm afraid his arm is messed up, Terri. Mr. McGregor, didn't you have a cast on that arm last night?"

"Yes, it came off in the water. I ran into the creek way up there at the other end of this field." He tried to turn to look back up the road, but the tarp held him tight. "Brakes gave out."

"Good Lord, you could've been killed!" Terri said. "What if we—"

Rust spoke up and cut her off. "Now, I could call an ambulance, but you look like you're just fine, except the arm and that cut on your head. You hold the arm tight next to you, like you're doing. Here, let me make a sling with your necktie." That done, he said, "I'll drive you into Finneyville myself, get you to the hospital so they can have a look at you.

How 'bout that? Won't have to wait for them to come to you."

McGregor nodded in great appreciation. "Good idea."

With effort he pulled out his good hand from the tarp and laid it on the nearest boy's arm. The boys appeared to be eleven or twelve years old. Long hair and fresh, friendly faces. "Thank you, boys. Charlie? Dewey? I owe you my life, I guess. Let me go to the hospital, and then I'll come back and visit with you—if that's all right."

Terri said it would be fine. Rust shrugged his shoulders, though, glancing at Terri and giving the impression it wouldn't be fine with him.

McGregor addressed the four of them in something near his normal voice. "My head's clear now. Tell me what happened to my friends. The last I saw of them, it looked like they wrecked their car over there."

Charlie assumed command, stepping up on the truck's footboard and pointing to the field. "They carried them away in an ambulance about ten minutes before you came sailing down the creek. They weren't busted up or nothing like that. Dewey ran to get my mother and I ran over there to 'em and they were talking and all. The woman tried to call for the ambulance, but my mom had already called. Can't see it from here, but the law and a wrecker man are over there now trying to dig out the car. It kinda got squooshed up in a dirt bank, like."

Rust said, "We'll have to go find your car, too. Charlie, why don't you hike over there and tell that deputy there's a car in the water up a ways in the creek. Hear now, we'd better be off to the hospital."

As Rust walked around the rear of the pickup, Terri reached over to pat McGregor's neck above the tarp. The touch of her hot hand sent tiny electric tingles cascading over his skin, up and down, nose to toes. It took his breath away.

She closed the door gently against the tarp as Rust climbed in behind the wheel.

Grinding through the truck gears, Rust apologized for the dirty tarp. It was the only thing he had around on a hot summer's day. Then he started talking about how lucky McGregor had to be and how, once, he himself had fallen down a ravine working on a road project. No one had found him until the next morning.

Letting the man talk, McGregor tried to gather his wits while his reaction to Terri's hot fingers played in his mind over and again.

Finally, McGregor interrupted. "Do you have a phone on you? I was thinking we could call the hospital and check on my friends."

"Won't do any good. Hospitals won't tell you a thing these days. Privacy law."

"I'll call them directly through to their phones."

Rust handed over his phone, but when McGregor rang their numbers all he got was a no-service answering voice.

"Eli? May I call you Eli? Did the boys say anything about seeing an orange pickup truck pull out in front of the Cadillac before it ran into the field?"

Eli looked sharply at him, then back at the highway. His face, which had been so warm and friendly back at the bridge, contorted into either a half-smile or a half-grimace. It gave him the smarmy politician look McGregor had seen last night at the Calvin House.

"Naw. Said they didn't know anything was happening until they heard a crunch and a horn blowing. They'd seen the car go by them on the bridge, but they were watching their fishing lines. What makes you think a truck pulled out in front of them?"

McGregor quickly put one and one together. One orange truck to another orange truck, the one he was riding in. He decided to shut up and replied, "Oh, nothing."

Feeling his head swim again, McGregor put his left hand on the dash to steady himself and accidentally knocked a ballpoint pen out of its dashboard socket. He fumbled it onto the floor and, reaching around, was unable to find it.

Eli said, "Don't worry about that damn pen. I get tons of 'em from the Manskar County Concrete people. They're loose with supplies, if you know what I mean, 'cause I buy so much road mix from them. You want a keychain or a ruler, let me know." He laughed.

"Now, come to think of it, I met an old orange pickup when I was driving up this way to Terri's house a while ago. Let's see, must have been around the first bridge out of Calvin Station. I'll show you. Man name of Poker Limbo driving it. That'd be Mama Limbo's son. Saw you over at Mama's early this morning. I know you've met her. You met Poker yet?"

"I've heard the name, talking with Mama and others," McGregor replied, "but we've not been introduced."

"In a way you have been. Last night out in the parking lot of the Calvin House, before the Tomato Boy got killed? You and your girl were watching a couple of old boys hootin' and hollerin' and runnin' around? That man with the tire iron, well, that'd be Poker."

"Oh. I see. But Mama said this morning Poker was in jail, somehow connected to the Tomato Boy murder."

"Sheriff let him out on bond. Brought the papers to Mama a few minutes after you left her place this morning. Said they're still investigating him, though. I saw you sneak out Mama's back door, by the way, after Camper clawed onto you." Rust laughed and pounded his steering wheel. "Way most people have to get away from him."

They came to the first bridge. Eli slowed and pointed out exactly where he had seen Poker's truck. Then they went on to Calvin Station and out the Ferry Road to the main highway into Finneyville. Several "Trust Rust" signs flew by, and each time Eli shouted, "There's one!" McGregor saw two or three "Sweep the County Clean with Grooms" signs, but to Eli they didn't seem to exist.

Eli asked, "Arm still okay, us bouncing so much in this old work truck?"

"Yes, thanks."

"Just a few more minutes, we'll be there." He paused, finger in the air, and then continued. "There's something else about Poker. I've been debating with myself, whether or not to say it. I have not—I say I have not—told this to the sheriff. Don't think I will either. So don't quote me. That old butt-in friend of yours, Poteet, ought to know it though. It's for his own safety."

Eli heaved a chest full of air.

"Early yesterday afternoon, I was checking on a road matter over around the county park by Mama's Emporium. Waved at a couple of park kissers sitting on a table and went over to pass out some literature to them. Turned out to be teenagers. Any rate, I was parked with the shed between us so I know he didn't see me. But I saw Poker Limbo drive up, out of that dirt road you take down to the river from the park."

"Really?"

"Now I don't know for sure, but I'd bet you a box of brand-new stop signs it was just about the time your Mr. Poteet got his window shot out."

"Damn! Poteet said it happened at one o'clock."

"Yep! That'd be right on the button."

McGregor and Eli looked at one another. Eli nodded.

At the hospital emergency room drive-up Eli asked if McGregor could walk in under his own power. McGregor assured him he could and thanked him again for the ride. "And I guess an extra thank you is in order for the information on Poker. I'll pass it on to Poteet."

McGregor unwrapped himself from the tarp and left it on the floorboard. Stepping out, he waved back at Eli and tried to act normal. He didn't want the man to have to go in with him.

As Eli drove off, McGregor noted the orange of his county work truck was a darker shade from that of Poker's orange. Which shade did he see on the truck that jumped out in front of Hood?

CHAPTER 8

In the emergency room waiting area McGregor spotted Hood standing hunched over in a corner furiously punching on her phone. To keep from alarming her, he untucked his bad arm from his tie-sling and held it behind his waist.

She looked up at him. "McGregorrr! My God, what happened to you? You're all wet. Where are your shoes?"

"You talk first, I'm fine. You okay?"

"Hell, McGregor, I wrecked Chesterfield! In that field full of flowers down from Poteet's. They put Poteet up in a room. They think he might have a concussion. Can't find anything else wrong. We were belted in with lap belts, but he still hit his head hard on the dash. We plowed into a dirt bank, head on. But by the time we hit it, we had slowed down a lot. What's your story? I expected you to be right behind us! Why are your clothes wet? What happened to your head?" She peeked under the bandage, frowning.

McGregor related his tale, hitting only the high points.

"Damn!" Hood cursed. "Damn, damn, damn! My Edgar's in the water? Let's look at your arm."

It took but the one glance and Hood was steering him to the nurse's station. She fished out his insurance card from his wet wallet as she whispered to the clerk that McGregor and Roland Poteet were the closest of friends. The clerk nodded, and in some kind of ER magic McGregor was in a wheelchair and rolling toward x-ray within minutes.

The radiology technologist cluck-clucked when the picture of McGregor's insides popped up on her PACS console.

"Was that good clucking or bad clucking?" McGregor asked.

"I just cluck when I get a really great shot. That's all."

Awaiting the radiologist's verdict in a curtained area, McGregor asked Hood, "Is Poteet awake? Does he seem okay to you?"

"Yeah. I feel like they're just being cautious. So the Buick went in the creek? All the way?"

"Afraid so. Let me make sure I didn't dream something. When I first came off the hill above the meadow I'm sure I saw a pickup truck pull out in front of you, and that's what caused you to crash."

"There was a truck. We were having such fun, and I started going too fast across the flats of that meadow. I tried to slow down, but the pedal practically hit the floor. I had hardly any brakes, and we were hitting small potholes like crazy. And then up comes this truck on the right and I mean out of nowhere, like it just rose up from a ditch on the side of the road. All I could do was swerve. I caught gravel on the left shoulder and we went speeding off across the field. The ground was mushy, and I figured we'd coast to a halt but we ended up hitting that dirt bank. Now that I think about it, I never even tried my emergency brake.

"Poteet had hit his head pretty hard, and my ankle was sore. My cell phone wouldn't work right, but somehow an ambulance and the cops showed up. I told the cops about the truck, but I really didn't get a good look at it. There was one thing I failed to mention to the cops on purpose. If I didn't know for certain that Poker was in jail I'd be tempted to say he was the man behind the wheel of that truck. Bearded, heavy set, big arms. I just saw a profile."

McGregor said, "Tell me the color of the truck."

"Well … it was orange! The color of Poker's truck."

"It wasn't a shade darker than Poker's?"

"I'm pretty sure it was Poker's shade. Yeah."

"Eli Rust's work truck is a dark shade. Now, let me lay this on you. Eli just told me Sheriff Buell let Poker out of jail this morning on bond, pending investigation."

"Then it was Poker!"

"Did the truck have duct tape on its fender?" McGregor asked.

Hood pondered. "It was too fast. I don't know."

"All right. Another thing. Rust saw Poker driving into the county park, up from that dirt road that goes down to the river. This was at the same time Poteet's window was shot out. Rust said he didn't tell the sheriff, and I was so bumfuzzled I didn't press him on why not. He asked me to tell Poteet but otherwise keep it quiet."

A doctor entered who claimed to be an orthopedic surgeon. "Mr. McGregor? Your arm appears to be unhurt. The bones are in place and your fracture is healing. We'll want to re-cast it probably Monday, so be in my office at 10:45 and I'll work you in before lunchtime. I'm sure he won't mind me telling you—Roland Poteet's knees are two of my best patients. Here's my card. What looks like abrasions to you on that arm is just mottled skin. For now, I'll put this splint and bandage on it. The cut on your head is minor. No stitches. But let's use these Steri-Strips on it for several days, and you should keep it very clean. You're showing no signs of concussion."

After the doctor finished, McGregor wanted to go up to Poteet's room. He held Hood's arm on the way, allowing her to limp slightly. But she said her ankle had loosened up and quit hurting. It felt good to hold her close, and he fought the urge to drag her into a corner and hug her tightly for about an hour.

Instead, he said to her, "There's even another thing about Poker. Last night, when I went to the restroom just before Poteet chased Leslie into the lobby, I saw Trussell in there, and I'm sure I heard Poker's voice coming from a stall as I was leaving. If it was his voice, that puts him at the murder scene. Ordinarily, I'd tell that to the sheriff. But remember my deal with Mama. I'm supposed to make sure Poker gets cleared. I'm in a quandary, an ethical dilemma."

"McGregor, you should have told us about the restroom first thing!"

"Yeah, well. Now I'm going to have to talk to Poker fast. Mama may have to hire me officially as one of his lawyers. Otherwise, I'll have to reveal what I know to the sheriff."

Poteet was asleep. The nurse with him said they shouldn't wake him. As the nurse hovered over the blanketed patient, McGregor sneaked a pair of hospital slippers from a cupboard.

Back in the corridor, he said, "I noticed that the sheriff's office is but two doors down from the hospital. I need to report my accident, and I want to have the brake lines checked on both cars. We both lost brakes, so evidently my hitting Poteet's pothole had nothing to do with causing my wreck. Somebody tampered with them."

It took a full hour to fill out the accident report. Sheriff Buell called in county attorney Red Wiley, who asked a set of questions of his own. Wiley called the wrecker man to have him check both cars for any sign of brake line tampering or steering problems. McGregor and Hood refrained from saying a word about Poker. Hood promised the men that after a rest she'd try her best to remember any details about the truck that pulled out in front of her.

McGregor knew he was walking a thin line, just shy of withholding evidence. But he concluded that if Poker were to deny being in the park, deny causing Hood and Poteet to run off the road, deny being in the restroom stall, then McGregor would have only suspicions. Withholding suspicions was not against the law. He felt his prosecutor self cringe in dismay.

Waiting for the wrecker man's response, they ate hamburgers and sipped Pepsi Zero. They agreed to be on first name bases, with one exception. The first name of Buell was to be "Sheriff." His actual name was Harris, and he said he didn't like it.

Red said, with eager friendliness, "Bob, it's time we come to an understanding. Sheriff doesn't have enough evidence to hold Poker for the time being. Mama Limbo signed the bond papers this morning on the disorderly conduct charge. She told us that she asked you to help investigate the Tomato Boy murder. Make sure Poker's name gets cleared and such. That Mama! She can come up with some good ones sometimes."

Sheriff spoke up. "We thank you for any information you might give us as a private citizen, Bob. Now, if you represent Poker as a lawyer, that's fine, too. It's your business. But unless you do represent him officially I'm going have to ask you to leave our murder investigation to us. It wouldn't work to have us and you both nosing around. We might step on each other's toes. You can see what I'm talking about, can't you?"

McGregor said he understood completely, and Hood nodded her understanding.

Then, McGregor fibbed a bit. "What I agreed to with Mama was to help her, quote, 'any way I could.' In no way do I intend to interfere with a police matter. I'm moving here, along with Hood, to assist Poteet for a while, to round up his old cars. Then, I'm to do his estate planning and such. Just out of curiosity have the state lab boys come up with any evidence or do y'all have any leads?"

Sheriff said, "The state's dug up quite a bit of evidence—"

Red interrupted. "Watch out, Sheriff. Bob's just pulled an old lawyer's trick on us, inserting a fast question. Something I might've done myself, in his shoes." Red peered under the table at McGregor's muddy socks and hospital slippers. "That is, if he had any!"

Sheriff said, "I wasn't going to say anything, Red," clearly irritated at his older colleague. "What I was going to say was that since the state's dug up some evidence from the scene, we need Bob to get Poteet in here soon as possible. We still need his statement, but we also need a fingerprint card and hair and blood samples. You know, to separate his identifications out of the scene debris. That all right with you, Bob?"

"No problem. We'll have to wait a day or so, though. The doctor says Poteet could have a concussion."

Red left the table to peer out the window. "Poor Roland. I sure hope he's not seriously hurt. Sheriff, you better tell Bob the rest."

Sheriff leaned in close to McGregor and Hood. "It's come to our attention that you're interested in the county as a source for writing a book about history. I know you're a lawyer and a former prosecutor and you're not going to interfere with our investigation if you say you're not. But just to put some moonshine in your Pepsi, so to speak, we'd like to make a deal with you.

"One, you lay off our investigation. Two, you talk Poteet into laying off politics, just let the old ways work their magic, you know. Things work out for the best in the long run around here, always do. Three, get him to talk to the Firstplacers Club, tell them he's out of politics. That way, the tomato growers will cooperate in their big tomato festival coming up next month. Four, make him stop threatening to sue the county about his damn pothole, for God's sake.

"Do those things, and here's the deal. Red and I will connect you to a person who has a big set of old personal journals. Person keeps them locked up in a cold vault because they're over a hundred and fifty years old! You get your hands on them, and you'll have enough material for several books. Make yourself a ton of money, Bob. Now, one caution. If you agree to our deal, you'll have to convince this person that you are in fact working on the investigation, instead of the contrary. Make sure this person believes you're helping us, and that we're helping you. In other words, that we're cooperating."

Red said, "Are you getting the gist of who this person might be that Sheriff's talking about?"

Hood leaned back, shook her head and rolled her eyes.

McGregor said, "Well, would this person happen to be Mama Limbo?"

Red said, winking at McGregor, "Damn, Sheriff! I told you he was a wise one!"

McGregor winked back.

Red, taking over for Sheriff, sat down and said, "Yes, it's Mama. She's kept her journals out of sight, but I happen to know where she stores them. I talked to the person at this place and he let me take a look once. I know a bit about historical documents myself and from what little I saw, these are the real things."

Red's tone became more amiable. "Just think about it, Bob. True original research from twenty volumes written by a person who founded the county and was in on all the hanky-panky that went down here in the early years. Why, you probably don't know it, but one of Andrew Jackson's cronies got his head blown off right over there in our Calvin House. You'll write bestsellers, sure as I'm standing here breathing."

McGregor asked, "If Mama keeps these journals so close to her chest, how are you gentlemen going to get them?"

"We have our ways, don't we Sheriff? Nothing underhanded, mind you, if that's what you're thinking. It's just that Mama might be owing us a favor or two soon. If anybody will make a deal it's Mama Limbo. If she gives her word you can bank on it. She is a Calvin, you know. You do as we ask, and I'll make sure Eli Rust repairs Poteet's driveway swimming pool and does it fast. Gets to the rest of the

Offshoot, to boot, quick as possible. What do you say? We have a deal?"

McGregor said, "It is interesting. Let me hear what the wrecker man has to say, first. Then, I'll need some time to think this over."

"No sir. Let's deal now!" Red demanded. "And, don't worry, we'll feed you enough information so that you can get Poker's name cleared—if he didn't actually kill Clyde. That'll make Mama happy. And that way you can keep your word with Mama and write your book, too."

McGregor held out his left hand. "Since you put it like that, you have a deal!"

His new partners beamed and they shook hands, Hood included, even though she could barely keep a straight face.

The wrecker man called back to report that he'd found puncture holes in the brake lines of both the Cadillac and the Buick. The brake fluid would leak slowly but would come out fast when the brake pedal was used a few times. He said the holes must have been made shortly before the cars were driven, else the fluid would have leaked by itself.

Red said, "Now you see, Bob, why we have to let the professional investigators work with no interference. We have ourselves a murderer on the loose in Calvin County. It's an awful thing! And this same person may be after Poteet. He needs to just lay off, go into hiding or something. Best you can do for Poteet is bodyguard him and write your book! Hear?"

"I hear." McGregor declared, and then asked, "When can I get my hands on these journals? Do I call you when Poteet agrees to shut down his politicking and talk to his Firstplacers?"

"You give me your word it's done, and Mama will deliver the books," Red replied. "And Rust will have men on the job within twenty-four hours. Guaranteed!"

Hood asked, "Sheriff, May I see the cars? I restored both of them and I'm dying to see what's left of them. I promise I won't compromise the investigation."

"Sure. You'll have to sign in and out. Chain of evidence stuff."

"Thanks. And I just realized we're without transportation. Poteet has more cars at his camp. May we get a ride there from anybody?"

"My chief deputy, Carlos Hernandez, is headed that way," Sheriff replied. "Y'all go with him. My boys have finished drafting their reports on both accidents, and Carlos will take a final look. And y'all come on to the picnic. Red and I need to get there before noon. With the killing and a murderer on the loose, I just cannot believe the picnic's still on. Don't quote me, but I figure Mama said it was on, and her being a Calvin—a live one—and the Tomato Boy being her cousin, everybody probably thought she knew the appropriate thing and just went along."

Carlos Hernandez was taller by a head and thinner than his brother, security guard Tomás. Standing in the heat beside his patrol car, McGregor and Hood waited for him. The chief deputy walked toward them in a confident swagger, his shoulders swaying with each stride. In his sharply creased uniform and aviator sunglasses he looked like a living police manual, aloof and strictly official. Turned out, he was affable and cooperative. At Hood's request he thumbed through his personal phone log for Mama's cell number. Driving from the station, they performed the required exchange of first names. With the idea in mind of a book-related interview, McGregor asked Carlos about his family.

Carlos said, "Tomás and I come from Mexican immigrants who arrived in Calvin Station in the 1820s. They eventually owned a large wagon factory. As soon as things settle down around here, I'd be happy to sit down with you."

When Mama answered Hood's call it was clear from listening that Mama was already at Poteet's hospital bedside.

Hood hung up and confirmed it by saying, "Mama will stay with Potty, I mean Poteet, until he wakes up, so he'll see a friendly face. She agreed it was best for us to get cleaned up and meet her later at the hospital." Hood winked at McGregor, signaling him not to ask questions.

Through Calvin Station and onto the Offshoot, they stopped for a quick view of the Chesterfield disaster scene. The shoulder of the roadbed where the orange truck had instantly appeared had a drop off of four or five feet where a driver potentially could hide a vehicle from view and pop up as if out of nowhere. Carlos completed a hurried reconnaissance and came back to say there were no clear tire tracks, just ruts in gravel.

Where McGregor had skidded off the road on the hill, they stopped again. This time they all got out. McGregor pointed out the potholes he had hit before leaving the blacktop. He showed Hood how he'd had a clear view of her car as it crossed the bridge. From this distance they couldn't make out the exact spot where the truck had been hiding.

The Buick's path to the creek was still visible in the mowed down flowers. The wrecker track was farther down the creek, suggesting the car had traveled several yards after it flipped.

Looking at the creek, McGregor felt chilled, as if he were still in the water. He began to shudder involuntarily. He tried to talk but couldn't. He tried to wave off Hood from hugging him but couldn't. The three of them stood in silence on the roadside for several minutes.

Hood squeezed him hard and whispered, "We were all lucky to get out of this one, Lumpkins."

McGregor leaned on the car to stare at his hospital slippers, trying to shut out the panic and breathe normally. Hood and Carlos left him alone. As his heartbeat began to slow, McGregor emerged from his cocoon and shook his left hand to rid himself of the finger tingles.

Carlos put an arm around him. "Listen Bob, I've helped a lot of officers get through trauma. I've been on the receiving end of some crap myself. You'll need to open up and tell the whole story soon. Janet will listen, I bet. And if you want to tell me about it in a day or two, call me. I'm on your side. I'll back you up, need be."

By the time they reached Poteet's driveway McGregor felt his normal self-control returning.

As a test he said, "Hey Carlos, I'm under orders not to ask questions about the Tomato Boy murder, but this is about my wreck. Am I right that they released Poker early this morning, and am I right that his truck was released to him to drive?"

"Uh, yeah that's right," Carlos replied.

"We left Poteet's home this morning a little before eight. Do you think Poker had time to drive up here and arrive before eight o'clock?"

"Sure. Are you thinking Poker messed with the cars?"

"Not thinking anything right now, just wondering. Does he carry a tool box in his truck?"

"Yeah, a tool box full of stuff. Poker's handy with tools and a hell of a mechanic when he wants to be."

"Is Poker a friend of yours?"

"Poker knows a lot of persons, I'm sure, but he only has two real friends in my estimation—his mama and the guy he was fighting with last night, man named Amon Trussell. Though, if you ever saw him and Trussell together you'd never think they were friends, the way they argue all the time."

"Tell us about them. We've only heard Mama's point of view. Come on in the house, and we'll make you a glass of sweet tea to go."

Carlos hesitated and then shrugged. After he called in his location, they left the car to saunter up to the porch. Carlos removed his shades and tucked a temple into a shirt pocket.

He said, "Well, let's begin with Trussell. He has some sort of head injury. County folk would be a lot more forgiving of him if he were more communicative. But he won't talk to anybody, and he drives around in that wreck of his running stop signs and red lights. We get calls all the time. When we're close by, though, he straightens up. So we're sure he knows *how* to act right. He lives in a shack on a hill above Pullwater Creek, above where his sister lives. I heard his sister and the boys were the ones who pulled you out of the water. If you need to know more about things than Mama's willing to say, you might get Trussell's sister to go with you and try to talk to him. I'd go along, but I know he won't talk around me."

Hood opened the door with a key Poteet had given her. They walked into the living room where they paused for Carlos to continue.

"Now Poker, you understand, plays dumber than he is. He's a pretty sharp ol' boy about a lot of things. I'd say he's close to forty. Played football in high school and set some records that weren't broken until Sheriff came along. Sheriff was a hell of a player. Anyway, Poker went on to the community college here, but I'm sure he never graduated. For a few years he worked for a guy who'd be his great uncle, Mama Limbo's uncle, man name of Earl Calvin. Mama is a Calvin—one of the reasons she swings so much weight around here. Earl now ... well, Earl owned lots of property.

"So when Earl and his wife died back in the nineties the Tomato Boy inherited the Calvin House Hotel and Mama got what's now the Tomato Emporium. The Tomato Boy bragged about getting the best of that deal. There's talk that Uncle Earl hid diamonds somewhere in the Calvin House or on the grounds. Since he died they've patched many a hole in many a wall in many a guest room.

"Before last winter the Emporium was just a bait-and-tackle place. Mama sold gas, that sort of thing. She kept that junkyard in the back with a small mechanic's garage for Poker to fool around in. I've never been back there—not many have—but word is Uncle Earl left Poker a bunch of antique cars and trucks. All of them hidden in sheds out in the woods on that hill next to the Emporium. Mama owns close to a hundred acres."

McGregor saw Hood's eyes light up with dollar signs. Carlos turned to her and said, "You'd be interested in the junkyard. I heard you're the one who restored that red Caddy. Did you do the Buick, too?"

"Sure did," Hood said, walking on to the kitchen, probably on a bit of air from the prospect of seeing Poker's cars. "Keep talking," she said, "I can hear you in here. I'll make you some tea."

Carlos raised his voice. "Mama had to work full time because old man Limbo squandered all her Calvin cash. Let's see. Mr. Poteet arrived here about this time last year, and after he put together the Firstplacers Club the members all helped Mama rebuild Earl's place into the Emporium. Word has it that Mr. Poteet co-signed Mama's loan—"

Hood shrieked.

McGregor again grabbed air where his handgun should've been. Carlos motioned McGregor to stay put; he eased around the corner in a squat, his hand on his pistol.

"Come on in, Bob!" he called out. "All clear."

Hood was leaning on the counter with the tea pitcher in hand, and she and Carlos were staring at the plywood on the kitchen window. A good part of it had been broken off and much of it pried away from the outside frame where it'd been nailed. When Carlos put his shoulder to the loose board and pushed, a hole appeared large enough for somebody to crawl through.

Carlos declared he would check inside the house, then outside. Having done both the day before following the shooting, he knew his way around, he said. Hood and McGregor were to stay in the kitchen. Gun in hand, Carlos left.

McGregor hoped Hood would be scared enough to want a hug, so he held out his arm to her. But she merely shrugged in tiresome resignation.

"Hell, I'm getting used to this," she said and continued pouring tea. She pulled bread from the pantry and cold cuts from the fridge.

When Carlos peeked in, he said, "Don't go anywhere. I still have to check the outside, and then I want to show you something. Looks like you sure had a visitor."

McGregor ate his sandwich, pretending to be as calm as Hood. They waited.

They heard the front door open and close. Carlos called to them from the direction of the art room.

Several of the Tommy Mathis paintings had been torn down from the wall. Two of the largest ones had been slashed.

"It's the only damage I've discovered," Carlos said. "I've called for backup."

Hood said, "The paintings, McGregor. Why, why, why?"

"Figurative stab in the heart, I'd say," McGregor replied. "It's likely to be common knowledge how much Poteet values them."

McGregor formulated a plan. He authorized Carlos to call in a small security guard firm that Carlos recommended as a competent outfit. Either Carlos or another deputy would stay to brief the guard upon arrival. McGregor and Hood would clean up, take one of Poteet's other cars back to Finneyville, and check on Poteet, let him know what happened.

They might consider staying at the Calvin House, Carlos advised, as he started talking on his radio.

"Yeah, right, the Calvin House," Hood murmured, "where they actually kill you instead of just scaring you."

At her bedroom door, Hood pulled McGregor inside with her and started undressing. "I've begun to get the willies now that I've thought about the break-in. You guard that damn door until I get out of the shower. Keep me from being knifed to death. Then I'll guard you."

McGregor sat on the bed once more, noticing his clothes were beginning to reek. Why could he not have gone first?

Hood yelled from the bathroom, "What I didn't want to say in front of Carlos was that Mama wants us to meet her at the hospital ASAP."

She peeked out the door. "By the way, how's your arm? You in pain or anything?"

"It aches like hell. But what about Mama? And hurry up. I'm stinking myself to death out here in these filthy clothes."

"I'm getting in the shower now, so come on in and listen. You turn your damned head, though."

The bathroom was thick with hot water fog, and although the shower door was translucent, it too was mostly foggy. Still, McGregor could see a pretty good outline of Hood squirming about in the shower stall. But for the wrist splint, he'd jump in there with her. The worst that could happen, she'd kick him out. McGregor said, "I'm listening."

Shampoo lather splattered exactly on the spot where McGregor was getting his best view. Hood spoke loudly. "Mama said her head waitress, Helen, has a sister who does all the photography at the crime scenes for Sheriff. The one we saw go into Clyde's room, I suppose. Anyway, Helen told Mama that her sister drinks too much and yaks to her about her work. This sister said they discovered that Clyde had a room cut out behind his pantry. You get to it by sliding out the refrigerator and going through a four-foot high cutout in the wall. It was full of ancient taping equipment and had some audio cassette tapes, labeled and organized. Dates, names and such. Then, Helen said her sister clammed up on her and wouldn't say anything more. Said that this morning, the sister got scared about something and left town!"

McGregor said, "We have to get to the hospital! I'll shower fast. If Clyde was doing what I think he was doing all

hell's about to break loose.   No wonder Sheriff and Red
wanted to shut me out!   Do you realize what conversations
Clyde was privy to in that hotel?"

CHAPTER 9

McGregor found a box containing Poteet's car keys. In the garage behind the guest quarter, he and Hood found a 1950 Ford station wagon and a 1957 Chevrolet Bel Air.

Hood gawked at the Ford. It had wood paneling on the outside of the doors, but the rest was lemon yellow. She said, "I sold Poteet that Chevy, another car I rebuilt myself. But I didn't know about this wagon. If still original, it'll have a V-8 with a hundred horsepower. In its day it'd *do* a hundred, too—with a couple of carburetors, the right headers, you know, the speedy stuff tacked on that they had back then."

McGregor preferred the Bel Air, and Hood agreed to take it but insisted on doing the driving.

After inspecting the brakes for tampering she checked the engine. "This blue beauty has what they called a 'fuelie.' It's a fuel-injected 283 cubic-inch engine with 283 horsepower. One for one. A horse for every cubic inch. They advertised that a lot."

Speeding up the driveway, they met a Silverado coming in with security guard insignia on the door. The driver flagged them down.

She was an attractive, athletic-looking African-American woman in her early twenties, dressed in a cap and green uniform. They undertook the regular Calvin County introductions. Her name was Lakisha Thompson, and she knew Poteet quite well.

"I know the house and I know Roland. That's why they sent me. I came here to a big crawfish party once, and Roland and I play tennis a lot at the Calvin House. Is he going to be all right from the wreck?"

McGregor told her the doctor thought so. Having decided to start taking notes, he pulled out a pocket notebook. Minutes were passing, but he wanted to hear anything Lakisha had to say.

She said, "Roland's a great tennis player, but you have to watch him. He cheats on the line calls. He's so good that Leslie Rion and I play him two against one."

McGregor asked, "Are you and Leslie close friends?"

"Close enough. I sure hate it that she's messed up in this Tomato Boy murder. I'll tell you one thing; I know she didn't do it!"

"Exactly how do you know she didn't do it?" McGregor asked. "We've met her only a couple of times and don't really know her."

"I know because I have connections over at the jail and was allowed in to see her this morning. She's torn to pieces, but she looked me square in the face with those eyes of hers. If you've met her, you know the kind of eyes I'm talking about. She said outright, she said, 'Lakisha, I did not kill Clyde Thacker!' And that's how I know.

"Says she wants her lawyer from California but can't get in touch with her. Says she's not saying a word to anybody around here until she can talk to that one lawyer, and they can keep her in jail for all she cares for right now. You don't think Roland believes Leslie actually killed the Tomato Boy, do you? If he's not on her side, the whole county will turn against her."

McGregor said, "We're on our way to see Poteet right now. I'd be surprised if he still believes it, if he ever did. We'll see you later here at the house and let you know. If I tell him you'll keep us informed on any details you might come up with about Leslie, I'm sure he'll be pleased. Deal?"

"You betcha."

"One more thing, Lakisha. Do you think the Tomato Boy was Leslie's father?"

"Well, she's not real open-mouthed about her personal life, you know. But she asked questions about him all the time. Wanted to know what I knew about him. 'Anything usual or unusual' was the way she put it." Lakisha looked around, brows raised. "She wanted to know if the Tomato Boy had any 'strange predilections.' I looked that up and still don't know what she meant. Do you?"

McGregor and Hood pretended to puzzle over the question. Lakisha said she had to go, that a deputy was supposed to brief her. Hood asked her for directions to the shortcut to Finneyville.

"You'll find Limestone Road on up the Offshoot past the home of Dimpsey Grooms. It'll be a right turn; take you straight to Finneyville. If you go that way, you'll get to see where most of the permanent tomato farm workers live. It'll look like a rough neighborhood, but it's not. They're just poor. I drive the county bookmobile and go up there all the time. Never had any trouble."

When Hood found the proper turn she read the sign aloud, "Limestone Road; Finneyville, 12 miles."

McGregor muttered, "God, she can test a man."

As they drove out of the steep mountains into the higher foothills, they came upon patches of fog. Along the way McGregor counted dozens of small homes built in clusters on the hillsides, clotheslines full and tricycles in the yards. Most of the houses were in need of paint. The roadway pavement was as bad as that of the Offshoot.

Hood said, "These would be the tomato workers' homes. I see some kids but no adults. I bet this time of year they work seven days a week, even on the July Fourth weekend."

Recalling Poteet's dislike of bullies, McGregor wondered aloud if Poteet had picked a fight with the tomato growers for reasons more personal than potholes and land development.

Hood said, "Possible. Make a note."

McGregor whipped out his notebook. "Top of the list, I'm adding, 'Talk to tomato growers.' You know, we met one or two at the Calvin House among the Firstplacers. As club members surely they would be willing to connect us to the growers who Poteet thinks are the most against him."

The sunshine of the morning was gone, replaced by a cloud cover. As the land flattened the road improved to new-looking blacktop. Hood gave the Chevy free rein.

"As feisty as any late model." she said. "I couldn't have done a better job."

McGregor commented that the seats were extremely comfortable and received for his kindly illumination a vicious glare.

McGregor lowered the sun visor. "This sky reminds me of Poteet's explanation of how the tomatoes get their afternoon sunshield? Those ladies at the Calvin House last night were talking about the fog from the river and were calling it a tomato fog? What was that all about?"

"It was strange," Hood answered. "They said about this time every July they start getting fog in the evenings. Then right around August first in most years, a tremendous fog rolls in from the river and surrounds Calvin Station for the night. They want to make it a part of the tomato festival and are assuming it'll happen again this year. They're talking about having a tomato fog party, an all-nighter at the Calvin House to jump-start the festival. Block off the street and such. It could be a wild one."

They came to a treeless plain. Tomato fields stretched outward—far to the north, far to the south. Here and there, they passed pickup trucks parked on the side of the road, grouped in threes and fours. Most trucks were of the beaten-up variety, but a few were brand new. Easily, a quarter of them were some shade of orange, and Hood pointed it out.

McGregor swatted his forehead. "Ouch! I shouldn't have done that. But I'm stupid. Orange is the state university's color. Orange and white. And this is a sports- crazy state. The more we drive around, the more we're going to see orange pickups. I'd say our suspect list for the truck that caused you to wreck has just ballooned to what, a couple hundred?"

Hood said, "Crap! You're right. And as your paint expert I'm the one who should have come up with that connection."

Outside the Finneyville hospital's main entrance stood the big man with the red eyes McGregor had seen sitting alone at Mama's Emporium. Hood parked beside an orange Jeep with "Sweep the County Clean with Grooms" signs on its doors, as a van plastered with "Vote Camper" stickers roared away from the lot.

The big man was chewing gum with his front teeth, and he tucked the tip of a shirttail into his pants at their approach. He said, "Hey, y'all, I'm Dimpsey Grooms. Y'all just missed Camper. The nurse shooed us out of Roland's room, so Roland asked me to wait for you out here."

First names were exchanged, and Dimpsey said, "Roland is awake and talking. Mama Limbo's with him. Y'all need to take better care of my buddy from now on, hear?" He grinned and chewed.

"How is Camper? Still campaigning hard?" McGregor asked. "I've met him, but tell Janet here about him."

Dimpsey implanted his wad of gum somewhere in his mouth and in excited chatter told Hood of Camper's wife having died and how the man spent all his time campaigning. He segued into what sounded like a memorized get-out-the-vote stump speech. Dimpsey had the habit of squeezing his droopy eyes shut at the end of most sentences, and McGregor found himself blinking rapidly in tandem.

"Okay, Dimpsey," McGregor said, "but we need to see Poteet now."

Dimpsey walked with them inside the hospital lobby. "I'm a history buff, Bob, and Roland said you need information on old county stuff. And I'm good friends with Tipsy Alcorn, who's our county historian and county clerk. I volunteered to call her and get you two together since Roland can't talk to her. Roland said y'all know why he can't.

"Well, she wants me and her to come by Roland's house and get interviewed by you. She says she wants to come over tomorrow. It has to be at Roland's, or she won't do the interview at all. She's the stubbornest woman in the county if you put aside Mama Limbo. Anyway, Roland won't get out of the hospital until tomorrow afternoon, they say, and she practically begged me for a look at the house, knowing Roland wouldn't be there. What about tomorrow, first thing, Bob?" He squeezed his eyes.

Hood nodded to McGregor to hurry up, so he quickly agreed to the meeting, "first thing," with the idea he could always call it off.

Poteet, though flat on his back, was all smiles. He expressed his sorrow about placing them in such danger. Mama said it wasn't his fault. She hugged Hood, then clucked and cooed like a mother hen over the cut on McGregor's head and the new splint on his arm.

Mama said, "Potty updated me pretty well. I left the picnic as soon as I heard. I swear I've never witnessed any such a two days in all my life since y'all got here. It's aging me fast!"

Hood kissed and patted Poteet.

He said, "The doctor told me I can't go home until tomorrow, since I get a headache when I sit up. I bet I put a dent in that dashboard."

McGregor said, "I'm afraid there's been a burglary at the camp. They broke in by prying off a piece of the board on the kitchen window. We can't tell that anything's missing, but in your art room they slashed a couple of the Mathis paintings."

"What?" Poteet sat up but quickly lay back down, grimacing in pain. "I can't believe it. What bastard would do such a thing?"

"Carlos Hernandez is looking into it, and we now have a security guard posted at the camp. She says she knows you. Lakisha Thompson?"

"Good! She can handle a gun and she's a fair tennis player, too. I check out books from her bookmobile all the time."

Mama was fidgeting. "Did y'all hear they let my Poker out of jail? I told him to go home and hide in his room and not to call anybody on the land line, which our sneaky young sheriff probably has bugged by now. Was that good legal advice, Bobby?"

"Perfect. And I want to talk to Poker very soon."

Mama nodded. "I'm gonna pop if I don't find out what you think about this taping outfit they found in that little room up in Clyde's suite."

"No offense," McGregor said, "but it shows that the Tomato Boy had what amounted to a psychological problem, a dark side. His taping system was said to be antiquated, but, whatever, it'd be enough to put Clyde in deep trouble if anybody found out about it. And now I know why Sheriff and Red want to keep me as far away from their investigation as they can."

McGregor had been living on adrenaline. And it was running low. Somewhere he found the energy to spill the details of the Sheriff Buell-Red Wiley deal with him to get Mama's journals.

Mama dropped her chin, speechless for the first time.

Poteet said, "Son of a bitch! Did you agree to all this?"

"Yes. I'd nearly drowned, and my head was still swimming. They're the law around here, so the best thing I could do was to take their deal and worry about getting out of it later."

Hood said, "McGregor, you poor thing. You're exhausted. But tell us what you think we should do now."

He replied, "Mama, you return to your picnic and have some fun. Check on Poker; keep him close to home if you can. I suggest we get a good night's rest. Something tells me tomorrow's going to be another big day."

Mama said, "I'll keep a leash on Poker. He can work in the café but not go to the picnic. He loves fireworks, but I'll make him watch the big show from the roof of the Emporium. Better view there anyway." After hugs, Mama left.

"Poteet," McGregor sighed, "I've a couple of details about Poker you need to know. And a few other things."

He told Poteet about sailing into Pullwater Creek, trying to make it sound as if it were merely a misadventure. He backed up to tell of the Calvin House parking lot excitement; the bathroom stall incident; the Rust revelation about Poker in the park at the time of the gunshot, and about their questions regarding the orange pickup at the Cadillac wreck. To wrap it, he revealed the fact that somebody had tampered with the cars' brake lines. Then he added, "Red and Sheriff firmly implied that you're still in danger with the murderer on the loose; that there's a connection between the murder and what's happened to you."

Poteet shook his head slowly back and forth. "I cannot *believe* all this is happening. This is *me*, Roland Goddamn Poteet, that I'm talking about, and even I can't take it all in. Y'all tell me the truth. Are y'all okay, for sure?"

They nodded, but not sidetracked by the drama, McGregor said, "Carlos Hernandez tells me I should try to talk with this guy Trussell if I want to find out more about Poker than Mama might be willing to say."

Poteet perked up. "Good idea. Yes sir, let's get that arranged. Mama's awfully protective of Poker."

Poteet asked, changing subjects, "Hood, do you think the slashed paintings can be restored?"

Hood answered, "We'll call Tommy Mathis and find out. Were they insured?"

Poteet said, "No, never got around to it. My cars are insured only for liability, what the law requires. Generally, I self-insure. McGregor, we'll need to go over that aspect of my finances.

"I'm grateful to you two. If you stick with me on all this, remember I know how to give a big bonus. You can count on that." Poteet sounded beat.

A loud knock came at the door.

Sheriff Buell peeked around the door, and when Poteet motioned to him with a finger he barged in with Red Wiley a half-step behind.

Sheriff coughed and hitched his belt. "Mr. Poteet, if you are up to it, I need you to identify a couple of things. I'm sorry, but this can't wait."

Red, stone-faced, waved McGregor and Hood out of the way and handed Sheriff two plastic bags.

Sheriff held up one of them. "When our wrecker operator went to clear out the two cars of personal effects the Buick was clean. Whatever was in there is now in the creek. But in the Cadillac he found two things. Do you recognize this one?"

Poteet, cold-eyed and alert, said, "I do. That's my driving cap. Why?"

Sheriff held up the other bag. "Can you identify this item?"

It looked like a broken piece of black plastic.

Poteet said, "No. What is it?"

"This happens to be the plastic handle broken off of a Sony cassette recorder, the same Sony cassette recorder that we now believe was used to strike Clyde Thacker over the head and kill him. The wrecker operator found it under the passenger-side front floor mat of your car!"

CHAPTER 10

McGregor listened to the somber Sheriff while carefully observing the deadpan county attorney. Red actually had his
tongue stuck in his cheek. Surely this ambush of Poteet was
nothing more than bad theater. But on the off chance it
wasn't, he needed to advise Poteet to keep quiet.

"Poteet, don't say—"

Poteet raised a hand to McGregor for silence. He
turned his head on the pillow to fully face Red and Sheriff
and asked, "Gentlemen, may I ask a couple of questions?"

Sheriff said, "Yes sir."

"Was your wrecker operator in the crowd at the hotel
around the time Clyde was killed, by any chance?"

Sheriff said, "Yes, he was. He signed the roster, saying he was in The Thumb."

"So Sheriff, you jump to the conclusion that I killed
Clyde and pocketed the handle when it came off in my hand.
Then I hid it in my car on the way home last night and simply
forgot to throw the blasted thing out the window, it merely
being a part of a murder weapon—completely understandable how a man might forget a silly thing like that!

"Or, just as easily, you could conclude that your man
who searched my car tailed Clyde up to the fifth floor,

whacked him over the head and fled with the handle in his own pocket. Then, conveniently, he planted it in my car, knowing I was one of the ones who found Clyde. Would you agree, Sheriff?"

Sheriff and Red burst into stilted laughter. Red said, "I told you, Sheriff, you're not going to faze somebody like Roland with the tough-cop routine. The man's been around enough blocks to build a city by now."

Sheriff said, "You're right. Roland, still and all, I felt like I had to make a big presentation out of it just in case you wanted to confess. We did check with your doctor before we came in. Don't want you to think we would be callous enough to pop in here to rough you up if you were still real sick. He said you're getting out of here tomorrow. That's real good. We still need your statement for the record and your fingerprints, hair sample and a blood sample. Just to clear you from the lab analysis stuff, you know. In the meantime, see if you can remember anything that might explain how this thing came to be in your car."

Red said, "In case you're wondering, we did interview our wrecker operator—strictly by the book. He has witnesses who vouch for him the whole time he was at the hotel. Besides, I take his word just like I'm taking yours, Roland." To McGregor and Hood, he said, "By the way, he's one of the ones who vouched for you two being in The Thumb. So don't get too sticky about him, hear?"

Poteet spoke up. "You were pretty good, though, Sheriff. You had me going!"

Poteet was fibbing to get along. But the attempted setup had McGregor miffed and he didn't appreciate Red's tone.

McGregor put his chin up. "Guys, Hood and I are leaving. We'll be staying at Poteet's place tonight. I'll pick up Poteet tomorrow and bring him over to the station in Finneyville—*if* he feels up to it."

Red snapped back at him. "Finding this handle in the car threw us a curve! Least thing it does, it proves that somebody wants damn sure to involve Roland in the killing. Or Janet, maybe. Or even you, for that matter, Mr. Bob McGregor. Think about that!"

"Should I be inferring something here, Mr. Red Wiley?"

"Our wrecker operator says Janet was alone in The Thumb for several minutes—"

Sheriff held up a hand. "Whoa now, Red, Bob. Peace! I arranged for a second security guard to stay here outside your room, Roland. Assumed you'd okay it. You'll have to pay the fee, of course."

"Thanks, Sheriff. It was thoughtful of you. Now I need to get some rest, boys. But, one more thing before you go." He turned to McGregor and winked with the eye not visible to Sheriff and Red. "McGregor and I are in the process of discussing the deal you made him this afternoon. I want y'all to consider changing your minds about McGregor helping you on this investigation as far as this guy Trussell is concerned. That nut's not going to talk to either you or the state boys. McGregor's a professional at interviewing witnesses, just like y'all. I have in mind that we send him up to Trussell's shack with the sister, Terri. Terri and the boys rescued McGregor, you know, and he's going to stop by there anyway to thank them. What do you say?"

Red said, "Why Trussell? What does he have to do with anything?"

McGregor actually was wondering the same thing, the recommendation of Carlos notwithstanding.

"Well, now come on," Poteet said. "I'm not asking you to reveal anything you're not supposed to, but y'all linked Poker to the murder because of something you found in his truck. You stirred Mama into a frenzy. Trussell could shed some light on whether Poker's mixed up in this thing or not. I'm trying to figure a way to calm down Mama with this idea. Where Poker's concerned she's liable to start throwing some serious weight around you boys. Plus, it'd help me get persuaded about getting out of politics."

Sheriff said to Red, "If Trussell knows anything I guess we could never get it out of him. The state people, either. Okay with me, as long as that's where it ends."

Red hesitated and then nodded, arching an eyebrow at McGregor.

To McGregor, Sheriff said, "Why don't you go on up there tomorrow morning? See what you can find out and report to us."

The doctor came in and ordered the visitors out.

Poteet held onto McGregor's splint as Sheriff and Red departed. He said in a low voice so Hood could hear also, "Offer that Terri money if you have to, McGregor, to get to see her brother. I think it important you talk to him."

He liked putting his money to work.

Down in the lobby, McGregor and Hood caught up with Sheriff and Red, and there they met the security guard coming in the front door. McGregor directed him to Poteet's room with instructions not to let anybody in without permission of the patient.

Sheriff gave McGregor Terri's number. When McGregor called her, she said the boys would be home for supper in half an hour; that he should come on over. He assured Terri he'd take only a few minutes of her time. Red pulled the phone from McGregor and asked Terri politely if she would think about accompanying McGregor for a brief interview with her brother tomorrow. He explained the reasons why and hung up.

Sheriff said, "By the way, Bob, Trussell's first name is Amon. That boy, Dewey, is his son. The mother's dead, so Dewey lives with Terri and her son, Charlie. Red and I arranged for the county to set up a foster home relationship for Terri to keep Dewey and it's worked out well. I'm proud of the way Dewey's coming along. Charlie is a good boy, too."

His tone was telling McGregor that Sheriff knew this family well.

"Terri lives on a trust fund set up for her after her husband died several years ago," Sheriff continued. "He was an insurance agent and handled the county's entire insurance business. We all thought a great deal of him. He hit the first bridge on the Offshoot going home from The Thumb one night. Car full of vodka bottles. You get the picture. A real shame, but he did leave Terri a whole bunch of insurance. She's around thirty now and lives in a house stuck up at the top of a road on the Calvin Station side of Pullwater Creek. You can't miss it if you're looking for it. Dirt road."

Red said, "That house could be a showplace if she'd spend money on it. She's on the lookout for a husband from what I hear, Bob, and may have some current prospects around here. So be careful in case somebody's watching you. She might try to latch onto you, too, you being a fair-haired outsider."

Hood said caustically, "With McGregor, she doesn't stand a chance! Does she, McGregor?"

McGregor felt picked on. He responded, "I'll try to maintain my professional composure. Why are y'all needling me?" McGregor noticed that Sheriff had taken a step back; had raised his pudgy cheeks toward narrowed eyebrows in an expression that McGregor couldn't decipher.

Red eyed the two of them with a grin. "Brings me to a nosy question that more than one person's been asking. Are you two an item or what?"

Hood moved her foot to hover over one of Red's tasseled Italian-style loafers. Pointing down, she said, "Why, looky down there, Red, we keep nosing around in the same investigation, like Sheriff says, one of us might end up stepping on the other's toes!"

Red jumped back.

McGregor drove this time, taking the short route once more. Hood dozed all the way. That made McGregor wonder if he should quit for the day, too, and perhaps re-schedule this meeting with the boys. No, he ought to get it over with.

At the camp, Hood hopped out, calling back to him in a tease, "Be careful with Terri!" She joined Lakisha, who had just rounded the corner in time to escort her in.

At the top of driveway McGregor turned right onto the Offshoot, toward the creek that he really didn't want to see again today. The sun was falling rapidly in the sky. But instead of the day cooling off, it was becoming hotter—and the Chevy had no air conditioning. Probably a car originally from up north.

After topping the hill overlooking Pullwater Meadow, he slowed when he came to the spot where the Buick had left the road. The roar from the creek seemed to intensify. Despite the heat, his gut chilled from the sound. In the creek it had been the incessant drumming noise of the rushing water that had so overwhelmed his mind. The memory of it would keep him awake nights for a long time to come. With deep fatigue creeping in he sped down the hill to get away from the sound, damning the potholes as he went.

He found the dirt road on the other side of the bridge. It was one-lane, steep and rutted. For the sake of the car and his nerves, he drove slowly up the hill.

A tangle of weeds began pressing the car from both sides. Long tree branches formed a dense canopy overhead. The humid air became ever thicker, harder to breathe. The earthy odors McGregor normally loved so much turned fetid, too intense. They bit the nose like acid. Slow insects collided with one another, buzzing and chirping and flying round and round as if in a soup. McGregor's skin felt blistered and raw, even though covered with a sheet of sweat. He had to use both arms to twist the steering wheel left and right. The new splint compressed his arm, squeezed his bones.

Was he having another panic attack? Or was it heat stroke? Was it anxiety from the anticipation of seeing Terri again? When he'd last seen her, *death* had a grip on his throat.

The picture of Terri's face calmed his nerves. In his memory, he felt her touch on his neck. Touch? Had it not been a caress? He reviewed how she'd done it, just at the exact moment when Rust's view was blocked. He recalled her mouth had been no more than a foot away from his eyes— her mouth, small and red-lipped like an unopened rose. The image braced him, and he became aware that he'd let the car stall to a halt on the hill.

He shook his head to force away the fantasy. Maybe he *should* turn around and come back later. He feared that if Terri appeared in reality as he'd been dreaming of her, he might not be able to control himself. No. He'd come this far. Besides, he needed her. Well, he shouldn't even think that. He needed to *see* her. That's all.

Finally, there was light at the end of his jungle tunnel. Spewing gravel the size of walnuts, he burst into a level clearing in the woods, perhaps a couple of acres in size. In the middle of the clearing stood a large, two-story farmhouse with a wing extending to the rear and two tall chimneys. As Red Wiley had intimated it was somewhat neglected, needing paint for one thing. Its tall windows were open to the air. Some cold-blooded souls still lived without air conditioning; how, McGregor didn't know. Would this Terri Williams be cold-blooded? He longed for a cold shower.

As he parked, a voice called to him from a screened-in front porch, built high off the ground. He climbed the five or six steps up and let himself in through the door to find Terri curled up on a davenport with several fluffy pillows. Above her, a slow ceiling fan with a coat of rust labored to circulate the dense air. It did such a poor job the several candles set along the edge of the porch never flickered. From inside the house McGregor could hear the boys shouting and laughing over the noise of a TV.

Terri spoke in a low sultry voice with a pleasing drawl. "I'm making the boys clean up the kitchen and cook a meal. Thought you might like to stay for supper."

Her blond hair was wet, combed back off her face— maybe from a recent shower? She was dressed in baggy shorts that showed her navel under a loose-fitting tank top. Her bare feet were tucked to one side on the pillows. The sunset light, filtered by the porch screen, gave her fair skin a thin pinkish glow. As if immobilized by the heat, she didn't bother to get up.

McGregor found words difficult. "Uhh, well," he stammered, "probably not tonight. As you know, I've had a rough day and I'm on my way to an early bed." Bed. Terri. Lovely thought. Visuals pummeled his brain, images unbecoming in a person who was supposed to be maintaining his professional composure.

"I, uh, thought I'd say thanks to the boys. And I wanted also to thank you in person for what you did for me today." He was thinking of her tingly touch but didn't dare say it, though he almost did.

"Oh, now," she said, "nothing more about that. How's your head and arm?"

McGregor stuttered out, "F-fine."

"Would you like a glass of sweet tea?" she asked.

She put her feet on the floor and leaned with care toward the table beside her. It held an iced tea pitcher, an ice bucket, and an extra glass with ice, all sweating with condensation. Her hand trembled in mid-air awaiting his answer.

"I'm having mine with a dab of George Dickel. How about you?" she encouraged, her nostrils flaring. From beneath a pillow, she pulled out a pint bottle.

His mind was telling him, "Oh boy, don't even go where I think you're going, McGregor!" But his mouth was saying, "That sounds nice. Thank you."

The sun moved down completely behind a shade tree and the porch darkened. McGregor watched Terri take a handful of ice and add it to the extra glass. She poured tea over the ice, about halfway up. The dab of whiskey she poured on top she followed with another delicate dab and then another. When she extended the glass up to him, it slipped a bit, but McGregor quick-stepped forward just in time to catch it—along with her hand.

"I'm sorry," she said, looking at McGregor's belly, instead of his face.

She slowly retracted her hand from his and just as slowly wiped away the wetness on a pillow, one side then the other. When she looked up, her moist emerald-gray eyes glistened in the fading light. She swallowed hard; McGregor watched her throat move up and down.

At the extreme periphery of his existence, he noted the blades of the old ceiling fan had given up the fight and quit turning. McGregor blinked away sweat drops falling from his forehead, his resolve to be a good boy melting away with them. He detected a question taking shape on Terri's face as her eyebrows arched in barely discernible jumps. He well knew the answer if the question was what he thought it might be.

McGregor realized he wasn't breathing. He sucked in lungs full of air, which seemed to break the spell between them. Terri blinked and averted her eyes to the fan.

"Look at that old thing." she said. "A little humidity and it just can't move anymore. Ever feel that way, Bob?"

McGregor drank. The icy-hot liquor felt marvelous to the back of his suddenly parched throat.

"I really didn't mean to stare at you like that," he said, recovering his ability to speak. "As I said, it's been a long day and, I guess … I don't know, I just couldn't say anything for a minute."

Terri spread out the petals of her rose-lips, in a soft and knowing smile. "Please. Sit here with me." She patted her hand on the cushion beside her. "Enjoy your drink. This is the time of day to ripen … quit talking … and just be. Know what I mean?"

He did. Man-oh-man, did he ever want to ripen, whatever that was. He took a step.

But from the house came a shout. "Aunt Terri, Charlie dropped the whole bowl of spaghetti all over the floor!"

Terri frowned and shook her head. A breeze suddenly blew through the porch. She heaved a sigh and hurried to the door. "That's all right, boys. Y'all come on out and say hi to Mr. McGregor."

They did, slamming the screen door behind them and jostling one another to be first to shake hands.

McGregor thanked them again for helping him out of the creek and told them to call him Bob. If they wanted to take him fishing sometime at Poteet's, all they had to do was call him and he'd come for them. They would fish all day and he would get to know them better.

Then Terri told the boys to go back inside and warm up a can of beef stew. If she didn't come in soon, they should start without her.

"I guess I can't offer you that supper, Bob, the way I'd planned. With those boys around, you never know what's going to happen next."

"No, uh, you never do. I mean, I have to be going anyway. Have you considered what Red Wiley asked you about over the phone?"

"I have considered it." she declared. And after a long pause during which McGregor thought her eyes were again focused on his belly, she said, "Let's have another drink before you go, and I'll consider it some more. The boys'll be fine in there by themselves."

Avoiding a direct reply, he said, "I can be here about ten or eleven o'clock tomorrow morning, if that would be convenient?"

"Well … the boys are going to an all-day church camp tomorrow, instead of regular services. I just don't know if Amon will be around, though. I should ask him first, maybe?"

"Okay. If you decide, call me at Poteet's. His number's in the book, I'm sure. Thanks for the drink. It was delicious. I'm pleased somebody around here can mix a drink without tomato juice."

She walked him to his car, stepping gingerly on the driveway gravel under her bare feet. As he turned toward her to say goodbye, Terri said, "When you come tomorrow … wear hiking boots. Make it eleven?"

By the time McGregor parked in front of the camp next to Lakisha's truck, he was truly worn out. The outdoor lights were ablaze, but Lakisha was nowhere to be seen.

He felt guilty for almost succumbing to Terri. No, that wasn't fair. What he'd almost succumbed to was his own fantasy.

He had no key, so he rang the doorbell. Eventually, Hood's voice through the door asked him for the password. He gave her the first expletive that came to mind. Hood was bleary-eyed but cheery. Why couldn't they ever be in the same mood at the same time?

He walked past her, saying, "I going to find some food, then my bed. I'm beat."

"I've heated two frozen dinners for you. I had a couple myself and then fell asleep on the sofa. So what did Terri say? Poteet's already called twice."

"I talked with the boys; made them agree to take me fishing here at the camp sometime soon. I think I assuaged whatever fears Terri had about going with me to see her brother. She agreed to go tomorrow at eleven."

"I'll call Poteet and tell him while you eat," Hood said. "He told me the Tomato Boy's memorial service is set for tomorrow at four. We should be able to spring our hospital patient in time to attend, don't you think? Clyde was not religious, it seems, so they're holding the service in the Calvin House lobby."

McGregor asked, "In the event this Trussell thing takes longer than expected, will you plan to pick up Poteet on your own?"

"Sure. You look terrible, Lumpkins." She kissed his mouth. "Sit down. I'll bring you your food. Iced tea to drink?"

"Thanks. Does Poteet have any whiskey around here to sweeten it up?"

"To go with what's already on your breath?" Hood asked, adding a sarcastic sweetener of her own to her voice.

McGregor grunted.

He consumed the trays of food before Hood hung up the phone. He was swilling his tea, with the sweetener he'd found in a cabinet, as Hood sat down with him.

She said, "Let's make a quick must-do list. Then I'll let you go to bed."

He hung his head. "You list, I'll listen."

"First, remember Grooms and Alcorn are coming over in the morning."

McGregor groaned.

"Second, since it's not even nine o'clock yet, you should be able to get plenty of sleep and still get up around four. That's when Lakisha's shift is over, and she wants to check in with us before she turns the place over to the new guard. We should have time finally to go over the entire situation here—have coffee and breakfast before Grooms and Alcorn arrive. If you'll cook breakfast in the morning I'll go out in the meantime to the garage and get that old Ford started. That way we'll have two cars.

"While you deal with the morning visitors, I'll stay in my room and prepare a schedule of activities for Monday. That would include new cell phones for us, and I'm thinking you'd best just go buy a car. Poteet's old cars definitely are not what we need for running around in. I'll probably rent a car for the remainder of my time here. And the doctor, don't—"

Would Hood drone on forever? His eyes closed on him as he stumbled from the room.

McGregor was snorkeling in Pullwater Creek trying to pick out his burgundy Buick within a school of Buick-shaped burgundy fish when Hood swam up beside him and started shaking him.

She was singing gently through the noisy swirl of water, "Time to get up, Lumpkins. Time to get up."

He jerked away and his snorkel stopped up on him. Gasping for air, he snapped awake. His legs were stiff and his arms were barely movable.

"Can't move," he said. "Leave me alone."

He was lying on his stomach, and Hood started massaging his back and neck.

"I knew you'd hurt this morning. But if we can get through this day, then on Monday we'll have a breather with just our errands to run and maybe a short chat with Poker. By then, Poteet will be home, and we can all relax and take a fresh look."

Her massage touched several raw muscles, and he turned over to face her in the dim light coming in from a hallway lamp.

"Okay," he said, "I'm up. Have you talked to Lakisha?"

"Yeah. Nothing happened during the night. No murderers, no burglars. The new guard's already on duty. Guess who it is."

"I'm too sore for games."

"It's Tomás!"

Hood patted him on the face. McGregor stretched, popping tendons and ligaments. His wrist started throbbing.

"Tomás, huh?"

CHAPTER 11

Hood invited Tomás to Sunday breakfast. McGregor watched him shovel pancakes and ham through that ever-present smile of his. As Tomás left for his outdoor post, he assured them he'd keep order at the camp after they were gone for the day. Lakisha, he said, would return mid-afternoon. They were on twelve-hour shifts.

McGregor allowed Hood to place a fresh butterfly bandage on his head cut. Then he cleaned up the kitchen while Hood sat at the table poring over a notepad, composing tomorrow's to-do list. His one-handed effort was difficult, and he silently fumed about having to be "protected" by the likes of Tomás—and by a woman. But his indignation couldn't be justified, he convinced himself. Tomás and Lakisha were there to safeguard Poteet's house, not him. Yeah, but still—

Hood said, "I got Poteet's Ford wagon running before I woke you. I'll take it and you take the Chevy again. While you're meeting with Grooms and Alcorn this morning, I'll call Mama and arrange our meeting with Poker for tomorrow."

Hood made a note and said, "Now for the murder. I suggest we review what we know about this idiotic place. You start at the beginning. I'll shut up and take notes."

Hood was in her officious mode, and it was beginning to piss him off. He said, "Okay, here goes. I cast aside a lucrative criminal law practice."

Hood looked up. "Let's stick to the facts, please, sir."

"I thought you were going to shut up."

"Go ahead."

"*Then* I came up here with one commitment in mind, that of working with an old rich guy we know and love to get his estate in order and to write my book. Simple. My best friend said so. The deal was sealed with a big money promise and a wonderful 1953 Buick. Life was grand."

Hood wasn't writing.

"You getting this down?" He poured more coffee. Hood frowned, pressing her lips tight in pretended agony, and started writing.

"Now, two days, one murder and, count 'em, four attempted murders later, I haven't seen any money and have no 1953 Buick. And, I've made yet another commitment, to wit: Investigate the murder—something I feel barely competent to do—and also the four attempted murders. By the way, make a side note. I feel barely competent to write a book. That probably should be somewhat relevant to the discussion. Paragraph.

"The second commitment concerns this improbable book. There's this big, ugly, crazy guy who drives an orange truck, you see. This guy probably tried to kill the old rich guy, probably burgled the old rich guy's house, and maybe tried to kill the rich guy a second time, along with the two of us. And maybe he did kill a beloved local celebrity. The crazy guy's mother is a Limbo nee Calvin. Put Calvin in capital letters! She offered me the use of a dead Calvin dude's journals, the journals being necessary for writing my book. But in order to see the journals, I must prove this crazy guy didn't do what all he probably did do, but mainly I must clear the good name of the crazy guy's mother, the good Calvin name. Paragraph.

"I was dragged through a creek and nearly drowned. And you wrecked the old rich guy, putting him in the hospital. Somehow, I'm sideways with the county attorney and probably with the county sheriff, neither of whom I trust worth a damn but with whom I have made a third deal. In that deal, I put my professional integrity at risk in order to obtain the very same dead dude's journals—the ones I was going to get in the other deal—by agreeing not to do what I agreed to do in the other deal. Paragraph.

"Before anything, though, I must interview this morning a nutty woman who only wants to see the rich guy's house at a time when he's not here because it used to be her house, okay? Then, I must interview the rich guy's neighbor. Now, the neighbor's not a bright light in my opinion. He's running an election campaign, using the rich guy's money I might add, in order to repair potholes which are going to be repaired anyway when I persuade the old rich guy to quit messing with the politics of the tomato growers. Oh, have I failed to mention the tomato growers?

"Well, these growers, damned if they're not anti-growth. No ma'am, no development for them. And that puts those dreadful people at odds with the rich guy. And at odds with the rich guy's Firstplacers Club, the members of which fear the anti-growth tomato growers but who are willing to fight them even though in so doing they risk serious, if unspecified, interference with a tomato festival that the rich guy has insisted they promote.

"And to top that, I'm on my way after the morning interviews to seek out a second crazy man who lives in a shack. What for? Don't really know, but the reason seems clear to the old rich guy and to the county's chief deputy sheriff. To achieve this third interview of the day, apparently I must hike up a mountain with a woman who's on the make and trying to seduce me. Paragraph."

"Wait, wait, wait!" Hood tossed down her pen. "What's this about her trying to seduce you?"

McGregor's mind screeched to a halt. "Oh, yeah, well, maybe I failed to mention that last night."

"Yes, I believe maybe you did."

"Well, she didn't really try to seduce me. I mean, she might have come on to me a little bit, but I think maybe she'd had something to drink, and…oh, hell, Hood, it was damned hot on that porch and after what I'd been through, I don't know, maybe I was weak for the moment and gave her the wrong impression. And—"

"Stop it, McGregor! I've never heard such bullshit. Either she put the make on you or she didn't. Either you liked it or you didn't. You're a big boy; which was it?"

"Okay, so she came on strong. Does that satisfy you? And no, I didn't like it. And nothing happened!"

Hood teared up in an instant. She squeaked, "Damn you, McGregor! Just when—"

She threw the notepad at him and ran from the kitchen toward her room, leaving McGregor stunned, with his coffee mug halfway to his mouth.

The doorbell rang.

McGregor sat still, blinking his eyes. He sighed and shook his head. The bell rang again. The psychologists say that if you want to elevate your mood, just smile. Like the Tomas smile.

On the third ring, he was squinting through the peep-hole. He saw the face of Tomas and opened the door to swap big smiles with him. Standing beside Tomas was one of his interviewees. Not Grooms.

"Hi there, I'm Tipsy," the woman said, straight faced.

"This early in the morning?" McGregor asked, trying to ignite his brain following the shakeup of Hood's melt-down.

She held up her palm to him. "Don't do it," she said crisply. "I've heard all the jokes before. I'm Tipsy Alcorn, the county clerk." She bustled past him through the doorway as if she still owned the place and turned back to him. "And I presume you are Mr. McGregor?"

"Yes."

She looked him up and down with bird-like movements of the head and then stared at his bandaged arm. "Sorry to hear about your mishap."

McGregor nodded to Tomás and closed the door. Tipsy was a five-foot-five, no-nonsense packet of energy. He took a deep breath. "Thank you for saying so. I want you to know how much I appreciate you being willing to come out here for the interview. Dimpsey said he didn't have to twist your arm much, but I had the feeling there's a secret he wasn't sharing."

She clicked away across the hardwood in her high heels into the living room, looking all around, and turned back to him, hands on hips.

"You're right, I guess. I've wanted to come back to this house ever since I sold it to Roland, but the s-o-b would never invite me. Can't blame him, probably, the way I bad-mouth him. I assume he's not here? Still in the hospital?"

"Uhh, no and yes, he's still in the hospital, at least for this morning. And you say you sold him this house?"

"I sold, he stole, is the way I put it. I supervised the building of this house from the ground up. I decorated it, I painted it—the inside anyway—and I furnished it."

Fat tears lurched from her eyes. All at once, her energy was gone and she staggered over to the sofa to plop down in a heap to sob.

McGregor wondered what it was about him this morning that was making women cry. He hurried to her side, grabbing a tissue box on the way.

"There, there, now." He patted her with his splint.

"Oh, I feel like a silly old lady." She wiped her eyes and composed herself as quickly as she'd decomposed. "Roland didn't really steal this house. He paid me over a million. It's the way he did it. He came right up to the door the day I moved in. He sat right there in that chair. And my husband, who's in the real estate business—we were just dumbfounded! Roland wanted to buy everything. Furniture, appliances, silverware, bed linen, everything. And he just acted so cocky, like he already owned my home and knew we would take his money. And he gave us an hour to make up our minds. My husband, being in the business, was jumping up and down wanting to sell. 'Double our money, double our money' was all he could say."

She pulled more tissues from McGregor's box and clattered away into the kitchen, dabbing at her swollen eyes. There was nothing to do but follow her.

"I don't know why I'm telling you all this. You have a kind face, Mr. McGregor."

"It's just McGregor, Mrs. Alcorn, to my friends. Or Bob, if you prefer."

She smiled for the first time, a bright pretty smile. "Just call me Tipsy. I am acting like it, aren't I? It's just being here, I guess. I've stayed awake at night dreaming of living here, what it would be like, the river and all, having a boat. I love being on the water."

She walked to the kitchen's picture window. "I suppose this is the window they shot out when they tried to kill Roland?" She reached out to touch the wood.

McGregor said, "Let me get you some coffee. Or, we have orange juice and, of course, tomato juice."

"Some tomato juice would be nice. I'm hooked on lycopene."

McGregor poured.

Tipsy said, "I'll tell you anything you like about the county for your book, Bob. I'm the county historian in addition to being the county clerk. I'll work with you, on two small conditions."

She had returned fully to her county clerk demeanor, the bird movements and the clipped speech. "First, I want a tour of the house, just by myself. And second, don't ever tell a living soul about what just happened here, me crying like a baby. Deal?"

"You have a deal, Tipsy, yes." But McGregor wondered. Why tour alone? As he reached out his bad arm for a handshake she took his fingers for a gentle squeeze. Did her tour have anything to do with fingerprints? Erasing prints? Or touching things to cover up prints? Was Tipsy the burglar? An attack on the paintings in the only room that's been changed by Poteet—would that be in her character?

"Have you heard that Roland calls my dream house a camp? Well, he does. It may be a damn camp to him, but to me—" She stiffened up her lips and probably would have continued blasting Poteet but for the doorbell ringing.

"That'll be Grooms," McGregor said. "Poteet says his timing is always off."

"His timing is off and he's a slob, to boot, and if Roland knew what was good for him, he'd steer clear of his fine and dandy neighbor. He's nothing but a big pretender!"

McGregor caught in her tone the possibility of another secret connection.

"I shouldn't have said that. I'm going to look around the house, if it's all right with you. I'll see you back here in the kitchen?"

"Yes, fine. But watch out for my friend, Janet Hood, in the guest quarter. I think she's upset and might not be in the mood to receive a guest. Oh, and please don't go into Poteet's art room. We believe we had a burglar who messed up some paintings in there."

"Art room? Burglar?—He has an art room? I'll just peek."

At the door, Tomás handed off Grooms to McGregor, smiled and left. Grooms marched in, carrying a bag of small chocolate doughnuts.

"Hope I'm not late. Saw Tipsy's car." He laughed. "You can't beat her at anything!" His boisterous mood was contagious. McGregor laughed and glanced at his watch. It was barely seven.

"This early in the morning, Dimpsey, late is a relative thing. I'm not Poteet, with my eyes glued to a clock. Come on in and yes, Tipsy's already here. She's touring the house on her own and will join us when she's finished."

Dimpsey said, "My first order of business would be a cup of coffee. Got any?"

McGregor poured him the last cup and walked across the kitchen to prepare another pot. With sideway glances, he assessed Dimpsey. The squeezing of the red eyes was more pronounced today, causing McGregor to conclude it was more of a neurological problem than a habit. Annoying, nonetheless.

Dimpsey Grooms—the politico wannabe. At first you note the corpulence, the blowzy jowls, the roadmap nose, and then, of course, the eyes. But what McGregor had learned of Dimpsey and observed first hand suggested that Dimpsey had a Willy Loman inside. McGregor sensed deep insecurity beneath the bluster and self-promotion. He knew little of Dimpsey's past, but he imagined a youthful, confident, capable engineer now turned into what sat before him—a beggar politician; a shaky, wobbly man with a bad tic.

Dimpsey took a double handful of doughnuts. As he munched, he fidgeted with the campaign button he was wearing and appeared to settle into a taste bud reverie.

When the coffee was on the make McGregor sat down, politely refusing a chocolate O. Then Dimpsey hunched over toward him, licking his fingers and squeezing his eyes.

"Bob, you seem like a real decent sort. I'll talk about your history book when Tipsy comes back, for sure. But while she's out of the room, I want to talk about something else." He slurped coffee and chewed for a moment.

"I'm listening, Dimpsey."

"Well, you've figured out by now, surely to goodness, that it was Roland who put me up to this campaign business, working me up about the potholes and such. Now I'd make a fine road superintendent, don't get me wrong. I have all the qualifications under the law, more than Eli Rust has. He has only a couple of years at some rinky-dink college, and … he's a bit on the nutty side. But the truth is I'm getting cold feet. I know I'm not much of a politician and what I really want to do is retire. I told Roland that, but he wouldn't listen. He's really pissed at Eli, you understand. But I didn't anticipate such a strong reaction from the tomato growers on this whole development issue. The nutshell is that they just want the county to stay the same. And … well, dammit, I'm beginning to think they may be right. Even if Eli *is* weird, he's done a good job overall. And ol' Red Wiley, he's correct, until we see what the state's going to do with the Offshoot out here it makes no economic sense for the county to spend any money on it."

McGregor said, "I like it when a man lays his cards on the table, Dimpsey. I don't mind interceding for you with Poteet. Right now, though, tell me more about these growers. I've met a couple of them from the Firstplacers Club, but I'd like to know more about them. I've only been here a couple days and I feel short of information."

Dimpsey reached down around his waist with both hands. He found his belt deep in a fold and ran his thumbs around the inside of it, trying to tug it up. He seemed not to realize he was doing it. "Okay," he said. Historically speaking, they've had a strong organization for fifty years or so. There are about a dozen families, all run by the old guys and gals. They have children and grandchildren in the business. The families have intermarried so much that I'm confused as to who owns what, or who has the say-so on things. They have a Calvin County Tomato Club that meets on Wednesday nights after church, in the First National Bank Building over in Finneyville. You should ask Tipsy to get you in this coming Wednesday."

McGregor nodded.

Dimpsey continued after a brief eye squeeze. "The growers easiest to talk to would be in the Vire family. Some of them are in the Firstplacers Club because they're also in the winemaking business. Then, let's see, there's Hernandez and there's Thompson. You should find them agreeable. I could go on."

"No, that's good." McGregor held up his hand. "The Hernandez family. Would that be the family of the brothers Carlos and Tomás?"

"Sure."

"And what about the Thompson family? Is Lakisha Thompson a member?"

"Sure. I believe you've met more of them than you know."

They heard noises from the hallway. McGregor again assured Dimpsey he would talk to Poteet about the election problem, and Dimpsey agreed to talk history whenever it was convenient. Then Tipsy and Hood came in, arm in arm and laughing.

Hood smiled lamely at McGregor and poured coffee for Tipsy and herself as they sat down at the table.

Tipsy said, "The only things Poteet added to this house seems to be his paintings, and it's horrible what some-body did to them. That room was my music room.

"Dimpsey, I don't know if it's the election or what, but do you have any idea who's trying to hurt Roland? Janet here says he thinks the tomato growers are behind the non-sense, trying to scare him away from supporting you."

Her tone was accusatory, and Dimpsey turned wine red.

"You make it sound like it's my fault, Tipsy. You know Roland talked me into running, and you know the growers as well as I do. Hell, they support you time and again when you run. And you're the one who hates Roland. What do you think is going on?"

"I don't hate Roland. In fact, Janet has been ex-plaining to me about Roland's life and such, and he's begin-ning to sound like a pretty decent guy. I may have been wrong all along, blinded to his good side by this house deal."

She turned abruptly to Dimpsey. "Listen here," she said, "what say we call it a morning, the two of us. Why don't you run along and let me have some privacy with Bob and Janet. I'll outline the history stuff I have to offer as quickly as I can. Then Janet and I are going to have lunch later. If I go along with her to pick up Roland from the hospital, he and I just might be able to mend our disagreements. We *should* do it in honor of the Tomato Boy's memorial service this after-noon. Lord, Lord, I'm gonna miss that wonderful man!"

She walked round the table and Dimpsey followed her to the front door, whispering to her as they went. Dimpsey called out a goodbye before they heard the door slam.

Hood put her fingers to her lips and threw McGregor an air kiss. She silently mouthed words to the effect that it was all right between them.

The returning Tipsy said in hushed tones, "I can't give y'all any specifics, but don't trust Dimpsey Grooms too much. People know I'm standing neutral in this election and they tell me things they wouldn't ordinarily say. Of course, we'll have to vote for Camper. Nobody else wants his job. As to who is going to be road superintendent, I've told Eli Rust to his face that I don't care for him or Dimpsey either one, and it's okay with Eli. He said he didn't care for me. Ha! But that Dimpsey is so clueless, he can't figure out who's supporting him and who's not."

McGregor said, "The truth is, clueless is a good word to describe Hood and me when it comes to this election. Tell us about it. You seem to be the first objective party we've met here. Obviously, it's an off-year election with only the two races. I got that, but why is it so upsetting?"

"All elections in Calvin County turn into backstab-bing brawls before they're finished. This was explained to Roland again and again by his club members. I would've said it more plainly by telling him to keep his arrogant newcomer nose out of this one. You've heard of mudslinging. Well, here, it's tomato slinging. In the next few weeks, you just hide and watch! You'll start seeing campaign road signs and yard signs with tomato splotches on them. I'm not kidding!

"You might think Camper Eskew's crazy for campaigning the way he does, being unopposed, but it's possible at the last minute somebody will mount a write-in campaign against him. And win, too! It's been done.

"It all has to do with that damned Andrew Jackson and the constitution his cronies dreamed up in the 1830s. It called for county offices to be elective, rather than appointive. That doesn't make sense in this day and age. For example, I should be appointed by the county mayor or the county commission, not elected. It's silly. What do I do? I parcel out car tags and marriage licenses and business licenses. I take the minutes at the county commission meetings. Do I exercise any real political judgment? No. So why should I be elected?

"The road superintendent and the assessor of property are elected on even-numbered off years. In August. The rest of us come up for election in August, two years from now. We all have four-year terms. More coffee?"

Hood poured. Tipsy lowered her voice again.

"The real deal is that it looked for all the world like the Tomato Boy was going to run for county mayor!" She sat back as though she had just revealed the date and time for the end of the world. She seemed extremely pleased that McGregor and Hood simply stared back at her like dunces.

"Damn! Y'all *are* clueless! Don't you see, with the new state law that goes into effect in two years, the county mayor is going to have lots more authority. Lots more power! Right now all he does is sign county warrants—you know, checks. He cuts ribbons at ceremonies and meets with the county commission. Even there, he can't vote unless there's a tie. With the new law, the really tough men and women will be attracted to the job instead of the political weenies.

"The county mayor we have now is on his last term and nobody but me ever sees him. Just about, anyway. Talk about a weenie! His secretary runs the day-to-day office. Wife's dead. He stays at home, usually, playing with his electric trains. You ought to see those trains. Has them running through little tomato fields. Pretty cute.

"Anyway, the Tomato Boy put out a trial balloon last month that he had a notion to run. He was sincerely shocked to find he had support from every section of the county. The county buzzed for days. But Red Wiley had announced way before that, on the day the governor signed the new law. Now, Red and Sheriff Buell are tight as Siamese tomatoes. And the way I hear it, Red wants to be mayor for two terms, eight years, and then turn it over to Buell for his own two terms, Buell being still a youngster.

"But word has it Eli Rust has a strong eye on the race. The reason he's so intent on winning re-election as road superintendent next month is that he can't afford to lose a race and then stand for county mayor in two years as a loser. See what I mean? That's what makes this election so big. With the Tomato Boy being dead, if Rust wins next month then that pits him against Red Wiley, two years from now. If you think this year's election's a hoot, wait until then!"

McGregor, thinking about the murder and about politics only secondarily, didn't quite know what to say. Was Tipsy not seeing the murder connection?

Hood shook her head and said quietly, "Good Lord, Tipsy."

Tipsy looked back and forth at them. "What?"

McGregor said, "Don't you understand, Tipsy, this election mess makes Wiley, Buell, and Rust suspects in the murder of the Tomato Boy!"

Tipsy looked stunned. "No! I hadn't thought about that. No." She made a face. "Nobody would ever think that. Not if you knew those men. Why, Red Wiley's as honest as they come for a lawyer. Oh, no offense, but you know what I mean. I've worked with all of them for years. Buell's a good boy. Politics is one thing, but murder? No. Never. Rust may not be well liked as a person, but he's an upstanding county official."

McGregor backtracked. "I shouldn't have put it that bluntly. My being a newcomer, I just had the thought, that's all. Politics aside, is there anything about the private lives of any of those guys that might make them want to see the Tomato Boy out of the picture?"

Tipsy looked at him thoughtfully. "Not that I can think of. The truth is I don't know that Clyde had any real enemies. Now, they still have that Leslie girl locked up. But if Clyde was her father, I can't see her doing him in, either. Can you?"

"Frankly, no," he replied. "Patricide can't be dismissed out of hand just because it's so repugnant, but it'd be the last thing I'd consider."

Tipsy said, "My view is an outsider came in and did it! Be on the lookout for that."

Hood cleared away the dishes. She said, "Tipsy, McGregor has an errand to run. Let's allow him time to get ready for that and you and I can tool around Finneyville, have an early lunch there. Tomás will take care of the camp. Sorry, I mean the house."

Tipsy said, "I have to go to church services at eleven. Visit with me, Hood. I'm a Presbyterian and we don't bite."

Hood asked Tipsy to excuse them and pulled McGregor aside, into the hallway. "Looks like I'm going to church. Forget my scene a moment ago. You go do your thing and I'll take care of picking up Poteet. I'll see you at the Calvin House for the memorial service if not before."

He pecked her cheek and said, "Ask Tipsy to keep quiet about our talk. I need you and Poteet to meet with me tonight to help me prepare a suspect list. With Tipsy's information on the election, he may be able to think of something more that would point a finger. At least we can finally talk to him at length. And don't forget to call Mama about meeting us tomorrow."

Back in the kitchen, he said to Tipsy, "By the way, do you have enough pull with the tomato growers to get me an invitation to attend their Tomato Club meeting Wednesday night?"

"Sure. Consider it done."

Walking into the guest quarters, McGregor almost collided with Tomás, who jumped back, losing his smile for the first time. "Mr. McGregor! I was just checking out the rooms here."

"I'm just plain McGregor. May I call you Tomás?"

"Sure thing."

McGregor decided to take the opportunity to ask Tomás about the tomato growers and invited Mr. Muscles back into the guest den. Tomás sat straight-backed on the sofa in apparent anticipation of a serious interrogation. He moved his pectorals up and down.

"Tomás, relax. I wanted to ask you about growing to-matoes. I understand you and Carlos are from a family of growers and I wanted to let you know that I'll be writing a book soon on the history of the county. Carlos promised me an interview, and I thought you might accommodate me also."

Tomás let out the breath he'd been holding. He fell back into the sofa. "I sure can. I'm sorry. Hey, can I be honest with you?"

"I want you to be honest, Tomás."

"Well, I thought just now you were going to lambast me about Janet. She told me earlier when she was back here crying, that if I didn't stop ogling her she was gonna whip my ass! I didn't know I was ogling her. I thought you were cor-nering me about what she might have told you."

McGregor had to laugh. "No, she didn't say anything to me. You have to understand Hood. First, she probably can whip your ass. She won a black belt in something or other. Second ... well, she's just a highly strung individual. Whatever she was crying about, she's over it. So tell me about your family."

Tomás smiled broadly and opened up. "Well, my Dad's still handles the business. Carlos and I decided to try something different, at least for a time. Sheriff Buell gets along well with the growers, and Dad found out Buell had an opening a few years back and had him hire Carlos. That was when I was still in college. We both have degrees in criminal justice. Me being younger, I'm cutting my teeth in the private sector. One of these days, either I'm going on the force with Carlos, or Carlos will quit and we'll start our own security team."

"Carlos doesn't want to be sheriff some day?"

"Yeah, he might. That is if Sheriff Buell runs for county mayor."

"If Sheriff runs, how soon would that be, the next election in two years?"

"Don't repeat this, but Carlos thinks now the Tomato Boy's dead, Sheriff Buell will wait a while and then announce for the next election even if he has to run against Red Wiley. But I don't want to talk politics, if you don't mind."

"Then tell me about your tomato farm."

"We run a big operation, and I've worked in all departments, from planting and picking to quality testing and water management."

"Was your dad upset when you and Carlos left the business?"

"You don't ever leave the tomato business around here, once you're in it. It's a family thing, if you know what I mean. But yeah, he's upset with us. We have two other brothers and they're staying on. Dad doesn't like anything to change and wanted us to stay in the business, too. Always said to us: Why mess up a good thing, boys? Said it was like him building us a big house and us choosing to live in a tent in the backyard. But Carlos and I like law enforcement too much, I guess."

"You must have some ideas about who killed the Tomato Boy, then."

Tomás studied the floor hard before answering. "Well, sure. But Sheriff, he's warned me you might ask about that and told me not to say anything about it."

Tomás stood up fiddling with his radio, a signal the interview might be over.

"I understand," McGregor said. "But I'd like to know why the tomato growers are so opposed to the new development on this end of the county?"

"Well, that's easy." Tomás walked to the outside door and opened it to leave. "Most of our workers live over here in the foothills. If the area gets developed, the workers can't afford to stay. We'll lose them, and maybe lose our farms in the process. The whole development idea stinks, if you ask me. It messes things up."

"You know Poteet is in favor of the development, don't you?"

"Yeah. But Mr. Poteet's a newcomer and he's a nice guy. He'll come around to our way of thinking sooner or later. That, or he'll get tired of fighting us. I hear he's plenty rich. He can live anywhere. Shouldn't be picking a fight."

"Just one more quick question. What do you know about Amon Trussell?"

"You gonna talk to him? Carlos says so. I don't know anything special about him. His sister's nice. I'm gonna see what's up with *her* one of these days. I like older women."

During the interview, Tomás had changed somewhat in McGregor's mind. He'd changed from a cocky tough dude, a young pony who wanted to horse around with Hood, to a congenial, smart fellow who maybe just liked to flirt too much. But saying outright to McGregor's face that he liked older women put Tomás back in the stable.

CHAPTER 12

McGregor now had the chance to relax for a couple hours. Hood and Tipsy had left, leaving him alone in the house. He showered and lay on the bed to stare at the ceiling. The morning's ill humor had left him.

What if Sheriff was privately planning to run for mayor this time and screw up Red Wiley's plans, and Red had found out? Red might try to frame Sheriff for the Tomato Boy killing. Or, Sheriff could be working a frame on Red. McGregor chuckled. This was fun. Politicians! But seriously, what he needed the most right now was access to the forensics from the murder scene. Without that, he was stuck with nothing but assumptions built from speculations. But he had to go forward.

He'd assume that all major events in Calvin County were connected because he believed that all *minor* events were connected. Therefore, he would assume that the actions against Poteet—and Hood and himself—were somehow connected to the murder. If it was a false assumption he'd find out soon enough and shift gears.

So far, Poker was the thread no matter how much Mama wanted to deny it. If Poker was behind the death threat, the gunshot, the brake line tinkering, and the burglary of Poteet's house, or even the murder, then the question became did he act on his own volition or did someone hire him? If the latter, who? Tipsy could well be right about an outsider being involved.

Tomorrow, he would deal directly with Poker and Mama. For now, the appropriate way to handle Amon Trussell would be to approach the issues tangentially. Why were Poker and Trussell at the hotel Friday afternoon and evening, and what were they fighting about? Has Poker ever expressed animosity toward either Poteet or Clyde? Upon leaving jail what did Trussell and Poker do, specifically?

When it was time to go to Terri's, he dug out his hiking boots from the closet and went out to the Chevy. A quick look underneath the car told him nothing was leaking and no bomb was ticking.

Driving across Pullwater Meadow, McGregor pushed away renewed fears of the creek roaring on the other side of the field by pondering the murder scene itself. The tableau was fixed in his mind: the Tomato Boy on the floor, blond hair thick with blood; a cracked cassette recorder; old audio cassette tapes scattered around. So far he'd been concentrating on motive and opportunity. What about the means?

If the cassette recorder was the murder weapon, then whoever killed Clyde likely had *not* walked into that room intending to commit murder. A person wouldn't contemplate killing somebody with a cassette recorder that might be found handy on the spot.

All indications were that Clyde had left the dining table to meet someone he knew. Say the killer walked into Clyde's room upset and angry. Though McGregor had liked Clyde somewhat, the man had expressed himself with a certain condescension. Whatever Clyde said or did, or failed to say or do, caused the killer's anger to intensify to fury. The killer grabbed the recorder and bashed him. Spur of the moment. Unplanned. Crime of sudden passion. And what are the main things most likely to boil the blood of a human being to the point of murder? Love, with its subsets of jealousy, revenge and hatred. Money, with its subsets of theft, extortion and double-dealing. Power, of course. A county official in Alabama had once said that he deserved his position, that God wanted him to have it for life.

As McGregor turned onto Terri's road, he urged the Chevy up the hill at a faster pace than he had yesterday, the choking vegetation no longer sinister but now merely overgrown weeds. Underneath the tree canopy, the air was fresh, light with pleasing scents. Money. Love and money. Love and money and Amon Trussell. Might Trussell be the murderer? Why had he not put Trussell on his preliminary list of suspects?

The best bet was that money played no part in the life of a man who lived in a shack and drove a beat up Ford over fifty years old. What could Trussell know that would make him angry with the Tomato Boy?

The clearing in front of Terri's house came into view. He didn't like it, but he was going to have to be tough on Trussell. And he'd have to be cool with Terri. He thought of her warm touch on his neck. Ah, God.

Terri was waiting for him on the porch steps, and she looked happy to see him.

"Hey, Bob!"

"Hey, yourself, and good morning. You look great! Can we see Amon today?"

"Absolutely! He came down the hill this morning, and I asked him about talking to you. He shrugged several times, which means 'hell, yes' in Amon language. He talks mostly with his body."

Terri talked with hers too, McGregor thought. She wore tight khaki shorts and a bright yellow T-shirt, and barrettes held back her hair on either side. She wiggled her shoulders and bounced on the tiptoes of her running shoes to the porch steps where she picked up a picnic basket for McGregor to carry. They walked around the back of the house to a trail which led almost straight up through a thicket of trees and bushes to switchbacks winding up the hill.

The basket was heavy, and Terri explained, "I'm bringing along lots of wine. Amon's a wine drinker when he can get it. He's not an alcoholic exactly, but he does like his wine, especially the local stuff from the west end of the county. We call it Vire Wine. They say it's a blend of local grapes and zinfandel imported from California."

The cadence of her voice was hypnotic. The words danced in McGregor's ears, and he could hardly make them out for watching her associated body language, the slight movements and gestures, the facial expressions. "And Amon likes dried snack food. I have plenty of sunflower seeds and such. He likes to stuff his pockets with them when he goes driving around town." All McGregor could do was nod and watch and fantasize until Terri moved on up the path.

At the pre-noon hour the day was clear and breezy, not horribly hot for a July fifth. The climb felt good to McGregor's stiff limbs, the breeze refreshingly cool on his face and bare legs.

Terri chattered about feeling guilty when she didn't attend church on Sunday. In response to the church questions she posed, McGregor lied, telling her he liked church but never seemed to find the time to settle down to one in particular. His old job had required working on weekends. McGregor sensed that Terri might have a problem with depression.

To upbeat the conversation he talked freely with her about his decision to move to Calvin County. She asked a few questions about his proposed book but gave the impression it didn't interest her much. He did not mention Hood, although he thought he probably should have.

Terri caught his arm and stopped him.

"Look up there through those poplars. That's Amon. I bet he's been spying on us and he's hurrying back to the shack to pretend he's surprised to see us. Watch him a minute, and you'll witness one of his problems."

They watched. Amon took three giant steps then touched a tree. He took four small steps and touched a tree.

Then, three giant steps, a tree touch; four steps, a tree touch; then giant steps again. On up the trail he went, repeating the cycle.

"If he misses count," Terri whispered, "he has to come back down and start over. Let's stay here to see if he makes it home and not interrupt him."

Far up the path McGregor could make out the roof of a building with a protruding stovepipe.

They squatted down side by side to get more comfortable. Terri suddenly put a hand on McGregor's knee to balance herself. A tingle shot up his leg to center itself in his groin. Damn! Just like her touching his neck. What was she, an electric generator?

She looked at him, removed her hand and smiled. When Amon made it to the shack, Terri said, "Let's go." She slapped McGregor's thigh and took off.

McGregor caught up, and because of the incline he was eye-level with her rear end, which was straining mightily to stay inside her shorts. He couldn't keep from noticing the outline of her thong. He warned himself to watch out and stay focused. But another voice reminded him that life was a journey, causing him to snicker silently. They broke out from the undergrowth of bushes into a clearing.

The "shack" was indeed a shack. It was constructed of mismatched plywood and wallboard, which, though tightly connected, had Insulation poking out at the seams. It had an over-sized window, open and covered on the inside with a bamboo shade. The stovepipe McGregor had seen was part of a sturdy brick chimney.

"Terri, how should I talk to Amon? Give me some pointers."

"Just follow my lead. You'll get the hang of it easy enough. Words don't explain Amon. You have to experience him."

She knocked on the door, which had a rusty revolver for a handle.

"Amon, it's me. I have Bob with me, like we talked about."

The door opened a crack and Amon peeked out at them with a surprised look on his face. "Hi, how am I?" he asked.

"Everything's fine. May we come in?"

He opened the door wide and they stepped into the one room. It was dark until Amon pulled up the blind; then, McGregor could see that the man kept a neat and orderly place. A cot was on one side, made up with military precision. On the other side was a wood-burning stove. Lining much of the wall space were shelves containing several books and a collection of canned goods. A large, squat table was the centerpiece of Amon's abode. Around it were three stained floor pillows. Amon sat down on a pillow and motioned for them to join him, Japanese style.

Terri said, "Amon, I brought you more snack food and some lunch. Chicken sandwiches with lots of mayonnaise. And look here. Vire wine!"

He pointed at the wine and said, "Fill 'em up!"

Terri unwrapped three large crystal wineglasses from the basket and poured, to the top for Amon and a more reasonable amount for McGregor and herself.

Amon slugged down half his wine and grinned. His face placid, there was none of the fear McGregor had seen before. The graying hair, combed to one side, and the two-day beard made him look like a 1950s Bohemian, a Bohemian poet who had wondered away one day while reading a poem and who never quite made it back to the fold.

"Amon, Bob has come to talk with you about anything you want to talk about. You know Mr. Poteet. Well, Bob here works for him."

"I know Bob. I saw Bob. Bob's funny."

Suddenly, with both hands Amon grabbed an imaginary steering wheel from the air and started driving himself around. Then he articulated, "Yes. Mr. Poteet. I like Mr. Poteet. He drives old cars. I watch him when he drives the red convertible. It's a Cadillac, Bob. He shines it. Too bad it wrecked. I saw it wreck.

"I have an old car, Bob. A 1955 Ford. It's green and white. They tried to make me stop driving. Terri made them test me. I passed the test. Made a hundred. Have eyes like a hawk, too. Terri said that Boy Tomato, that ol' Blondy, was real happy. But I don't care about him."

With a sigh, Terri interjected, "Now, Amon, it was the Boy Tomato who arranged for you to be re-tested, not me. You were happy that he was happy. Remember the insurance he helped you get?"

Amon stared into space. Then he pulled out an envelope from inside his shirt and handed it to McGregor. "The Boy Tomato gave me this."

McGregor surveyed the document within. "An insurance policy. Well, congratulations, Amon! It seems you love cars and love driving them. So do I."

Amon said, "I love cars and I love driving them."

Terri beamed at her brother. The joy McGregor saw on her face astonished him. It magnified her beauty, if that was possible.

She gushed, "Amon, I'm so happy that you've decided to talk! I do wish you'd come to the house more often and talk with the boys the way you're talking now. You know Dewey loves his daddy and Charlie loves you, too. And you know Eli would like to see you more."

As soon as she said *Eli*, a shadow crossed Amon's face and his eyes veiled over. Terri quickly added, "Of course, you do as you please. I'm not trying to make you do anything." She adjusted a loose barrette. "Anyway, we're not here to discuss any of that. I'll get your meal ready, and Bob wants to say a few things to you." She poured wine.

McGregor, uncertain how to proceed, sipped more wine than he should have. If Amon saw the Cadillac accident, he needed to pursue that. He forged ahead.

"Amon, I was wondering. When you saw Mr. Poteet wreck his red car, what caused the car to wreck?"

"A pickup truck."

"That's interesting. Can you tell me who was driving the pickup?"

"Naw."

McGregor realized he'd asked the question as if he were a first year law student. He rephrased the query.

"Amon, did you see who was driving the truck?"

"Yep."

"Who was it?"

"I like Mr. Poteet because he waves at me. Other people out there don't wave at me. Poker waves at me. Poker is good."

This last comment he pointedly directed at Terri.

Terri said, "I know he is, Amon. It's just that he scares me sometimes, although I do like him just fine."

Trussell stared at her with wide eyes that said he knew her liking Poker was a lie.

McGregor asked gently, "Was your friend Poker driving the truck?"

"Poker drove with me when I came home from jail. He followed me home. Poker knows who drove the truck."

Terri assumed the protective sister role. "Bob, I think he's saying in his own way that you should ask Poker."

McGregor veered to another path to get back to talking about the Tomato Boy. He had let the mention of him slip past. "When you and Poker had that fender-bender down at the bridge, what did the cops find in Poker's truck?"

"A tape."

"Why were the cops interested in a tape? Can you tell me?"

"Yep."

McGregor had done it again. "Okay. Why were they concerned about the tape?"

"The tape had blood on it."

"Where did the tape come from? From the Tomato Boy, uh, the Boy Tomato?"

"Naw, from the front seat."

"Was it Poker's tape?"

"Yep." He held out his glass. "More wine, please Terri. Give Bob more wine."

Terri filled the glasses, drained hers in a gulp and re-filled it. McGregor glanced away from Amon's cool, pene-trating eyes. Although he was practiced in the art of making eye contact, Amon was a challenge. He picked up the wine bottle, pretending interest in the label. It said 15.2 percent alcohol. This interview could deteriorate quickly. He needed to sharpen up.

"Okay. Let's see. Whose blood was on the tape?"

"Poker's blood."

"How did Poker's blood get onto the tape?"

Amon slugged the wine again. "Poker cut his finger."

Amon grabbed a sandwich and ate in silence until he finished the entire foot-long sub and his wine. Twice, McGregor started to speak, but Terri shook her head at him.

Amon picked up his air steering wheel and started driving again, making acceleration and braking noises through clenched teeth.

Terri put down her glass. "I think we need to go, Bob. When Amon adds sound effects it means he wants to be alone. He never, ever, likes to drive with passengers."

She left a full bottle of wine on the table. Amon ig-nored it along with their good-byes and kept on driving. He was on a long trip.

About halfway down the hill McGregor was trying to place the bloody tape in context when Terri paused, sat down on a stump and opened the basket.

"Bob, look what I found!" She pulled out a half-pint of tequila and a couple of bottled waters. "We didn't get a chance to have our lunch. How about a picnic?"

She pulled McGregor down to sit on a fallen log. Sunlight twinkled down around them through the oak leaves and danced in spots on the ground. It was the heady wine or it was Terri or it was the day finally heating up, but McGregor suddenly felt his face grow thick and heavy and hot.

Questions formed and half-formed in his head, but he couldn't take his eyes off Terri as she downed a couple of swallows of the liquor and passed it over to him. He never drank liquor straight and actually thought for a split second about refusing to do so now, before he hefted the bottle for a long pull. He followed it with the entire contents of the water bottle and fell backward into the grass growing off the trail. Terri took another sip, and then fell with him, accidentally spilling the remaining tequila on her face. McGregor started laughing and realized it was his first carefree laugh in many weeks.

He raised himself up on an elbow, his face almost touching hers. He had the clear intention of asking her about the exact relationship between Amon and the Tomato Boy. Instead, on impulse, he gently licked the tequila from her face. He kissed her lips and she returned the kiss. Then big teardrops formed and ran down the sides of her face and into her hair.

"Terri! What's wrong?" She was the third woman today he'd made cry.

"Oh, your questions back there just made me start thinking about poor Clyde. You mentioned blood, and now all I can think about is Clyde's head cut open the way they said it was."

Taken aback, McGregor said, "Yeah, it was something awful."

"I dated Clyde," she said flatly.

"Dated him? When?"

Through a series of whimpers, she explained. "About a month ago. He'd started all that talk about wanting to be the new county mayor, and all of a sudden I just got real attracted to him. I couldn't help it. You're the first person I've told about that. It was secret. Turned out, Clyde liked secrets. That's what he said. Why do men like secret affairs so much?"

"Hmm," said McGregor, disheartened and disappointed. "I don't know. Same reason women like them so much, I suspect."

Terri laughed then. "Yeah."

"So what happened with you and Clyde?"

She wiped her tears and said, "Clyde broke off the whole thing one day. He didn't give any excuse. I thought at the time that Leslie Rion, the woman they have in jail, had something to do with it."

No longer feeling amorous, McGregor went back to detecting. "Tell me, are you sure you never told Amon what you just told me? Or, do you think somehow Amon found out about you and Clyde?"

She shaded her eyes from a sunbeam that had bored its way through the leaves. "Sometimes I feel like Amon knows everything that goes on around here. He's always watching people. They never seem to notice him, but I do. That's why I came up here with you today. If Amon ever opens up we could all learn a thing or two. Some of it we might not want to learn."

Her eyes fluttered then, showing a slight tinge of fear.

"What?" McGregor asked.

"After Clyde dumped me, one day the boys went on an overnight church camp. Amon came by the porch. He can always tell when I've made a Vire Wine purchase, it seems. Anyway, I think I overdid the wine, and, well, I might have let it slip. I know I was thinking about Clyde when Amon was sitting there. I just can't remember if I was saying out loud what I was thinking. Amon acts so stoic, sometimes even I forget he's there."

She jumped up. "Let's go! I bet it's not even one o'clock yet. We have time for a pitcher of margaritas to go with our sandwiches before you have to leave." Taking the picnic basket, she started down the trail.

Margaritas?

Back at the screened porch again, they were both out of breath. McGregor missed a step going up and reflexively put out his bad arm to catch himself against the doorframe. The pain buckled his knees. Cursing, he rolled back down to the lawn and lay there clenching his teeth.

Terri turned motherly and assisted him up on the porch into an ancient wicker chair, which groaned under his weight but held him. He cradled his arm until the pain eased. "Sorry about that," he said.

Terri went in the house for a wet towel and came back wiping her face. Then she cleaned McGregor's sweaty face for him, careful to avoid the taped-up cut.

"You're a good nurse," he said.

"You stay right there, Bob."

She went back inside and returned with a pitcher of iced margarita mix and a large bottle of tequila. With a cigarette lighter she started lighting the candles that lined her porch floor.

McGregor looked at the tequila bottle with dread. He said, "I don't know, Terri. I'd better get to your bathroom for a minute. You have any ibuprofen in there?"

Angry about his arm, which was becoming a real disability, he washed down four of the pain pills he found and performed his other bathroom task. He resolved to get away from Terri. She was a lush, no matter how pretty she was. This much drinking could lead to trouble. Back on the porch, however, his resolution dissolved immediately when he laid eyes on her.

Terri had reclined on her davenport, propped up on pillows, and was sipping away at her drink. She held out a margarita for McGregor to take. With no hesitation he accepted it and tossed an extra pillow on the floor to sit next to the davenport.

"That arm better?" she asked.

"Oh, yeah!" he answered and drank heavily from the wide brimmed glass, splashing some of the green stuff onto his white shirt.

Terri laughed again, watching him try to swipe it away. "Goodness," she said, "I don't know why I spilled the beans about me and Clyde. I guess with him gone, it doesn't matter much, but I feel guilty about the whole thing—I mean about telling you, revealing a secret."

She put a hand on his head and ruffled his hair. "If Sheriff ever found out, you know it'd make me a suspect in his eyes." Then she pleaded, "You won't tell him, will you?"

He couldn't imagine Terri as a murderer. "Your secret's safe with me. As long as you didn't kill Clyde!" He looked up at her and scooted around on his pillow to face her. "Did you kill him?"

She stared deep into his eyes. "I did not kill Clyde Thacker."

McGregor put his drink on the floor next to a candle. He pulled himself up and sat down next to her on the davenport. She handed him her drink, and he placed it carefully on the table. He rested his cast on the seat back and leaned down to her face. This time, he stared long and hard into *her* eyes. They were liquid, opaque and glistening—and totally unrevealing. This would be purely a judgment call, he thought.

His lips an inch from hers, he said, "I believe you."

As they kissed wildly, twisting and writhing, McGregor wanted nothing in life more than to rip off her clothes and make hot, senseless love to this charmer of a woman, this delicate, tender, and seductive woman. Make sweaty love, in the daylight, unrestrained and uncontrolled—right on the porch. He wanted to, she wanted to, and so they did it.

When it was over they lay panting ear to ear so that they barely heard the grinding gears of a vehicle coming up the steep road.

Terri gulped, "What's that?"

McGregor cursed and disentwined himself. The noise was coming from a good distance. Lurching about, they smoothed down their clothes, and McGregor tumbled into the wobbly chair across the porch. He was sitting there upright with drink in hand when an orange pickup truck broke into the clearing slinging gravel—Eli Rust's work truck.

A dozen birds screeched in unison and fluttered from the yard as Eli halted at the porch, under the shade next to the Chevy. Terri continued straightening her clothes, her face still flushed and eyes wide with worry.

"Hey, Terri!" Eli bellowed. "I brought the boys home early so we could all go to the memorial service. Thought the boys needed to witness the biggest funeral the county's ever seen!"

The porch being higher than the truck, McGregor was able to look down through the windshield at Eli's face, which was screwed up into furrows.

The boys had the truck door open and started piling out with camp gear in their arms. To get out of their way, Eli, with a hearty laugh, leaned over onto the hood of the Chevy with both hands.

"Hi, Mom!"

"Hi, Aunt Terri!"

They all three squeezed through the screen door at once. The boys gave a simultaneous "Hi, Bob" to McGregor and rushed into the house. Eli stood with arms crossed, his face a giant question mark as he surveyed the two of them, the table of alcohol, and the pillows strewn on the floor.

"Well, ho, ho! We're having some afternoon toddies for the bodies, I see. Mind if I join in?"

McGregor rose to shake hands, offering his left. Eli, mixing up his hands awkwardly, finally took McGregor's left hand with his right, shaking it with his palm to the back of McGregor's hand.

Terri looked stupefied, so McGregor played host and said, "No, not at all, Eli, help yourself. We're having margaritas to take the heat off. Boy, it's turned into a real scorcher of a day, hasn't it?"

"Well, I was thinking it was a bit cool for July. It's getting cloudy, looking like rain again. But whatever." He poured a drink, mix only, and sat on the davenport with Terri, putting his arm around her.

Terri, composing herself, leaned into his side. "Bob just came by to see if the boys might want to ride around with him in that old car, maybe take us to Clyde's memorial service. Says he's feeling attached to the rascals since they saved his life and all. Didn't know they were at camp, so we just started talking. Bob's interested in the history of the county and gonna write a history book is what I understand."

McGregor thought she lied evenly, convincingly.

"That right, Bob?" asked Eli. "I can tell you all about the history of the roads. The Old Military Offshoot out there'd make a book to itself if the story was ever told."

McGregor replied, "I'd be interested in hearing it sometime; I really would. But right now, I have to be going. Sure y'all don't want a ride over to the hotel, Terri?"

"No, Eli can take the boys. They're used to riding all over the county with him." She looked up at Eli's big face. "And me, well, I just don't feel like going. I'm just going to sit here on the porch and have another drink. To Clyde's memory, I guess."

"You drink too much, Terri," Eli said. To McGregor, he said, "I've been telling her that and she won't listen."

Eli walked to the door of the house. "Hurry up, boys!" he called. "We want to get a good seat over to the hotel."

He turned back to McGregor. "Be seeing you over there, Bob." Suspicion on his face, he eyed the two them for a moment and went on inside. They heard him stomp up the stairs.

Terri edged over to McGregor and whispered, "Damn, that was close. I didn't expect anybody for another couple of hours." She finished off her drink.

"Are you and Eli dating, or what, Terri?"

"I'll explain it later. The boys need a father. And, oh, I don't know. Let's talk about it later. Why don't you come back here instead of going to the service? We could ... push more buttons?"

"I don't think that would be the wisest thing. Besides, I promised Hood and Poteet I'd meet them at the hotel. Poteet's supposed to be released from the hospital."

"Who's Hood?"

McGregor sighed. "She's a friend. Janet Hood. I'll explain that one later, too. I'd better go now." He squeezed her arm.

He turned the car around and waved at Terri, leaving her on the porch steps looking forlorn.

McGregor was halfway down the long hill wondering if Rust could have figured out what he and Terri had been up to and whether Hood might be able to do so in her omniscient way. He slammed on the brakes.

"Son-of-a-bitch! Hood!" he roared to the trees and the weeds, causing the birds to cry out their own insults. Rust leaned on his car hood—his cold car hood under the shade tree.

Immediately, his head cleared of its alcohol buzz. The day's infatuation with Terri vanished. He had to tell Terri what he'd realized; plus, now was the time to ascertain a few facts, while Terri was still somewhat pliable. Down the winding road at a curve he spied a side trail through the brush large enough for a car to fit.

He eased the Chevy along the trail until he was well away from the road. He came to a clearing and turned the car around. Interestingly, from this perspective there was a break in the trees, looking down the hill. He could see the bridge over Pullwater Creek and the Offshoot as it headed toward Calvin Station. He waited.

He heard Rust's old truck lumber down the hill. He watched for it to come out past the foliage and onto the Offshoot. Finally, it appeared and roared off into the distance. Satisfied, he headed back to Terri's.

She must have sensed he would return, for she was sitting on the porch steps as though waiting for him, this time sipping from a mug. He hoped it was tea or coffee.

"I was wishing you'd come back," she said, "but not for the same reason I was wishing it before. We need to talk."

They re-entered the porch and she poured him a mug of iced tea. No whiskey this time.

"Thanks. Terri, I agree we need get some things straight between us. I couldn't leave it the way it was. First, tell me about you and Eli, and then I've a confession to make."

Terri blew out all the candles on the porch. She had changed her clothes, was dressed now in white linen slacks and a starched white blouse. She looked prim, formal. He was reminded that he needed to get back to the camp for his own change of clothes, before going to the service. He'd have to hurry.

"Well, all right." Terri said. She sat down on the davenport's edge. "I don't have any secrets when it comes to Eli. It's just that we don't go around broadcasting our relationship, you know."

Losing her slow drawl, she explained rapidly that she'd decided the boys needed a man around, a role model. Amon never would be able to raise Dewey properly. Both boys were at the age when a man in their lives would make a real difference in how they managed their teenage years. Because Eli was divorced and he and Amon had been such good friends in years past, and Eli had taken a liking to the boys and they to him, and Eli was, frankly, an attractive guy, she'd found him to be a strong possibility.

Since the death of Clyde on Friday, she'd been thinking that Eli now had a good chance of becoming county mayor. That would mean the boys would have a person close that they could really look up to. They could be somebody in the county. She didn't want to put her relationship with Eli in jeopardy. And that meant she couldn't see McGregor anymore.

"I hate it because I really do like you, Bob."

It was McGregor's turn. He confessed, "I've been working on renewing an old flame with a girlfriend, and I don't want to harm that relationship, either. I've known Hood, er, Janet, ever since college. I think I might be in love with her all over again. She's in the car restoration business and she came up here to work with me, work for Poteet just for a couple of weeks to help with his old cars. We're both staying at Poteet's place for the time being."

Terri smiled an ordinary, non-sensuous smile. "Let's be friends then, all right?"

"You got it! Now, I would appreciate answers to a couple of questions. I'm stumped wondering about Amon and Eli. Back at Amon's when you mentioned Eli, Amon changed his demeanor instantly, and not for the better. And now you say they've been friends for some time. Tell me about them."

"Amon and Eli *are* buddies. And years ago they went out of town to work on a big job together. That was when Amon had his accident that put him in the shape he's in now. They were working for a big highway construction and paving company when one day Amon was out by himself on a new road doing some soil testing. It was raining that day and had been for several days in a row. Amon was struck by a hit-and-run driver, as far as anybody can figure out. It was muddy as muddy could be out there. And the best guess from what tracks were left was that Amon fell into a big mud pile somehow, and the pile slid all the way down into a big gully. He was down there overnight mostly buried before anybody found him …"

McGregor got the creepy feeling he'd heard this tale before from Eli, but with Eli as the main character.

"… It was Eli who reached him first. Amon had a bad head injury and stayed in the hospital for weeks. Eli talked the company they were working for into paying Amon a bunch of money in exchange for Amon and Eli never saying anything about it. You know, file a claim or anything. I only have bits and pieces of the details. But it seems it was important for the company to maintain a perfect safety record at the time, so they coughed up money to both Amon and Eli. Eli has always held a strong grudge against the men who ran that company.

"Often, whenever Eli sees Amon for any good period of time, Eli will start drinking heavy, which he usually doesn't do. He's against alcohol, you see. Then, he'll start cussing those company men, whoever they are, and say the most vile things about them. He says sometimes at night he can't sleep. Says he lives the night Amon spent in the gully over and over, like it was him that had been down there. Says it's weird. Anyway, Amon lives on the interest from that money and when he dies, it'll all go to Dewey. But something snaps in Amon when he sees Eli. We're hoping it'll go away, the more they see each other with me in the middle, so to speak."

"Do you think Eli has any knowledge of your secret affair with the Tomato Boy?"

"Nooo. No way." She looked at him sharply. "And if he ever does find out about it, I'll know who told him!"

"Don't worry. My lips are sealed. But you said Amon might know about it."

"Yeah, that is a problem."

McGregor reached over and patted her arm, saying there were two other problems she needed to be aware of.

"First, I'll be visiting with Poker tomorrow and probably again later in the week. I'll let you know what I find out if it involves Amon."

"Oh, God! That damned Poker Limbo! I can't stand him, but Amon likes him so much."

McGregor stood up to go. "You told Eli that I'd just stopped by. That means he knows nothing about us talking to Amon, is that correct?"

"Yes. I didn't see any need to tell him. He gets protective of Amon, always wanting to know who he talks to."

"Well, the problem is that Eli put both his hands on my car's hood getting out of the way of the boys rushing in. The car's been in the shade all this time. He would have felt it cold. That'll tell him the car was parked here long enough to cool down. You should go ahead and tell him I was here for an hour or so. I'd come up here looking for the boys and we began talking about my moving here and how I'm a former prosecutor and such. He needs to know I'm not a threat to him. Tell him I talked to you about Janet Hood. That'll throw him off enough so that I don't think he'll be wondering about what might have happened between us."

McGregor opened the door to leave and Terri hopped up and ran over to him. She hugged him and asked him how long he expected to live here.

"Two years is the plan."

With her head still on his chest, she said, "If for some reason, it doesn't work out with Eli and me and you and that Janet, will you come back to me?"

"Yes," he whispered huskily, "I think that's a strong possibility." It was a lie.

Or, maybe it wasn't. In the shade of the tree canopy down the road, McGregor stopped the car. He braced his aching wrist behind his neck and leaned on it. Lying was strictly against his personal code. Philanderers disgusted him. His mood tanked. These mood swings were becoming wide, as wide as Hood's. Why was he doing what he was doing?

CHAPTER 13

It was apropos to the return of the morning's dark mood that a dark cloud should roll over Pullwater Meadow when McGregor crossed it as he headed back to the camp. Rain sprinkled the windshield. McGregor tuned the radio to a local station. The weather report predicted two or more inches of rain during the night. A flash flood watch would be in effect beginning at midnight.

A newscaster announced that the Tomato Boy's memorial service would be held as scheduled at four. A reporter already on the scene said that attendance would be limited to close friends and invited guests. No mention was made of family. The public would be welcome at a graveside service whenever the medical examiner's office released the body, which it was expected to do within the week. McGregor had been given no actual invitation to the memorial service.

At the camp he assumed the positive, that he was invited, and made a fast change into a suit and tie. He and Terri had neglected their picnic sandwiches when they'd turned into love animals on the porch. So, being an animal, he started wolfing down some carryout chicken he found in Poteet's mostly empty refrigerator.

The remorse he felt for the porch activity with Terri robbed the food of any taste. Although he and Janet Hood— maybe he'd start calling her Janet—had exchanged no formal commitments of late, he felt as close to her now as he ever had.

Tomás suddenly came striding into the kitchen, his great smile preceding him by a few feet. Lakisha followed him.

"Hey, man, that's my food!" Tomás barked.

McGregor coughed on a bite. "Sorry. I didn't know."

"It's okay, just joking you. I had all I wanted. Made you jump, didn't I? Lakisha's here early so I can go to the Tomato Boy's service on the way home. I'll give you a ride there if you'd like."

A subtle request lay underneath the friendly offer. McGregor, having learned to read around and through the actual words of his new friends in Calvin County, accepted the ride. Who knew what he'd blow on a breath test, anyway?

Lakisha promised she'd come in and have supper with the camp household later. Her father would be representing her family at the service, she said. It was those of the older generation who enjoyed the friendship of the Tomato Boy. They remembered him as the cheerful kid who ran around the Calvin House playing fun tricks on the staff. At her age she didn't know him well, but she liked him because he'd done something through the years to benefit every club, every school, the sports teams, and had been especially charitable to her bookmobile.

"Whenever I saw him," she said, "he always acted like he was leading a parade or something. In a way I admired him but I also felt embarrassed for him."

When McGregor and Tomás stepped out onto the front porch to leave, a fierce, blowing rainstorm assaulted them. Using umbrellas from a porch stand, they hustled into the security SUV. McGregor checked the time on the dash and made a mental note to buy a new watch.

Tomás said, "We don't really need to worry about the time. The service is by invitation only. There should be plenty of room."

"Who planned the service?" McGregor asked.

Tomás explained that the hotel's head clerk had put together a list of nearly two hundred persons and cleared it with Sheriff Buell and other county officials.

Then Tomás cleared his throat. "Carlos wanted me to explain a couple of things to you that he couldn't say to you, him being the chief deputy. Back door stuff. Seems he's okay'd you in his own way. You see, this Tomato Boy murder has Sheriff Buell and Red Wiley mystified. Carlos knows they've tried to freeze you out of the loop by promising you Mama Limbo's old journals and promising to get the Offshoot re-paved. Carlos thinks that you being a prosecutor and a newcomer you could weasel out more information in certain areas than they could."

"Former prosecutor," McGregor corrected him.

"Any rate, here's the deal. Carlos is afraid Sheriff and Red are going to try to pin the murder on Poker Limbo. He thinks it's true that Poker is into this thing up to his nose hairs, but Poker's just not the kind of man to strike another man dead. There's some bad in him, but a lot more good than bad. Personally, I disagree. But that's Carlos and he's usually right. You met Poker, yet?"

"In a roundabout way, yes. I've met Mama and you know that she and Poteet are good friends. Poteet says he wants me to find a way to get Poker out of this situation, if possible, because of that friendship. I'm hoping to finally meet with Poker tomorrow for a sit-down chat."

"Good thing," Tomás said. "You should know that Sheriff and Red suspect Poker of sending that death threat and firing that shot. The burglary at Mr. Poteet's and the brake line thing, well, that's up in the air. Then, there's that piece of information that Janet mentioned—that somebody in a truck caused her to run off the road in the Cadillac? Nobody knows what to make of that. But Carlos says even if you put all those things on Poker, nothing adds up to his doing the killing. 'Coincident, but not related.' His words.

"The problem is that Carlos found a cassette tape in Poker's truck with blood on it when Poker wrecked the day of the murder with that idiot Trussell. That's why he arrested Poker on suspicion. It had Sheriff and Red jumping for joy. And this is what I'm getting to. When they sent that tape off to the lab, Carlos saw it. And it had a lot more blood on it than when he first found it!"

Tomás glanced at McGregor for a reaction. McGregor allowed the statement to dangle in the air for a long moment. He considered saying nothing, but decided Tomás was waiting for him to express the unspoken accusation.

"If that's the case," McGregor said, "and the extra blood comes back as Clyde Thacker's blood, then either Sheriff or Red may be trying to pin the murder on Poker with hard evidence."

"Yeah. You said it. And Carlos eventually would have to go along or suffer the consequences."

In silence, Tomás drove slowly to avoid the potholes, which now brimmed with rainwater. After turning right onto Ferry Road toward the Calvin House, he sped up.

He said, "Poker refused a lawyer and denied having anything to do with anything, but he gave conflicting stories on where he was and what he was doing at the time of the window shooting and at the time of the murder. Sheriff's looking for anybody who saw him at the hotel, other than out in the parking lot. He's not been questioned on the burglary or the brake line thing. No legal cause to bring him in. The forensic experts found nothing in Poteet's art room except what they now know are Poteet's fingerprints. Which reminds me. Carlos said Poteet came to the office today to give his statement and provide prints and hair and blood samples after Janet picked him up from the hospital. So those matters are taken care of."

Tomás parked behind the Calvin House in a security-reserved spot. The rain stopped pounding and settled down to a hard drizzle. He said, "Turnabout's fair play, did you find out anything from that idiot Trussell?"

Knowing that McGregor was going to visit Trussell was one thing, knowing that he *did* visit Trussell was something else entirely. Was somebody spying on him? If so, was his activity on the porch observed? McGregor couldn't say anything about Terri and the Tomato Boy, but he wanted to give Tomás something. The truth, though, could hurt Poker more than could be assessed at this point; plus, a niggling suspicion told McGregor that Carlos and Tomás had more than one tomato plant growing in this pot. He decided in favor of shading the truth with some gray.

"No, I didn't get much. But I'm going back to see Trussell again because I'm convinced he knows something. He may be protecting Poker or somebody else. After I get to know him better, I think he'll trust me more."

Tomás turned on his smile. "I'll report that as a maybe. Carlos said to use me as the go-between for any information you pick up."

Tomás opened the door, but McGregor stopped him. "Speaking of turnabout. If I keep on the Trussell track for Carlos, will he tell me about the forensic evidence from the murder scene?"

Tomás shed his smile and focused on McGregor's eyes. "You are good, McGregor. I'll ask."

Under umbrellas they splashed to the lobby. McGregor re-evaluated Tomás once more, begrudging him several plus marks. In the business of law enforcement, scruples were hard to keep. Sometimes you had to choose sides. Sometimes you had to change sides.

In the hotel lobby dozens of folding chairs, sedately draped with black cloth, faced the ancient fireplace with its ornately carved mahogany mantel. The mantel was partially overlaid in dark red and green fabric. A large photograph of the

Tomato Boy—as an adult—had been placed on a dais in front of a podium. On either side of the dais were poster blow-ups of the can label photo of Clyde as a youngster.

The chandelier shone brightly in the otherwise gloomy atmosphere. Many persons were seated; just as many stood about in clusters, chatting with heads low. A man played mournful music on an organ.

McGregor moved just inside the door and backed up to the wall. His interest settled on the dozens of tall tomato plants, drooping with ripe fruit and assembled in big pots to create walkways from the front and rear lobby doors to the seating areas. Shorter plants were stacked on low shelves around the dais. There were no flowers anywhere, just the tomato plants. And the oddity amused McGregor. They couldn't let Clyde be Clyde. He had to remain the Tomato Boy forever. Suddenly, McGregor felt pressed for meaning. Did he truly comprehend what was going on here?

He reached over to the tomato pot nearest him on his left and touched a leaf. He took a hefty tomato as large as his fist, tugged it gingerly from underneath a leaf and turned it slowly within the light of the burning chandelier. An insight occurred, one he should have had already. Calvin Countians weren't mere food producers, purveyors of tomatoes; they were *farmers*. They tilled. They cultivated, hands in the soil—connected to it. They lived wholly dependent on earth, water, wind and fire. And their brains and brawn. Before this, McGregor in his educated arrogance would have understood the tomato as a symbol of the soil and felt good for being so enlightened. Now, he understood that to a farmer the tomato didn't represent the soil, it *was* the soil.

This thing he was holding, a thing of skin, pulp, pith, core and seeds was not the end product of a linear world, but part of a cycle. Most likely, the Tomato Boy—or the idea of a Tomato Boy—*had* become a representation, a symbol of the current prosperity of the county commonwealth in all its forms. Prosperity in the late summer of the seasonal cycle was tallied in tomatoes and not in new roads, condos and boat launches. The killing of the Tomato Boy was a blow against the status quo, an intrusion from the other world where such things as development did count. How had Tomás put it? Development stinks? Maybe it does.

To record his thoughts, McGregor whipped out his notebook and scribbled the heading "Tomatoes—For the Book" on a clean page. Now, what were the words? Prosperity of the commonwealth? Intrusion? Status quo? Ah, God, an alcoholic hangover was lurking just around the next thought. He jotted down "Development Stinks" and let it go at that.

McGregor looked around and saw Tomás talking to Carlos, who fidgeted with his polished gun belt while listening intently. On the other side of the room, Sheriff and Red stood shoulder to shoulder staring off into space, wearing grief-stricken masks. Eli and the boys were nowhere to be seen. McGregor wondered if Rust claimed he wanted to bring the boys here as a ruse to check on Terri after somehow finding out about the meeting with Trussell.

McGregor spotted the backs of the heads of Mama, Poteet and Hood. He eased down the aisle and took an empty chair beside Hood.

After exchanging hushed greetings with the trio, he let Hood whisper in his ear. She told him to look across the aisle when he could do so inconspicuously. He let his head drift to the right. Leslie was over there sitting beside a woman, their two chairs set apart from the rest. They were dressed in formal black and wore corsages of cherry tomatoes. Leslie's facial profile would easily match a template of Clyde's.

Hood whispered again, "That's her mother beside her—her mother, the lawyer."

"Interesting," McGregor said as the organ music ceased and a man approached the podium.

Hood said, "That's the county mayor. The one with the electric trains."

The mayor said words of welcome on behalf of the Calvin House. The service would be informal. He used stilted language to describe his long relationship with Clyde and the Calvin families of old. Try as he might, McGregor was unable to remember what the man said as soon as he said it. Then, the mayor introduced Tipsy Alcorn, handing over the cordless microphone to her. Tipsy paused with head bowed as if collecting her thoughts.

Eventually, she spoke evenly and respectfully. "Clyde Leslie Thacker, age 41, is dead."

"Clyde Leslie?" McGregor whispered to Hood. But she shushed him, so he listened up to what Tipsy was saying.

"Today we have gathered to pay him tribute and to memorialize the short time we had with him. We grieve for our loss. We give our deepest sympathy to his daughter, Leslie Rion, who is our new friend, and to her mother, Stacia Rion, who has traveled from California to be with us today.

"Our dear friend Clyde, our beloved Tomato Boy, has passed from our midst, but his memory will live with us and in this hotel he loved so much."

She continued with sentimental stories representative of Clyde's benevolence and how he paid attention to children and the unfortunate. She recounted the oft-told tale of how his "sweet baby face" was selected to illustrate the labels and advertising for the great Calvin County Tomato; how because of that, the county had been blessed and would remain in his debt down through the years to come.

"On a bed table in his room," Tipsy said, "Leslie found a simple poem written in the hand of the Tomato Boy. Maybe something he jotted down in the middle of the night. She wants me to read it today. It says:

> My life was but a shadow of red
> by eyes
> glimpsed then gone,
> leaving in the minds behind the eyes
> perhaps
> a small wonderment."

She explained that although Clyde was not a frequent church-goer, he had once told her in a personal moment that his favorite religious song was "Ave Maria." In the same breath, he had mentioned to her that his all time favorite song was "California Dreamin'."

The two songs might sound a bit strange together, Tipsy said, but she and others, Leslie included, had decided it would be appropriate to perform them. She motioned, and a boy choir marched in from the hallway, the boys each wearing a red choir robe garnished with thin green collars. The boys sang "California Dreamin'" melodiously, and then Tipsy assumed a position at the microphone stand.

She thanked the boys for the time they had spent in rehearsal at short notice and for their fine rendition. The Tomato Boy, she declared, would have been proud.

Then, in a rich voice McGregor could hardly believe was coming from such a small woman, Tipsy sang "Ave Maria" a cappella. It was a captivating performance, and McGregor could hear many sniffs from behind him. Hood quivered beside him, touching his arm. Mama and Poteet held hands.

McGregor glanced at Leslie. She sat with back straight, pensively elegant and without tears. Only her hands moved in her lap as she slowly kneaded them. Her mother cried quietly. McGregor had to admit it. He was touched by the simple service, by the idea of a life well lived, and by Leslie's grace. His eyes welled up.

After several mourners stood at their chairs to give personal testimonials to the great character and loving nature of the Tomato Boy, Tipsy called to a man at the dais to step forward and close the service. He did so with a long, eloquent prayer about people and place; something about time, then sunshine. McGregor lost track. He wanted to speak to Leslie and meet her mother, the lawyer.

But with the "Amen," several mourners jumped to hurry over to clutch at the women in black and reduce themselves to crying once more. Leslie merely stared at them and held out her hand. McGregor's timing was off. He decided it was best to leave the county to its grief.

Poteet and Hood were tired and wanted to go home. Mama was too overcome to talk, managing only a whisper that she'd see McGregor tomorrow. McGregor learned she was in her own car, parked in front as a family member.

It was the threesome again who drove the Offshoot. A fresh storm cell raced through the mountains directly overhead, the thunder and lightning unsettling and thwarting McGregor's attempts to talk. Hood, at the wheel, cursed and fought the old Ford wagon to stay even moderately in control.

In front of the camp, Lakisha met them with umbrellas. To their supreme delight, she had brought in a home-cooked meal large enough for an army. She joined them at the kitchen table and turned serious.

"I got to thinking about the break-in," she said. "In my kind of job, I'm a suspicious you-know-what. I wondered if the slashing of the paintings was a diversion. So, I checked the phones. Sure enough, look what I found!"

She produced five plastic ovals, listening devices she said. "They get power from the phones, so now that they're disconnected they don't work. But I have to warn you. There may be others. Could be hidden anywhere."

With Poteet's consent she brought in debugging equipment from her vehicle and scoped out the house. She found no more bugs, but she advised that they talk only where they believed it to be completely safe.

After she had donned her rain gear and left them, Poteet put a finger to his lips, motioning McGregor and Hood to follow him. They obeyed, walking behind him to the study, which was a cozy, expensively furnished, and windowless room off the main living room. Poteet closed the door and pressed a button on the wall, which caused a hissing noise to come from the door frame.

Poteet smirked at them. "Don't worry about bugs in here. After I bought the place I had a firm from up north

I'm familiar with to come down here and completely soundproof this room. It's my sanctum sanctorum, the kind of room I've wanted for years. You wouldn't believe how many business secrets I've lost to prying eyes and ears and what it's cost me. I bet Tipsy didn't even notice this morning that the room is actually a foot around smaller than when she built the house. I also had them turn it into a storm shelter with thickened walls and its own HVAC and telephone systems."

The first thing that caught McGregor's eye was another Tommy Mathis painting. A departure from landscapes of sunny Tuscany, this one pictured a reclining, naked blue woman.

The wall opposite the door was devoted to a series of photographs chronicling Poteet's pre-Calvin County business and social life. McGregor recognized handshaking senators and presidential candidates. To both McGregor and Hood, one eight-by-ten photograph stood out from the rest and they took a closer peek. It showed a young, long-haired McGregor hugging an alluring Hood who had short hair, the two of them standing under a sign that said Earth Day. Poteet had added a small plaque that read: Future Earth Movers.

Hood pecked McGregor on the cheek. That particular Earth *Night* had been their first night. McGregor's stomach knotted in guilt.

They settled into a couple of leather wing chairs to watch as Poteet opened a cabinet door to reveal a well-stocked bar. He mixed a pitcher of Beefeater martinis, plopped olives in glasses and poured. After the first sip Poteet sank heavily into a chair and said, "Let's talk!"

McGregor insisted on going first, hoping his stomach would relax. He told them of Grooms wanting to quit the race. Poteet was stunned but said they should discuss that revelation later. Then McGregor, with Hood's help, divulged what Tipsy had said about the county mayor's race coming up in two years and who all wanted the office. Poteet said the

Wily-Buell dynasty being contemplated was news to him, but again waved off discussion.

McGregor objected. "Not satisfactory, Poteet! You can deal with Grooms later, but you should tell us what you know about these possible suspects! It bears on who has been trying to kill you or scare you, whatever. And who's trying to pin the murder on you by planting that handle in Chesterfield. The tomato growers may not be behind this at all."

They stared at Poteet, waiting.

"Look," said Poteet. "I knew the Tomato Boy wanted to run. There was some talk in the club meetings about the others, but I focused on the business aspects of the club, the festival and such. I'm not one to speculate about politics because I don't enjoy politics. I put Dimpsey up to running this time because I thought he wanted the job, and it was a way to keep the Offshoot from tearing up my cars. It was that simple."

McGregor decided to let his explanation pass for the time being. He was antsy to tell them about the rest of day. He gave them a short version of the Trussell interview, and ended saying, "Both Terri and I believed Trussell was telling me that Poker knows who ran y'all off the road."

His martini giving him the bravado to bend the truth with a straight face, McGregor wedged in the information about the relationship between Terri and Eli Rust without giving any hint of the Terri and McGregor porch love. He left out the story of Terri's affair with the Tomato Boy.

Then he told them of Amon Trussell slipping in the mud pile down the hill at a job site years ago. Hood and Poteet dropped their chins when McGregor revealed how Eli, while driving him to the hospital yesterday, had tried to empathize with McGregor's frightening experience in the creek by telling the tale as if he, Eli, had been left overnight in a ravine.

"Eli holds a strong grudge against that company he and Trussell worked for," McGregor declared.

Poteet breathed an "Uh, oh."

"Yeah," McGregor said, "Uh, oh, is right. To me, the Eli-Amon connection was a mind bender. I don't know what to make of it."

Privately, he was worrying about how Eli might take it if he found out about the porch liaison.

Hood asked, "Is this Rust a fruitcake, maybe? Tipsy vouches for him, and I don't think she'd do that lightly. Poteet, you've retired to some kind of bedlam. Maybe we should make a list of who we think is sane and start from there. It'd be a short one. Lakisha is one, and I think I'd add Carlos Hernandez, and I guess Tomás, so far as I can tell. I think he's a sweetie!"

She cupped her mouth as McGregor squinted at her.

He said, "Speaking of your sweet Tomás, I've had two informative conversations with him."

Once finished with his quick review of tomato farm life from the point of view of Tomás and the news that Buell might not wait his proper turn to run for county mayor, McGregor said, "You may want to fill up those glasses again when you hear this. It's a bombshell!"

To their bug-eyed stares, he let them in on what Tomás had revealed on the way to the memorial service about the bloody tape.

Hood tossed back her drink, almost choking on her olive, and quickly poured another.

Poteet dropped his shoulders and said, "So, we have some kind of conspiracy working in the sheriff's office against Poker, and Carlos goes and creates another conspiracy to uncover the first one and involves you, putting you adverse to Buell and Wiley! Good Lord!"

McGregor, having resolved nothing, listened to Hood and Poteet reveal their activities of the day. Leslie had been released from jail as soon as the mother, Stacia Rion, had arrived this morning by private charter from California and threatened Red Wiley with a million-dollar lawsuit. Mama

Limbo had met Stacia at the airport, briefed her on all the events and taken her to Calvin House.

Poteet and Tipsy had reconciled this morning. Poteet had sworn her in as a Firstplacer, on the spot, from his hospital bed. In their bargain Tipsy compelled a promise from Poteet to never again refer to the house as a camp. Instead, he was to call it by the name she had given it when her pastor had blessed it—Sweetwater, the name of her ancestral home in Calvin Station. It had burned years ago as had the previous home on the same town site, and that home had been built in 1823.

Mama and Tipsy had coordinated the county to finalize details of the memorial service and gain approval by Leslie. The women had then spread the word that Leslie was to be treated henceforth as the Tomato Boy's daughter and heir and afforded the graciousness her status deserved. There had been no objection.

"Okay, okay," interrupted McGregor. "But tell me about the mother also being a lawyer."

"Well, she is," said Hood, munching her olive this time. "She swore to Mama that Leslie was Clyde's daughter. In her view, Clyde was a playboy and she didn't want him to know about Leslie. By the way, Mama never knew Clyde had a middle name. Leslie became obsessed with finding out about her father, against her mother's wishes. Mama seems confident she can weasel more stuff out of Leslie and is going to talk to her tomorrow and let us know tomorrow afternoon."

Poteet asked, "Where do we go from here, McGregor?"

McGregor hated not being able to confide how he had Trussell at the top of his list of possible murderers, but that info had to remain sealed for the time being. How long, he didn't know.

He said, "Poker should be our prime target. But listen, I don't care how we feel about Leslie, the fact remains that when Poteet walked into that room Leslie was there. We can't begin dismissing her as a suspect until one of us talks to her. Instead of Mama doing so, I'll do it first thing in the morning." He looked at Hood expectantly.

"Well, McGregor, I object to that," she said. "So just wipe your little peevish expression off your face and listen. I think we should give Mama her chance. She knows Leslie better than us. You and I should stay on our schedule and run our errands. That Ford's not going to hold up long. We have to get cars, and I guess buy one for Poteet, too. Let's all go see Mama at the Emporium tomorrow afternoon as planned and interview both her and Poker. Take as long as it takes. What do you say?"

McGregor had to agree she made sense. Poteet nodded assent on top of a tired sigh. But his eyes suddenly gleamed. He said, "I'll go with y'all to the Ford dealership tomorrow. I've been hankering for a brand new pickup. And Hood's right, y'all need better transportation. Hell, let's all get new trucks! I'm buying!"

Hood said, "Hallelujah baby! Martinis for Poteet every night! Now, Poteet, you look worn out, and McGregor you look like you've been through the creek again. I say we all go to bed. How about breakfast at seven?"

McGregor and Hood left Poteet as he climbed the stairs to his room. In the guest quarter Hood said goodnight, went inside her room and closed the door, leaving a disappointed McGregor to stare at her doorknob.

McGregor was slumped on the edge of his bed, looking inside his mind at Leslie's face and trying to convince himself she was no murderer, when he heard a tapping at his door. In a change of heart, he now wished Hood would leave him alone. But it was not Hood knocking; it was Poteet. He motioned McGregor to follow him back to the study.

Poteet uncorked a bottle of wine. "Nightcap? Here. Let's smoke, son." He pulled out a wooden cigarette box and they lit up long Marlboros. McGregor waited, his fatigue turning to exhaustion. The tobacco tasted good, though, and so did his double-sips of wine.

"Oh, man! What's this wine?" he asked. "It's a mouthful!"

Poteet held out the bottle. It was a 1994 Caymus Special Selection, an all time McGregor favorite.

Poteet chuckled. "I know your wants, boy. So, tell me what happened between you and that Terri Williams? As the saying goes around here, she's a firecracker!"

McGregor debated. His resolve to keep his secret dashed itself off the walls of his skull until it finally self-destructed. Poteet was not a man you normally lied to. Anyway, remaining silent much longer would simply cause Poteet to guess the truth.

"I have to admit it, Poteet. She got to me. Now, nothing happened! We messed around and that's all. Some kissy-face. But I tell you what; I sure *wanted* more to happen. I left her soon after Eli and the boys arrived, but I went back after they were gone and talked to her about being just friends. So, I guess I escaped the firecracker unscathed."

Poteet merely grinned. He asked, "Did Eli get any notion of what had transpired?"

"I think my cover story will play."

"So, how are you and Hood doing? I get the impression Hood has a renewed interest in your maybe becoming a solid pair again."

"I love Hood. I've always loved Hood. But, listen, since I've been on her merry-go-round a long time, I'm wondering if we can ever get off and go on with our lives."

"If you let me vote, it'd make me a happy man to see y'all married. As you know, Hood's like the daughter I never had. And you, why I've always thought of you as one of my own. I think you know that. I've spoken with Hood outside your presence. She's so close to wanting marriage, she might spring the question herself. I think she's going to make a strong play for it. After I'm squared away again here, you two should take a trip, use my dime, and maybe go check on some old car I have warehoused. Work a little, play a little. Enjoy."

Poteet could be charming in his old school way. McGregor marveled at how attached he was becoming to this man, and said, "I'd appreciate that. I'd love it."

Then Poteet leaned over to him. "Did you know Terri Williams and Clyde Thacker had a recent hot love affair?"

Now Poteet was sly. That much was a given. But you had to know him for years to discern exactly how artfully cunning he could be. Was it for this question that Poteet had invited him here? Were his soothing words mere softening up. Had Poteet spoken the truth about his feelings for Hood and for "one of my own?" Or had that been calculated as just the right way to touch McGregor's heart? Hard to tell. Poteet had obviously already surmised the effect Terri would have. Poteet was probably about eighty percent sure Terri would have spilled the beans on the Clyde affair and equally as sure Terri would demand secrecy as soon as she revealed it. So, how to proceed? How much could he refrain from telling Poteet and still pass this contrived loyalty test? Poteet prized nothing more in a friend than loyalty, other than promptness, of course.

McGregor drank, though he felt sober as a rock now. He lit another Marlboro and eyed Poteet, and then he broke his promise to Terri.

"Poteet, I have to hand it to you. I've paused long enough now so that you know the answer to your question. If you know about the affair, then it's no deep, dark secret. Who does know, exactly?"

Poteet said, "I believe that in the last few months I became Clyde's only confidant in such matters. So, I know. Now you know. And Terri knows, of course. I think that's it. But I think Terri knows that I know. I think Terri figured I would tell you. How much of her passion today was calculated to put you in the frame of mind to keep her secret?"

McGregor was flummoxed and angered. "Come out with it, Poteet!" he demanded in sudden indignation. "Do you suspect her of killing Clyde or putting Trussell up to it?"

"Trussell? My God! Does he know about Terri and Clyde? I haven't schemed it out that far. Should have. But I always think of him as an innocent babe, his being about fifteen minutes shy of a full hour, you know. Holy shit!"

McGregor said, "I think he does know about it. Terri was drinking with him one afternoon and said she thinks she could've revealed it to him by thinking out loud."

"Listen, McGregor. That Clyde was a huge make-out artist in his younger days in California. With Terri, he reverted to his old ways. He played with her, and then tossed her away like he would a bad tomato. If she ever put it to her brother in those terms—"

McGregor asked, "Still, why would she want me to know about the affair?"

"I don't know," Poteet said. "My only thinking was that she'd tell you to throw you off her own tracks, or get you on her side in case I told you. Anyway, she has a reason to have hated Clyde, and that's why I insisted you go spend some time with her after Carlos Hernandez came up with the idea. I thought it best you go in cold, without my suggesting anything."

"Poteet, I don't want you sending me anywhere cold. I wish you'd quit conniving. I need to know the unvarnished truth about this situation you're into—that you got Hood and me into. Don't toy with me anymore. If there's anything you need to tell me, now is the time. And don't bullshit me!"

Poteet looked stunned. McGregor disliked talking to the old man this way, but he needed somehow to shake him up.

"Okay, McGregor, don't melt down on me. You want truth? I'll tell you some truth. Then, let's go to bed.

"When Hood was in here, you were telling us Trussell's story about how he was injured? Well, it sounds all too familiar. I think that company he and Eli Rust were working for just might be my old paving and road construction company, Poteet and Johnson. There was a point in time, many years ago. Can't put my finger on the year. Any rate, we were trying to sell the company to a big national outfit. Our safety rating was a primary selling point. Our reputation was crucial. My memory's vague, but I recollect the company paid off a couple of guys who we thought tried to take advantage of the potential sale situation. You know, faking an accident and soaking us big time, them knowing our precarious position. I ordered the lawyers to offer them money to go away and not file a claim or anything. Lawyers said they took it and we never heard from them again. Seems the so-called accident involved a man knocked down on the side of one of our roads under construction, and they didn't locate him for something like twenty-four hours. Supposed to have a bad head injury, but the lawyers told us the whole thing was bogus."

"Good Lord, Poteet. The crap that you can get into!"

Poteet checked a watch and declared it bedtime for certain. Before they parted, McGregor suggested a few points of procedure. They would inform Hood of Poteet's recollection of the paving company incident, and Poteet would try to dig up a file on it from his former attorneys. Whether to mention anything to Hood about Terri's affair with Clyde was left an open question.

Later, McGregor tossed and turned in bed, damning his libido to the hell it deserved. Why could he not have admitted even to Poteet that he'd had sex with Terri? Was he in some form of denial? Over and over, he listened to himself say to Poteet: "Now, nothing happened!" Poteet was no fool.

Not for the first time he forced himself to come to terms with the oft-learned lesson: The one thing that makes a man happiest in life is the one that makes him the unhappiest. He reviled himself as a lying, cheating scoundrel. Thereafter, he slept soundly.

CHAPTER 14

Monday morning brought a clear sky. The Sweetwater men commenced the day early with coffee on the back deck, Hood not being up yet. The normally chatty Poteet fell into silence, staring at his mug. McGregor reclined in a lounger. The fireball sun ascended the sky through the close green foliage packing the hill of the opposite riverbank. Steam rose in geysers from the surface of the Big Turkey. Ducks and ducklings skimmed about the surface without a quack and without a visible purpose.

Envious of the ducks, McGregor closed his eyes and twitched his nose, which was tingling from the morning air, so redolent with lavender. Without warning, the smell of Terri's hair came to him, a remembrance so strong he thought if he opened his eyes she would be right there nose to nose with him. Perhaps he'd go see her tomorrow. He needed a reason, though. What about asking her questions regarding Leslie? He could ask her—

Hood broke his reverie when she opened the screen door and stomped across the deck. Her hair was whacked out and she looked in a mood.

"I don't know why I'm drinking *hot* chocolate," she whined, "if this is going to be another suffocating day. The humidity is already way up!" She threw the chocolate over the railing. With a magazine she fanned herself and looked at McGregor, an eyebrow raised as if inviting an argument.

In some unfathomable way she probably sensed his thoughts of Terri. It would be nice to have mental privacy, but with her around, forget it.

Then she said, "I know you two piss ants went back to the study last night after I went to bed. What's up?"

After the men strained to clear their throats, McGregor pointed to Poteet. In the same detail as before, Poteet reiterated his tale of the fraud exacted on Poteet and Johnson.

Hood threw up her arms. "You're a walking, talking twist of fate, Poteet. Of all the places in the world a wealthy man like you could retire to, you pick the exact spot where these men live!"

Poteet faced her, "What can I say? I never heard the names of those men back then. My lawyers were J. Hollis Edwards and his crew of high-priced scalawags." He turned back around in his chair to McGregor. "I shouldn't say that about them. No offense, McGregor. I always trusted Hollis. If you hadn't come up here to help me, I was going to call him. I'd be surprised if they don't keep records for a good long time, wouldn't you? So, let's give them time to open up this morning and I'll call them."

Hood turned toward McGregor. He told her about Terri and Clyde. "There was just too much to talk about last night."

Not being burdened by jealousy, Hood merely shrugged and tied down her hair with a kerchief.

Across the river, the sun crested the treetops in a blinding flash. Shielding his eyes, Poteet said, "I now declare it daytime! Let's eat breakfast."

McGregor and Hood followed him into the kitchen. Tomás trooped in after them from the front porch, waving the bug-sweeping equipment around the room; Lakisha had briefed him on the telephone bugs. He said he was tired, up for too many hours. Poteet invited him to breakfast.

By dividing cooking duties four ways, the sulky group had breakfast on the table in ten minutes flat.

"Okay, Tomás," McGregor said, "I've reported what we talked about to Poteet and Hood."

Poteet and Hood spoke up together, Hood giving way to Poteet.

"Young man, I don't want to sound ungrateful for the information, but you could be involving us in some political intrigue we're best left out of."

Tomás responded, "Hey, Carlos said he thought long and hard about it. But you being who you are in this county and already getting political by backing ol' Grooms, he figured if he was going to get any help in this thing, you were the one to give it to him. Who else would he go to? Our daddy and the rest of the growers had just as soon see Poker go down as anybody else. Other than Mama and you, who else cares a whit for that guy?"

"But, good Lord, Tomás," Hood said, "surely they care who really did it. They don't want a murderer running around loose. When we talked to them, they seemed genuinely horrified by that prospect. Do you think they know who did it and don't want to prosecute him? Or her?"

"Naw, they don't know. They just want a quick trial. Get it over with, so Red can run for mayor without the disruption. For the most part, they're good men, but when it comes to politics in Calvin County ..."

McGregor saw that Tomás wanted to say more, so he asked him, "For example?"

"Well ..." Tomás hesitated. "When Sheriff ran for sheriff two years ago he was chief deputy in the department. He brought in a couple of prostitutes from Manskar County—couldn't find any here—and set them up in a house. Then in front of a reporter and photographer, he arrested them. Here's another one. The Millraineys have been making whiskey here for generations. Sheriff busted up a still and claimed it was one of Millrainey's. It was big news because no sheriff had ever had the guts to bust up a Millrainey operation. Of course, it was a dummy still. But old man Millrainey went along and took a fine and promised never to make whiskey again. Under-the-table money had to have changed hands. I don't hold it against Sheriff. That's politics."

Hood said, "You're cynical. Like McGregor, here."

McGregor said to Tomás, "Yesterday you didn't want to say who you thought killed the Tomato Boy. What about now?"

They waited for Tomás to chew a piece of toast.

"One thing Carlos and I don't know is exactly how much Sheriff and Red confided in y'all. If I said the words *hidden room*, would they mean anything to you?"

McGregor replied, "They didn't confide anything. They told me to keep my nose out of it. But in the few days I've been around, I've developed some sources of my own. As to the hidden room, do you mean the room the Tomato Boy built behind his refrigerator, which was full of 1980s style recording equipment and cassette tapes?"

Tomás smiled. "Yeah, that's it. Far as they can tell, Thacker had three rooms bugged, the three suites comprising the rest of the fifth floor of the Tomato wing. Sheriff found an old cassette tape player at a pawn shop and over the weekend he and Red listened to the tapes that were found in Thacker's suite. Red's secretary also listened in to transcribe in shorthand if need be. Last night she told Carlos what she had heard. She's a friend of Carlos from high school days, you see. Still stuff going on with 'em on the sly, you know. You don't have to tell him I said that.

"One tape was of a conversation between Red Wiley and another attorney. Dated a few weeks ago. Red talked about two things: 'the project' and 'the paving company.' Carlos thinks Thacker knew what those references meant. Thacker announced for mayor the day after that tape was made. Thacker probably thought he could use the information to pressure Red out of the race.

"Red also said on the tape that he assumed Eli Rust would be his major opponent in the mayor's race. Without explanation, Red said that 'the paving company' could be used to make Rust think twice about running for mayor."

Tomás held up a hand and chuckled. "I have to tell y'all about this one! Seems our current county mayor and Tipsy Alcorn were up in a hotel suite one time. She was talking seriously about a county commission meeting, but he was talking about his damn trains. He has an electric train set-up in his house and plays with them all the time, sort of like a fanatic. Tipsy starts squealing on the tape because the mayor is apparently chasing her around the room making choo-choo noises at her! The mayor tells her he wants to poke more coal in her boiler, and then there's the sound of her screaming and the door slamming!"

After the laughter, Tomás continued, "The secretary told Carlos that most of the tapes contained meaningless stuff not worth discussing. Her guess was that Thacker mainly just listened in on the guests, not recording much."

Poteet poured a round of coffee. He asked, "So what's the upshot of all this as it relates to us?"

Tomás answered, "Carlos believes the stuff directed at y'all is connected to the murder. Somebody found out about Thacker's taping system and got hold of a tape that relates to both you, Mr. Poteet, and to Thacker. He or she wanted to scare you both out of politics. Scaring Thacker went too far. Carlos highly recommends that you publicly disavow any political ambitions, behind the scenes or otherwise. It might be the one thing that saves your life! You should stay right here at home for the time being and call the newspaper for a phone interview. With your clout you can get it on the front page. What do y'all think?"

Poteet said, "Fine with me. All I really ever wanted was my road repaired, but that's not worth dying for. I don't care about politics, never have. So I'll stay here this morning.

The glaziers are coming to work on the window, anyway. I need to be here."

McGregor said, "I still want Carlos to let us in on the crime scene forensics."

"He's thinking about that. He won't even tell me."

McGregor continued, "Then here's what I suggest. We'll talk to Poker. If there's anything there, we'll report it to Carlos through you, Tomás. Poteet, you should announce to the local paper that you're out of politics. That should satisfy the growers. Tomás, if you and Carlos will keep quiet about my helping you, Sheriff and Red should keep their end of the bargain and get me Mama's journals and get the Offshoot potholes repaired."

All at once, McGregor's arm started hurting, which made him want to get to the doctor's. He pointed to the arm and said to the group, "The orthopedist gave me an early appointment. Let's get started."

Poteet escorted McGregor and Hood to the front porch. "If y'all want pickups, get the F-150 with the extended cabs and handy extra seats. My deal still holds. I'm buying! Y'all make the deals and I'll have the bank issue a check."

McGregor and Hood took the Chevy and made several stops in Finneyville. By the time they arrived at McKool's Ford, McGregor had a new cast, a cell phone and wristwatch.

A man wearing plaid pants with an orange sport coat and puffing a cigar came strolling out of the showroom. McGregor parked, and as he and Hood walked down the line of F-150's they found the dandy dresser approaching them to be Glenn McKool, a talker and a zealous Ford man. From one angle McKool's thick hair looked like a toupee, from another it looked real. Poteet had called, McKool said, and a shop worker would be driving back the Chevy to Poteet's and would bring in the Ford wagon for a check-up.

McGregor, having fun, allowed himself to fall into the exuberance of the buy, and before it was over McKool had

him in a roomy tomato red truck with all the goodies Ford
had that lent sparkle to a new pickup. Hood, on the other
hand, said she had to think of the environment. In the back
lot she picked a used baby blue mid-sized Ranger with manual shift and a mere four-cylinder engine.

At paper signing, McGregor seized the opportunity.
"Glenn, in Hood's and Poteet's car accident I'm sure you've
heard about by now, there was an orange pickup that figured
in the deal—its driver maybe even causing the wreck on purpose. We know of Poker Limbo and his orange truck. Are
there others around our part of the county that would look so
similar you could mistake them for his?"

McKool had let his cigar go out some time ago. Now
he wobbled the stub of it around in his mouth and looked
baffled. He laughed, which made his hair bounce and look
like a toupee again. "Are there any others that look similar?
You kidding? The whole damn county's full of orange pickups. Especially ones from the old days, when it was the thing
to do to have any vehicle with the university colors. Plus, the
county work trucks and even the fire trucks are all orange."

"I was afraid of that," McGregor said, "but I had to
be sure."

"Interesting, though, you mention ol' Poker. You can
tell Roland that Poker came in here several days ago, or
maybe a week, maybe two, wanting to know if I would order
him a new pickup and if the money had come in for it yet.
Had no idea what he was blabbering about, and when I called
Mama she said to ignore him.

"And let's see now. Similar to Poker's huh? You
know that girl they have locked up for killing our Tomato
Boy? She came in the showroom some time before Poker
did. Couple of weeks, something like that. She asked if I had
any old, cheap pickups. Said she liked orange and said one
like Poker Limbo's would suit her. I found her one like it on
another lot and sold it to her. Saw it not long after that,
parked in front of the Calvin House. But Terri Williams was

sitting in it. In the passenger seat. Roland'll know who that is. Y'all watch out for her. She's a firecracker."

After one more stop, this time at Kroger for groceries, McGregor and Hood arrived back at Sweetwater to find Poteet puttering with the front porch flower pots.

"Nice trucks," Poteet said, helping to lug in the grocery bags. "But I can tell from your faces you have news. Damn, I'm dying, y'all, stuck here at home."

When the three were seated in the study Poteet waved off profuse thanks for the trucks, both hands flying in the air in excitement. "What's up?" he asked.

McGregor said, "We ran into a talkative car dealer, name of McKool."

"Yeah, yeah, Glenn McKool. A good member of the Firstplacers Club."

McGregor conveyed the new information about Poker's mystery truck and Leslie's Poker-lookalike truck. "The whole orange truck thing is screwy, but it is a thread."

Next, McGregor said to Hood. "As to Poker, we have an interview shortly. But as to Leslie, I've a question— may I have a date with you tonight for dinner at The Thumb? We'll try to sit Leslie down for a conversation. Regardless of what Mama might have learned from her this morning, it's time I talked to her myself."

Hood agreed, and for lunch she prepared soup and sandwiches. In a great, selfless act she served the men. Ladling the soup, she boasted about grinding down McKool on the price of the trucks.

Poteet had called several Firstplacers, all of whom were relieved by his acquiescence to the powers-that-be and the halting of Dimpsey's campaign. The newspaper had promised to print his interview as a news article on tomorrow's front page, and Poteet in turn had promised several full-page ads to tout the upcoming festival. After the meal Poteet repaired to his study to phone his old law firm again and press for faster progress in tracking down the firm's records.

The glaziers had replaced the big kitchen window. McGregor and Hood paused before the expansive view of the great back lawn and the river beyond. Sunlight glittered on the water in dazzling white splotches, causing McGregor to wonder how many billions of photons were being reflected his way. The scene must have touched Hood in a less scientific way. She put her arm around McGregor and gave him a love pinch on the neck.

"I could live in a place like this, I guess," she said, as if in a dream. "With you out of the car thief mess ... If I keep getting good vibes from you ... Nah, let's talk about that later. Right now, duty calls. I'm going to my room to phone my office. No one has called me since we left Montgomery. That could be bad. I'd better find out."

She left McGregor standing at the window. A cloud sailed by to extinguish the dance of water-light, but McGregor could still feel the skin pinch on his neck. Ah, God. Hood could stroke a man. He decided to renounce forever any interest in other females until he could discover what it was Hood wanted from him.

He composed himself and called Red Wiley's office. Red was out, so he left a cryptic message: "Bob McGregor has complied. See newspaper front page tomorrow morning. He expects road crews to be working Wednesday morning, starting with swimming pool."

Later, McGregor and Hood convened in the study with Poteet. Poteet locked the door and said, "Even though it's killing me, I've decided not to leave the house today. So I called Mama and invited them over here. She's glad to do it. Like me, Poker's climbing the walls. She said we won't recognize him. One of her staff is a former beautician, and she's given Poker a make-over."

McGregor said, "Fine. Look, no matter what goes down this afternoon, we can't let Poker leave until we get something out of him. Offer him money. Or hell, offer him a new truck! Anything to make him talk. If he refuses to open up, I say we threaten him with our going to Sheriff. I can use the 'I can't withhold evidence' ploy on him."

They went to the front porch to wait.

CHAPTER 15

Mama's Oldsmobile sputtered to a stop in the driveway. She waved and honked at them. The man who stepped out of the car was indeed a new man. "Make-over" didn't describe Poker's new look. Poker was handsome—in a rough way. He'd lost a few pounds, or maybe it was just that his beard was absent. His hair was tinted a golden brown and had been cut much shorter and brushed over with a part on the side. To top it all he wore a blazer with a striped tie.

Poteet welcomed Mama as though he hadn't seen her for weeks. He shook hands formally with Poker, as did McGregor and Hood. Poker nodded with friendliness and mumbled his hellos. Poteet assembled the group in the study where he had set out an assortment of sweet tea and soft drinks. Hood had prepared a tray of sandwiches. While Poker was feeding at the food tray with his back turned, Mama slipped a note to McGregor and the others.

It read: "I talked to Leslie. Have information. Will have to wait till Pk. leaves us. First things first!"

They settled down with Mama and Poker on a short sofa together and the three inquisitors in chairs facing them. Poteet's chair was a recliner and he eased halfway back.

McGregor thought that up close, Poker, with his fluffed-up, sprayed-in-place hair, looked like a hard-nosed alcoholic turned preacher. Several shaving nicks around a few acne scars made the conversion appear only partially successful.

Poker was disconcerted and seemed self-conscious, arranging his tie and fiddling with his blazer buttons. So they talked of the weather and how bad the storm had been last night. The memorial service had been nice, and it was good to see that Leslie was going to be welcomed into the community.

They waited while Poker settled down. Poteet unconsciously checked his wristwatch.

Mama straightened up and blinked away a tiny tear. "Poker has some things to get off his chest. We've talked to each other more in the last two days and nights than we have in the last two years. I've been at fault in so many ways I can't count them. Poker's been upset with me for a long time, but he says he just loved me so much he couldn't come to me and tell me. Now, what my boy has to say will definitely come as a shock, so get prepared. My faith is in our friendship, Potty."

She turned to her son. "Poker, dear, tell them in your own words what we talked about last night. It needs to be said straightforward. If we don't get it out in the open, we can go no further. Like I told you, Potty is the best friend we have and I told you how much I trust our new friends here. So just open up with them, the way you did with me."

McGregor flinched inside. Any time a lawyer says to a witness, "Tell the court in your own words ...," instead of simply, "Tell the court ...," it's an unconscious admission that what the lawyer's really thinking is, "Tell the court what I told you to say but say it in your own voice, the way you normally talk."

Poker spoke. In a guttural bass, not altogether unpleasant, he said, "Mr. Poteet, I have a confession to make. It was me who shot out your window. I never thought once about hitting *you*, I just wanted to break the window. I shot at it up real high, close to the top."

Poteet sat stone still and gape-jawed. Then he pushed his foot-rest down and managed to say softly, "Go on, son. Let us hear it all."

The big man scooted to the edge of the sofa, put his elbows on his knees and looked at Poteet with sad eyes. With his voice beginning to crack, he declared, "And, I punctured the brake lines on both them old cars. I can explain it all, I really can."

Poker's jaw began to quiver. "And, and ..." he said and hung his head. "I've been bad, Mr. Poteet. Real bad!"

Poker wept.

The giant shoulders heaved and tears gushed. McGregor felt paralyzed. Poteet and Hood stared wide-eyed. Mama hugged him and took one of his great paws between her hands. Poker's arms and legs shuddered; then his entire body shook in what seemed to be the anguish of the broken-hearted. On and on.

Mama started crying. Hood teared up. Poteet, finding himself, moved over to the sofa to sit by Mama.

A person can cry for only so long. Finally, Poker regained some control. Poteet passed him a box of tissues and patted his arm.

McGregor thought what he had witnessed might be completely honest. No matter what the man had done, he deserved a bit of admiration for his courage. Was the person causing the most problems for McGregor—beginning the first hour in Calvin County—going to be the one best hope for solving the Poteet riddles, the murder and all?

Mama prepared a plate of sandwiches for Poker, who loosened his tie and hawked into a handful of tissues. Poker consumed the food in five whale bites, as McGregor counted them on his fingers in a way that only Hood could see. She frowned at him.

McGregor, familiar with interviewing fretful witnesses, said, "Poker, just take it easy now. Thanks for telling us what you did. It takes a strong man to admit something like that. We appreciate it. I want to skip over most of the details for the moment. One thing is extremely important, though. When you punctured the brake lines, did you put anything in Poteet's Cadillac? Did you slip anything under the floor mat?"

"Naw. Never did that. What thing?"

"Sheriff Buell found something, that's all. If you don't know about it, I can't say what it was. Under orders not to. Now, we had a break-in here at Poteet's yesterday morning. Some paintings were cut up in the art room. Did you do that?"

"Naw. I don't know nothing about that." Poker clenched his lips and asked if he could smoke.

Poteet said, "Sure." And he flipped the switch on a floor air filter while lighting a cigarette himself.

Poker sucked on an unfiltered Pall Mall as if it were a straw in a thick milk shake and asked, "Can I have a drink? I mean a real drink?"

Poteet prepared a light bourbon for him and poured iced tea for everyone else. They waited.

McGregor decided the exigencies of the moment required him to bring up the subject of Amon. He said, "Poker, I've spoken to Amon Trussell up at his place on the hill. Amon confirms what I myself saw, that somebody driving an orange truck pulled out in front of Hood and Poteet, causing them to wreck. He wouldn't tell me who the driver was. Was it you?"

"Naw. Me and Amon were up on the road going up to Terri's house. There's a place up there off the road, a turn-around place where we park at night sometimes and drink beer and stuff. You can see the Offshoot from there. The truck what pulled out in front of y'all, Mr. Poteet, was a truck that looked just about like mine. But I was in mine. We went up to Terri's and called 911." He paused.

Poteet asked, "And is there more? Did you see the driver?"

"Yeah, I'm pretty sure it was the Manskar man, except he had a beard, and the Manskar man don't have any beard. Has a moustache, that's all."

"Who is this Manskar man?" McGregor asked.

Poker looked at Mama, apparently for reassurance. She nodded at him.

"The Manskar man is who got me into this whole thing to start with," he said. "It sounds stupid now that Mama's talked to me about it. Makes me feel like an idiot. This man comes up to me, you see? It was one day when I was hidin' in the junkyard from Mama. Says he's from over Manskar County way. Says he buys old pickup trucks for top dollar to put in museums. Wants to buy mine for fifteen thousand dollars! I liked to shii … I mean, well, you know. And anyway, I offered him the keys then and there, but he said 'Not now.'

"He pulls out a whiskey bottle and we take a slug, you know, to seal the deal. Says as how people like you, Mr. Poteet, are real evil men. Says you loaned money to my Mama to fix up Uncle Earl's place just so you could steal it from her. Says that's how rich folks operate, how they get rich in the first place. Asks as how weren't you always there at the café and always playing up real cozy-like to Mama. Says you and that Yankee bitch Helen—sorry, but that's how he said it. That Helen and you were outsider con artists, gonna take everything we own. Says the Tomato Boy is losing all kinds of money at The Thumb 'cause of me and Mama competin' with him and says that he's in on the con, too, never mind that Mama and me are his cousins."

Poker tossed down the rest of his drink and lit another cigarette from the end of his first one. He sat back, seeming to organize his thoughts.

Poteet said, "Good Lord!"

McGregor said encouragingly, "Go on Poker, we're listening."

"Well, you see this Manskar man, I don't know, he's like a real smooth talker. By the time we finish off that bottle, he gets me to believing all this bullshit, I mean, all this stuff. And, well, I'm real worked up about it, you know, and get to bragging about what all I'm gonna do to y'all. You know, to protect Mama. He tells me if I agree to do it all his way, that he'd deliver a check to ol' Glenn McKool and tell him to hold it for me. After that I'm supposed to go over to the McKool Ford place and pick me out a brand new truck. It'll be all paid for, and then he'd come to get my old pickup soon's I get my new one.

"He says you love two things, Mr. Poteet, and nothing else and nobody else matters to you, you being so rich and so evil and all. Says you love this house here and all your old cars. Says you treat people like toys. I'm terrible sorry, Mr. Poteet, but he just made it sound so true. Mama says it all has to do with me being jealous about you and her. I don't know, but y'all do spend a lot of time together, and me and Mama used to be a real pair, you know, back when we worked for Uncle Earl and all and since Daddy died."

Poker blinked back tears. Poteet held up a hand. "It's okay, Poker. Just keep talking."

"Now, Mama, she says she hadn't been paying me much attention ever since you'd come into her life. I just feel awful about this, Mr. Poteet. I feel like a stupid kid. Can I have another drink? I'm about to die. My feet are killin' me in these stupid loafers. Can't I just slip 'em off?"

Poteet said sure he could and mixed him a good strong drink this time.

Poker tugged off his shoes, shook his head like a dog coming out of water, and jerked off his blazer revealing huge wet underarms on his blue shirt.

He lit a Pall Mall and slugged a gulp of dark bourbon. "Anyhow, the man never delivers that check to McKool, says he decided to make me do the nasty stuff first. He says I should send you a note telling you that you were gonna be shot. Soon's I do that to show my bona fides, he says then he'd send that check to McKool. Then I'm to shoot out your kitchen window and he tells me how to go about doing it.

He even slips me an old rifle with a good scope on it. Says to throw the whole thing in the river when I do it. Says to do it on the day before the big picnic, so everybody'll hear about it. Says to do it from the bottom of that dirt road down from the park, you know, straight across the river from here. Says the next day I'm supposed to puncture your brake lines. Well, I got put in jail as y'all know and barely made it over here in time to do that. Wish to God, that damn Carlos would've just kept me in the can and none of these wrecks would've happened." He shook his head.

Mama leaned over and whispered to him. He said slowly as if to get it just right, "Oh, yeah. I'm real, real sorry, Mr. McGregor, about you getting wrecked in the creek. And, Miss Hood, Mr. Poteet, I'm real sorry about y'all wrecking, too." He looked at Mama for more reassurance and she nodded to him.

McGregor asked, "But the man still has never delivered the check to McKool, has he?"

"Don't know. After he didn't get that check over the first time he promised, I went up to see Amon one day and the Manskar man was there. So I accused him of going back on the deal and he says Amon was gonna do the other things we talked about and would do it for free. Amon didn't want no truck. So, me and Amon we get in a fight. And the Manskar man said he'd changed his mind again and would buy me the truck and that's when he started talking about having me do stuff first. Said he'd heard Mr. Poteet and the Tomato Boy were gonna get the bank to foreclose on me and Mama right after the Fourth of July. And I had to make sure I did what I was supposed to do in order to scare you off and make you move away or something. I forget just what he said. At the time it all made sense to me. He was a pretty slick talker."

McGregor said, "Now, Poker, listen to me. Did the Manskar man talk you into doing anything to the Tomato Boy?"

Poker looked at Mama. Mama said, "Tell them what happened."

"Well, I was supposed to shoot out Mr. Poteet's window the afternoon before the picnic, like I said. Last Friday. That morning I was to go over to the hotel and talk to the Tomato Boy about meeting me up in his room around dinner time. Said me and Amon could do it together. He said to tell the Tomato Boy that I wanted to talk to him about a tape I'd found. To tell him I wanted a thousand dollars and for him to leave my Mama alone. Said it'd scare the Tomato Boy and he would leave us be. Wouldn't tell me why it would scare him, exactly. Said I had to trust him. Said he guaranteed the Tomato Boy would never say anything to the cops or anybody else. Gave me an old tape to show to him. Said to set up the meeting, then we were to go to the hotel but hide somewhere in the building and not actually meet with him. Made us go over it all until we got it straight. Said McKool would be open on the Fourth and I could go order my truck." He looked over at Mama with a face of despair.

Poker badly wanted that truck, McGregor thought.

McGregor asked, "So what happened Friday?"

"I showed the Tomato Boy that tape and set up the meeting. He got real scared and said he'd meet with me. Made me feel good, seeing him squirm, too. Then Amon, he got it all ass-backwards and thought we were supposed to actually go to the meeting, instead of just hide at the hotel. He headed off to the hotel and I chased him down in the parking lot. Ran him all the way from there to the river before I caught him. Some punk guard chased us. But we lost him. Then, when we finally went back to the hotel and snuck in a side door, I made Amon hide with me in the restroom. Then, all hell broke loose out in the big room there, and me and Amon snuck out the side door again. He got in his car and I got in my truck and we headed back to his place, but Amon turned around again at the bridge on the Big Turkey and yelled at me that he was going back to the hotel. I had to ram his old car to stop him. Banged up my truck pretty bad. Amon, he gets crossed up in his brain all the time."

"Keep going," Mama prodded gently.

"So, Carlos, he throws us in jail when he finds the tape I showed the Tomato Boy when I set up the meeting."

Poker sat back exhausted and Mama resumed the story for him. "Poker cut his finger trying to pry open his glove box with a screwdriver to hide the tape when he saw the cops coming to the wreck. We think the tape is the so-called evidence they have on him. He never listened to the tape since his player had quit working. Says it was just an ordinary cassette tape. Besides, the Manskar man told him nothing was on it."

"Mama," McGregor said, "I need to hear it all from Poker. Now, Poker, I know you know Leslie. Do you know anything about her driving an orange truck that looks a lot like yours?"

Poker licked his lips and thought about the question for a long moment. McGregor ordinarily could listen to a witness in rapt attention for hours on end, but for some reason now, as Poker paused, McGregor's mind wandered. He couldn't stop it. The thought struck him that yesterday at this time he'd been on the porch, that marvelous old porch, squeezing Terri's firm body. He tried to force the picture from his mind.

"Yeah," Poker said, finally. "Leslie always said she didn't have a ride out to the café, but I saw her driving a truck like mine one time. She came up to Terri's house in it one day." He laughed a throaty heh-heh, and shielded his face from Mama with a hand. "She caught me and Terri on the porch."

Mama punched him with her elbow and laughed with him.

McGregor was listening with only the half of his mind that wasn't on Terri. And it took a second for what Poker had just said to sink in. Poker had been telling an eye-opening tale, but this revelation jerked McGregor's bones. His entire body tensed up. He jumped in his seat and croaked, "What? What did you say? On the porch doing what?"

The question was too loud, too accusing. The rest of the crew recoiled and looked at him. Hood gave him the old Hood glare, which told him she knew something was up with him and Terri. He sank back in his chair.

"I … I just didn't hear it clearly. Sorry I jumped at you. You were on the porch with Terri when Leslie drove up? What were y'all doing?"

Mama said, "Now then, Bobby, we're all grown-ups here. What do you think they were doing on the porch in the heat of an afternoon? Folks all over the South doing it." She and Poker kept laughing with Mama elbowing him, like a teenager.

To McGregor, the idea of Poker and Terri on the porch, on *their* porch, was so repulsive he thought he would throw up. All he could think about for the moment was Terri languidly reclining on those pillows, sipping her margarita and holding one out for him—so perfectly sensuous, her knee bent, her body so receptive. God! Terri and Poker?

He managed to say, "So, it seems that Leslie and Terri," he could hardly say her name, "and Terri are friends, do you think?"

McGregor knew his voice was shaky and Poker just looked at him, a question mark on his brow. Mama eyed him, too.

Poteet sat back in his chair and sipped tea. It was Hood who came to McGregor's rescue. "Poker, what we need to know is whether Terri and Leslie see a lot of each other? Does Leslie know Amon, for instance?"

"Uh, I don't know. I think Terri is the first person Leslie ever met when she moved here. The Tomato Boy got them together, you know, when Terri and the Tomato Boy had that fling!"

At that, Hood and Poteet stiffened. McGregor knew he should shut up, but he couldn't. He had to act as if he had no knowledge of any fling with the Tomato Boy. "Fling?" he asked incredulously. "Terri and the Tomato Boy had a fling?"

"Uh, yeah. That's supposed to be a secret. I guess I let the old cat out of the bag, didn't I?—Fur, claws and meows. Yeah, they got it on, I mean, sorry, they dated. For a couple of weeks back about a month or so ago."

Poker's face flamed red and he gushed, "Made me mad as hell! I can't put it in words. But Mama calls Terri a firecracker. Says she has a way of wrappin' a man up in a knot. Says her husband, before he died, you know, used to be jealous as hell. Wouldn't let her even look at another man." He looked at Mama with a frown. "Mama says Terri's like honey that men stick to like ants. Can't get her out of their minds, you know, once they get glued to her. That right, Mama?"

Mama said, "Terri is a well-meaning sort, how she takes care of the boys and puts up with that nutty brother. But she likes powerful men to fall for her so she can control them. Way I figure, she looked at Poker and saw something raw and healthy about him, him being so gruff and wild sometimes. Had to get her hands on him. Tame him."

Hood gave a blowing glance to McGregor, with the kind of fierceness in her eyes that curled his toes. Then she asked Poker, "And did Amon know about this, about Terri and the Tomato Boy?"

"Sure. And, man was he ever mad, too, because the Tomato Boy had helped him keep his driver's license and the insurance on his Ford. Supposed to be his friend. That's another reason he got so mad when he found out from the Manskar man that the Tomato Boy was trying to steal mine and Mama's café. That's why I had to fight him then. He always fights when he's disturbed about something. Gets mean!"

McGregor's internal lawyer struggled to gain control over the part that had become the jealous fornicator, and fortunately, the lawyer won the fight. McGregor waved off a follow-up question from Hood and said, "Now, think carefully, Poker. Around the time you and Amon were hiding in the restroom at the hotel, did you ever lose sight of him?"

"Well, now I think about it. Yeah, I did. See, I had to go to the pot real bad. I mean real bad! I was all tore up and nervous. Amon didn't want to hide with me in the stall 'cause I was right there on the pot. I made him stand in there with me, anyway, so I could keep an eye on him. Told him to hold his damn nose. I did flush a lot, but he motioned to me that it was getting to where he couldn't breathe. So he ran out the door. I couldn't just get up and go chase him down!"

"Now, think carefully," McGregor said. "Did Amon have time to go up to the Tomato Boy's room? You said he thought he was supposed to actually go to the meeting."

Poker looked to Mama for guidance, but Mama shrugged and said, "Just tell him what you think, son."

Poker said, in a return to his former gruff attitude, "I think you're trying to say Amon killed the Tomato Boy! That's what I think." His eyes bulged at McGregor.

Poteet moved over to sit by Poker. "No, that's not it, son. It's just the one tiny detail that we need to know. Not whether Amon killed Clyde, just whether he had time to go up to Clyde's room before he came back to the restroom. Please think about it and give us your best answer."

Poteet's stroking worked and Poker calmed down. "I say that yes, he had the time. I was stuck on that pot a good while. Just when I thought I could quit, it'd hit me again."

McGregor asked gently, "How did he act when he came back?"

"Well, let's see. He came back acting like he was driving, you know, making car noises. He does that to tell you not to talk him. Amon talks with his body. You have to be around him to get the whole picture. Mostly, he was looking for his sunflower seeds. Dropped them somewhere, he said. You don't want to get between him and his damned old seeds.

"So, I didn't talk to him, just pulled him into the stall with me. I cleaned up fast and then some man came in the restroom and Amon just had to go out. He said something to the man and the man told him to leave him alone. And that's about when we started hearing screaming from way down the hall. And we got the hell out of there.

"Mr. Poteet, I need to ask you to forgive me. If you can't, you can't. But I can't talk no more. Don't know what else to say. I'm ready to take my medicine."

Poker stood up, disheveled now. A shirt button across his middle had popped open to show a hairy belly; his pants had slipped down past his waist. He combed his hair with his fingers and scrubbed his hand across his face where a beard was rapidly returning.

Mr. Hyde was being released, thought McGregor. Poker struggled back into his loafers and flat-footed it to the wet bar where he poured a giant bourbon, straight up, and drank it down in gulps. Mama shrugged. McGregor and his cohorts shrugged and joined Poker at the bar.

Poker and Mama decided to take their drinks out to the porch to await the verdict. Mama still had lots to tell them about Leslie, she said. While Poker buttoned himself up in his blazer, she pleaded with her eyes for a favorable outcome. Her face wrinkled into big worried furrows; then she turned away. Poteet walked them out to the porch, leaving Hood with McGregor.

Hood hissed at McGregor, "All right! Just what the hell happened between you and that Terri? Tell me the truth!"

McGregor had an inkling of what poor Poker must have been experiencing. Did he have the courage of Poker to come clean? Maybe it took more courage to lie. Had Poker lied?

"Nothing happened to give you any details about!" Then McGregor thought joking might calm her down. "I had lust in my heart, that's all, Hood, I swear!" He laughed and tried to take her arm, but she pulled back. "Terri's a good-looking woman," he said. "Mama is probably right about her. You're just feeling jealous, now that you and I are getting along better. You know what I mean?"

"I'll tell you what I know. I know that soon as I can, I'm going to have a woman-to-woman chat with this Terri character and you better be telling me the truth!" She made as if to punch McGregor in the groin, causing him jump back. "You think you're clever, but you're really just a moron."

Crap! He'd have to get to Terri first thing tomorrow, for now he had a perfectly good reason to go see her again. One good thing about Terri, she could lie convincingly.

Poteet walked in and sealed the door. He assessed the two of them with a broad grin, which faded when they said nothing.

He asked, "What the hell are we going to do, McGregor? I hope your conniving brain has schemed out a plan, because I'm at a loss. It's a new feeling for me, and as they say around here, I ain't likin' it. My big concern is for Mama. She has that wonderful combination of grit and frailty … and well, I'm close to her."

Taking a seat, McGregor said, "My plan is that we take Poker's story at face value and simply forgive him his trespasses. What good would it do to prosecute the man? Or, what, sue him? It buys us time, grants us a continuance, so to speak.

Poteet was nodding hard. "Good. It's the old no-harm-no-foul rule. And he *is* a widow's son."

McGregor continued, skipping Poteet's reference to the Masonic "plea" for now. He said, "I don't think Red and Sheriff really care who's responsible for the gunshot and the brake lines. Probably, they're afraid that tracking down those items could lead them to the tomato growers who want to keep you out of politics, and that would be information they don't want. If we excuse Poker, that keeps you tight with Mama. I get the feeling she's expecting it, and keeping you and Mama friendly is the main thing, as you intimated. Friendships are more important than cars.

"Regarding what we pass on to Carlos through Tomás, we tell them exactly what Poker owned up to. And tell them we don't care. We cajole Carlos into holding the information until the lab results on Poker's bloody tape come back. There's a chance the extra blood won't match with Clyde's. Without such a match they'd have nothing on Poker for the murder, just his confession about what he did to us."

Hood asked, "You don't think Poker's the murderer, do you?"

"Don't know. Right now, Amon's on the list. Jealousy and revenge. He gets confused and can't control his anger. He was a jealous brother. Plus he wanted revenge for what he perceived as the Tomato Boy trying to hurt Poker and Mama."

Poteet said, "But, if you reveal the Amon situation to Carlos, then you have to reveal the Manskar man connection with Poker and also the Tomato Boy-slash-Terri love affair. And that would give Poker just as strong a motive as Amon."

Hood said, "I'm confused. If it were up to me I wouldn't make any decision until McGregor can talk to Leslie, maybe tonight if things work out."

McGregor realized he was still fumbling with his mental picture of Poker and Terri engaged in porch copulation. Because of that, he wasn't thinking clearly. The confusion of his cohorts wasn't helping. "Sorry," he said, "but I've had a second thought. We shouldn't let Poker off the hook for nothing. Prudence dictates we attach strings."

He explained the need to have Poker pay for the property damage. "The problem is that his acts were criminal as well as civil wrongs. And it's unethical for an attorney to promise to drop criminal charges on the condition that a person pays civil damages. It's too close to extortion. At the point we learn enough facts to reasonably corroborate his confession; we will have a duty to alert the authorities."

Hood and Poteet agreed to abide by McGregor's dictates.

Yet, in the time it took Poteet to call in the defendant Poker from the porch, McGregor's mind raced with more second thoughts. The awful porch scene in his mind could not be real. It was beyond reason. If Poker lied about Terri, as surely he had, then his veracity in total must be questioned.

The crying frenzy had an effect favorable to Poker and Mama. Therein lay the rub. Without those remorseful tears, McGregor wondered, would he have devised the plan of action that now seemed one-sidedly advantageous to Poker? And what about the blazer outfit? How many times had he watched the ugliest wretch of a dirtbag car thief walk into the courtroom newly dressed up and cleanly cut? Had Mama rehearsed the witness? She'd had him cooped up for two days. Is that why Mama didn't want to talk at the memorial service? Had she been unable to face him while in the middle of coaching Poker? She had sat next to Poteet, hugging and holding hands. A schmooze job?

When everyone had reassembled and Poteet had sealed the door, McGregor stepped to one side out of the lamplight and continued forming nasty inferences about what Poker and Mama might be up to. Or Poker and Amon. What kind of influence do you have over a man when you can force him stay in a restroom stall with you?

He decided a light sentence for Poker was still the operative way to deal with the situation. Besides, right now he wanted to hear about Mama's talk with Leslie. Mama couldn't get away with lying about that with Leslie available to confirm or deny—unless Leslie was part of Mama's conspiracy. McGregor noted Poker had combed his hair, buttoned up his blazer and straightened his tie.

Poteet announced the verdict, as McGregor had outlined it. "We decided to take your word as a gentleman, Poker. We will excuse you for shooting out the window and causing the car crashes. For the time being. It's understandable how you were suckered in by this Manskar man. But you must understand we can't withhold evidence of a crime indefinitely. If you continue to help us solve this murder, maybe you won't ever be charged with anything."

Poker and Mama sighed with relief, hastily accepting Poteet's terms, including paying for the property damage.

Mama said, "Potty, this is the best gift I've ever received from anybody." She dismissed Poker to drive away in her Oldsmobile; Poteet would lend the Chevy to Mama later, assuming it had been returned from McKool's by now.

"Mama, my dear, we're running short of time," McGregor said. "Fill us in on Leslie, if you're up to it."

"I'm up to it," she replied with a big grin. "I met her this morning in her room at the hotel. She made her mother leave us because they're not getting along. Stacia was against Leslie coming out here and cut off her money. So Leslie hitched a ride with a Calvin County trucker she found out in California. That trip wasn't exactly a fun time, and she blames her mother. I know the old trucker and Lord knows what he might have tried to do to Leslie on a thirty-six hour trip.

"Anyway, for a while she put off introducing herself to Clyde, just observing the town folk and getting the feel of the place. She discovered me and I hired her. She ran into Lakisha Thompson at the work-out gym at the Calvin House. And Lakisha told her you knew Clyde as well as anybody. Then y'all played tennis together, right? Lakisha gave her the background on the whole county. I told Leslie, myself, how the Tomato Boy was given his name and all.

"Anyroo, she finally told Clyde who she was. Clyde was shocked! Mainly, he told her, because he'd had his eye on her and would have asked her for a date, except that he was seeing Terri Williams steady at the time. That Clyde, he was something, wasn't he? Okay, so Clyde was happy, but he made Leslie promise not to say anything to anybody on the grounds he was gonna run for county mayor, and it wouldn't look right for him to have a love child. Leslie said that Clyde had a thing for secrets, and she was finding out that a lot of others in the county did too."

Mama paused and turned for a quick glance and a smile at McGregor. He shifted his legs in response. Hood pursed her lips and gave him satanic slit-eyes.

Mama continued. "Leslie was hurt that Clyde didn't want to make a big announcement about her, but decided it was okay because she just liked being with her father. Leslie and Terri came to be friends. And they were all happy for a while.

"Now get this. Leslie met Eli Rust at the gym. Eli is a big ol' boy, and Leslie found him good looking—y'all have to remember she's from California. God help her! She approached Eli and discovered he was divorced and a big-shot county official. Eli invited her for coffee. And, let's see now, it was then that Eli told her he was attracted to Terri Williams. Well, Leslie was learning fast about Calvin County secrets and kept her mouth shut about Terri and Clyde. But Eli tells her he's suspicious of Terri, thinks she's having a secret affair. Not with Clyde—but with Poker! He says because Poker is always around Amon, he's always around Terri, too. Says the thought of it gagged him!

"I don't know why nobody thinks my boy has the right to date women. But Leslie says to Eli, that she'd met Poker many times by then and couldn't believe Terri would date him, him being the way he is. Now I'm going to let that stuff pass, these attitudes they have about Poker, circumstances being what they are. But I can tell y'all, if a person don't like Poker, then they don't like me! It's a family thing. Between us here and the fence post, Poker had just that one dance-around with Terri and that was it!"

Mama grew stone-faced and seemed to ruminate on what she'd just said. Then she blinked several times and smiled.

McGregor had a sudden case of dry-mouth and nodded to Poteet who said, "We understand, Mama. Give us the rest."

"Okay, so Leslie was in a pickle. She knew for certain that Terri and Clyde were lovers, okay? She thought Eli Rust was simply imagining a relationship between Terri and Poker. But Eli was fixated and said to her something like this: "If I had a truck like Poker's I could play some tricks and make Poker look bad, break up him and Terri. You take this money and go buy an orange truck like Poker's old thing."

Well, it could never hurt to have a county official as a friend, Leslie was thinking. So she played along and bought an orange truck from Glenn McKool. She drove it a day or so, even took Terri out shopping in it. Eli did take the truck, but before he did, one afternoon Leslie drove it out to visit Terri at her house. And then and there, she caught Terri and Poker on the porch!"

McGregor groaned; his mouth was so dry it hurt to swallow. He went to the bar and mixed a drink. Mama pressed on.

"Leslie, when she drove up, she saw Amon up in the trees, evidently spying on those two on the porch. Now I'm still debating whether to tell my Poker that he was seen by Amon that day. Should let sleeping dogs lie. Y'all don't say anything to him.

"Terri yelled at Leslie, begging her to keep quiet, saying she could explain. But Leslie was real upset and she wheeled out of there crying. She met Eli to hand over the truck, and without thinking through the consequences, she blurted out what she'd seen on the porch. Eli took the news by making weird faces and pounding a fist in his hand.

"Back at the hotel, Leslie also told Clyde about Terri and Poker. Clyde threw a fit. Hard for me to imagine. I don't think I ever saw Clyde mad. But my boy can make a man jealous as all get out, I figure. So Clyde said he had something on Poker and showed Leslie that old tape system. Said an unknown man from over in Manskar County came to the hotel two separate times. Said he got him on tape both times, and the second time the man was talking to Poker.

"Now, Bobby, we have to find that particular tape! Poker says he did meet with the Manskar man at the hotel one night but can't remember what was said. Said they were drunk, at least he knows he was."

McGregor said from the bar, "You're right. That tape would be the only evidence corroborating Poker's testimony if he ever has to testify about this Manskar man. It would be extremely useful." McGregor was suffering from a sick stomach and realized he sounded theatrical, like an actor trying to sound lawyerish.

Mama nodded and continued, "Leslie scolded the Tomato Boy big time for having the tape system. So Clyde made a deal with her; she thinks just to keep her quiet. That afternoon, they drove up to Nashville to see a lawyer. Leslie said the lawyer was old as the hills and was squint-eyed like a snake. Clyde signed a will, leaving her almost all his property. Then he promised to make her a partner in the hotel right away.

"Leslie's mother is leaving today. I suggested Leslie talk to Bobby and Janet. She wants y'all to come to the hotel tonight for dinner."

McGregor asked, "What did Leslie end up doing about Eli?"

"Let him go. Thought he acted too strange, talking about roads and dirt and politics and tricking Poker and such. And you know those crazy faces." Mama crinkled her own face to mimic Eli in a well-done impression.

"Now that's it, I can't talk no more. But Bobby, you come see me at the Emporium tomorrow. I'll have one of those old books for you to look at."

CHAPTER 16

McGregor enjoyed cogitating in silence with his friends for a while after Mama left. Suddenly tired of the mystery, he gazed at the Earth Day photograph of the young Janet and Bob, which was hanging directly opposite his chair. No more than three hours after that photo was taken, they were making love in the bed of his pickup truck with floor mats for a mattress and McGregor's dirty laundry for a blanket. He'd been on his way to the campus Laundromat when he'd stopped to chat with Hood and Poteet, who were planting a tree on the commons with a hundred other celebrative Earth acolytes.

Poteet brought him back to the present. "I'm concerned about Leslie," he said. "Now that it's gone public that she's Clyde's daughter, the killer could be wondering if she ever listened to those tapes."

Hood said, "My head hurts from all these details."

Poteet said, "Yeah, what about Leslie putting the moves on Eli? And that damn situation with the orange truck has popped up again."

Hood commented, "I have an if-if to see whether we're thinking the same thing. If the Manskar man drove the truck that pulled out in front of us, a truck like Poker's, and if that is the one Leslie bought for Eli, then bam! Eli is connected to the Manskar man."

McGregor said, "Stop and think, though. What you just said requires the Manskar man to actually exist, as Poker claims. For the sake of argument, let's suppose he does exist, and he meets with Poker at the hotel. Assume Clyde listens in and records that meeting. Suppose Poker admits to the Manskar man that he intends to harm or kill you, Poteet. That could be the basis for Mama concocting a tale in which Poker points the finger at the Manskar man for all of Poker's crimes in order to be excused by us. What if Poker put the Manskar man up to doing the dirty work, instead of vice versa?"

Poteet asked, "You're implying that Poker's lying outright! And are you implicating Mama in this?" His tone was that of the stern professor.

McGregor leaned toward Poteet with hands outreached and said, "Look, the conundrum of the orange truck makes it convenient for Poker to say he didn't pull out in front of you, that the Manskar man did it. Amon Trussell left it to Poker to tell me who was driving that truck. To me, if Poker punctured the brake lines it stands to reason he drove down the road, hid by the wayside and made sure you ran off the road. The Manskar man may be nothing but a phantom."

Poteet lit a cigarette, his eyebrow twitched; he looked McGregor up and down, but said nothing. McGregor felt as if he were undergoing a Poteet-style re-evaluation. He'd been through them before.

"Let's start over," McGregor said. "Assume Poker is brighter than he makes out. Let's say today's crying scene was a ruse—for argument's sake, Poteet. Let's say that on account of Terri, Poker was as jealous of the Tomato Boy as the Tomato Boy was of him. So Poker dreamed up this conspiracy that you and the Tomato Boy were trying to hurt Mama. Some kind of alcoholic delirium? He concocted a plot to get rid of both of you. Mama finds out about the tape this morning from Leslie—the one with Poker on it. Tells

Poker. Poker confesses to Mama—the exact reason why he does we don't know yet. Mama tells him to go ahead and confess to you the smallest of his transgressions, relying upon your probable willingness to forgive—for her sake."

Poteet's eyes narrowed and a vein popped up in his neck.

Hood said, "I don't like it. Not plausible!"

McGregor waved her off. He said, "I still think, all things considered, it was best to excuse Poker as we did for now. But we've yet to hear the full truth from him. Plus, I think Mama put him up to what he said today and how he said it. You noticed she invited me to look at one of the journals tomorrow. She thinks she has tamed my suspicions and needed to hold out that carrot to keep me tame."

The agitated Poteet said, "You don't seriously believe Mama's capable of that kind of disloyalty, do you? Good grief, man, she doesn't have that kind of treachery in her! She's a kind-hearted woman."

"I'm sorry. But you hired me to tell you what I think, and I think you and Hood are being snookered. You can mark Poker off your own murder suspect lists, but he's still on mine, right around Amon Trussell's name."

Hood asked, raising her voice, "Out of curiosity. Who else?"

McGregor shouted, "Leslie! That's who!" Emotions were seething, so he decided to leave. "I'm going to my room," he declared. "Y'all stew over all this madness as long as you want."

Frankly, he thought, he'd confused himself. Going out the door, he heard Hood sending him a parting shot. She said loudly, ostensibly to Poteet, "And I bet Terri's not on his damn list at all!"

In the solitude of his bathroom, McGregor turned the hot water tap on in the wide soaking tub and watched it fill. Scooting in under the bath tray, he laid his cast on the tub side and tried to relax, neck deep. In addition to the vast temperature differential, tub water was softer than creek water. Regardless, he had started reliving his trauma in the creek when a tappity-tap-tap sounded at his bathroom door.

"McGregor, it's me," said Hood's voice.

He responded sourly, "I'm in the bath! What do you want?"

She walked in on him and sat on the edge of the tub. She tucked her top lip under her bottom lip.

Ah, God, what a woman. What now? "Hood, I'm naked here for Christ's sake! I have a broken wrist that hurts like hell. Can I not have one minute of privacy?" He pulled the bath tray over as a shield. "What do you want?"

"Ordinarily, my little nudie, I'd let you pout, but I think you're in need of an intervention. And we are need of reconciliation."

He shrugged and sighed.

She said, "How'd you feel about Poker's breakdown in the study. Be truthful."

Tranquilized by the hot bath, McGregor could find no reason to avoid an answer. He admitted, "At the time I thought his rendition of events was honest." He looked up at her. "But it doesn't mean I shouldn't have second thoughts!"

"No, but I'm saying just don't rely on them so heavily. Look, you're used to pounding the truth out of witnesses and such, keeping your emotions to the side—if you had any. It made you an asshole lawyer, but I could live with that so long as I didn't have to live close to you." She nudged his shoulder, playfully.

McGregor remembered the many phone calls from Hood he'd failed to return during his early years on the Task Force. Hood had been building her business then, and she was also hard to contact. But in the last couple of years they'd had some good times, even though he'd usually been just as preoccupied. He'd learned to manage time.

"But up here," Hood was saying, "I'm seeing a lot of the Bob McGregor I used to know, the emotional and kind-hearted one. I want to encourage you to give a little when dealing with Poteet. Don't blow this gig, you know? I told you I had the jitters about you moving up here. Maybe you should lie low. You'll get the journals just by keeping Poteet out of politics."

"Hood, I see your point. I'm not going to lie low. Let's drop it for now."

Later, when McGregor walked out of his room, ready to go to The Thumb, Hood was coming out of her door. He held her steady gaze and received from her that certain communication, that flicker of the eyes—*the* signal he used to get when it was time to go to the bedroom with her. Hood giggled. McGregor's heart thumped. Then together they realized that Poteet and Lakisha were in the guest den watching them.

"Hi," Poteet said. "Hate to intrude on your staring contest, but Lakisha has shared some background on Leslie with me. You should hear this before you go on your date."

Lakisha sailed right into her story. "When I first met Leslie, I thought she was just a lost soul drifting in from California. I invited her to play tennis with Roland and me, and she seemed to get along well in town. Like I told you before, she asked me a lot about the Tomato Boy. Then I noticed she was running around, shopping and stuff, with that Terri Williams." She stopped for their reaction.

"Was that bad?" asked Hood, sounding overly hopeful, it seemed to McGregor.

"Well, it was good that Leslie was making friends. But I had to warn her. I had to warn her that Terri had just quit a secret love affair with *Sheriff Buell.*"

Hood plunged into a chair and slung her head back, rolling her eyes. To keep from pounding his head against the wall, McGregor took a chair and slumped. Poteet nudged Lakisha on.

"Okay. Well, yeah, they'd had a big one going for a couple of years, off and on, you know how it is. That's why Terri's brother Amon got away with so much for so long, why Sheriff conveniently blamed most of Amon's mischief on poor old Poker Limbo.

"So I told her to watch out because Sheriff, he's the jealous type and if he got mad at Terri, and I knew he was, he might take it out on her friends. A way of punishing Terri. He's that type."

McGregor, irritated beyond patience to hear of yet another man in Terri's life, moved to sit on an end table next to Lakisha and tried to remain focused. He said, "Tell us what Sheriff Buell is capable of doing, say, if he discovered Terri was dating somebody right after she quit him?"

Lakisha thought about it. "My guess is he'd kick somebody's butt if he could. Sheriff's cool on the outside most of the time. On the inside he's thinking about women all the time. Didn't hire me when I applied for a deputy slot, but I don't think it was because I'm African-American or nothing like that. He just knew I'd keep my distance from him."

CHAPTER 17

Going out the door for their "date," Hood prodded McGregor. "We have a much better suspect in our randy Sheriff now, don't we?"

"Yeah."

"Ol' Sheriff. If you're unfaithful at home, you can't be trusted in any other part of your life, either. He should know that, right?"

"Right." Ah, God.

They were getting into Hood's truck when Poteet called to them. His former attorney had phoned and said the Poteet and Johnson file was missing; that he didn't recall the incident, and that the young attorney who would have handled the case was long gone, having moved to Oregon and dropped out of sight. "For now, we're dead-ended there," Poteet said.

Hood drove the Offshoot and was making the turn toward the Calvin House when a siren whooped behind them. Hood pulled over.

It was Carlos and he was in a snit about something. He grunted an invitation for them to come back to his patrol car. They climbed into the rear seat. Sweat ran down the back of Carlos' neck, even though the air conditioning was on full tilt.

Carlos stared out the windshield. "Bob, Janet, I've bitten into a hell of a rotten tomato! I got to spit it out and spit it out fast!" He wiped his face with a handkerchief.

McGregor asked, "What happened? Did Sheriff find out about us working together?"

Hood put a friendly hand on the shoulder of the chief deputy, and Carlos turned to face them.

"No. But I've made the biggest blunder of my life. If Sheriff does find out now, it'll be my job, for sure. And Sheriff's not a man to mess with if you don't have the goods to back yourself up."

Hood said, "What are you talking about?"

"That damned Jimmy Henry! He was responsible for bagging, sealing and labeling the Thacker crime scene evidence to send to the lab. The lab called not long ago, and thanks be to the Almighty, I was there to take the call. Jimmy Henry labeled two different cassette tapes as the one found in Poker's truck. You understand? He labeled one correctly, but labeled one of the tapes taken off Thacker's floor as the Poker tape. That's the one I must have seen. The lab guy said of the two tapes labeled "Poker Limbo's truck," one tape had a smear of blood, the other had a lot more. Jimmy Henry thought through his procedure that day and figured out how he'd made the mistake. Said his dog was sick that day. My God, just think what I've been accusing Sheriff and Red of doing! If they find out I thought they planted evidence, I don't know. Hell, I'd have to leave the state.

"Listen here, please don't ever mention what I had Tomás tell y'all. I guess I just wanted to be sheriff so bad I jumped to the wrong conclusion. Man, how could I be so stupid?"

McGregor said gently, "Okay, calm down, Carlos. Nobody's perfect. You know we aren't going to say anything. And Tomas won't. So nobody's ever going to know about it."

Carlos couldn't come out of his hyper state easily. "It's the damn lousy pay schedule for deputies. All we get are the rejects from the city police force, and if you know anything about the Finneyville force, that's a hell of a reject! Jimmy Henry, goddamn him, works like a demon, but he's not worth a shit as a deputy. How could you even make out two labels the same way, two times in a row and not realize it? Shit! Shit!" He pounded the dashboard. "And I think I'm smart enough to be sheriff?"

Hood said, "Carlos, you're being too rough on yourself. You deputies have to trust each other. It's just one of those things that happen. You'll get over it. It'll be fine."

He responded, "Y'all are lifesavers. Y'all find out anything from Poker, by the way? Ah, hell, don't answer me. I don't want to know. I'm leaving the investigation up to the powers-that-be. From now on, I'll take my orders and hope to keep my job. Y'all go on now. I owe you a big favor."

McGregor said, "There is one thing you could help us with, Carlos. Tell us the lab results from the crime scene."

Carlos sighed. "Okay, just keep it confidential. The blood on the *true* Poker tape matches Poker. The blood on the other tapes from the suite matches Thacker. The state's experts found four things of note. One—several dried sunflower seeds in the carpet outside the Tomato Boy's suite. The carpet had been vacuumed not thirty minutes before Thacker was found. Two—there was a ballpoint pen just inside the doorway of the suite, between the carpet and the floor molding, an advertising type pen from Manskar Concrete and Culvert Company. We checked. Manskar Concrete started passing them out about a month ago. That pen had a tiny speck of Thacker's blood on it, but it was too far away to have been spattered, they believe. It had to have been moved, you know, the sort of thing that'd fall out of a pocket. Three—Leslie Rion's fingerprints are on many of the tapes found, even though she claims to know of only one specific tape. That's a discrepancy we haven't chosen to hit her with yet.

"The last thing is one I don't know what to make of. It's a letter from Mama Limbo to the Tomato Boy. She tells him she has no idea where the old journals are and says, I quote, 'You stay the hell off my back, you hear me, boy?' It was on the floor when Thacker was hit because the blood on it was consistent with the blood distribution pattern on the floor around it. Y'all know Mama has those books, so she was lying to her cousin for some reason."

McGregor asked, "No fingerprints on that pen?"

"Just smudges in motor oil and dirt."

Hood said, starting up her truck, "I feel like I'm back in the game! Carlos woke me up. Before he pulled us over, I was daydreaming again about packing up and going home."

McGregor's interest had grown ten-fold. He thought of that particular pen he'd seen in Eli Rust's truck on the way to the hospital and Eli saying it came from Manskar Concrete. And it was Amon who had a penchant for sun-flower seeds. Was it possible that his suspicions of Mama and of Leslie would be justified?

The lobby of the Calvin House was empty of guests. They asked the desk clerk to page Leslie. That done, they introduced themselves, casually dropping Poteet's name as their employer, in the process. Ethan Townsley was the clerk, the head clerk. They complimented him on the well-planned memorial service and offered their condolences.

"How is Mr. Poteet? The hotel's real concerned for him, and not just because he's the biggest tipper in the county, either." Ethan chuckled.

"He's pretty good. I'll convey your regards." McGregor said. Then, tapping the counter with his fingers, he asked, "Do you get much business from visitors driving over from Manskar County?"

"Not much, no."

"Out of curiosity, can you tell me the last time anyone from Manskar County came in? Mr. Poteet said to ask, said it was important."

"Well, let's see. It was less than a month ago, I guess."

McGregor pulled out a hundred-dollar bill. "Mr. Poteet said if you remembered a Manskar person coming in, then I should give you this and ask you if the Tomato Boy met with the person. He has reason to believe a Manskar County man might have something to do with Mr. Thacker's death. Mr. Poteet said it was urgent to find out anything you might know. And to keep it confidential that he'd asked."

Ethan palmed the currency and asked them to come behind the desk and into the office.

With the door closed Ethan said, "There is something. I tried to tell Sheriff Buell about it, but he seemed not to take it seriously and just went on asking me other questions. I'll show you what I showed him. Mr. Thacker seemed upset about this guy. Highly unusual!"

Ethan pulled out of a file drawer an eight-by-ten photo. "Mr. Thacker shot this with his cell phone camera on the sly and had me enlarge it on the computer."

The picture showed a man striding down a hotel corridor heading in the direction of the camera. He wore a tight shirt revealing a muscular torso and broad shoulders. His shiny shoes reflected the corridor lights. He had a thick mustache and short, light hair. His facial features transmitted ferocity.

Hood commented, "He looks like a man on a mission."

"Yeah," said Ethan. "I get the same feeling. I was on duty the two times he came in, about a month apart. Has the voice of a first-class alley mugger. The first time he came in, I called Mr. Thacker's attention to him because he paid cash in advance and wanted a suite. Paid rack rate. You know, full price. Mr. Thacker usually reserved those suites for the local dignitaries and only charged them half-price."

Ethan started to say something more but changed his mind. McGregor figured he'd thought of the taping system, which he surely knew about by now.

"And the second time?"

"The second time, I notified Mr. Thacker again—same reason. And Mr. Thacker seemed scared. I'd never seen him scared about anything, so that's why I remember all this and why I think this guy ought to be checked into. Thought about doing it myself, since Buell wasn't interested. But Mr. Thacker already checked the address the guy gave us. It's the local jail over in Manskar County. Bogus, we figured. Something he pulled out of the phone book. My idea was to publish the picture and see if anybody knows him. Buell didn't even stick around long enough for me to suggest it."

McGregor asked, "May I borrow the photo for Mr. Poteet to look at? He can't leave his house, because we all believe somebody's still after him. Would you also look up the dates when this guy was here and phone Mr. Poteet tomorrow when you get a chance?"

"Sure." He ran a copy of the photo and tucked it in a folder. "And tell Mr. Poteet we're all thinking of him."

Leslie walked into the office.

"Hello, you guys. We finally get to meet again. You've met Ethan? Good. After talking to Mama this morning, I've been on edge. I'd like you to be my guests for dinner."

Leslie was wearing her glasses. She had a new hairdo, short and full, and wore a low-cut blouse under a classy waist-coated pantsuit, tailored tightly to expose her curves. It was hard to see her as a lightly clad waitress serving red drinks at Mama's. Well, not so hard, really.

Hood said, "We'd be delighted. I'm famished."

"How's Roland?"

"Taking it easy for the time being." McGregor said.

Leslie seated them at the same table where they had visited with the Tomato Boy. She said brightly, "We have rack of lamb tonight, the specialty of the house. Or, if you'd prefer a steak, my chef prepares a delicious blue cheese filet mignon."

The Thumb had two other sets of diners, seated on the other side of the bar at the far side of the room and clearly out of earshot. McGregor would have preferred the seclusion of Poteet's study, but they were here and the timing was finally right.

After placing their order for wine and dinner Leslie said, "I've taken over management of the hotel on legal advice from my mother that I don't have to wait for probate to keep the business going. Leslie used a whiney voice to mimic that of her mother and said, "In Tennessee, the decedent's real property vests in the heir or heirs."

"I'm almost certain she's correct," McGregor said. "Mama Limbo told us that you and your mother aren't getting along."

"She didn't want me to come here. I came anyway and she's angry. She's gone back home."

Then Leslie gushed, "I've assumed tonight that we're on first name bases. I feel like I know the both of you so well already. I don't know why, but since we first met at Mama's I feel comfortable with you. Mama loves you both and already thinks the world of you after only what, two, three days? And she loves Roland."

It pained McGregor to hear how much Mama loved him, considering his recent accusations against her.

The waiter arrived to serve the wine, a fine pinot noir. McGregor said, holding up his glass, "Our condolences to you, Leslie. I propose a toast to the memory of Clyde Thacker!"

While dining they conversed about the hotel business, about Poteet as a businessman, and about McGregor's book. Leslie was thrilled to learn of the book.

"If recent events are illustrative of the history of our fair town, you should be able to write volumes of best sellers."

As the table was being cleared, McGregor anguished over his questions for Leslie. He wanted desperately to know her view of the Poker and Terri porch scene, but not with Hood present.

He said, "Leslie, we're ready to hear what happened when Clyde was killed."

"To tell you just that is the reason I asked you to dinner," she said. "First, let me say I think the murder is connected to this insane taping system my father had. Back in California, he worked for a film company where he dubbed sound effects onto film during the editing process. And he was a man who loved secrets. Nobody knows why. Mama Limbo said she would tell you about the system."

"Yes," said Hood, "and though it's bizarre, even with all his celebrity, your father could have been downright bored living here after the bright lights of California, so to speak."

"That's as good an explanation as any."

McGregor asked, "Did Clyde at any time have a large collection of tapes? From what we've heard only a few recordings were found."

"He had several more tapes than Sheriff claimed were found! And they were labeled with dates and a cryptic code he used. He told me he would put selected persons in selected suites and listen in to their conversations, their noises, and tape what he might want to listen to again. Periodically, he'd erase or destroy the recordings. The only one I know of for sure is the one I told Mama about, the one of Poker and some man talking. During my interviews with Sheriff Buell, he displayed all the tapes he supposedly had. I didn't see the Poker tape. I would have recognized it because I picked it up once and it had a crack in its plastic. I did tell Sheriff Buell about it. So he knows Poker was taped."

McGregor looked at Hood to make sure she saw the significance of that last. Sheriff could have possessed the Poker tape, but not shown it to Leslie. If so, it could be their basis for a case against Poker.

McGregor said, "Please go ahead and tell us what happened up there that night."

Leslie frowned and started her story. "When my father left you guys here at this very table, I followed him out. I'll tell you why in a minute. He didn't see me and went in the restroom across the hall. He stayed longer than seemed necessary. I became distracted when a customer asked me something or other and never saw him come out. I knocked on the door, but nobody answered. The Firstplacers in the lobby asked for more drinks. I served them and called my father's room. No answer there, either. But he could have been there anyway. Father was quirky and often refused to answer a ring. So I went up. The door was already opened a crack, and I went in and started to call for him, but there were tapes scattered all around on the floor and a chair was turned over. Then, I noticed the refrigerator was pulled out from the wall. I just sort of froze with my mouth open, knowing something was wrong. Oh yeah, his tape recording was done in a small room he'd carved out of the pantry. You go in it from behind the refrigerator." She looked at Hood. "I know, it sounds ridiculous!"

Hood nodded to her nervously. Although Hood seemed as enthralled by the account as McGregor, the expression on her face was cold. McGregor wondered if she was sensing something he was missing in Leslie's account.

Leslie's lower lip quivered and she hunched her shoulders together. "I went into the little room, but nobody was there. Then I heard voices coming from the bedroom. That's when I hid behind the kitchen counter. The voices moved in my direction. I couldn't even tell if the voices were those of men or women. Then I became certain that one was my father's. They were talking very low and didn't seem to be angry. The kitchen's a part of the main room, and I was afraid I could still be seen. So I crawled behind the refrigerator. I heard my father mutter something. It was his voice, but I couldn't understand the words. Then I heard him say loudly, 'What the ...' and that's when I heard a thud and another thud, like somebody falling.

"I was petrified! I couldn't breathe and I couldn't move. My heart felt like it was going to explode! I think I blacked out for a few seconds. When my vision cleared I didn't know where I was for a second. I didn't hear anything so I crawled out into the kitchen and reached up into a drawer to get a knife but couldn't find one. I tried not to make a sound. I stood up, and there was Roland standing over my father, who was laid out on the floor!"

Tears come then. Who could blame her for crying? It took a few minutes, but with encouraging words McGregor put her back on track.

"I squatted and crawled to the refrigerator and then realized that wasn't the way out. All I wanted was out! Roland had killed my father. And when I ran he chased me! I thought he was going to kill me, too, and the only thing I could think of was to get to the lobby where the crowd was. The elevator opened and I jumped inside. But Roland barged in. He kept grabbing me and I fought him. I got out on the lobby floor and ran, but he still chased me. Then somebody grabbed him and I fell into a chair. I think I was screaming. Somebody was screaming, anyway. There isn't much I recall after that until I was outside the hotel. Sheriff Buell finally calmed me down. He explained that Roland had walked into the room and found my father on the floor and me in the kitchen."

They allowed her several minutes to compose herself. Then McGregor asked her, "Can we get you a drink or something?"

"No. I'll be okay."

She had pulled off her glasses to cry and when she looked at McGregor with those penetrating eyes, McGregor melted inside. She looked so meek—and innocent. But the deep V in her blouse kept attracting his attention. Mixing empathy with sex was wrong, but he couldn't stop it.

Hood was watching him. For her benefit he feigned a lawyer's deliberative detachment and asked calmly, "What were you going to tell your father when you followed him out from The Thumb?"

"Oh, yes. That! I'd seen a man in the lobby by the fireplace. He was talking with somebody in the crowd. You see, one night my father snapped a photograph of a man who had come into the hotel. He showed me the picture and kept it in a file in the office. He said that if I ever saw the guy I was to let him know immediately. I think he was frightened."

McGregor pulled out his folder from Ethan the desk clerk. "Was it this man?"

Leslie gulped. "Yes, that's him. How did you get that picture of him?"

He said, "I'm sorry. I can't talk anymore about this unless you come to Poteet's house. He has a soundproof and bug-proof room. I mean, can we really trust this hotel not to be bugged?"

The hotel had a wedding booked tomorrow. On Wednesday it would host an all-day emergency seminar for farmers because the university extension service had found tomato destroying nematodes in the soil in Manskar County. So Leslie chose to meet at Sweetwater on Thursday.

McGregor and Hood headed out Ferry Road for the Offshoot. Once south of Calvin Station they saw no other vehicles. Hood was strangely quiet. McGregor said, "I'm rolling down my window. I need to smell earth." Hood turned off the chugging a/c and rolled hers down, too.

It was another humid night, hotter than ever. Probably still up in the nineties. McGregor laid his head into the wind imagining lying out in a field of flowers. The moon was out, high in a hazy but starry sky.

As they crossed McGregor's lifesaver bridge, Hood said, "So tell me. Is Leslie still third on your suspect list?"

"Not sure."

Hood kept on. "What about the part of her story where the Tomato Boy visits the restroom? You know who had to have been in there if Poker's story is true. You think

Clyde held his nose and carried on a polite conversation with the gentlemen in the stall? Poker's rendition left out any mention of Clyde coming in. I'm beginning to have my own doubts about Poker."

McGregor said, "I'm too tired to care about Poker right now."

His mind had shifted to Hood's dress. It had inched way up. Her moonlit thigh muscles were twitching as she flung the wheel about to maneuver the truck between potholes. Without thinking, McGregor unbuckled his seatbelt and scooted over to her.

"Can you smell that stuff out there? It's making me drunk!" He eased his hand onto her lap.

Hood said, "Mmm. McGregorrr. I don't know—"

She hit a pothole, a big pothole. They weren't going fast, but the unbelted McGregor bounced up high and came down with his elbow onto Hood's knee, causing her to hit the gas pedal hard and twist the wheel sharply. The light truck spun sideways as they bumped across one pothole after another. Hood quickly braked, but by then the screeching truck had skidded and torn its way across the gravel on the roadside to within a yard of the vast field of wildflowers.

Hood, using cuss words only she knew, fished out from her purse a small flashlight and went out to survey the exterior of the truck. McGregor, meantime, rubbed his head, sore from banging the cab roof.

"Nothing wrong out here," she called out. "You still all right?"

McGregor grinned to himself, feeling giddy. He climbed out of the cab and raised his arms to the sky, grateful to escape yet another left hook from fate and thinking, "Ain't life grand?"

He shouted to the flowers of the meadow and the stars above, "We're alive, Hood!"

He grabbed her before she knew what was up. He hugged her tightly and swung her by the hips with his good arm until they fell to their knees into the deep mass of meadow blossoms. Then he gently pushed her out to arms' length to scrutinize her face in the soft light. He counted four tiny trickles of silver sweat. If he spoke, he was afraid he'd say something stupid like I love your sweat. So he tried to show his affection on his face. In response, Hood let form on her mouth that particularly radiant and special smile she kept in reserve for him.

His senses raw, he pulled Hood down into the depths of the tall flowers all the way to the moist loam. But Hood put a hand on his chest and pushed him over to his side. Directly into his mouth, she whispered in a hot breath, "Hold that feeling, Lumpkins."

He held it as Hood went to the truck. On his back, the moon in his eyes, he held his breath and savored the lingering whisper still swirling in his mouth. When Hood came back she had with her the truck's plush floor mats.

On her mats, placed carefully into the flowers beside McGregor, Hood reclined. She held out her arms. McGregor closed his eyes. His incoherent thought was something about the thrill of life, of making love to Hood one more time before he might die.

Back to reality, Hood said, "Hot damn! Man when you get in touch with your feelings, you get in touch with mine, too! What a ride!"

McGregor, breathing hard, said, "I ... I ... yeah!" But all at once his sixth sense went on the alert. A tingle shot up his neck. Hood started to say something more, but he caught her arm.

"Listen!" he cautioned her. "There's somebody out there watching us!"

They arranged their clothes fast and threw the mats back in the truck, but neither could see anyone or anything in the field. Hood made one full sweep of the area with her headlights before speeding away.

At Sweetwater, as they stepped from the truck, Lakisha walked out of the moonlight. McGregor said, "Lakisha, one quick question, please, before we go in. I assume you know of Amon Trussell. Is he known hereabouts as a peeping tom?"

"He's not a window peeper if that's what you mean, but he stares at you. In a way that makes you wonder if he knows what you're thinking. I believe I saw him right here early this evening watching *me*, but it was getting dark at the time and it could've been somebody else. What really made me think of him was my knowing about that old trail down by the river.

McGregor asked, "What trail?"

"There's a trail that starts near the river just north of Roland's property line. It runs over the hill and past those huge Pullwater Springs, you know where the creek comes from, past the old mill there and on down to Pullwater Hill, Terri Williams's hill, where Amon lives. From there it winds into south Calvin Station, down to the old quarry. It'd be easy for Amon to get here on that trail."

As Lakisha walked away, McGregor sighed, "We've been too busy to look over that map Poteet said he had. We've left geography out of our considerations."

Poteet was sitting at the kitchen waiting up for them. He eyed their wrinkled clothes with suspicion. McGregor blushed, which was something he rarely did. Hood smiled.

Poteet reached down and pulled a twig of dried flower from McGregor's pant cuff and said to him, "My, my. I've a feeling our Scotsman might be reverting into a Celt. I hope your intentions toward my daughter here are honorable, sir." He held the twig up high and affected a Scottish accent. "Och! You hae a bit o' heather stuck to you still, laddie."

Hood laid her hand on McGregor's cast and giggled her fullest bubbly giggle. Poteet pounded the table, laughing.

"Okay, Poteet, knock it off!" McGregor said.

Poteet's laughter wound down to a more serious chuckle. He said, "Let's get this murder solved so I can get out of this damn house and start living again. You two sit down and have a decaf and fill me in on Leslie."

McGregor prepared the coffee. Hood said, "First, Lakisha, outside a minute ago, said she thought she saw Amon Trussell out in the woods this evening and told us about an old trail down by the river that runs all the way to Calvin Station. Tomorrow, we need to look at your map."

They told Poteet what they'd learned from Leslie and that they had scheduled another meeting with her on Thursday. Poteet issued low whistles and exclamations during the storytelling. Finally, he asked, "Do you think she told the truth? Do we take her off the suspect list?"

With sudden truculence, Hood jumped in front of McGregor's response. "No. There's no way to corroborate her version of events. She had a huge motive for murder. Just look how she's taken over the Calvin House. It could all have been planned. Could be she coerced Clyde to leave the place to her in that will."

McGregor was taken aback.

Poteet said, "Now Hood, you're sounding like McGregor and his attack on Poker and Mama. There wouldn't be some jealousy showing up here would it? I mean, did the Celt Man melt down when Leslie cried? Huh?"

Hood started to defend herself, but stopped abruptly. "Well, all right! So what? I have as much right to be skeptical of Leslie as he does of Poker and Mama. Besides, I don't like her."

McGregor changed the subject. "We have other big news. We think we have a picture of the Manskar man!" He related the discussion with Ethan. "So, we hope Ethan will call tomorrow. He'll have the dates of when this guy showed up. Here's the photo."

Poteet stared at it. "I recognize this man! Can't call his name or where I met him, though. It's not the face; it's the eyes. Yeah. Definitely. I've had some dealings with those eyes before."

McGregor told him about the meeting with Carlos and what forensics had found.

Poteet said, "I'm glad we're off the hook on the bloody tape issue. What do you make of the other items they found?"

"The sunflower seeds and the pen? Not much, but there are connections. Amon Trussell eats sunflower seeds. Rust had a pen in his truck similar to what Carlos described. The letter from Mama on the floor with blood on it? It shows that Mama and Clyde were in some kind of controversy. Over the journals, it sounds like. We know she was his strong business competitor. But let's stop. Have y'all ever been plain brain tired? Well, that's me."

Then Hood said, "Me, too. If I go to bed, will you two promise not to hold a secret meeting behind my back?"

They promised.

Poteet glanced at a phone message pad. "Tommy Mathis called me. I'm supposed to ship the slashed paintings to him tomorrow. Marigail Mathis has already started work on a portrait of the Tomato Boy, a life-size rendering, and will finish soon. Clyde paid up front."

McGregor said, "Have the security company get you a driver when you go out. I'll try to see Amon once more. Then Hood and I will go to Mama's and have a quick look at her journals. Hood can bring the Chevy back home." As he'd hoped, Hood didn't say anything about going to Terri's with him.

McGregor followed her into her room with the general idea of spending the night with her. But she was all business. "If I can trust you alone with Terri, I'd like to stay here in the morning and deal with my shop office on the phone. But I do want to go with you to Mama's." She arched a brow. "Can I trust you?"

"You can trust me," he replied, as she ushered him out the door.

CHAPTER 18

Tuesday morning's skies were gray. Television weather showed a band of rain coming in from the west. McGregor exercised while formulating the words he wanted to say to Hood. He tried her doorknob and found it locked, so he decided to let her dwell on last night without his interference. Poteet wasn't up, but had left the Big Turkey watershed map on the kitchen table for him. After studying it he left the house about nine, not even seeing Tomás. Where was Tomás?

On his way to Terri's house, he slowed down coming to the site of last night's lovemaking in the flowers. He sniffed the air, but the flowers were moist and drooping. His nose had a memory, though.

Who owned this meadow? He had to know. It and the creek stirred his emotions like nothing he'd experienced from any other particular spot on Earth. Any leftover fear of the creek had dissipated, replaced by something he could only identify as respect, and what else? Sympathy? The coming development would surely harm this place. After he received money from Poteet he'd try to buy as much of the meadow as he could. His mind flashed to Tipsy and her attachment to Sweetwater, and he was gripped by a yearning to protect "his" meadow, to save it. McGregor in the past had left such noble desires to the environmentalists.

Up Terri's road McGregor pulled the red truck onto the side trail where he'd stopped before to wait for Rust to leave. Sure enough, he could see the depression beside the roadway where the orange truck had been hiding. From his angle of vision he supposed a person could see the face of the driver, but it would be difficult given the distance. With binoculars, maybe.

Poteet's map denoted Amon's back-trail as the Military Cut. The new theory said that the perpetrator of the sneak attack on their cars' brake lines—Poker, or whoever—had used the trail and slipped out of and back into the woods within seconds. Poker had not been asked about his exact movements when tampering with the cars. That was a big mistake. But McGregor's task at hand was to talk to Amon about the Manskar man and about what had really happened in that restroom.

As he exited the tunnel of overgrowth and drove into Terri's clearing the first thing he saw was the rear end of an orange pickup sticking out of an open yard-side shed door. He noted the license plate number in his book.

Climbing from the car, he heard, "Hi Bob!"

The words sliced hot through his body. Terri's sultry voice was calling from the other side of the porch screen, the screen opaque from reflected morning light.

He coughed, "Hi up there. Uh, mind if I come in?"

"Please come ... in."

McGregor thought, ah God, here I go. He opened the door a crack and stood there. "Hope I'm not interrupting. Sorry I didn't call first. Decided to drive up, spur of the moment." He felt unprepared for this visit.

"Have a seat, Bob. I'm glad you're here. I was thinking about you. Like I made a wish and, presto, you showed up!"

He didn't move and Terri smiled. And then she turned and bent over, her back side toward him up in the air.

She was wearing sandals, cut-off jeans and a T-shirt. On her left butt cheek, there was a hole in her jeans the size of a half-dollar, showing nothing but pink skin.

She started lighting a series of candles in tall glass holders. Into each holder she poured a liquid. He realized those candles had been lit the two times he'd been here, but he'd not paid them much attention other than wondering why she burned candles in the heat of the day.

McGregor said, "I wanted to ask you to walk around your property with me," he said. "I need the exercise and I'm interested in your home. Just how much of the property around here belongs to you?" He stepped back to the yard, looking around and hoping she'd follow him off that damned porch.

She joined him, saying she owned three hundred acres extending from the Offshoot, over Amon's hill, and down to a trail near the Big Turkey called the Military Cut. He wanted to ask who owned Pullwater Meadow, but decided to stay on subject.

"Tell me about the Military Cut."

"It's just an old dirt road. Hardly anybody uses it."

"I'm curious. Did you or the boys see anybody on the trail last Saturday morning?"

"I didn't. No reason I would have. It's been months since I was over there. Don't know about the boys." She reached and squeezed his hand. "The boys are gone for the day, in case you were wondering."

He started to respond just as something caught his eye far up the hill, toward where Amon's shack would be. He asked her, "What's that white thing up there flapping in the wind?"

She squinted. "Oh, that? That's a thing Amon plays with. He has a pole up there close to his house where he flies flags. Different days, different colors. It's just one of his secrets."

"Listen, does Amon have a cell phone or even a regular phone he could use to call Eli when he sees I'm at your place?"

"No phone and no electricity up there. I bought him a cellular once, but he cooked it on a spit over a fire. Go figure. Amon never talks on a phone. I don't know how Eli finds out when you're here."

She put her hand to her forehead and peered into the woods. "Looks like we're alone, Bob. Can you see that tree house up there?"

McGregor said he thought he could see it but he really couldn't, the foliage was so thick.

"Can Amon spy on the porch from up there?"

"Yeah, he sits in that house or perches on a limb. He was there this morning. Usually, I don't pay him any mind. If you try to keep up with Amon, you'll go as goofy as he is."

McGregor looked for the white flag again. It had gone, but in its place there suddenly appeared a yellow flag with a black outline.

"Hey! The flag changed," he said.

"Yeah, that Amon!" She pulled on McGregor's hand, sending the familiar tingle through him. They walked round to the rear of the house.

"I was hoping to talk to Amon again today, actually," he said with nonchalance.

"No … not today, Bob. He's been sullen lately. Not a good time."

Well, hell, he thought. But something needed to be accomplished. He casually pointed to the tail of the orange pickup. "Whose truck?"

"Eli keeps it over here as a second vehicle for me. He uses it sometimes; sometimes I do. My old car won't run half the time." She pushed the shed door open wider to reveal a tan 1978 Buick.

"Hey, look at this!" McGregor exclaimed. "I love Buicks." He touched the car. "Nice wax job. So did Eli buy that old truck from Leslie Rion?"

Terri released his hand and looked at him quizzically. "Why, yes. Back when Leslie and I were on good terms."

"I didn't know y'all were friends? You're not anymore?"

"Nope. I guess I didn't mention it, but I knew early on she was Clyde's daughter. She found out about me and Clyde, and I thought it seemed okay with her. Then she had a change of heart. I've wondered if she was the one responsible for breaking us up. In some things she said, I could tell she was afraid I'd marry Clyde. If you've met her, you probably can tell she's a snot!"

She grabbed McGregor's cast and said, "Come on, let's get back to the shade. I made sun tea yesterday and it's great."

He told her he had to go. But she tugged on him and he followed her, strolling behind her with his hand cupped over his eyes to keep from seeing that hole in her jeans.

On the porch, Terri stooped to re-light a candle that had gone out.

"Where *are* the boys this morning?" he asked as evenly as possible.

She poured him a glass of tea. "Just gone, that's all. You know, summertime. Hey, I need to run in for another glass. You have a seat. Take a deep breath, lots of deep breaths."

McGregor plunked down in the old wicker and breathed heavily, wondering why he was being so compliant with her directions. Where were the flowers he smelled so strongly? He'd noticed nothing growing in the yard more than the ordinary petunias and marigolds.

Terri came back and poured tea.

"What's that marvelous aroma floating around out here?" he asked. "Since I arrived in Calvin County I've been blasted by various smells like nothing else before. This whole area has to be the sweetest smelling place on Earth!"

She laughed and laughed. McGregor watched her, listening to her voice rise and fall in pitch. He thought, simply a perfect laugh! Was he was being charmed all over again? At least he was hearing laughter today rather than crying.

"What? What's so funny?" he asked.

She sipped and eyed him over her glass. "I don't know about the rest of the county, but here on the porch, it's the oil, Bob. I put oil in the candle holders. It's made special for me by my massage therapist who's also a kitchen chemist. It's called aromatherapy." She said teasingly, "Surely, you know about that?"

"Of course, but I don't get massages. What's in the oil?"

"Oh, you'll have to get a massage from Karen. She has oil for stress and one for creativity and other stuff. I asked her to make a batch for me that would work as a love potion, an aphrodisiac thing. It's what you smell now."

She jumped up. "Come in the house, I'll show you something."

He followed her with caution, wondering if it could be true. Could he have been affected by a love potion? If so it would be the most ridiculous thing that had ever happened to him.

"Terri, did you have that oil on the porch Sunday afternoon? When you and I—"

"Sure I did. It works every time. C'mere." She led him to her bedroom.

The room was smallish, with a high ceiling and big windows. A four-poster bed took up much of the room.

Terri pointed to a silver appliance on the floor. "That's a diffuser. I put my oil in it and it heats up and blows all around the room. The oil is a mixture of secret ingredients, but mostly it's made from ylang-ylang." She flipped a switch on the diffuser.

"Ylang-ylang?"

"It means flower of flowers. Comes from Asia. Just stand here a minute with your eyes closed and breathe through your nose."

He did as instructed but smelled little. He was about to say so when his mind filled with visions of naked women running through flowers. In a blink, he visualized the hole in Terri's jeans and the pink skin. He opened his eyes and shook his head. He had to stop this.

"Maybe it does work," he said.

"What were you thinking of?" she crooned at him, as she stepped over to him and put a finger through one of his front belt loops.

He looked down at her, at her hair, her throat, her wet lips, her glazed-over eyes. It was a moment of truth. Would he talk or would he act? He chose to talk.

He unhooked her finger from him and edged toward the door. "Well, I was thinking of women running around nude." He smiled. "Have you ever used the oil on Eli?"

"Nooo. I don't even allow him in the bedroom. It doesn't work on his type is what Karen said."

They leaned inside the bedroom doorframe, facing each other. She said, "I haven't forgotten our agreement, but I had a dream about you last night. You were making love in a field of flowers. Have you ever done that?"

This was more than he could handle. He stood up straight.

"Have you been spying on me, Terri?"

She cringed. "No, I—"

Just then, they heard the gunning of an engine near the top of the road, the churning of gravel. Terri sprang from his grip and ran to the front window.

"Damn! It's Eli! How in the hell does he know when to come up here and bust up our get-togethers? Hurry up and sit down in a chair or something here in the living room. Let's tell him you're here to pick up the boys to go fishing. That s-o-b!"

Eli burst through the door, but stopped short, finding McGregor and Terri chatting quietly in the living room, drinking their tea.

Terri scolded him, "Eli, don't you know how to knock?" She went over to peck him on the cheek and punch his big arm. "You should call me first."

Eli was red-faced and sweating. "Oh, sorry, Hon, I guess I wasn't thinking. Sorry, Bob. How are you? I don't know what I'm doing sometimes, Terri. I get so worked up when I'm not with you. I guess I just had to see you all of a sudden. What can I say?"

"Oh, don't say anything, you big boob! Let me get you a glass. Have some iced tea. Settle down. Bob was hoping to get the boys to go fishing today over at Poteet's, but they're out running around somewhere."

She left them, and Eli sat down to squirm and grin.

McGregor decided to let Eli speak first. Finally, the man said, "So, Bob, why didn't you call first about the boys? Oh, never mind. What have you been up to? I mean, you know, how's it going?"

"Fine, just fine. Did you see my new red truck outside?"

Terri walked through the room on the way to the tea pitcher. Eli's eyes followed her in fascination. He rambled on about trucks, how red was the best color for a pickup and how he was sick of orange trucks and wished he had a red one.

McGregor wasn't going to leave immediately as he'd done before. He wanted to size up this man, let him talk. Besides, another theory was forming in his mind, based on a history book he'd once read about military roads and signal flags in the days before the wire telegraph.

McGregor asked, "So, Eli, I've been wondering where your office is. Do you operate out of Finneyville or Calvin Station?"

"Have the main one in Finneyville, but I go to the one at the old quarry there south of Calvin Station some days. Why?"

"Just thought I'd get together with you soon, talk about the old roads and such. For my book."

Terri's shock at Eli's arrival was changing to anger. McGregor saw it on her face and it wasn't pretty.

She asked Eli, "You were at the quarry today, weren't you sweetie? I thought you had to work all day on those old Bobcat earth movers you bought." Terri must have sensed Eli was vulnerable and decided to pounce on him. "What's the real reason you came up here right now? Has something happened I need to know about?"

Eli replied with a blank face. "No, the Bobcats are up and running. They're old as the hills but run pretty good. Dangerous as hell, if you don't know what you're doing. Then I, well, I just wanted to see you, that's all."

Terri bristled even more at the obvious lie. She said, "Well, I'm tired. I'm sorry if I sound mean, but why don't you invite Bob to the office now. I think I want to be alone!"

McGregor and the startled Eli watched as she stomped to her bedroom and slammed the door.

Eli said, "Women! Let's go, Bob. But not to the office, not today. Have other things to do"

Outside, Eli said, "I'll follow you down the road. By the way, you read this morning's newspaper yet?"

"No, I just had fishing on my mind. Didn't want it cluttered with the news. Why?"

"Why? Because Roland's on the front page talking about getting out of politics. Paper says Grooms is backing out of the race. You tell Roland I said it's about time! I got a call from Red Wiley first thing this morning. Says the money will be freed up to re-work the Offshoot, if that's what I want to do. Said he thought it'd be a good idea. You've met him, I assume. Pushy bastard!"

"Eli, I had a thought. Why don't you come over to Poteet's house? Tell him yourself what you think about the newspaper story. Y'all need to get back to your friendly ways. If you're going to repair the road now that the money's there, no reason why you can't mend fences."

Eli looked stymied. He stared hard at the ground and his voice changed to a low growl. "I don't believe it's a good idea right now. Just leave it at that for the time being."

He climbed into his work truck and backed up. With his thumb he motioned McGregor to get going in front of him.

McGregor took his time maneuvering the new truck downhill through the ruts. Eli stayed on his tailgate. In the rear view mirror, Eli's face grinned at him. At first glance, the full-faced grin looked hard, malevolent. At next glance, though, the same grin looked friendly.

McGregor thought if the situation were reversed, would he be buying Terri's limp excuses for her keeping company with Eli? Answer: Hell no! So Eli might do something foolish to stop him from seeing Terri again. What might that be?

At the Offshoot, Eli turned toward Calvin Station and McGregor turned toward Sweetwater. Watching Eli fade away in the mirror, McGregor punched in Terri's phone number.

"Terri? Bob. Sorry if I upset you. You okay?"

"Yeah. You didn't upset me. I just had to get away from Eli and his questions."

"I've had a second thought about your question to me before Eli came. Love in the flowers? It was Amon who spied on me last night in the meadow, wasn't it? And he told you about it, right?"

"Yeah. I was just going to play a joke on you. Why did you get so mad?"

"I got rattled. I'm sorry. You said you remembered our agreement and I have it in mind also. But I want you to know I love that ylang-ylang. And, I wanted to warn you. I don't think Eli's buying our excuses. Is he the kind of man to get violent if he's jealous?"

"Eli, violent? Never. He's just a big old lug. I know his ex-wife. Never laid a finger on her. I asked her because Eli's so big and all. The only time she ever saw him mad was when he talked about Amon or politics. Now he can *talk* real ugly, like I told you."

McGregor knew it was an ambush, but he decided to do it. "Terri. Tell me if this is too personal. But Lakisha Thompson told us about you having an affair with Sheriff Buell. How about him? Is he the violent type if he's jealous?"

After a pause, Terri said weakly, "I guess I failed to mention that item. We'll have to talk about it sometime." Then, out of left field, she said, "Can I come over to Mr. Poteet's if we're going to keep talking?"

McGregor thought about the soundproofed study. It might be best to see Terri away from her ylang-ylang from now on. "Sure," he said. "How about late this afternoon?" By meeting her in Hood's presence, he might be able to free his mind of her sexuality. It sounded right.

Terri said, "I'll have the boys fend for themselves for supper and drive over," she said. "About four?"

As McGregor curved around the driveway pothole at Poteet's, he was reevaluating having Terri and Hood in the same room. His phone rang.

"McGregor? Tipsy Alcorn here. Roland gave me your number. Say, I'm in a rush but thought you'd like to know. Eli Rust just called me with a bunch of questions about you and Janet. Wanted to know if y'all were married was the main thing. Truth is, I don't know, but I told him I didn't think so. You aren't, are you?"

"No, Tipsy, we're not married. What else did he want to know?"

As he spoke the question, McGregor arrived at the front porch. Tomás was loading Hood's suitcases into her truck. Good God, he thought, she's found out about Terri and she's cutting out!

Tipsy was saying, "Nothing else, really. He beat around the bush, talking about Grooms dropping out of the race, but I could tell this marriage thing was the real reason he called. … You there?"

"Sorry, Tipsy. Have to go. Thanks for the heads up."

"Tomás!" he yelled. "What's going on?"

"All hell broke loose down at Hood's business in Alabama," Tomás shouted back. "She's been firebombed! You better go in and talk to her. She's been on the phone for an hour—ordered me to pack her stuff for her and load up."

McGregor rushed into the house. Hood was upstairs in Poteet's bedroom, standing in front of a computer console. She had her cell on one ear and Poteet's desk phone on the other. She acknowledged him with a sharp nod toward Poteet's list of received emails.

"Okay," she was saying, "I'm waiting."

An email popped up and when she opened it there appeared a drawing of a man's face, a man who looked a whole lot like the Manskar man.

"Got it, Sergeant. Thanks." She hung up the cell and punched the computer's print button. Into the other phone, she said, "Poteet? Yeah. Looks like the Manskar man! Listen, McGregor just walked in. Let me go so I can talk to him. See you in a minute."

Hood lunged into McGregor's arms. "Oh my God, Lumpkins. It's a mess!"

Her shop had called her with the news that her office in the front of the garage had been torched that morning. When the workers arrived the place was already ablaze. The cars were untouched, but her office was history. A homeless person, sober and sleeping in one of Hood's unused work trucks outside the shop had given the cops a good description of a man who had run from the building. The police artist created the drawing.

"McGregor, what are we going to do? The Manskar man bombed me!"

McGregor's training took over. He settled Hood down on Poteet's bed, urging her gently to calm herself. "We'll get you down there immediately. If the fire's out and it's just the office, stuff there can be replaced. Maybe it's not going to be as bad as you think."

Hood started to shake. McGregor hugged her until she struggled from his arms and ran to the bathroom. He heard vomiting noises.

After a few minutes it grew quiet, and then McGregor heard the shower running. He found a robe in Poteet's closet for Hood and put it inside the bathroom on a hook. While he waited for her, he stared at the police artist's sketch. After college once, Hood went through a phase using five-dollar words when she'd said, "Nobody defiles Janet Hood with impunity." Ever how it was said, the meaning was clear, and it was true. He planned his next moves.

Hood came out of the bathroom wearing the robe, went to her room and dressed. McGregor pocketed Poteet's .45 and with Tomás they all waited for Poteet, silently collecting their thoughts.

When Poteet arrived he introduced them to his new personal bodyguard, the man who had guarded him at the hospital. Tomás took him outside for a briefing.

Sealed in the study, the Sweetwater crew of three went over the known details of the attack on All Hood's Cars. Then Poteet fired off a list of his day's developments.

He had shipped the paintings to Mathis from Finneyville, where he'd run into several Firstplacers around town. The whole county was abuzz from the news contained in Poteet's newspaper article. The Firstplacers were holding an emergency session today at the Emporium to revamp the tomato festival, now that the growers would be supporting it.

Sheriff had Poteet in for a joint interview with Leslie to go over every tiny detail surrounding the murder. Leslie had coolly admitted touching several tapes, having forgotten about it because of how brutally she'd been hustled off to jail and questioned. Sheriff's few leads weren't taking him anywhere. The state's investigator had been called to another case.

Poteet said, "Outside Sheriff's office, Leslie told me that she knows about Ethan, the clerk, giving us the picture of the Manskar man and said she hadn't brought it up with Sheriff and Red, she was still so mad at them.

"Eli is holding a press conference today at four o'clock sharp in Finneyville to announce he's starting work tomorrow on the Offshoot pavement.

"But I saved the big news for last. I stopped by to see Ethan. The Manskar man was at the hotel on May fifteenth and again on June fifteenth. Get this! On May fifteenth, Sheriff was there, staying in one of those top floor suites with his wife, one of the suites that Clyde had bugged. Suppose Clyde got Sheriff and the Manskar man on tape?"

McGregor said, "And the timing would be right on June fifteenth for that meeting Poker had with the Manskar man. We have to tell Sheriff about the picture Ethan gave us and the police sketch, but we must do it carefully."

It was time for McGregor to outline his plan of action. First, he'd hire Tomás to drive Hood to Montgomery and help her check out the situation there. As soon as he could get over to the Tomato Emporium, he'd get a firm identification of the sketch from Poker. Then he would hunker down in the study here and choose the most likely suspect for the Tomato Boy murder. He'd work that suspect up one side and down the other. If he met a dead end, he'd start over on the next most likely. That was how he'd cracked car theft rings; that would be how he'd crack this case.

Hood said, "As far as I'm concerned, McGregor, you work for me as well as for Poteet. Work openly, Sheriff and Red be damned. Don't hire Tomás. I'll pay him to drive me to Montgomery and stay with me as a bodyguard. As soon as I persuade him to go, we'll leave. We'll report by phone when we get to Montgomery. Should be about six hours from now.

As Hood edged to the door, she shouted, "You two get together tonight and sort out all this stuff! Stay up all night if you have to, but make a plan and make it good! This shit is serious! The Manskar man messed with my cars and I want him bad! If y'all don't get him, I will!"

It was noon when they stepped to the front porch for Hood and Tomás to depart. The sky was dark with imminent rain. As Tomás affixed a tarp to the truck bed, McGregor clung to Hood until Hood pushed him away. He was worried for her; suddenly afraid he might never see her again.

McGregor drove to the Tomato Emporium with Poteet and his muscled guard as passengers. Poteet would retrieve the Chevy following the Firstplacers Club meeting, which might continue until early evening. McGregor was parking when the rain started in a hard downpour.

Mama was running around in a flutter, trying to seat the many unexpected Firstplacers. Shaking umbrellas and shedding hot raincoats, they expressed worry about the weather and how the rain might affect the tomato crop if it kept up when early July was supposed to be much drier. Poteet and his muscle joined them.

Mama made room for McGregor in her tiny office. She handed him a book—a Clayton Calvin journal. She offered him a pair of white cotton gloves and said, "Take a look, Bobby, and have fun."

"May I see Poker for a quick question or two?" he asked.

"I'll send him in as soon as he gets his chores done. About half an hour."

She hugged him and left. Through the partly open tomato tapestry, McGregor counted around thirty persons, all of them demanding lunch.

He sat in Mama's desk chair and carefully opened Clayton Calvin's Journal Number One, but he couldn't stop thinking of Hood. He called her.

She said Tomás had talked to Carlos. The sheriff's office was in turmoil over the investigation. Carlos had suggested to Sheriff that he change his mind and bring

McGregor in on all the details of the murder, but Sheriff had vetoed it.

With Hood off his mind temporarily, McGregor erased the clutter in his head for an examination of Clayton's journal. The cover was soft brown leather with gold tooling as a border. The headband on the ribbed spine was a bit loose from age so that McGregor could peek in to see the hand-sown binding. The pages showed little aging, and the attached green marker ribbon was pressed between the last two pages. But the book fell open to its third page where two loose sheets were tucked. The papers were a copy of the Tennessee private act establishing Calvin County, dated the tenth day of October "in the Year of our Lord, being One Thousand Eight Hundred Twenty Seven." It was signed "Sam Houston, governor." McGregor knew that before Houston went to Texas, he was governor of Tennessee, about the time Andy Jackson was elected president.

The journal contained neat, almost delicate handwriting with wide margins. In the middle of a sentence near the top of page three, the word "telegraph" popped out at McGregor. Clayton Calvin had written the entry back in the spring of 1827, five months before the county was formed.

McGregor felt goose pimples as he read:

"Rained hard for third day. When I most need my telegraph, flags are useless, for the Military Cut is in deepest fog! Few horseback stewards arrived at parade veranda this morning. Stewards in attendance reported mush on roads. Travel near impossible! My Second Jackson Man may well be bogged down or lost to a sinkhole. I await his arrival with trepidation. Most recent Letter from Scd. J. M. proved he had little faith in my discovering identity of the Murderer of First Jackson Man last month. I will produce that Coward for hanging or Will Refuse Office of Sheriff of new county!!"

With fascination, McGregor eagerly read on. In a digression from the day's events, Clayton expounded that because of his position as master of the Calvin House, he was a "funnel for local gossip and tidings of all sorts."

His stewards had polled the men who would populate the new Calvin County with the result calculated as:

"… the ultimate and natural desire of my constituents, soon to be, is that we go forth as one, quite apart from this Manskar ilk of avaricious men, who have not the backbones of slugs!"

The next day's entry was short:

"Was Dry Today. Several stewards were able to appear at parade veranda, telling me my Second Jackson Man is on the move! But appears weary."

McGregor read and re-read the following day's much longer report, with the hair on his neck rising:

"A Steward arrived parade veranda late—carrying distressing word of import. Jackson Man stopped over at Manskar Court H. Conferred with Sheriff Halfacre. Stwd. had 'a special servant' lend the ear. Halfacre ordered extra whisky. Halfacre asserted he will find killer by haling in the men of the county for questions, one and all, if necessary. Simpleton! How crude. Also Halfacre desires Jackson Man to force me to accept Halfacre's men to cut my new roads. Ho! Had assurance from Halfacre of no interference from Manskar when Calvin County established. This is brazen deception from an old friend! THEY will NOT control my county! The first Manskar sawyer to cross the Big Turkey with a blade, I will hang! I have my own sawyers and will build my road to suit me and me alone. I now await my Second Jackson Man with my wits sharpened."

Calvin skipped two days' entries before picking up the story:

"… underneath the Great London Chandelier, I attenuated the Jackson Man with several pulls from my best jug and by my soft wit and unrivaled charm. He spoke freely. Halfacre's hidden animus toward me was fostered by my short dalliance last year with his new wife. Perhaps his antipathy is justified.

"I explained to the Jackson M. that I have in my possession the musket ball that shattered the skull of his predecessor as the poor man sat in a chair under the same Chandelier then hanging above us. I acquainted him of my discoveries of late. That ball is of military origin. It is stamped with the mark of the Manskar Foundry and it must have come to us in the delivery of a gross of balls to the Calvin Station Militia depot on 2 April, present year. Our killer is, thus, a local man with authority to enter our depot. I have that authority of entry as Captain of the Militia. Four other men have the authority of entry. I am not the killer. The killer, thus, is most probably one of those four men!! The Jackson M. was properly impressed by the logic. On matter of roads, he assures me he will back me fully over Halfacre and his Manskar road men. I will be the most Powerful Man in my Calvin County!!"

The tale of old-fashioned power politics caused McGregor to generate a brand new theory, all about present-day power politics. *Control* of the coming development was one of the keys. In a county such as Calvin, the sheriff, in 1827, was then and was today the single most powerful county official. In two years time under the new law, that hat would be passed to the county mayor. McGregor needed more intelligence on the background of Calvin County Sheriff Harris Buell and his connection to Manskar County.

He stared at the fascinating journal and became anxious to see Terri for what she might reveal about Sheriff. But damn it! Hood would not be there. Could he control himself in Terri's presence without Hood?

"Mama said you wanted to see me!"

McGregor jumped. He looked up to find that Poker had walked in and seated himself. Shaken a bit, McGregor removed his gloves, put them and the journal into the plastic holder and wiped his face with a handkerchief.

"Hey, Poker. I won't keep you long. I know you're busy and I'm busy." Although Poker was wearing more of his new wardrobe, he looked disheveled. His hair was in a tangle; he was unshaven, his face gray.

"Are you all right?" McGregor asked. "You look ill at ease. Relax."

Poker leaned his chair back on two legs against the wall. "I'm fine. You're the one that looks weird. What do you want?"

McGregor decided the quicker the better. "Does Amon ever use a telephone?"

"Naw. Hates them."

"Do you know anything about Amon using some sort of signaling system to communicate with Eli Rust?"

"Yeah, he uses a bunch of stupid flags. Eli says it helps to keep Amon's mind busy. Keep him out of trouble. Now is that all?" Clearly, he wanted to leave.

"Just a couple of more things. Now, this question's personal, so you don't have to answer, but I am leading up to something important. How many times were you with Terri on her porch in, shall I say, a romantic situation?"

"First, tell me why you want to know. You sweet on her?" Poker's color had returned to his face and he leered at McGregor.

"No, I'm not sweet on her. But I'll tell you why I want to know. Amon saw you two on the porch at least once!"

That brought tomato red to Poker's face. "That sorry shit! How do you know that?"

"Leslie said so. That day she drove up in her orange truck we talked about, she saw Amon lurking in the woods watching. So, how many times?"

"Just the once. Terri said she was sweet on the Tomato Boy and would never do it again."

"How did that make you feel toward the Tomato Boy?"

Poker slammed down his chair and rose halfway out of it. "Bob, gonna say this one time and one time only. I didn't kill the Tomato Boy! I know that's what you're getting at. And I don't like it one damn bit!"

"Okay, okay. So what are you going to do now that you know Amon saw you?"

Poker squeezed back into his chair. "That's for me to know and you to find out!"

McGregor quickly changed the topic. "Let's cut to the time you and Amon were hiding in the restroom at the Calvin House, the day of the murder. Did the Tomato Boy come into the restroom? I've a witness that said he did."

Poker squinted. "I left that part out at the meeting over at Mr. Poteet's. I didn't know if y'all were going to turn me in or not. But, yeah, he did come in. Amon went out of the stall to talk to him and mumbled something. The Tomato Boy said, 'I'm going to my room now. It's after six o'clock.' Said it like he expected us to follow him."

"Is that when Amon couldn't take the smell anymore and left?"

Poker hung his head. "Yeah. It sure does make it seem like ol' Amon did the killing, don't it?"

"Points in that direction. And I'm suspicious that there's more of a connection between the Manskar man and Amon than you might know. Would June fifteenth be about the date you and the Manskar man met at the Calvin House?"

Poker thought about it and nodded. "Yeah, about then."

"Now, look at this. Do you recognize this man?" McGregor held up the artist's sketch of Hood's fire bomber. He didn't want Poker to know of the hotel photo yet.

Poker took the sketch. "This looks a lot like the Manskar man. Sure does. Where did you get it?"

"It's a police artist's conception of a man who fire bombed Janet's business down in Montgomery this morning. Did you know she had a car restoration business down there?"

"Yeah, Mama told me. So what happened? Anybody hurt? Janet okay?"

McGregor was pleased Poker was showing some human concern. He gave Poker the few details he knew.

"That man is bad news!" Poker jumped up. "It's after two o'clock here, after five someplace. I'm going to go get us a couple of Potions."

Alone, McGregor mulled over his next move. He didn't want to unleash Poker on Amon. But it might be the only way to get Amon talking. Amon Trussell, McGregor was beginning to suspect, really was a sorry shit. Regardless of the man's disability, McGregor could develop no sympathy toward the sneak. Unless Amon's lurking was just his way of protecting Terri. He could understand that, and if true he would change his opinion.

Poker came back with two giant mugs. He drained half of his and lit a cigarette. He turned over Mama's "No Smoking" sign and used it as an ashtray. McGregor, grinning, accepted an offer of a cigarette. They smoked and drank. McGregor waited for Poker to say something.

"Bob," Poker said. "I want to ask you something. You for real? You on my side like Mama says you are? Or, you just a fancy-pants lawyer jerking my chain?"

McGregor thought quickly. His answer had to be persuasive. If Poker would open up, this murder could be solved.

He picked up his glass of beer and drained it in several swallows. He crashed the mug down on Mama's desk, making Poker jerk backward.

Leaning over the desk, he stared Poker straight in the eye. "Poker, I promise I'm leveling with you and I'm on your side. Do you promise to level with me? And I mean you give me everything?"

Poker grinned and finished off his beer. He carefully removed the paraphernalia from Mama's desk. Scooting to the edge of his chair, he put his left elbow on the desk. "Arm wrestle me, Bob."

McGregor put his good arm up and connected thumbs with the big boy. They each clutched an edge of the desk with their free hands. Poker counted to three.

After breaking his wrist, McGregor had purposely added strength to his left arm by lifting more weights than usual. He'd put up a good fight.

As he realized he wouldn't be able to put McGregor down right away, Poker's grin faded to an ugly frown. McGregor called on all his reserves to maintain the illusion that he thought he could win. With his broken wrist hurting like hell pulling on the desk's edge, he strained as hard as he could. Poker applied more pressure. McGregor's face bulged as he clamped his teeth even harder. Poker slowly moved McGregor's arm toward the desktop, but no more than half-way. McGregor groaned loudly. He could no longer breathe. Poker gulped a breath and with a loud shout and a monstrous heave, put McGregor flat on the desk.

They sat back in their chairs, McGregor limp as a rag, Poker heaving in laughter with great har-har's.

Mama rushed through the doorway. "What's the damn racket in here? What's happening?"

Others peeked into the office. McGregor couldn't talk at first. Then finally, he said, "Mama, get us more beer! I think Poker and I have come to terms."

Poker jumped up. "I'll get 'em." He growled at the onlookers, who scurried away.

Mama sat on the desk looking at McGregor. "Poker arm wrestled you, didn't he, son?"

McGregor nodded. His right arm hurt, but his left arm had hardly any feeling.

Mama said, "That's a real good sign!"

He motioned with his head for Mama to look at the sketch of the Manskar man down on the floor. He told her the situation. Mama immediately phoned Hood. As she spoke, she ducked outside the office.

Poker came back with more beer and held the mug to McGregor's lips for him to drink. "You got some grit in you, Bob! Now, it's time to swap punches. I'll go first." He grinned when McGregor moaned. "Just kiddin.' Here, drink some more."

McGregor's left arm quickly returned to near normal, but he pretended he still couldn't move it so that Poker would continue ministering to him. Though much of this battle of brawn was for show, as far as McGregor was concerned, he had to admit that it made him think better of Poker again. Poker could well be the genuine article.

He persuaded Poker to agree to a full interview, during which they would go over Poker's activities in detail. Poker set the meeting for his next day off, Thursday, in the morning out in the junkyard where they'd have privacy.

Then Poker escorted him to the front veranda. McGregor flexed his left arm and Poker grabbed it and started gruffly massaging it with a few twists.

"You got a good arm there, Bob! Here's how to make the feeling come back." He slugged McGregor's shoulder hard with a friendly fist.

McGregor dove into the rain.

CHAPTER 19

It was a difficult drive back to Sweetwater. Out of one torrent of rain, he would hit another. His intuition fired at him from all sides, telling him to find a way to apply what he'd learned from Sheriff Clayton Calvin's journal to his investigation. But the rain bested him. He focused on the slapping windshield wipers and the edge of the road. And Terri and Poker on the porch.

Parked in front of the Sweetwater porch, he stayed in the truck hoping for a break in the storm. The unguarded house surrounded by water-heavy mist and fog looked grim and unfriendly. He kept the engine running and with it the air conditioner. It was a little after three o'clock, so he had close to an hour before Terri would arrive and Lakisha would show up for duty.

He forced his brain back into operation. How should he question Terri? It was a delicate matter asking someone about an old love affair. With Hood gone, he thought seriously about rescheduling Terri. But Terri had the boys to consider. He shouldn't expect her to change plans just because he was afraid of being alone with her. The determining factor was that Eli would be at his four o'clock press conference. The timing could not be better.

A horn beeped behind him. It was Lakisha coming in early.

Together, they went into the house and checked it room by room. After McGregor changed into dry clothes, they sat in the kitchen and he told her of Terri's imminent visit and his intent to conduct the interview in the study.

"You going to shut yourself up in that room with a vamp like Terri Williams?" Lakisha asked. "You crazy! You want me in there to guard you, don't you?"

McGregor huffed, "She's not a vamp. And I can take care of myself, thank you."

The doorbell rang and Lakisha ran in front of him to answer it. Terri came in with no umbrella or coat, not soaking wet, but wet. McGregor found her a large towel in the laundry room, and they left Lakisha unsuccessfully shielding a big grin with her hand. McGregor closed the study door.

"Have a seat, Terri. May I offer you a drink? I can make coffee, if you're chilled."

"Let me think about it," she said with a smile. She cocked her damp head to one side, wrapped herself in the towel, and sat down. McGregor thought of her having wet hair the first time he'd seen her on her porch.

"Where's your friend?" Terri asked. "It's Janice, right?"

"Janet. She had to return home. Some pressing business matters." His stomach knotted up at his mention of the name.

McGregor busied himself adjusting the air controls to a higher temperature for Terri, though his own face was beginning to burn and the closed up room was suddenly stuffy. Then he pointed to the refrigerator and looked at her.

Terri said brightly, "I'd like tequila but I'd better stick to Coke. I bet the growers are beginning to fret with all this rain. It's supposed to be dry the first part of July."

McGregor found no Coke or other soft drink. He decided on the real thing.

"Let's have a short bourbon," he croaked. Clinking ice and pouring, he stammered, "I ... I wanted to get some details from you." As he handed her the drink Terri met his gaze with expectant eyes. Luminous, translucent eyes. He was sure he could see her thoughts.

McGregor found a seat in Poteet's recliner opposite Terri. "You didn't bring any of that ylang-ylang with you, I hope. God, Terri, I feel like a kid on a first date, all of a sudden. You have that effect on me, somehow. Let's just have our drink and chat for a moment. Then I do have some serious questions."

He lit one of Poteet's cigarettes and Terri put her fingers up to her lips, signaling she would like one. He lit it for her in his lips and handed it over. They puffed in silence and drank. Terri shivered and pulled the towel more protectively around her. Was she afraid of him? Did he look like a Celt, ready to jump her? He felt foolish.

Terri shivered again. But this time she couldn't stop. McGregor jumped, put his drink aside and crushed his smoke. Without thinking about what he was doing, he motioned her to come to him. She stood, stubbed out her own cigarette and gulped the last of her drink. She scooted onto his lap and wrapped the towel around both their heads. In the towel darkness she kissed him hard.

With long breaths, McGregor smelled her wet hair, her wet clothes. His body's response to the olfactory sensations was instantaneous. His nose was on her neck when he felt awareness of the outside world slip away. Outside was outside and he was inside. The chair, already reclined, toppled over backward from their weight. And they fell to the floor, groping one another and tearing off clothes.

When it was over they lay still. McGregor searched his mind for the equanimity he believed he should have. It wasn't there. He said, "No regrets, but this has to be—"

"I know, babe. We have to quit. From now on, I'm going to be one woman for one man! Eli is generous to the boys and they like him, and I ... well, I like him. But I want you to always be my friend. I don't have many friends, you know."

Her candor touched him. "We'll be friends," he said. "Always."

They were dressed and standing near the bar with fresh drinks when Terri brushed her hair with her fingers, put her chin up and said, "Hey. You want to know about Sheriff and me, don't you?"

"Yeah. I do, and if you don't mind telling me the more personal details, I assure you I'll keep your confidence."

They sat together on the sofa.

She said, "I'll tell you what I know. Sheriff is married to the county mayor's daughter. She stuck by him back in the high school days when a girl accused him of hitting her and he got in trouble. So I don't think he'd ever leave his wife, just for that. Just about everybody at the time believed the girl's version. His wife is pretty well connected in Finneyville—and he has a big fear of not being connected. Family connections kept him from being expelled from school. So that's Sheriff in a nutshell.

"Some months after he was elected he came to my house one day investigating a fight between Amon and Poker. That day, I'd put my ylang-ylang mixture in my candles out on the porch for the first time. On a whim, I decided to try it out just for fun, I guess. Well, it was a hot day and he … it was like he just melted!"

"Melted?" McGregor asked. "He melted … on your porch?"

"Do you want those kinds of details?"

"No. I guess not."

"Okay. We started meeting in those fancy Calvin House suites, and he made me bring my aromatherapy diffuser each time. It was weird, like he became addicted to my oil. I fell for him and wanted him to get a divorce, but he never would. We went off and on, off and on, for months. I was always scared that somebody might find out about us. Lakisha Thompson did find out. And then Clyde, he found out somehow. Never knew how. Clyde put some moves on me one night at the Calvin House as I went sneaking out the back after meeting Sheriff. Moves, and then ... you know.

"This was just a few weeks ago and Clyde had just announced that he'd run for county mayor in two years, like I already told you. I hate to say this, because really I'm not a mean person. But I was tired of having to sneak around with Sheriff, and I told him goodbye; that it was over. Sheriff was ... heavy-handed. Clyde was romantic. Clyde was fire and ice, fire and ice. I was off balance and ... excited. I wanted to be around him all the time. Anyway, for some ungodly reason, I told Sheriff how I felt about Clyde.

"Now, Bob. Nobody knows that I know what I'm about to say. When I told Sheriff about Clyde—the afternoon I said goodbye to him—we were sitting in his patrol car in the parking lot of the Calvin House. And wouldn't you know it, Clyde walked out of the hotel to the pool house. He didn't see us, and Sheriff yelled to him in a fit of anger and jumped out to go talk to him in front of the car. They were some distance away, and I could tell they didn't think I could hear them, me being closed up in the car with the air blowing. Sheriff warned Clyde to stay away from me. Clyde warned him right back that he would mail something. I heard the word, but it wasn't plain. Gonna mail this something to the newspaper! Sheriff threatened to pistol whip Clyde, and he put his hand on his pistol and unhooked that little snap button. Clyde saw him do it and just laughed. Then Clyde waved to me and took off. Sheriff yelled after him that he'd get him.

"Sheriff drove me home, and I pretended I hadn't heard anything. He hasn't spoken to me since. I never asked Clyde what he had on Sheriff because he didn't know I'd overheard them. I think he suspected it, though. Anyway, Clyde dumped *me* a while after that."

McGregor pulled out the police sketch of the Manskar man and asked Terri if she'd ever seen him.

"Yeah, he's the guy that came to talk to Amon not long ago. Then Poker came over, and they went without me to Amon's place. Amon told me later that he'd been in another fight with Poker. Had something to do with this man, but Amon wouldn't say what. I'll tell you one thing. This guy scared me to death. I got mad at Poker because I thought Poker was the one who tangled up Amon with the guy. I do know that it had something to do with trucks. Sounds silly, but that's all I could get out of Amon about it. Who is he?"

"We don't know. But I believe he's tied to the murder somehow. You know of any connection between this man and Sheriff?"

"Nooo."

"Reason I ask is that this man was at the Calvin House on the same night Sheriff was staying there with his wife in a suite. Last May; on the fifteenth."

"May the fifteenth? That was my birthday! Sheriff was supposed to meet me that night for a celebration. He told me he was called out on business and couldn't meet me. That sucks! Damn, I hate him! You say he was with his wife?"

"I think Clyde had a tape recording of Sheriff with something on it that would hurt him badly, and Clyde threatened to reveal the tape. Now, if that's true—and it's still a big if—do you think Sheriff would stoop to murder to get hold of the tape? Think hard, because your answer is important."

Terri replied, her tone hard and menacing, "If it had anything to do with his *precious* wife, he'd do it."

McGregor switched to the thornier issue. He strained to keep his voice level. "Leslie said she drove to your house one day in an orange truck. That's the reason I asked about that truck at your house this morning. Leslie said when she drove up to your porch she caught you and Poker having sex."

Terri jerked to the other end of the sofa. She eyed McGregor hard, lit a cigarette and stutter-stepped to the bar where she mixed a heavy drink. After sloshing down half of it she turned back to reveal a tear running down her face. She puffed hard, and then dropped the cigarette in the sink.

"Has Poker said anything to you about that day?" she asked.

"He said y'all were together once on the porch, but you told him you were with the Tomato Boy, so it could never happen again."

"Damn that Poker! It's true that we were on the porch when Leslie drove up. But if I know Poker, he exaggerated the rest of what he told you. We never did anything!"

McGregor sighed with relief and slumped, resting his head on the sofa back and hoping he could make himself believer her.

"It was a hot Saturday, first hot day of the year. The boys were gone for the day and I didn't see Amon up in his perch. I decided to sunbathe on the floor of the porch where the sun would reach my entire body if I stretched out. I had on a bikini and I took the top off to put lotion on. My ylang-ylang concoction put me right to sleep. I was on my tummy and didn't hear Poker at first. Later, he told me that his truck had conked out down my road a ways and that he left it in a turn-around spot off the road where he and Amon go a lot of times. And he just walked up to the house and found me lying there. Anyway, I woke up but only about half-way, you know, and turned over before I knew what I was doing. I was still real dreamy. And he was kneeling beside me with his shirt off! He was all sweaty, and he fell over on top of me."

Terri blushed and swigged more of her drink. "I don't know how to say this without embarrassing myself. But Poker, he did it ... well, you know what I'm saying! He never even unzipped his pants or anything, you know what I mean? I don't think he had been with a woman for quite some time.

"I was completely awake by then. You can believe that! I was pushing Poker off me when we heard Leslie drive into the clearing from the road. She drove up all the way to the porch, and you know how high the porch is. Well, she just sat down there in her truck staring up at us, then turned around and started driving away. I called to her, but she didn't return, just yelled something back at me. Then, she wouldn't talk to me after that. From her view of us down in her truck looking up, she probably thought we were both naked.

"I really didn't blame Poker that much for what he tried to do. But I didn't tell him that. I told him to keep it quiet, that the Tomato Boy must never find out what he'd done. As far as I know, Clyde never did. I was afraid of what he might do to Poker, you know. One thing, though, see how pale I am? I haven't sunbathed since then."

"Okay," McGregor said, "believe me. I'm beginning to understand the mixed-up sentiments and opinions a person can have about Poker." Still, he hated the idea of Poker even touching Terri. But to press on, he had to shake off the vision. What he was about to reveal would hurt her.

He asked, "Did you know that Leslie, at one point, had her eye on Eli? That Eli wouldn't go for her, at least openly, because he was secretly attracted to you? That Eli suspected you and Poker had a thing going, believing that Poker was always coming up your hill to visit you under the guise of seeing Amon? And, that Leslie told both Eli and Clyde about you and Poker?"

Terri's mouth fell open. "That bitch!" she screamed, and she burst into tears.

Then she grabbed her stomach and vomited on the floor where she stood. When she fell to the floor, McGregor ran to her and tried to hold her. Crying and vomiting! First Hood, now Terri.

McGregor's stomach churned from the smell, but he knelt on the floor with Terri and hugged her. He was going to have to learn to be more tactful. He could well have phrased his question differently. It had to be the Poker thing that kept him off kilter.

Terri threw off his arms. She leaned up against the barstool legs. McGregor wet a cloth and gently wiped her face, then started cleaning up the mess on the floor.

"So that's why Clyde quit me!" Terri shouted. "All this secret shit! I hate it. I hate Poker and I hate Amon and I hate Leslie! And I hate you for telling me!"

She fell crying into his arms. McGregor wasn't feeling all that good about himself either.

Terri had been gone more than an hour when Poteet returned home from the Emporium. McGregor, laden with guilt once more, had paced the floor for a time before settling down in the living room to flip through the suspect list in his mind.

Just as he finished telling Poteet the information about Sheriff and Clyde swapping threats and what he'd learned at the Emporium from Poker, Hood called on the phone line in the study. The ideas he'd gleaned from the Clayton Calvin journal had to wait to be discussed. They went in to talk to Hood over the speaker phone.

Hood reported that Tomas was being a great help, taking charge and working with her to create a to-do list. The two of them were safe at Hood's home at present. Tomas was not going to leave her side for a moment, she said.

That last sent a prickle through McGregor. He had a split-second vision of Hood talking on the phone as she sat on Tomas's lap, drinking wine and being tickled by her new lumpkins. "Is he there now?"

"No, he's checking the outside."

McGregor outlined for Hood what he'd just related to Poteet. "Let's not take the time for details, but after I read some of the Clayton Calvin journal today about the old sheriffs around here, I made a conclusory jump. I've come to suspect Sheriff Buell more than the others. It's logical, believe me. And I'll go over it with Poteet in detail."

Hood said firmly, "Okay, y'all put your heads together tonight and see what you come up with. I need to decide how much I tell the local cops here. If I reveal what I know of the Manskar man, they'll contact Sheriff Buell for sure and give it away that we know about this Manskar asshole. Also, Tomás wants to inform Carlos, thinks it would be part of our bargain to do so. What do I do, McGregor?"

"Tomás should go ahead and consult with Carlos and tell Carlos I'll be calling him. I've a plan in mind that I want to bounce off Poteet tonight. To make it work, I'll need Carlos. Don't tell the cops down there about the Manskar man yet. "

Poteet left the study, and McGregor continued, "Take care, Princess. I'll call you tomorrow. If the word of our county officials is any good, they'll start work on the Old Military Offshoot first thing. We'll see. Oh, and Princess, Tomás knows that bodyguarding doesn't literally mean staying side-by-side, right?"

"I'm sure, Lumpkins, that he knows how to perform his duties around the opposite sex. He'll conduct himself as professionally as you did interviewing Terri. Bye."

Hood. McGregor could never get the upper hand.

McGregor and Poteet dined on microwave food, and then hunkered down in the study. McGregor refused the glass of wine Poteet offered him, so Poteet poured one for himself and said, "Give me your ideas, Celt Man. I'll be your sounding board."

"You tell me if I'm being too egocentric," McGregor began, "but the bombing of Hood was calculated to make *me* leave Calvin County. The bombers—plural—wouldn't know Hood well enough to understand she can take care of herself. They figured I'd run to protect my poor, helpless woman. My working premise is that the Manskar man is being managed by someone who would think Hood a weak woman, the type possibly who thinks all women are weak, i.e., Sheriff Buell, Eli Rust, Poker Limbo and maybe Red Wiley. The Manskar man fits the profile of a hired gun.

"But, contrarily, if he is the primary actor then I'd be looking for an accomplice here who would have something to gain by cooperating with him and who could be manipulated by him. That would necessarily include Mama Limbo, Leslie Rion, Poker Limbo, Dimpsey Grooms and Amon Trussell. Let's dispense with that notion first.

"I trust your judgment of Mama. She's crafty but not treacherous. Leslie had a lot to gain by the Tomato Boy's death, but she's young and I believe she would think she'd have more to gain if Clyde lived. I'm convinced Poker can't manage himself, much less help a killer and a bomber manage a conspiracy. Dimpsey could be manipulated as evidenced by your running him for road superintendent. But the Tomato Boy's death would only hurt his chances of election, not help, since you were to get Clyde's support for him. Amon would be utterly unwieldy, undependable.

"Back to my working premise. Mama, Poker or Leslie could have hired the Manskar man, but none has the political clout to back up what he or she might order the man to do. To run the Manskar man, you need the kind of clout that makes you certain you can get away with it. Of the people I know, that leaves Sheriff, Eli and Red.

"Before I get too far afield in my analysis, let me say that yes, I've thought of Terri Williams. But I know her well enough to believe her single vice is persuasive lying. Getting jilted by Clyde was merely part of the game. You win, you lose."

"Who then? Name him. Or her."

"I have to focus on the motive most likely to drive a person to murder and firebombing. Red and Sheriff could well be in a private shootout for the mayor's office. To control the levers of the law well enough to thwart an investigation of the Manskar man, Red would need the total support of Sheriff. But Sheriff wouldn't need Red. Sheriff could do it on his own as the chief law enforcement officer of the county. In other words, Red and Sheriff together would have the necessary clout—or Sheriff alone would have it. Eli Rust wants the mayor's office, but right now he doesn't seem to have half the clout needed to protect the Manskar man. Eli would need to partner with either Red or Sheriff. I don't see that happening.

"But look at Eli closely. No one really likes him except Terri and the boys. Now why not? I believe it's because he possesses a seething, underlying contempt for everybody. You. Dimpsey, Red. Mama disdains him and says other business people do, too. But she told me she was afraid to openly commit to Dimpsey, although she supported him. Why? I think she sees in Eli that same contempt, a prideful righteousness, a controller. Eli committed criminal fraud on Poteet and Johnson. That makes him the only known criminal in the bunch.

"It comes down to Red, Sheriff or Eli. I've only been here a few days so to some extent I have to depend on my gut. Because both you and Hood are in danger—and me— I've got to choose. For now Red is out. He had more to lose than to gain, I'm betting. Between Sheriff and Eli, I pick Eli. My gut says the man is twisted somehow."

Poteet said, with no hesitation, "I pick Sheriff. And Sheriff alone, not with Red. He threatened Clyde over Terri and believes no one knows it. He has the personality to carry through on the threat. With his probable connection to the Manskar County sheriff, or at least the sheriff's office over there, he could find the Manskar man to do his bidding. The Manskar man even gave the Manskar County jail's address when he stayed at the Calvin House; a mistake. Plus, the Manskar County folk want the coming development on their side of the Poplar Mountains. Sheriff as county mayor, not giving a damn about the development because he doesn't want to antagonize the tomato growers, would be well suited to reject the new deal, handing it on a silver platter to Manskar. Whereas Rust would want to keep the development with all its attendant road construction, regardless of how he might try to assuage the growers by denying it. With me so far?"

"Damn good analysis, Poteet. Go on, convince me."

"Sheriff gave nothing more than perfunctory attention to Ethan's offered photo of the Manskar man," Poteet continued. "He knew all about the Poker and Amon Trussell relationship—and thus, how they could be used as patsies. He easily could have slipped the plastic handle under the mat in my Cadillac. And he was at the hotel on the night the Manskar man was there. They could have been taped or at least overheard by Clyde, as they made plans to kill Clyde and set up Poker and Amon for the fall."

McGregor countered, "You're still mired in the development issue and can't see the forest for that particular tree. You boil it down, in the majority of cases, a person murders out of hate or rage. I'm new here. I looked at the forest first, then boiled it down to one tree, the person most likely to possess hate or rage."

Poteet said, "Okay, we agree to disagree. What's your plan?"

McGregor replied, "I want Carlos to arrange a meeting at Amon's shack for Thursday or Friday, depending on the weather. I want Sheriff and Red, Carlos and me there. I want Poker there to prod Amon, to push his buttons. We'll persuade Eli to go by telling him Amon wants him there. If we can goad Amon into talking about the Manskar man, I can spring the photo and the sketch on them all at once. I hope to provoke the guilty party into taking some kind of preemptive action that will reveal him. Let's call it Plan A. What do you think?"

Poteet rose and with formality said, "Well done, Celt Man. Go for it! Fire the next round. The only thing that still haunts me is that I've seen the Manskar man before. I wonder if I was at the Calvin House one of those nights he was there. I wonder if he thinks I saw something I don't even know that I saw and he wants me out of the way, too. You know, my friend, if we jump too far into this crowd, we could find ourselves in deep water."

"I've already been there," McGregor muttered.

CHAPTER 20

By six o'clock on Wednesday morning, McGregor was up, refreshed and ready for action. While he was shaving, Plan A swirled in his head. Soon as it was time, he'd call Carlos.

It had rained intermittently during the night, and the weather forecast said the sunshine this morning would be short lived. Severe thunderstorms were expected, starting mid-day.

Poteet, having consigned his bodyguard to the television in the guest quarter, met McGregor on the deck for coffee where they watched the sun peek out. Poteet had a leg cramp. While he stretched and popped, he complained about not being able to play tennis lately. He feared he no longer had the knees of a twenty-year old.

Poteet dialed Hood for her morning report. McGregor could tell from Poteet's reaction that Tomás answered the call, which caused McGregor to burn his lips on his coffee as a malicious thought crossed his mind. If Hood and Tomás were having an affair, wouldn't that clear the way for Terri and him? Why have such thoughts? The Terri lust had to be over! For a host of reasons.

Poteet told Hood that McGregor had a brilliant plan and handed the phone over.

"Morning, Princess," McGregor said. "Did you and Tomás survive the night together?"

Hood huffed back at him. "I know your wicked mind. If you must know, Tomás performed his assigned tasks to perfection! And that's all I'm going to say about it."

Damn it! She'd flipped him again.

"Give me back to Poteet. I'll let him tell me how brilliant you are. I'll need convincing."

Poteet took the phone and left McGregor for the sanctity of the study.

In the distance, McGregor heard the grinding noises of heavy machinery. He walked round the side of the house and up the drive. Halfway to the Offshoot, he saw road-working equipment being parked at the swimming pool hole and workers scurrying back and forth. Great. At least the grand pothole scheme was working.

Turning to go back, he heard a shout, "Ho there, Bob!"

It was Eli with hands cupped to his mouth. "Tell Roland I'd like to see him up here, soon as he has a chance!"

Back at the house, Poteet was off the phone. "Hood sounded much better, even cheerful. She thought your plan complicated, but what isn't up here, she said."

"Eli is up on the road with his machines and wants you to come see him"

Poteet ventured, "If he's the murderer he's up to no good. If he's clean maybe we can finally make peace. How will I tell?"

"It's a risk. I'll drive you up there to save your bad knee. First, I want to call Carlos"

Carlos already knew from Tomás about the artist's sketch and photo of the Manskar man. He was skeptical about Sheriff being involved, but just to get Amon to talk— and McGregor's production of the sketch and photo—it might be worth a bold gamble. If none of them was guilty, what would it hurt to meet? Tomorrow would be the earliest possibility because of the coming thunderstorm today.

At the top of the driveway McGregor stayed in his truck, and Poteet hobbled up to see Eli. McGregor watched as the two political foes shook hands tenuously and Eli started talking. He wasn't close enough to hear voices distinctly.

Eli strutted around, arms waving. Poteet did a lot of nodding. Eli put his arm around Poteet a couple of times. McGregor wagered with himself that Rust had cooked up a deal to get something out of Poteet to keep the road crew working on the entire Offshoot. Elections come and go, he thought, but this is the way the county's future gets sealed up tight—a couple of good old boys wheeling and dealing on a back road, a good month before the voters would "decide."

Back in the study with more coffee, Poteet reported he'd struck a couple of tentative bargains.

"Eli wants a secret meeting with you, me, and Dimpsey. After he wins the county mayor race, he wants to arrange for Dimpsey to be appointed road superintendent to fill his vacancy. Then, if Dimpsey does a good job he'll have no problem running for his own four-year term for road superintendent unopposed. We keep the deal secret for now. But once Eli wins the current election, he said he'd start building the political roadbed for Dimpsey to come along and pave it. Eli will announce for mayor sometime in the weeks following this August's election.

"Now, he wants you at this meeting so I can mediate the two of you on what he called his Terri Williams problem. Said he thinks Terri has a crush on you, you being a bigshot from out of town and such. He wants your assurance, face to face, that you won't interfere with them. Said he thought I could persuade you he was the right man for Terri, able to raise the boys and all. Said if you pursued her, he figured he'd lose her to you. Get this! He said we had to meet today and settle it, because tonight he's going to ask her to marry him!"

McGregor hung his head, silently cursing.

Poteet was still talking, "There at the end, Eli was practically begging me to intervene between you two. I felt sorry for the guy, frankly. I agreed to do it—assuming that you'd have no problem with it. This is the perfect way to get back to normal, providing we can get this murder solved."

In some ways Poteet was plain gullible.

With the hard rain coming in around noon, Poteet said Eli would shut down his road operations, and then meet them at his office at the old quarry outside Calvin Station at one o'clock sharp. With the quarry gate closed, nobody could bother them there.

Poteet explained that the quarry had been childproofed after a teen drowned there a few years back. Kids used to sneak in to swim in a giant rainfill hole there, a hole as big as a small lake with water thirty feet deep in some places. The road department still needed the quarry for its gravel, so the county spent a good deal of money to seal off the entire quarry, which was nothing but a huge hole in the ground. Poteet had been there once. He said if you stood at ground level inside the quarry, it appeared to be surrounded by high cliff walls. An automatic gate had been constructed at the quarry entrance and fences erected around the perimeter. Eli operated the quarry works from an office and garage and stored much of his road equipment there, small loaders and such.

Poteet, excited, said, "Tell me your thoughts, Celt Man—quick because I have something more to tell you!"

McGregor said, "Okay. I have no problem playing along for my part on the Terri matter. But at first blush, the whole matter of Grooms seems to me to be strictly a gratuitous gesture on Eli's part. What does he gain by Grooms becoming road superintendent?"

"Good question. Eli's probably assuming he would retain political control of the department if Dimpsey owed him his job. Now, let me tell you this. Eli said that if we could all agree as I outlined, he wanted to ask us about a disturbing piece of information he's obtained about Sheriff. Has something to do with the murder, but he's not telling what it is until we settle our differences. He did volunteer that he thought Sheriff was a vindictive character. He and Terri had a talk last night and it caused him to remember something Sheriff said to him about the Tomato Boy."

McGregor grew uneasy. Had Terri told Eli she had visited here yesterday and that they had discussed Sheriff? Worse, had Terri revealed the full extent of what had happened here in the study? Poteet left for the kitchen to prepare breakfast. McGregor sat down to ponder.

With Eli out on the Offshoot working, McGregor decided on a phone call to Terri. There was no answer. He thought about driving over, but Eli might follow him. There was the old trail out back. He could take it—go see her for the last time as a single woman. No, Amon would spy him there and report to Eli. Next, he dialed her cell phone but with no more luck than before. What could Terri have told Eli? Most likely, it concerned Sheriff and Clyde swapping threats, but maybe she'd failed to tell McGregor the whole story.

At breakfast Poteet was pleased with himself. He chattered about having his road repaired and about Dimpsey taking his rightful place without needing to run a campaign. He allowed he might donate to the Rust campaign chest, in recompense for having talked Grooms into running.

As Poteet rambled on McGregor pushed the food around on his plate. Finally, McGregor held up his hand. "Whoa. You're getting way too happy about this. You do this sort of thing often. You get these wild visions of how great the future's going to be. Have you stopped to wonder why Eli wants to meet at the quarry? Why there? Why not here? Why not a neutral place, say in Finneyville?"

Poteet blinked several times, as if he'd caught Dimpsey's tic. "Yeah ... well ... I guess he doesn't want us seen or overheard. Should I call, have Eli meet us here? Should we meet at all? What about Plan A?"

"Let me think," McGregor said. "If Eli is innocent, then we can solve problems quickly, return you to some normalcy. At the same time, find out more info on Sheriff.

I'm feeling pushed here because of the bombing. If Eli is the murderer, then this meeting is a set-up."

"I want to go," Poteet said. "I'm convinced that as of now our man is Sheriff. Plan A might never come off because Sheriff might see it for what it is—a set-up. I'm going, whether you go or don't go." Poteet was hot. "I guess I've minimized to some degree how I really feel about that road out there. I want it asphalted, macadamized, graveled, concreted, cherted, corduroyed, or even grassed, but, by God, I want *something* done to it!"

McGregor locked eyes with the red-faced Poteet. After a long thirty seconds, McGregor blinked. "Okay, we'll go. I work for you. But I'm taking that .45 of yours. And I won't take any chances."

Dimpsey was answering his phone this morning and agreed to come over for a talk. He arrived grumpy and squeeze-eyed, complaining of lack of sleep lately and about having no good friends other than Roland and Camper Eskew. All Camper would talk about, he griped, was the Tomato Boy murder.

Upon hearing Poteet outline the possible understanding with Eli, Dimpsey's world clearly brightened. McGregor watched the curious fellow transform into a man of ideas about road construction and proper maintenance. Holding office without having to campaign met with his complete approval, never mind what he'd said before about retiring.

Dimpsey said, "Now I have a bit of news myself. I received a phone call this morning, early. I didn't recognize the voice. It said words to the effect: 'Roland Poteet is your friend. You tell him I have information about the murder of Clyde Thacker that I can't give to Sheriff Buell. If he wants to know, I'll meet that lawyer of his at The Thumb.' Then he said I should tell you that he's a messenger from a group of developers in Manskar County. Said you'd understand. Said he'd call me again and then he hung up. What in the world do y'all think that was all about?"

They asserted they had no idea but for him to get in touch immediately whenever the man phoned again. Then they ushered Dimpsey out the door with instructions to be ready for pick-up around twelve thirty.

When it was time to leave McGregor put on a lightweight windbreaker, snug around the wrists and waist with tight elastic. He tucked the pistol in the back waistband of his pants. He put on his favorite sneakers and an oiled cotton rain hat. When looking in the mirror, he shivered.

McGregor drove his truck to within a few feet of where the roadway began its steep decline into the quarry. The road ended at a high steel gate topped with barbed wire. He stopped to get his bearings, ignoring Poteet and Dimpsey's chat about how the value of their real estate holdings should be going up soon. He saw that, indeed, a chain-link fence ran the entire perimeter of the top of the quarry.

The sky was darkening ominously in the west, but here the sun shone through a mix of fast moving, puffy clouds. A tiny strip of color on the distant southern horizon caught McGregor's eye, a bit of yellow against the green of foliage. McGregor smiled to himself. It was Amon's telegraph in operation.

One of the first questions McGregor would have for Eli, if he could push it into the conversation, was if Amon had ever mentioned the Manskar man to him. He was debating whether to let Eli see the photo and the sketch. They were tucked under the front seat. It depended on what information Eli might have about Buell. He'd have to play that gambit by ear.

Poteet noted it was one o'clock and urged McGregor on. As they descended to the quarry, the gate opened. Eli was standing on the other side of it. He waved to them and sallied over to shake hands with Dimpsey through the truck window. Dimpsey squeezed his eyes and shook hands vigorously.

"Glad y'all could make it," Eli said. "Let me deal with the gate, and then I'll hop in the truck bed and ride with you to the office. Go slow. We got mud around here! And you know about the rainfill, right? The big hole full of rain here at the quarry? If you're not careful, you'll get in the mud and slip off into it."

Inside the office, Eli had arranged a line of straight chairs in front of an ancient metal desk, which looked like war surplus. The room was tidy and strictly utilitarian. Two doors were in the back. One had a restroom sign and the other a sign reading "Danger-Authorized Personnel Only."

Eli was cordial as he prepared instant coffee, prattling about the big storm on its way and how weather played such a powerful role in road maintenance. Since the newspaper story, he'd received "countless phone calls and emails" congratulating him on "winning the election."

As Eli passed around cups of steaming black coffee, McGregor noted a tremble in the man's hands. This guy was fighting anxiety or was high on caffeine.

Eli apologized on behalf of the county for the long delay in re-working the Old Military Offshoot. If he'd had his way, he asserted, the road long since would have been repaired. Dealing with the tomato growers on one side and the developers on the other, frankly, was a thankless task. Nobody understood.

"But now," he said, "Let's get down to business."

Eli and Poteet reiterated to Dimpsey their earlier discussion concerning Dimpsey becoming road superintendent. Dimpsey could hardly contain his delight. Finally, he jumped from his chair and offered his hand to Eli.

"Eli, I'm not sure why you're doing this, but I want you to know I'll be your biggest supporter when you're mayor!"

Eli said, "Good! Now that it's settled, Dimpsey, you just relax. Since we're all friends here, you can listen in on what Bob and I have to say. I have no secrets about the way I feel toward Terri Williams. I want her to marry me."

He went on to explain to McGregor that his behavior around Terri was caused by stress on his "faculties" from the election campaign and the murder of the Tomato Boy. He segued into a lengthy rant about the Tomato Boy's incomprehensible desire to be mayor, his never having held an elective office.

McGregor saw Eli's eyes dilate and tiny sweat beads pop out on his forehead. Was Eli losing it? Was he on drugs? Not caffeine, but cocaine? Suddenly, Eli seemed to realize he was babbling and stopped in mid-sentence.

"Roland," he sputtered, "Uh, please, uh, proceed with your mediation as we talked about this morning. I'll shut up about Clyde Thacker."

Poteet, looking unsure of what he was supposed to say, finally turned to McGregor and spoke. "Well, McGregor, as far as I can tell, Eli here wants to get some assurance from you that you have no intention of pursuing Terri romantically. I think it's big of Eli to come forward and say what he thinks. Seems to me, it's a straightforward way of setting aside any jealous feelings and can be the beginning of a good friendship between the two of you. Eli can be invaluable as a resource for your book. And with his knowledge of automobiles and given the fact we've all just elected him mayor, why I think he could help you oversee our setting up my car museum that I once had the Tomato Boy talked into."

Poteet looked at Eli with raised eyebrows and then back to McGregor.

McGregor started to speak, but thunder cracked above them, causing them all to flinch. Rain began pounding on the metal roof of the office. He had to raise his voice to overcome the noise.

He said, "Well, I guess it's my turn. Eli, I think I had a kind of infatuation with Terri, talking to her about the boys and about my book and all. Best I can tell it all stemmed from her face being the first one I saw when the boys pulled me out of the creek. I never confused infatuation with love or anything like that. By the way, I don't think I ever formally thanked you for getting me to the hospital. That was a great help. Now, as far as Terri is concerned, I promise I'll not visit her or in any way make it difficult between you two. I think you *are* the right man for her. She speaks highly of you and, if I had to guess, I'd say she's in love with you."

McGregor hardly could believe he was mouthing such hackneyed nonsense. It was as if he'd been tossed into a group therapy session in a nuthouse. And he was the biggest nut there.

Eli stuck his hand under a large blueprint on his desk and pulled it back quickly. He was sweating profusely now. He wiped off his reddening face with a swipe of a big hand. Instead of looking mollified by McGregor's conciliatory gesture, he seemed suddenly furious. He breathed deeply, jerking his head with his mouth open. McGregor wondered if he was about to have a heart attack or stroke. Eli stood and leaned over his desk toward McGregor. Then his face morphed into the exact same full-faced, malevolent grin McGregor had seen briefly in his rear view mirror as Eli had followed him away from Terri's house yesterday.

Eli bellowed, "Why, thank you very much, Bob McGregor! You goddamned son of a bitch! That's awful damned kind of you!"

The door to the "Danger" room opened up, and out stepped a man holding two long-barreled revolvers leveled at the group. He was tall with a bushy mustache. Short hair. Dressed in black. He fit the photo and the sketch. He was the Manskar man.

Through his frozen grin and clenched teeth, Eli shouted, "Come on in and join our little party, Victor! Search these bastards. You three stand up! Get your hands up!"

Poteet jumped up fast, and as eyes went toward the movement McGregor whipped his left hand to his back.

The Manskar man said, "Oh, no, no, no!" He leveled a weapon on McGregor. "Everybody in Tennessee goes armed. I wouldn't have believed it if you weren't carrying a piece. Get it, Eli."

Eli reached around McGregor, pulled out the .45 and unloaded it, tossing it into a desk drawer. Back behind his desk, he said, "Why Bob. You didn't trust Rust?"

Pockets were emptied, cell phones confiscated.

Poteet kept looking at the Manskar man. Then he shook his head. "Victor! That's who you are! You're Victor Helminth!" To McGregor, he yelled, "Helminth was a low-life road foreman of mine—until I had his ass fired!"

Eli reached over the desk and pushed Poteet hard on the chest, back into his seat. McGregor punched the off-guard Eli squarely in the face with a left hook, bowling him over his desk chair and onto the floor behind the desk, flat on his back. McGregor jumped on top of the desk as the Manskar man—Helminth—fired a round into the ceiling and then pointed the gun again directly at McGregor. McGregor froze, almost in mid-air.

Eli shook his head and slowly rose up, wiping a drop of blood from his nose. He laughed. "That didn't hurt a bit, Bob."

The rain had let up but a clap of thunder exploded around the building and lightening directly above turned the room blue. The lights dimmed and blinked on and off. The captors looked up at the light fixtures, and, stepping off Eli's desk, McGregor sneaked two eight-inch screwdrivers that had rolled from beneath an in-out file holder. The lights held steady, and Eli helped himself to one of Helminth's revolvers as McGregor slid both screwdrivers up past the elastic band around his cast. Eli's attention focused on Dimpsey, who had sunk back into his chair.

Eli yelled at Dimpsey, "You dipshit! I'm about to get even with your fat ass!" He put the barrel of his revolver to Dimpsey's temple. "Did you honestly believe for one second that I would turn over *my* department to somebody like you, you sniffling, double-crossing lying bastard!"

Dimpsey squealed, "I didn't double-cross you, Eli, honest. I stayed completely loyal and I kept quiet just like you told me."

McGregor and Poteet looked at each other and then at Dimpsey in bewilderment.

McGregor murmured, "Oh-shit. I know what happened."

Eli pressed the gun harder against Dimpsey's skull and spat out, "Why don't you be the one to let our other friends here in on the details of our secret. Go ahead, tell them!"

Dimpsey, eyes squeezed tight, said, "I got fifty thousand dollars from Eli to quit the race. I'm so sorry, Roland, I'm so sorry!"

Eli said, "*All* the details. Nothing matters now. Tell them!"

Dimpsey simpered, "Give me a drink, please, Eli."

Eli pulled a pint out of his desk drawer and took a pull, then tossed out the remainder of Dimpsey's coffee and poured the cup full of liquor. Dimpsey knocked it off in one long swallow.

Dimpsey managed to say he'd been the one to approach Eli and offer to get out of the race for a hundred thousand dollars. They had settled on fifty and Helminth had met him at the hotel and paid him off. "It was way last May, Roland. I've been living a lie ever since. I wish I were dead!"

"Well now, weasel-worm," Eli said, "you're about to get your wish." He turned to Poteet. "This sorry asshole took my money. Then, he just had to talk while he was taking it. Vic tried to shut him up, but he babbled on and on. Vic let him. Had no idea that crazy Thacker was taping the whole thing. The whole goddamned thing!"

Dimpsey squeaked, "He was?"

"Yes, he was, you stupid prick. Then Thacker tried to blackmail me. Not just to quit the race, but to leave the county. Move away. That perverted, blondy-haired California son of a bitch tried to make me, Eli Rust, move

away from my own county! From my people! Break the trust
I've built up all these years." Eli slugged again from the bottle. "Damn! That's cheap shit, but it's *good.* Why I ever quit
drinkin' I'll never know."

He pushed Dimpsey's head back with a handful of
the man's chin fat and stared at him. "I had Vic set up the
two village idiots as patsies. Then I got the tape from
Thacker and then I hit him. Like this!" He struck Dimpsey a
vicious blow on the side of the head with the gun barrel.

McGregor jumped toward Eli again, but Helminth
shook his head at McGregor and moved quickly to cover
him. Dimpsey slumped to the floor and Eli looked at
McGregor.

"What is it Bob? Oh, Vic, I think Bob might be
wanting a margarita. Fix him a margarita, Vic! And get him a
pillow." Eli pulled a cell phone out of his pocket. "You go
to the calls received menu on this little dandy belonging to a
woman named Terri Williams, and it'll say the last call was
from 'Bob'—this morning. You trying to get an early morning date, Bob? Or you taking the boys fishing?"

"Eli, man, it's time." Helminth interrupted. "We
need to move fast! Quit yakking with these chimpanzees and
let's get on with it!"

Eli yelled in a blast of spittle, "You shut up and do
your damn job! Go check the mudslide! They'll be here any
minute."

From Helminth's wide eyes and dropped chin,
McGregor surmised that the Manskar man had just now real-
ized that his partner might not be simply a common criminal.
He might be crazy.

Helminth took a breath and went over to peek into
the rain, fighting the wind with the door.

McGregor said, "What's happening, Eli? What do
you intend to do?" It was a play for time, time to try to figure
a way out. McGregor believed Helminth was capable of
shooting them in cold blood at any second. Probably Eli,
too.

"Well, Mr. Playboy. Let's see. Did you happen to notice that big pile of mud out there? Seems our landscaping dirt's been sliding all night and all morning toward the rainfill hole. I started thinking last night after I had me a real good shot of that cheap shit. Now why couldn't some men I know come over here and just slide down into the rainfill hole with that mud? Vic over there thought it was a great idea, didn't you Vic?"

"Sure did!" said Helminth, coming back to the group. He put his hand on Poteet's head and forced him to look up at him, eyeball to eyeball. Helminth shook the rain from his face and scrutinized Poteet. Poteet's eyes darted left and right, but he maintained composure. McGregor was proud of the old soldier for not breaking. Helminth said, "Y'all found my little bugs, you bastards. That made me mad. Eli came up with the idea to invite you two and this Dimpsey dipshit here. I figured it'd be such fun, I came up with the names of two other guests."

A horn honked outside just as another wave of rain and thunder roared through the quarry.

Eli shouted, "That's them. Be careful. Let them get all the way in, then muscle them over here."

Eli went to the door and opened it enough to put his face and arm through to motion the new arrivals inside. Then he hurried back to the desk. He said to Helminth, "Good, they closed the gate like I said to. It'll lock automatically."

Through the office door marched Poker and Amon. Poker slapped water from yet another set of new clothes. He stomped his muddy boots on the mat and looked around. Amon was standing stock still, his eyes wide. Poker glanced at the gun pointed at him, then over at McGregor. He grimaced, seeing what he'd walked into.

Helminth said to them, "Don't say a word or even twitch unless I tell you to. Is that clear?" Poker nodded. Helminth searched them. Amon asked Eli to make the man stop. Helminth shouted, "I said don't say a word! Is that clear, birdbrain?"

Poker yelled, "It's clear to him, asshole. And don't call him birdbrain!"

Helminth said, "Ohh, look who's giving orders! How about I just shoot the birdbrain now and get it over with, just to see how mad old Pokey Pokey here can get?"

McGregor intervened, hoping to stop the escalating violence. "Eli, are you telling us you killed Clyde Thacker just to stop a blackmail scheme?"

"Well, since your ears will be full of mud directly, I'll let you hear my juicy story. First of all, you could have saved your butt, Bob, if you'd just left with that gal of yours when Vic bombed her. But no, you had to get one last screw out of my Terri, didn't you? That's when I decided to get rid of the whole lot of you. I was going to live with Grooms; shut him up only if I had to. Poker and Amon are such nitwits, they'd never figure out anything, even after that stupid Buell charged them with murder. But Roland, my friend, you had to go regardless. Sooner or later, you'd figure out it was me and Amon who fleeced you that time. I'm bringing Vic into my operation when I'm mayor and if you ever saw us together, you'd remember. I was right, too. You seeing him with me today, you recognized him right away. So I intended to nail you no matter what. Vic here had a talk with Thacker and I saw he wasn't budging. So I devised a plan to set up Poker and Amon for the killing. Detailed—even to the point of planting that recorder handle in the Caddy to make like Poker put it there. I have a tape where Poker admits to taking money to shoot you, Roland, compliments of Thacker and his taping system. But you're a hard man to kill accidentally. So, when the mud started moving last night and Bob already wanting me to cozy back up to you, I figured this was a good way for you to go to your spot in hell."

He turned in fury to McGregor. "Then Bob sealed his own fate yesterday at your house, Roland. Infatuation, my ass! That's right, Bob, she told me. I, of course, forgave her.

And she promised nothing would ever happen again. How sweet! I told her I'd make up to you, and we'd all go on with our dear sweet lives. Ha, I mean lies. Like hell! You knew she was mine and you went after her anyway. So since I included you in this party, I figured to get the whole damn bunch of you. Thacker got his for prickin' Terri, now you and Poker'll get yours for prickin' her. I'll deal with that bastard Buell in my own good time!"

McGregor thought fast. These guys couldn't afford to put bullets in them, if they planned to push them into the rainfill. The bodies would be recovered. That was the key. He'd just have to wait for the right moment and try to overpower them. He also needed to communicate with Poteet and Poker so they could all move simultaneously.

Eli moved to the door. To delay him, McGregor said, "But Eli, Amon's your friend! Can't you leave him out of it? Plus, he's Terri's brother."

"Leave him out? Now there's the real beauty of my plan." He came over and squatted between McGregor and Poteet and lowered his voice. "You see, Amon thinks he slid down the mud into that big ditch off that road we were working for Roland's company. He didn't. I pushed him! He was refusing to go along with the lawyer's deal with me and Vic to squeeze the company for some quick cash. The lawyer told me to get rid of him. Ended up just great. He really was hurt! Had no memory of what happened. The lawyer talked up a good deal with the company and we skedaddled."

Poteet asked, "You mean the lawyer was in on it?"

"He cooked up the whole thing from the beginning. Screwed y'all good."

"Where's he now?" Poteet continued. "Isn't he a loose end?"

"Naw. Vic here knocked him off soon as I decided to run for mayor. Where'd you do him, Vic, Oregon?"

"Portland," Helminth responded. "Hey, Eli, its time, man!"

McGregor tried to keep Eli talking. "But Amon won't give anything up. Like you said, his memory's gone."

"If you must know, he's getting flashbacks. One day he'll remember. He has to go now that I have the chance."

"What are you planning? Just dumping us over the side?"

"Naw. Too neat. I need y'all to cooperate and get in your trucks. See, it's like this. We're having our nice friendly meeting, which by the way, I taped a while ago. Learned that from our dear departed Firstplacer Boy. We meet, see, then Poker and Amon come in. They're in a fight, see, and they get into Poker's truck and the truck's in gear and they accidentally roll close to the rainfill, in the mud. And I crawl through the mud and get two chains hooked onto Poker's truck. I'm the hero, see what I mean? We get them to shut off the truck engine and put it out of gear. Then you and me, we get in our two trucks and try like hell to pull them out with the chains. The slide gets worse all of a sudden and starts to pull all three trucks into the rainfill. I get out of my truck just in time. But y'all don't ... unfortunately. You and Roland go down in your truck, chained to Poker's truck. It all happens fast. Oh yeah, the dipshit goes down on his own. He's too fat to crawl out of the mud when it starts its big slide. Then Vic, here, he conveniently disappears out of the county. I'm left as the only witness to a horrible tragedy. Y'all, of course, will be heroes. Died trying to save Poker and Amon. I almost die trying to save all of you. I'll be the new county celebrity. I'll take my rightful post as the real Firstplacer in this goddamn county! It's downright brilliant, is it not?"

Eli had forgotten one thing—to keep his voice down, and Amon had heard him. Amon leaped passed Helminth, unmindful of the gun, and tackled Eli broadside. But Helminth was quick. He hit Amon hard on the back of the head with the gun grip, and then pointed it at Poker who had moved toward him.

Poker growled, "For that, Manskar man, I'm going to kill you!"

Helminth just laughed and Eli stood up. He stood Poker next to McGregor's chair. Helminth got Poker's keys and went outside, stuffing his revolver in his belt.

Eli opened another bottle of bourbon and downed a mouthful. He picked up the phone and dialed 911. He shouted, "Hey, Eli Rust! I got a big mudslide here at the quarry, got some trucks stuck in it. Drivers might be hurt." He hung up and waited thirty seconds, then called back. "Eli Rust again. Forget it. No help needed."

Eli smirked at them. "Covering my ass. I'll explain that it looked like we had Poker and Amon out of the mud, then the dirt pile moved and caved in and sent the trucks sliding away. Nothing I could do. Happened so fast!"

Poteet said, "Eli, think it over, man. You'll never be able to live with yourself. Think of Terri and the boys. Somehow, somebody will figure out what happened. What about Helminth, for instance? He knows. What if you get sideways with him some day when you're mayor, say? You gonna to kill him, too? He might get you first. Think about that. You can still stop all this, plead insanity to killing Clyde. We'll forget about today, no harm done really. You'll get off and still get to marry Terri."

Poteet, the new mediator, was giving it a good try.

Eli looked at Poteet blankly as if he had not heard a word. Then he said, "Hey, Poker. Reason I pulled you into this thing is that Leslie told me she caught you and Terri. Terri won't talk. So tell me, how many times did y'all do it? Huh? How many? Tell me, or I'll shoot you where you stand."

Poker said, "Leslie lied. When she came over that day, I was there to see Amon. Terri thought Amon was spying on her, so we tested him. That's all. I pretended a couple of moves on her. That's what Leslie saw, but she got mad and wouldn't listen to us explain."

Poker's rendition surprised Eli, and he stopped to ponder it. He asked, "You going to tell me Terri faked it with Thacker, too?"

McGregor, seeing Eli nonplused, tried to wedge more confusion into his alcohol-fueled brain. "That's right, Eli. It was all a fake. Clyde and Terri made it up to test Leslie, see if she really loved Clyde as a father or was just after his money. Terri was just friends with Clyde. That's all."

Eli must have wanted to believe it. He shrugged and went to the door to open it and stare into the rain, but still pointing his gun at his captives.

McGregor thought, if they died today and Terri had to live with this maniac, at least it would go easier for her if Eli thought she was more pure. Poker looked at McGregor with something like respect in his expression, as if he'd finally made up his mind about him.

In a rapid-fire whisper, McGregor hissed, "Listen up! They can't shoot us. Our bodies have to be found to back up their story. We can't have bullet holes in us. So, we jump them when we can and take the chance they won't immediately shoot, all right?" Poker and Poteet nodded. And McGregor slipped one of the screwdrivers to Poker.

Helminth came in covered with mud. "Damn stuff's slippery as hell! Almost went over myself. The trucks are fixed up with the chains and all. The dirt pile's beginning to move. Let's get 'em out there!"

Helminth muscled Dimpsey off the floor and with difficulty dragged him out the door. When he came back he had a rope looped under his arms. "That damn mud's moving, Eli. I'm tying myself to a post." He slung Amon over his shoulder and took him outside.

After that, Eli ordered everyone outside. He sent Poker out to his truck. McGregor and Poteet watched as Poker slipped and clawed his way to the old orange truck where Amon sat slumped over in the passenger side. Eli's plan was complex, but McGregor could see it working in all its devilish detail. An investigator later might be suspicious of

Eli's account but never be able to prove it happened otherwise.

Helminth tied a rope under the arms of Dimpsey, who groaned but didn't wake up, and jumped into the bed of McGregor's truck to pull the big man in after him. Then he wrestled the rope from underneath Dimpsey and hopped down. Eli ordered McGregor and Poteet into the cab of the red truck, with Poteet in the middle seat. Then he climbed in after them on the driver's side. Eli backed up the truck toward Poker's truck, toward the lip of the rainfill. To the rear-end of the red truck's frame, Helminth connected a chain, which apparently he'd already laid out and which extended all the way to Poker's rear bumper.

Eli said, as all three of them looked over their right shoulders, "You might note for the record that my transmission has gone out on my truck. Tsk, tsk! It'll give me a reason to cry and whine to get more money out of the county for new trucks. 'I could have saved those poor men, if the county had bought me a new truck like I asked for,' I'll plead."

To the right side of the red truck, the great pile of dirt groaned like a mountainous dinosaur waking up. It moved suddenly toward them and toward Poker's truck, which lurched toward the lake. And the chains tightened. The red truck squawked. They all twisted to look out the rear window.

Amon suddenly rolled out of his side of Poker's truck and tried crawling in the knee-deep mud around him. He made headway, but Helminth drew a wrench from a pocket and gave it a throw. It beaned Amon on the forehead and under a geyser of blood, he collapsed backward, deep into the mud. Poker shot out of the cab and climbed into the bed of the truck to look for him. The rolling mud was up to the truck sideboards now and Amon had gone from sight. Poker bounded to the tailgate and jumped into the mud where the chain was hooked. He grabbed the chain and started hoisting his way forward. Helminth found another set of wrenches in Eli's truck and started throwing them, knife-like, at Poker.

They bounced off his tough hide. Pulling free of the sucking mud, Poker raced toward Helminth. Helminth fired off one round from his revolver, but it missed by a wide margin. Poker was on him fast with an arm around Helminth's neck.

Eli said menacingly to McGregor and Poteet, "Don't even think about it, you two. I'll put a bullet in you and bury you under the Offshoot where nobody'll ever find you. Watch Vic. He'll stomp Poker to death! That's the way he likes to kill."

Helminth did work himself out of Poker's grip, knocked Poker down in the mud and started stomping him. But Poker pulled his screwdriver out of his belt under his shirt and stabbed Helminth in the thigh. Helminth slipped down and Poker put the screwdriver through the Manskar man's thick neck and twisted it hard. Blood spurted high into the air.

Eli yelled, "Victor!"

As he spoke, the dirt pile and the surrounding blanket of mud heaved in a great avalanche-like wave. The movement sent Poker reeling back toward his truck, and Helminth flopped around until he disappeared.

Eli said, "Oh, shit!"

Poteet screamed, "Celt Man. Now!"

In a slashing arc around Poteet, McGregor hit Eli with his cast hard across the bridge of the nose. The revolver fell to the floor between Eli's legs. Eli was stunned. McGregor fought off the wrist pain, opened his door and tried to pull Poteet out with him. But Eli grabbed Poteet by the shirt.

Poteet shouted to McGregor, "Run, run for the office. Get my .45!"

Eli whacked Poteet's head against the dash. McGregor got out and sprinted toward the office.

But Eli found the gun and fired. The bullet whizzed past McGregor. Instinctively, he dove for the ground—to land on his broken wrist. He lay prostrate, immobilized in pain. As his head cleared he heard an engine moving toward him and looked around to see Eli coming at him in a Bobcat. McGregor knew the Bobcat to be a small, agile earth mover. Eli would be on him in a flash. He was a goner.

But Eli drove past him instead of running over him. The Bobcat wheeled around and stopped. It was now between McGregor and the office. Eli was going to toy with him.

Through sheets of rain, McGregor saw that wicked grin. Another rumbling sounded behind him. He glanced back. His truck, with Poteet in it, was moving backward. The cab of Poker's truck was already near the rim of the lake. He had to do something.

He looked back around as he heard Eli gun the engine of his Bobcat. There! Over there was another Bobcat. McGregor ran to it, slipping and sliding, and climbed on, expecting a bullet at any time.

He had operated a Bobcat only once, when Hood had replanted her entire yard. About all he'd learned was how complicated it could be to the untrained. Its bucket operated by foot-action against floor pedals, its motion by hand-action on two levers positioned either side of the seat. He had one good hand.

He fired up the Bobcat and raised the bucket up just as Eli slammed into him. McGregor reversed and stopped. The throttle was on the side of his bad arm, but he managed to turn it up to full speed and push forward the handles to run squarely into Eli. Eli's Bobcat wobbled, but stayed upright. Eli laughed loudly, backed up and crashed forward to ram McGregor. Two more hits and McGregor was thrown clear of his machine. He ran again, slipping and slopping. Eli was on his heels in no time, his Bobcat's tires whining as they spun in the mud.

Even with mud-grip tires, McGregor knew Eli couldn't climb a steep hill going forward in a Bobcat, so the only place to go where Eli couldn't was up onto the great pile of slush. But if he did that, he'd be digging his own grave.

McGregor stopped and turned around. Turned to face the bucketful of dirt and mud Eli had scooped and lifted high in the air. By goosing the Bobcat's engine with amazing skill, he let the slime dribble out around McGregor. McGregor backed up.

Eli shouted to him over the roar of the rain and the Bobcat engine, "You want to make love now, Mr. Playboy? How about I bring Terri over and y'all get it on? Huh? How 'bout that? How about a margarita now, Mr. Playboy?"

McGregor shook his head to fling the mud from his eyes and saw his truck and Eli's truck sliding inexorably toward the brink. Poker's truck was almost gone from sight. The door to his red truck snapped open and, best he could see, an arm reached up from the mud. Poker's arm. Poker emerged from the mud that was waist-high and pulled on Poteet, who tumbled out of the truck and fell on top of Poker. Poker had saved Poteet. It had happened in a flash.

McGregor yelled back to Eli, taking a chance that Eli was feeling all-powerful, "Hey, asshole, before you kill me, turn off that engine. I want to ask you something."

Eli, with his mighty grin, switched off the Bobcat and the arm lowered itself with the bucket to the ground.

McGregor said, "I wanted to ask you to let me take you up on your offer. Let me have sex with Terri one more time. She said you had a pencil. Let her have one more good one before she marries somebody who will never have the power to turn her on, much less do anything about it."

Eli pulled out his revolver, climbed down and stalked toward McGregor. He shouted, "I'm gonna blow your balls off!" He stalked to within an arm's reach of McGregor and slowly lowered the weapon to McGregor's crotch.

When the nose of the gun touched him, McGregor bent his knees deeply as if in a quick flinch. He looked squarely into Eli's eyes and put his arms behind his back. He pulled out the screwdriver. When Eli's eyes flared, McGregor jumped. He caught Eli's wrist and the revolver in the vice of his legs just as the revolver fired behind his butt. He felt the heat of it. Taking the cue from Poker, he plunged the screw-driver into Eli's neck up to the hilt and twisted.

Eli let go the revolver and began stumbling in small circles. Then he reached for McGregor, blood spurting in a fast rhythm. McGregor stepped aside, and Eli pitched forward into the mud heap. One leg jerked twice, and then he went limp.

CHAPTER 21

An hour after arriving at Finneyville's hospital, McGregor and Poteet had been able finally to telephone Hood. McGregor, happy to be alive, had related to Hood a play-by-play of the day's events. Then Poteet had commanded she charter a private plane on his dime and fly with Tomás back to Calvin County.

Now, it was shortly before ten p.m., and McGregor was sitting in bed at Sweetwater wearily making notes on a legal pad. He heard tires screeching outside. The door to the guest quarters slammed open, and Hood shouted his name. He heard Poteet, who was stretched out on the guest den sofa, direct her to the bedroom.

She peeked around the doorframe. "Hey, Lumpkins."

McGregor dropped the pad and spread his arms. "Hey, yourself, Princess. Come here!"

The relief of seeing her brought wet eyes to McGregor. Hood wiped her own eyes and lay down beside him. She whispered in his ear, hugging his head tenderly to her breast, "That was a close call. I'm so sorry I wasn't here to help. Is Poteet still okay out there? Bring me up to date. How's Poker? How's your arm?"

McGregor spoke softly. "Poteet's head is a hard nut to crack. He has a bad bruise, that's all. Poker has a broken wrist just like me. He broke it twisting Poteet out of the truck. My wrist will survive, they tell me, but I'm sore all over."

Woozy, McGregor tried to recall what Hood already knew; then, he gave her the gist of the latest details.

The rain had turned to drizzle before moving out around five. After a long search Amon Trussell had not been found. Sheriff was presuming that he and the Manskar man had gone over the lip of the rainfill with the trucks during the mudslide. Recovery operations were scheduled to begin at dawn.

Nobody knew how, but Dimpsey must have slipped out of the truck bed. He was found in the mud. The last McGregor had heard he was scheduled for surgery with a fractured skull.

There came a knock at McGregor's door, and Poteet limped in. After a brief reunion with Hood he crawled into bed next to McGregor.

"I can't talk," Poteet said, carefully adjusting a pillow under his head and closing his eyes. "Are you telling her what Carlos told us?"

McGregor said, "Yeah. Let me back up. Carlos said that by one o'clock this afternoon, Terri finally realized that something had to be wrong with Eli, based on his babbling at her house after he'd drunk himself silly late last night. He'd slapped her around and found out from her that we were interested in Sheriff as a suspect. He left her at dawn, making her promise not to leave the house until he returned in the afternoon. He apologized meekly for hitting her and promised her that by the end of the day, he'd have his fences mended with Poteet, and with Dimpsey and me. All morning she debated whether to accept the apology, and finally decided that she'd be nuts to do so. She didn't want to call Sheriff directly, so she started to call Carlos. That's when she discovered Eli had cut her phone line and stolen her cell phone."

Poteet was quietly snoring, and McGregor lowered his voice. "She was scared and searched until she found Eli's spare keys to that orange truck. As luck would have it, the ring had a key marked 'quarry gate.' She took the boys to her minister's house in Calvin Station where she called the sheriff's office and talked to Carlos in his patrol car by radio.

"When Eli made that call to 911 and then called back immediately to cancel it, the dispatcher informed Carlos, telling him Eli sounded drunk. He decided to drive out to the quarry to check out the situation. He called Terri back to have her follow him in case he needed her, because they fully expected to find Eli alone and drunk at the office.

"From the top of the quarry, they saw the trucks in the mud. Eli was banging me around in my Bobcat. Dimpsey was lying in the bed of my truck with his feet dangling over the tailgate. Eli started chasing me in his Bobcat, me slipping and sliding. They reached the gate and Terri opened it. They drove in to see Eli holding the gun on me then me stabbing him with the gun going off. So there—I have witnesses that I didn't murder the bastard."

McGregor let Hood's eyes shower him in silent affection and cool his raw nerves. He drifted away. She kissed his fingers and gently placed his cast—his new cast—under the covers. He felt her pull the sheet to his chin and tuck it around his shoulders.

The following Sunday afternoon, on the hill above her home, McGregor watched Terri Williams hover over her brother's grave, her arms around the waists of Charlie and Dewey. Other than the minister, she had invited only McGregor and Poker to attend the brief service.

A gentle breeze rustled leaves on the hillside tulip poplars, delivering upon the small group a slight fragrance and a few brown, worn-out blossoms. Tears rolled down the face of young Dewey, who held a single rose in an outstretched hand. The minister spoke tenderly about human beings struggling to make sense of life and death. As the minister offered a lengthy prayer, McGregor resolved to let Charley and Dewey take him fishing. He needed peace. And he needed to start making a difference in a positive way and perhaps learn something from the life of the beleaguered Amon Trussell.

Back at Terri's house, the minister departed. Terri had a rental car and was taking the boys to visit her late husband's parents over in Manskar County. The boys were waiting in the rental, and by prior arrangement Poker went to his car to wait for McGregor to have a private visit with Terri in the living room.

"Terri, I'm so sorry things turned out as they did. I want to go fishing with boys after a while. I don't want them to think I'm a monster."

She nodded to him and put her head on his chest. For a time he held her close in the silence of the warm room. As he was beginning to notice ylang-ylang in the air, the boys shouted for Terri and she lifted her head.

She said, "I'll think about it. Bye, Bob."

Poker had some trouble wrestling Mama's Oldsmobile through the ruts down Terri's road with only one arm. About halfway down, he turned to McGregor. "This is the last time I'll drive this old road. I ain't said it to nobody, but I had a good hold on Amon's body there in the mud. Had to turn him loose if I was gonna get Mr. Poteet out of that truck. I hope Amon was dead. Do you think he was dead, Bob?"

McGregor felt his throat constrict as he fumbled for a placating answer. "Had to be by that time, Poker. You did the right thing."

Poker reached over and touched McGregor's knee with his wrist cast. Then he grinned, shook his big head, and said, "Mr. Poteet told me it was all right to call him Potty."

It was stated with finality, and McGregor saw no reason to respond.

When they were crossing Pullwater Meadow, McGregor asked, "Poker, do you have any idea who owns this field?"

"Sure. Everybody knows that. Potty owns it."

When they arrived at the Tomato Emporium, only a few cars were parked in the lot. Mama had closed the place to the public for a private gathering in honor of Poteet and those persons who had helped him through the last several days. Poker cut the engine and pulled out a red permanent marker.

"Let's sign each other's cast, Bob."

McGregor inscribed his name on Poker with a flourish. On McGregor, Poker carefully printed the words: TO MY FRIEND BOB, POKER LIMBO.

Inside, Poteet was waiting for them. McGregor pointed his finger at him and said, "I found out who owns Pullwater Meadow."

Poteet said, as he took Poker by the elbow, "Oh yeah? Talk to me about it sometime." He led Poker away.

McGregor left them in the café near the door and for a minute watched them clown around as they anxiously peeked out the windows.

In the lounge, he pulled up a chair to join Hood, Mama, Tipsy, Sheriff Buell and Red Wiley at a table. At the next table, Carlos and Lakisha were hooting at a joke that Tomás was telling.

Red was saying to Mama, "Yeah, well, Dimpsey will recover they say. It's a crime to sell your candidacy after you formally declare, but Sheriff and I decided so long as he moves away from Calvin County, as he claims he'll do, no reason to press it. As to Poker, theoretically what he did looked like attempted murder. But we know he didn't intend it, and we'd never get anything more than a misdemeanor out of the grand jury. With misdemeanors, if the victims don't want to prosecute, we usually don't. So there it is. Poker's clear!"

Mama jumped up and hugged Red and Sheriff. It embarrassed Sheriff and he said, "Poker's getting a new truck, huh?"

"Yeah," Mama said. "Potty said to him, 'Next time you want a truck, best thing is to just ask me for it.' So Poker did! He told Potty he wanted a black one this time. Said he hated orange."

Sheriff asked Hood, "Did you get the Caddy and Buick down to your shop?"

"Yesterday. They're in bad shape, poor babies! And Poteet's Tommy Mathis paintings are being repaired, too. Are we assuming the Manskar man is who broke into Sweetwater?"

McGregor said, "Yeah, he admitted as much at the quarry. Yelled something about us finding his bugs."

A voice from behind the bar called out, "All rise and make way for drinks! Made fresh from today's tomatoes."

They turned to see Leslie carrying a tray full of red drinks in mugs and Helen following her with a second tray. Everyone stood up. Leslie was decked out in her old Tomato Emporium server's outfit, a short red skirt and low-cut blouse. The men ogled her. McGregor, as was becoming the norm, had trouble peeling his eyes away from her.

Hood, of course, noticed it and punched McGregor on his new cast. "Down boy!" she commanded under her breath.

Her tone was playful, but when McGregor locked pupils with his guru, Hood's dark eyes scalded him without mercy. In the hubbub, no one else seemed to notice when she stepped sideways to join the group at Tomás's table. McGregor cocked an ear and heard her mutter to Tomás, "I can't control the son of bitch."

Was Tomás becoming her confidant? He and Hood were at a precarious point. Any comment or careless flirting could swing them apart.

With a red Potion in hand, Leslie said, "I wanted to serve drinks at Mama's one last time." She held up her glass. "Here's to the Tomato Boy, and long live his memory!"

"To the Tomato Boy!" they responded and gulped their delicious Mama Potions.

Red said, "Hey, let's all be serious a moment. When they bury Clyde this week I'm publicly stating that he saved the county from a terrible injustice; that he was working as my agent to capture these crooks; that I had nothing to do with that taping system, but as it turned out it was a great idea of his. I'll say that the Tomato Boy gave his life in the performance of his duty as a citizen of Calvin County. And that the public should raise up his memory to stand as an example of personal sacrifice. During the festival next month we'll pick a day and declare it as the annual Tomato Boy Day. At noon that day we'll conduct a minute of silence."

McGregor understood that around here the lies would never cease. He might as well learn to live with them.

Poker yelped from the cafe. Everybody hurried to converge at the café windows. Out in the parking lot, its air brakes hissing, a truck rolled up pulling a vehicle hauler. Poker and Poteet went outside. The others stayed put to let them have their moment of private friendship.

The lone vehicle on the hauler was a gleaming black F-150. When the man rolled it to the ground, Poker hopped inside and cranked it up. Poteet slid into the passenger seat, and with waves to the group the two pals roared off down the highway.

McGregor said, "The gift of that truck, Mama, is probably only the beginning. Once Poteet starts throwing his money around, he can't stop." He turned to find Hood back by his side, and he put his cast around her waist tightly to hold her where he hoped she'd stay forever. "We can attest to that, can't we Hood?"

Hood giggled her sweet bubbly giggle and pinched him just under the wallet in his back pocket. In the wallet was a fat check.

Gary McKee lives in New Mexico but habitually frequents
Tennessee and Alabama. A lawyer, who for many years limited his practice to county law, McKee is also a commercial mediator. He developed
the Bob McGregor Mystery series while co-authoring and editing legal
manuals for county officials. Soon to be published is the second book in
the series, *Tomato Fog*, a Bob McGregor Mystery.

McKee is currently writing the first installment in a series of
historical mystery novels. *Calvin House, Book One*, is about the backwoods
philosopher-detective, Sheriff Clayton Calvin, who founded Calvin
County in 1828 with the help of the shadowy Jackson Men and one mys-
terious and very "generous" Jackson Woman.

LaVergne, TN USA
24 February 2010

174061LV00003B/48/P